praise for
THE ELIZAS

"A book you won't be able to leave sitting on the nightstand for long."
—*Harper's BAZAAR*

"From a possible murder attempt to amnesia, prepare for tons of juicy plot twists!"
—*Cosmopolitan*

"A dark and twisty mystery that will keep you guessing until the very end."
—*Marie Claire*

"A story blending Hitchcock, S. J. Watson, and Ruth Ware."
—*Entertainment Weekly*

"An eerie tale of manipulation, inception, and betrayal that will leave readers questioning their own memories—and reality."
—Jamie Blynn, *Us Weekly*

"This captivating thriller will keep readers rooting for Eliza—and trying to guess what is fact and what is fiction."
—*Real Simple*

"A brilliant narrative about a confused young woman struggling to separate fact from fiction in her life . . . Highly recommended for fans of eventually justified 'paranoid woman' characters who descend in a direct line from Charlotte Brontë to Ruth Ware."
—*Booklist* (starred review)

"A spine-chilling thriller that blurs the lines of fact and fiction. Electric and smart, with a witty protagonist readers won't soon forget."
—Mary Kubica, *New York Times* bestselling author of *The Good Girl* and *Every Last Lie*

"[Shepard] pays close attention to cinematic details, practically projecting Eliza's descent into personal nightmare, where she cannot be certain of her own memories, onto a silver screen. A delicious Southern California noir riddled with muddled identities and family secrets."

—*Kirkus Reviews*

"This intriguing story is as disconcerting for readers as it is for Eliza. Shepard weaves a complicated and ultimately chilling tale that will keep readers turning pages."

—*RT Book Reviews*

"Equal parts fun and disturbing, *The Elizas* delivers a heavy dose of psychodrama and a punchy, contemporary voice."

—*BookPage*

"A dark, twisty labyrinth of a psychological thriller with a fascinating, complex protagonist whose growing paranoia kept me in constant suspense."

—A. J. Banner, *USA TODAY* bestselling author of *The Twilight Wife* and *The Good Neighbor*

"Provocative . . . Eliza's voice draws readers in, and her unreliable memory creates tension. Gillian Flynn fans will be satisfied."

—*Publishers Weekly*

"A solid choice for psychological thriller aficionados."

—*Library Journal*

THE ELIZAS

a novel

SARA SHEPARD

ATRIA PAPERBACK

NEW YORK   LONDON   TORONTO   SYDNEY   NEW DELHI

ATRIA
PAPERBACK

An Imprint of Simon & Schuster, Inc.
1230 Avenue of the Americas
New York, NY 10020

First Atria Paperback edition January 2019

ATRIA PAPERBACK and colophon are trademarks of Simon & Schuster, Inc.

For information about special discounts for bulk purchases, please contact Simon & Schuster Special Sales at 1-866-506-1949 or business@simonandschuster.com.

The Simon & Schuster Speakers Bureau can bring authors to your live event. For more information or to book an event, contact the Simon & Schuster Speakers Bureau at 1-866-248-3049 or visit our website at www.simonspeakers.com.

Interior design by Kyoko Watanabe

Manufactured in the United States of America

10 9 8 7 6 5 4 3 2 1

Library of Congress Cataloging-in-Publication Data

Names: Shepard, Sara, author.
Title: The Elizas : a novel / Sara Shepard.
Description: First Atria Books hardcover edition. | New York : Atria Books, 2018.
Identifiers: LCCN 2017026988 (print) | LCCN 2017029053
Classification: LCC PS3619.H4543 (ebook) | LCC PS3619.H4543 E45 2018 (print) | DDC 813/.6—dc23
   LC record available at https://lccn.loc.gov/2017026988

ISBN 978-1-5011-6277-0
ISBN 978-1-5011-6278-7 (pbk)
ISBN 978-1-5011-6279-4 (ebook)

To Charles Vent

"We are only falsehood, duplicity, and contradiction; we both conceal and disguise ourselves from ourselves."

—BLAISE PASCAL

ELIZA

I'M SCREAMING AS I wake up. The sound is sucked away as soon as I open my eyes, but it leaves a mark on my brain, a quickly fading handprint in wet sand. My throat is raw. My head is pounding. I struggle to look around, but all I see are blurred shapes. There's an acrid taste of booze in my mouth.

Way to go, Eliza. You dodge a bullet, and you do this?

I picture the upgraded suite I'm missing out on because I'm too wasted. When I arrived at my suite in the Tranquility resort in Palm Springs late Saturday afternoon, I opened all the blinds in all the rooms. I stripped off my clothes and lay atop the bedsheets in only my underwear. I sat in the enormous empty tub and later warmed my ass on the heated toilet seat. And then, against my better judgment, I unlocked the minibar and belted down several bottles of vanilla-flavored Stolichnaya in quick succession. It tasted so good. Like an old friend.

As I drank, I stood on the balcony and stared into the courtyard seven flights below. It's a perfect square, that courtyard, made up of flagstone paths and flower beds. The space is divided into secluded quadrants that invite privacy . . . and scandal. The lore about this

1

place is that in the early sixties, a wannabe starlet named Gigi Reese was murdered in that courtyard. Bludgeoned in the head, apparently, probably by some local goons she got mixed up with. When they first found the body, officials ID'd her as another blonde actress named Diana Dane—the two women looked very similar. The public mourned for Diana Dane, who'd danced alongside Danny Kaye in a few pictures. *What a tragedy! A life cut short! We must find her killer, pronto!* Then Diana Dane returned from a USO trip to Japan and told the world she was just fine, thank her lucky stars. When the coroner got the dead woman's true identity sorted out, the Hollywood headlines barely mentioned it. They were still talking about what a relief it was that Diana Dane was okay. No one cared who'd offed Gigi Reese. The mystery is still unsolved.

After I finished my third mini bottle of vodka, I was feeling loose and reckless, so I figured I might as well go all out. I ordered room service, telling the guy taking my order, "Oh, just send up one of everything, especially the desserts." While I waited, I looked at the hand towels in the bathroom. They were soft, yet substantial. Unforgiving. I tried to imagine Gigi Reese's killer using such a towel to muffle her screams. Or maybe he knocked her out quickly, and she hadn't had time to make a sound. I ran my fingers over the spaceship-shaped alarm clock next to my bed, noting the sharpness of the tip and the heaviness of its base. It would make a good bludgeoning tool.

But now, when I turn my head to check out the space-age alarm clock again, it's not on the bedside stand. In fact, I don't even *see* the bedside stand. Light streams through a window, too—but isn't it nighttime?

A face emerges above me. "I think she's awake."

It's my mother's crinkled forehead, her wire-frame glasses, the sunburned nose from Saturdays spent kite surfing. She is so incongruous in this setting I assume, at first, that I'm still dreaming.

"What are you doing here?" I ask. It is an effort to speak. It feels as though there is someone sitting on my face.

My mother licks her lips. "Eliza." Her voice cracks. Trembles. And then she sighs. It's a big sigh, sad and long, gloomy and defeated. "Honey."

Honey. It sets my heart thumping. My mother only calls me *honey* when I've done something to really shake her up. We've been through things, me and my mom. I've scared her one too many times.

"W-what's going on?" I croak.

My stepfather, Bill, shimmers into view. There are mussed tufts of grayish hair above his ears. "Don't worry, chicken. You're going to be okay."

I remember the scream I'd made upon waking. "Did something happen?"

Gazes slide to the left. I spy my stepsister, Gabby, slouched in a doorway. This isn't my hotel suite at *all.* And what I'd thought was the typical crushing, sticky-mouthed descent into a hangover doesn't feel that way anymore, not completely. I notice a machine standing to my left. Green LED numbers march across a screen. The beeping sound is rhythmic, organic, matching the cadence of a body—my body. There's an IV pole with bags and tubes next to me, too. The goopy liquid in the IV bag is tinged an inorganic, vampire red, but when I look again, the liquid is thin and clear.

"Why am I in a hospital?" I whisper.

Again, no one speaks. A slick, cold feeling creeps down my back. A voice prods from somewhere deep. *You've got to get ahold of yourself.* I hear clinking glasses and a strain of "Low Rider" on the stereo—but *what* stereo? My vision swirls. *Stop staring,* someone says. And: *I've been looking for you.*

I try to grab the memory, but it's a petal blowing off a patio. Someone's screaming. Then . . . nothing. When was this from? Is it even real?

I try another question. "What day is it?"

"Sunday," my mother answers. "Sunday morning. You've been asleep for a while."

3

"Why am I in a hospital?" I ask again. "Please. Somebody tell me."

Bill clears his throat awkwardly. "You were found at the bottom of another pool last night."

I blink. In a way, I'm not surprised. This is, what, the fourth time I've almost drowned? The fifth? No wonder my family seems fatigued.

"The one at the Tranquility resort?" I ask tremulously.

"You don't remember." Bill says it like a statement, not a question.

I glance at my mother. She's staring down at her chest, biting her lip, so she doesn't see when I shake my head—but then, it's clear she already knows. I hate that I'm disappointing her—*scaring* her—but . . . I *don't* remember. Again.

"Where's my phone?" I ask.

My mother's face shifts into a mix of anger and annoyance, her favorite way to deflect fear. "Eliza. The last thing you should be worrying about right now is your phone."

Bill leans forward. "It's true. The doctors want you to rest. You need to get your strength back up."

I crane my neck and look at Gabby. Her expression is grave behind her round glasses. A sliver of memory from last night suddenly wriggles through. It's nighttime, a few hours after my minibar and room-service binge. I am standing on the pool deck at the Tranquility, but I don't know why. Every other time I've been at the pool, it's been pleasantly crowded with lounging bodies, but in this memory, the area is empty, as though everyone has just evacuated. Waves bob tempestuously on the water. Towels are thrown haphazardly across chairs. An upended cup sits on a table, a balled-up napkin printed with the resort's logo has missed the trash can and lies on the concrete. The diving board wobbles, as if someone has just jumped off . . . and dissolved into nothing.

The sky is very dark in the memory, opaque black velvet. The air is a cleansing kind of chilly, like there was a sudden drop in barometric pressure wicking away all the humidity. I can practically feel my

4

heels ticking against the hard tiled pool deck. I stand near the water, looking around frantically—*for what?* And I feel scared—*but why?* And then I hear footsteps. There's a confusion of movement, and I trip. There's a yelp—*my* yelp—and a stranger's laugh. The water is shockingly cold when I hit it belly-first. My useless limbs flap, I try to paddle, but I quickly give out. Air leaves my lungs. My shoes fall off my feet as I sink to the bottom. I can't swim. I never learned.

I inhale and detect the faintest hint of pool chlorine in my nostrils. I hear that "Low Rider" riff again. A cold sweat breaks out on the surface of my skin. "Did they find him?"

My mother's lips part. "Who? The person who pulled you out of the water?"

Once again I feel those strong hands pushing me from behind. Once again I hear that laugh. A high-pitched, mocking, *satisfied* laugh.

"The person who pushed me *in*," I whisper.

Gabby's blonde head shoots up. My mother's face turns red, and she pokes her head into the hall. "*Nurse*," she says in a panicked voice.

Now I am shaking. "No, seriously, someone pushed me!" My voice grows louder. "Someone pushed me into that pool! We have to find him! Please!"

"Eliza." Bill's face is large and close. "No one pushed you. You *jumped*."

"Like every other time," my mother murmurs into her hands with a sob, just as a nurse walks into the room with a gleaming syringe.

I cower back on the bed. My eyes bulge as the nurse steps closer. "No!" I cry, but it doesn't matter. The nurse isn't listening, and neither is anyone else. It's not so crazy they think I jumped. I have a bit of a track record of this kind of behavior. But I didn't go into that water willingly—this I know for sure.

Someone wanted me dead.

■ ■ ■

The clock on the wall of my hospital room says 3:15, and judging by the sunlight, I have to assume it's now Sunday afternoon. I must have fallen asleep from the shot the nurse gave me because, she claimed—they all claimed—I was having another episode. The whole way down, milliseconds before I lost consciousness, I argued with the room this wasn't a repeat performance. I wasn't delusional like all those other times. I was telling the truth.

Now, the room is silent and still. I don't know where anyone is— maybe my family has left. In many ways, I hope they have.

I feel around on the little bedside table, hoping my phone is there. It's not. It's discomfiting not to have my phone by my side, like one of my senses has been taken away. I've missed hours of news. I've missed random snaps from celebrities I've never met and friends I never see and distant family members I don't really like. I've missed emails about shoe sales, makeup sales, and emails that proclaim *Free shipping today and today only!* Maybe I've even missed an email from my editor or agent. I want to Google this hospital to make sure it's reputable and search for news of last night's incident at the Tranquility. I want to Google the meds in my IV drip, and ask Siri why all hospitals smell like sadness, and also confirm with Siri that my family actually drugged me to keep me quiet.

Okay, it had been a major slip to drink. I'd promised my family I wouldn't after my surgery and treatment. Only, it had tasted so *good*. Once I'd started, I couldn't stop. I'm not really very good at re-fraining, to be honest. Willpower isn't my strong suit. But drinking was my only slip, and it didn't dull what I know. Everything I'd said to them about someone pushing me is true. It happened. I know it.

There's a knock at the door, and I shoot up. A guy in a faded blue shirt enters. He's sandy-haired, with black plastic glasses that were probably hip about five years ago. He's got a weak, wimpy half smile and long, thin fingers with carefully manicured nails. I arrange the sheets around me so that my ass isn't exposed and pull my hospital gown tight. I wish the gown were any color but white. The fabric matches my skin tone perfectly.

"Miss Fontaine." He extends his hand. "I'm Lance Collier, with the Palm Springs PD. I've been assigned to your case."

"You're a detective?" My voice leaps. The world blossoms.

He sinks into a plastic chair next to my bed. "I have a few questions for you. I hear you're going to be with us for a while longer."

"What do you mean?"

"I was told your family would like you to take a few days to recover in psychiatric."

My heart sinks. "No. *No.* I wasn't trying to kill myself."

Lance turns his head to the right. His neck cracks noisily, and I wince. I have never liked the sound of cracking joints. "What I see"—he flips a page—"is that two passersby rescued you from the bottom of the Tranquility resort pool last night. True?"

I shrug. "I guess."

"And you can't swim, right?"

"That's right."

"So what were you doing in the pool?"

"Someone pushed me."

This doesn't even elicit an eyebrow raise, which surprises me, considering the last time I made this claim I got a needle jammed into my bicep. "Did you see the person who pushed you?" he asks in an even tone.

"No, but I felt hands on my back."

"But no face. So you can't be *positive* you were pushed."

I lick my lips. "Are you saying I'm lying?"

He crosses his legs. The clock on the wall ticks loudly. "Miss Fontaine, it's come to my attention that you've had some issues with suicide attempts in the past."

I inwardly groan. "Yes, but that was . . . before."

"Before what?"

"Before her brain tumor."

My mother rushes into the room, never mind that this is a private meeting. Bill follows. Gabby pulls up the rear.

"Um, hello?" I say awkwardly, defensively.

My mother turns to the detective. "She tried to drown herself four other times last year. Three were in hotel swimming pools and a hot tub. The fourth time was in the Pacific Ocean—Santa Monica. She kept saying she had to. Someone was after her. Someone was trying to hurt her. Finally, about eleven months ago, a doctor gave her a brain scan, and it turns out she had a tumor pressing against—"

"—my amygdala," I interrupt, desperate to regain control of this. "It's this part of your brain that tells your body how it's supposed to respond to emotionally charged situations."

"I'm aware of how an amygdala functions," Lance says.

"That's why you see all those suicide attempts on my record," I say. "But the doctor got the tumor out. I had treatment, and I'm better now. Last night was different. I wasn't trying to die. Honest."

"It's just so *similar*, chicken," Bill says quietly. "The drinking, the fear that someone was after you . . . everything about the situation is the same."

"Well, it's not the same." I look around the room and see tilted mouths, downcast eyes. "It's *not*." It comes out like a whine.

There's a small, condescending smile on Lance's face. "How about you walk me through what you remember?"

I try to grab on to that memory of the strong hands on my back at the edge of the pool, but the shot that nurse gave me—a mixture of drugs I'm unfamiliar with—is making even reality seem dreamlike and unfathomable. "I walked out to the pool. I stood there. Then I felt this *whoosh*. I was pushed from behind, and I fell in. I was in a public place. Weren't there witnesses?"

Lance studies his notes. "According to the report, there were no witnesses besides the people who rescued you. By the time they saw you, you were already in the water, and they said no one else was around. They pulled you out, laid you on the deck. One of them gave you mouth-to-mouth."

I feel itchy. It's harrowing to hear the details of your almost-death. I notice, out of the corner of my eye, that my mother has her lips pressed tightly together.

"Are they sure no one else saw?" I ask. It seems impossible. There were hundreds of guests at that resort when I checked in. The lobby was clogged with guys in Maui Jim sunglasses and women carrying raffia Tory Burch handbags.

"There was a thunderstorm—the pool area had been cleared. The staff wonders how you even got onto the deck—it was roped off."

I'd climbed over the rope? My patent leather booties had five-inch heels. What the hell prompted me to do that?

"Who pulled me out of the water?" I ask. "Who was it?"

He looks again at the notebook. "Someone named Desmond Wells. Know him?"

I crane my neck at the notebook, too. Lance has written the name *Desmond Wells* in all caps along with a Los Angeles area code and phone number. The name doesn't ring a bell. "Does he work at the hotel?"

"He said he was a guest."

"So what about video surveillance? Didn't *that* pick up what happened?"

"There normally are security cameras in the pool area, but the power was down because of the storm."

I snort. "And I bet it snapped right back on after I was pulled out of the pool, huh?"

"This isn't a conspiracy, Eliza," my mother says, almost inaudibly, her voice tinged with that sad, scared bitterness again.

"How about people at the bar? I was talking to someone there, I think, before I went to the pool. Can you interview them? Maybe they saw something. Or *I* could interview them, actually. Do you happen to know where my phone is? I could call the bar and straighten this out."

My mother looks aghast. "You were at a bar, too?"

I clear my throat. I'd promised I wouldn't go to bars after the tumor surgery. Just like I promised I wouldn't drink, period. I look at Lance. "I-I just went for some atmosphere. I wasn't drinking."

Lance coughs awkwardly. "The lab did a toxicity report on you. Your blood alcohol level was sky-high."

I can feel my family's gaze upon me. It sucks to be caught in a lie, especially such a foolish one. But sometimes lying's my natural response. The lies come out of my mouth involuntarily.

Lance flips a page. "Anyway. The police who responded to the 911 call spoke to two men who rescued you, and they said they'd never seen you before, and they didn't know where you'd come from. Can you describe who you were talking to at the bar, Eliza? Did you get a name?"

I swallow hard. I have no idea.

"Was it a man? A woman? Anything?"

Still nothing. I'm not even sure I *was* talking to someone.

"Can you tell me which bar you were at? I could look into it."

According to the big binder in my room at the Tranquility, the resort has six bars. D'Oro's, the casual one off the lobby; The Stuffed Pig, for business dinners; Trax, with the DJ; Meritage, a wine bar; Shipstead, the nautical-themed martini bar; and Harry's, a tiki bar. So I have a one-in-six chance of getting it right. *Stingers,* buzzes a little insect in my head. I drank a stinger last night. How had *that* come about? That's not a drink I usually order.

"Ah. Here it is. You were most likely at the Shipstead. That's the only bar whose door leads to the pool area." Lance looks up from his notes and squints at me. "It's possible, though, that you don't remember the night properly. There's the issue of your toxicity report, for one thing. And I happened to get a look in your bag, too—I found . . . well, I suppose you know what I found."

"What?" my mother gasps.

Lance is still looking at me. "Are you sure *that's* not why you fell in the pool? Maybe you were too wasted to realize what you were doing?"

I try to swallow, but my throat is so dry. I can picture the label of the bottle he found. It reads *Xanax, 1 mg, twice daily.* "I don't suppose you noticed all the *other* things in my purse, did you?" I finally say. "All the vitamins? Metabolic maintenance, immuno drops, Metformin, CoQ10?" I give Bill and my mother a self-righteous glance. "It's everything the doctors ordered me to take to keep the tumor from coming back. I'm *trying.*"

"We know you are, chicken." Bill pats my arm. "We know."

"Are you on any other prescription medications?" Lance asks.

This is unbelievable. "I'm sorry, but do cops usually ask these sorts of questions?"

"Actually, I'm a forensic psychologist. But I have ties to Palm Springs PD, and I report everything we're speaking about to them."

I scoot away from him in the bed. "We're done, then. Conversation over." I've had enough of talking to shrinks.

"Eliza." My mother crosses her arms over her chest. "Honey, please. He's just trying to help."

"Too bad," I say, like a toddler. *And stop calling me honey,* I want to add. It's just too incongruous . . . and heartbreaking.

"I promise I can help put the pieces together for you," Lance says. "But for this process to work, you have to be a willing participant. So how about you tell me if you took any other meds last night before you fell into the pool?"

I chew the inside of my cheek. I hate the turn this has taken.

"You know, even just mixing Xanax and alcohol can give you blackouts, memory gaps, and—"

"That might be true, but I didn't take all those last night," I cut him off. "You're not listening to me. This isn't a memory gap. This really *happened.*"

Lance looks at me easily, but I detect a slight smirk on his face. As he shifts in the seat, he's lined up squarely with a poster of a curly-horned mountain goat in the hall. His head tilts just so, and it looks like he's the one with the horns.

"Let's talk about the drinking," Lance circles back. "So why drink so much? Were you upset about something?"

I stare down at the sheets. "No."

"You sure?"

I look him square in the eye. *Focus,* I tell myself. *Breathe.* "Of course I'm sure."

"And what prompted this visit to Palm Springs, anyway?"

Why the hell does *that* matter? "I don't know. It's . . . pretty there. I like the dry heat. I like art deco. And I like hotels."

"You should have told us you were going, sweetie," Bill chimes in.

This takes me by surprise. "Am I on probation?"

"You promised us you'd tell us if you went anywhere outside LA," my mother says.

I push my tongue into my cheek. I did?

Lance sits back in the chair and crosses his ankles. "That must have been tough to have a brain tumor last year, huh?"

I wrinkle my nose. He's using his Shrink Voice. I've heard a few of those in my day. "It wasn't that big of a deal."

"You don't have to downplay it. Cancer scares the shit out of everyone."

"Of course it scared her," my mother says. "As a kid, she *worried* she was going to get a tumor. She worried about a lot of things. Illness. Death. She was an unusually anxious child. And then she *got* a tumor. She was beside herself."

"Mom," I warn.

My mother shrugs. "But you were."

Lance peers at me expectantly. I swallow hard, readying my own version of what it was like to have gone through brain surgery and recovery at twenty-two years old. The thing is, though, my mother is right. I *was* a strange child. A kid who worried. A kid who had obsessions, obsessions that still exist today. I was that kid who lined a storage bin with silk, climbed in, shut the lid, and lay there for hours, pretending, absorbing, *fantasizing*. I used to make my Barbies strangle, bludgeon, asphyxiate, stab, and hack apart one another. I was that kid who hanged every one of my stuffed animals from nooses in the closet doorway, pinning miniature suicide notes to their plush bodies. My mother found those suicide notes. She asked me why I'd done such a thing. I didn't have the vocabulary for it at the time, but I guess I was just curious about how someone could sink to that level of despair. I identified with that level of despair, though I didn't know why. It came from somewhere deep inside of me, a place I was too young to understand.

Maybe my errant amygdala was to blame. Being diagnosed with the tumor was a bit of a paradox for me—it was nightmarish, yes, but it also kind of explained why, sometimes, I made very strange and unhealthy decisions. It was like a get-out-of-jail-free card. I was no longer responsible for my actions.

"Look, it wasn't fun, but I got through it," I answer. "And I'm doing well now. I have my own place. I have a job. I even wrote a book."

Lance raises an eyebrow. "A book?"

"A novel. *The Dots*. A publisher bought it and everything."

"How about that!" Lance glances around at my family. They shift from foot to foot. "What's it about?"

Gabby makes a loud throat-clearing sound near the door, but when I try to catch her eye, she doesn't look up. "It's a coming-of-age story," I say.

Lance nods encouragingly. He probably expects me to tell more, but I don't want to. The last thing I want to do is explain my creative endeavors to my family. This is my achievement, not theirs—they didn't foster it in the least. They aren't artists. They aren't even readers. They'll deem it silly, probably. Frivolous. Melodramatic. They don't even know that it's publishing in a month. I hope they miss it entirely and never read a word, because then I won't have to hear their misinterpretation.

"Eliza, let's try and think this through," my mother says. "You had a shock last night, and I think you need some time to rest. If you don't want to stay in this hospital, maybe consider this place instead." She fishes in her Band-Aid-colored bucket bag and hands me a pamphlet. It takes me a moment to make sense of the words on the cover. *The Oaks Wellness Center.* There's a picture of people sitting around a farmhouse table, eating soup and looking joyful and serene. *Psychiatric treatment in a relaxed, soothing environment,* reads the cover.

Acid rises in my throat. "No way."

"The last year has been hard for you," Bill says. "It's okay to admit you're going through a rough patch again."

"This isn't a rough patch!"

"It's okay, Eliza." Lance puts his pen in his front pocket. "People with serious illnesses often have psychological relapses."

"I. Didn't. Jump. Into. That. Pool," I tell the room. "I felt . . . hands." I hold up my two shaking palms and make a shoving motion. "I don't need a rest. My tumor isn't back. And I definitely don't need a *psych ward.*" I look at Lance. "Can you at least ask around again, see if anyone saw anything, or if there was a backup video? Or even just ask the bartender on duty if they saw anyone with me in the bar that night?"

"But you seem like a nice girl, Eliza," Lance says. "Would someone really want to hurt you?"

My brain catches. A *nice girl.* It's comical. On the other hand, *am* I someone a person would like to hurt—even kill? Someone must have consciously made the decision to thrust me forward into the water. Someone must have hated me that much. It has to be someone who knows me. Someone who knows I can't swim.

Sometimes I pick flowers, beautiful flowers, off people's lawns.

People I don't even know. I don't do anything with them. I smell them, drop them, and sometimes step on them.

I can be cruel and withhold affection.

I'm a liar. A fabulist. It's probably why I wrote a book so easily post-tumor.

A lot of my decisions don't make sense. I piss people off. I burn bridges. I do nothing to repair them usually, either.

There are certain things I don't remember at all, huge chunks gone. I've been told the tumor's to blame, but sometimes I wake up with a residue of shame over me, as gritty as sand. And sometimes, I still get the feeling I've done something. Something awful. I just don't know what. So maybe someone does hate me that much.

I jut my chin into the air. "I guess that's for you to find out, isn't it, Lance?"

Lance looks at my family. My mother raises her eyebrows. Bill breathes out, looking heartbroken. Gabby is trying to morph into the wall. And then I glance at Lance's notebook again. He has flipped to a sheet of lined paper with the heading *Eliza Fontaine*. But he hasn't written a single thing. No testimony. No details of my attack.

It doesn't take me but a moment to get it. In his mind, there *was* no attack. He has sided with my family. I'm just a crazy girl. I don't know what's real.

I look desperately to Gabby, hoping she'll speak up in my defense, but she's pointedly consulting her phone as if we're all just inappropriately loud strangers she's stuck sitting next to on public transport. And for a moment, I entertain the idea that perhaps there is a third girl in the room, a different Eliza, and they're talking about *her*, not me. After all, I'm the Eliza who's better. I'm the Eliza who just had a few too many drinks. I'm the Eliza who remembers hands at her back pushing her into the water. I'm the Eliza who has the niggling worry that someone might have done it on purpose, for something I deserved.

That last bit strikes a dissonant chord. Only, no. This isn't like the other times, those paranoia-fueled plunges brought on by a twisted lump of abnormal cells. Someone really *is* after me. Whatever happened to me this time, my fear is completely and unequivocally justified.

I just wish someone else believed it, too.

An excerpt from The Dots *by Eliza Fontaine*

Once upon a time there was a girl named Dot, and she loved her aunt—her namesake—Dorothy. They were two peas in a pod, Dot and Dorothy. Two dots connected by a solid, straight line. They could finish each other's sentences. They looked very much alike. Sometimes, Aunt Dorothy joked that Dot was a clone of herself, a perfect genetic match. Dot hoped so, because that would mean great things for her future.

Her aunt's full name was Dorothy Ophelia Banks. With her pale skin and violet eyes, the story went that, as a teenager, a modeling agent plucked her off Henry Street in Brooklyn and told her she was going to be a star. She went on to model for a brand of mints that weren't quite as good as Tic Tacs, an airline that was plagued with technical problems just months after taking to the skies, and a brand of butt-hugging jeans that should have been the next Jordache but never caught on. Soon after, she married a tycoon who'd invented a new type of contact lens. She bounced around New York doing the club circuit, socializing, making friends with writers and playwrights and countesses and people who had fleets of helicopters; one man had his own spaceship. She was the type of woman who could charm any person in any room. She could wear a silk jumpsuit and platform heels; she was proud to traipse around in a thong bikini. A trapeze school in New York City opened; she was a natural at high-flying and spent a little time with a small postmodern circus. She did stand-up comedy at smoky clubs and always got belly laughs.

Two years later, she ditched Mr. Contact Lens and dated a man working for the government, changing her wardrobe to tweedy shoulder-padded power suits and dark Ray-Bans. Rumor had it she was activated by a phone call one sunny Sunday morning and went undercover in Tunisia. Assuming her undercover identity, she learned to parachute. She took up puppeteering. She raised champion Airedales. Later on, tired of DC and espionage, she moved to Los Angeles and married a film producer who promptly died, though not before giving her a son, Thomas, who then died, too. She joined a cult in New Mexico and made pottery. She wrote a novel called *The Riders of Carrowae* and spent years editing it. She distilled her own whiskey. She sold off a tech stock her late husband purchased in its infancy; with the handsome capital gains, she bought a house in the Hollywood Hills that had a clichéd but lovely view of the Hollywood sign off the back deck. She submitted *Riders of Carrowae* to agents. Everyone rejected it.

She went to parties. She flirted with men. People gave her gifts, mostly museum-quality jewelry and keys to safe-deposit boxes. She frequently gambled in Vegas—her favorite casino was the Golden Nugget—and always won. And then her niece, Dot, was born. And that's when everything changed. Dot became the center of Dorothy's life.

Dot thought Dorothy was the most amazing person ever. The hours she spent with Dorothy were magical. She disappeared into Dorothy's walk-in closet in the hotel bungalow where she'd made her residence and emerged in Dorothy's furs, gowns, and jewels. Dorothy took pictures of her and told her tales of where the outfits came from—a mink from a prince who'd fallen in love with her, a diamond necklace from a director who wanted her in his movie, a handmade beaded shift from when she was in a *Vogue* photo shoot, though her photos hadn't made the issue's final cut. Dorothy spritzed Dot with her signature scent she'd had a Portuguese perfumer concoct for her out of bergamot oranges. Then they played Oscar Night, Dot strutting on the red carpet, Dorothy conducting the interviews. Other days, they played Funeral, Dorothy settling into a silky coffin she kept in a back room, Dot weeping for her and giving a heartfelt eulogy. Often, from inside the coffin, Dorothy stage-whispered lines to add to the speech.

They spent days in bed eating Oreos and Brie and watching *The Third Man* and other old noir films. They wrapped Dorothy's Hermès scarves around their heads—Dot's favorite was the one printed with prowling leopards—and tooled around town in Dorothy's Cadillac convertible. They made up stories—Dot told the beginning, Dorothy the middle, as middles were hard, and Dot the denouement.

Dot needed Dorothy. It wasn't that she didn't love her mother, but there was something so *familiar* about Dorothy. So recognizable. Her aunt sharpened who she was; she made Dot's existence feel important and meaningful and tethered to a larger, brighter, bigger something. Dot pitied those who didn't have a Dorothy in their lives. That's what made what happened later on so tragic. When things soured, when things got tempestuous, it wasn't just a hurricane-level disaster. It was an exploding atomic bomb.

This is that story.

ELIZA

THE NEXT MORNING, as I'm adding antioxidant powder to the smoothie I'd had delivered from a juice bar down the street, I hear my mother's voice in the hallway. Most of what she's saying is garbled murmurs, but I clearly make out the words *paranoia* and *illness* and *suicide*. A conversation about me, then. Naturally.

Moments later, she blusters into my room with a confrontational look on her face. She stops short when she notices I am no longer in my gown.

"Am I a picture of fashion or what?" I gesture to my clothes. I'm wearing an oversized Lakers T-shirt, acid-washed jeans, and Keds. A nurse brought all of it up from the Lost and Found; the dress I'd worn at the resort had been ruined by pool chlorine, and I hadn't packed anything else. "But beggars can't be choosers, I guess."

"You're checking out?" My mother's voice cracks.

"Yep." I try to sound rested, sober, healed. I hold up my phone. "I even got this back."

My phone had been across the room the whole time, on top of a plastic bag that contained my ruined dress and shoes. A nurse finally noticed it this morning, and I'd pounced on it hungrily, scouring Google News for evidence of someone pushing me into the pool. There was no evidence. Whatever happened to me didn't make any feeds, not even a local news report, not even the Tranquility's Twitter account. Though I suppose bragging about random women lying facedown in the resort swimming pool probably isn't the best PR strategy.

"A-are you sure you don't want to stay another day?" my mother asks.

I give her my healthiest smile. Inside, I'm shaky, but I have to do this. I have to leave. I have to prove that what happened to me really happened. And I have an idea. One that doesn't involve being stuck in here.

My mother hurries over to the nurse who happens to be in the room tidying up for the next patient. "Where's the physician on duty?" she murmurs. "Can you find him, please?"

The nurse ambles slowly to the door and peers into the hall. "Don't see him anywhere."

I slide off the bed and look at my mother. Her face is pale. Her violet eyes have narrowed on me, and I know what she's thinking. She wants to talk a doctor into forcibly keeping me here. But I did the research: they'd have to get a court document to make me stay against my will. Such a thing would take days, maybe weeks. For now, I'm free.

As though he's sensed the tension, Bill appears at my mother's side. She quickly fills him in, and he looks just as concerned. But I'm not going to be persuaded. Not by them.

"At least let us drive you home, Eliza," Bill finally offers.

"I can take a cab back to the resort to pick up my car. No biggie."

The nurse shakes her head. "No, dear, you can't get behind the wheel. There's too much medication in your system."

And just like that, we're walking out to the parking lot toward Bill's Porsche Panamera.

My father died when I was very young—I barely remember

him—but my mother was lucky to hook up with Bill thirteen years ago for this car alone. He opens the back door for me, and I sink into the leather seat and shut my eyes, relaxed by the sudden growl of the engine. Who knows how my car will get home from the resort's parking garage?

Gabby slides into the backseat, too, her hands flat across her thighs. She gives me a sideways glance, grimaces slightly, and scrunches against her door. "I know, I know." I gesture to the Lakers shirt. "They said they washed this stuff in Clorox, but they should have burned it."

Gabby's smile flickers. "I guess it's better than wearing the gown home."

"Totally," I agree, because I think this is her idea of a joke, and I think she's being kind, and I need her on my side.

Bill inserts a paper card into the automated pay booth, and the barricade lifts. Soon enough, he turns onto the I-10. Drab desert sweeps by. We've got the SiriusXM business channel at a low volume. No one is talking. Clearly they want to; I can feel it in the air, crackling. Everyone would love to scream at me how it was a terrible idea for me to have checked myself out. It wafts off them like sweat.

Gabby shifts next to me, and I sneak a peek at her. She's typing furiously on her phone. "Whatcha doing?" I ask, as though we have conversations all the time.

She flips the phone over, concealing the screen. "Um, just work stuff."

"Anything interesting?"

She flinches, then slips the phone in her bag. "Not really."

She looks out the window, though there's nothing to see. Gabby's got a long face, a sloped nose, a shrub of light hair, and a turned-down mouth. I was nine when my mother met Bill. Not long after their first date, he and Gabby appeared at our house for dinner, and I had stared Gabby down. I'd been told she was my age, and that her mother had died of pneumonia. But with her pink-tinted, plastic-framed glasses and Shirley Temple curls, Gabby looked more like seven. She wore hard black shoes with thick soles that made her feet look large and cloddish. And there was something about her expression that reminded me of a big gray rain cloud. When I stomped my boot, she flinched.

"You're still at that infinity-scarf place, right?" I ask brightly now, as the car hits a pothole in the road. "What's it called again?"

Gabby stares at me for a moment, and I wonder, briefly, if I've made this up. Maybe she never worked for a company that makes scarves that cleverly hide headphones and neck braces and colostomy bags. It seems, all of a sudden, quite fantastical—and also sort of lame.

But then she says, "Yes. I'm still there. The company's called That's A Wrap."

"And you took the day off to bring me home?" I squint. "That's really nice of you. I really appreciate it."

Gabby flinches, and I wonder if she thinks I'm being sarcastic. It's not like we're the best of friends. So I give her a sweet, grateful smile. When she smiles back, her eyes are full of sadness. "We were worried," she says softly.

"She's volunteered to take you to your follow-up appointment, too," my mother adds.

Gabby's phone pings again. I try to look at the screen, but she tilts it in such a way that I can't see what she's typing. A car swishes past us; for a moment, someone in the backseat meets my gaze. I am struck, suddenly, with a blinding sense of fear. I breathe in sharply. The world recedes. My brain folds in two.

When I come to, I see only my reflection in the window. My dark hair is shoved into a greasy ponytail. My bruise-colored eyes look bloodshot. My small, delicate features, normally moderately lovely without makeup, look bloodless and haggard. I glance around the car. Gabby stares at me nervously. My mother eyes me from the front, her lipstick halfway to her mouth. Have I said something?

Done something? Made some sort of sound? The lane next to us is empty. There isn't a car behind us or ahead of us for a quarter mile.

I straighten up and pretend nothing has happened. I glance at my own phone, smiling secretly at the text I'd sent just before getting into the car . . . and at the response I'd received. *Just you wait,* I want to tell my family. *I'm going to show you all.*

An hour later, my family pulls up to my rental, a 1920s bungalow in Burbank that's not far from the Warner and Disney lots.

"How about we come in with you?" Bill says as I yank open the back door and slide my legs out. "We'll help you get settled. Get you into bed. Make you some dinner. I can do a good chicken noodle soup from a can." He chuckles as if this is legitimately funny.

"Thanks, but I'm fine," I say, grabbing my mess of discharge papers.

"Can I at least walk you to the door?"

Instead, I let him give me a hug. Bill is a man who gives bear hugs: big, emphatic squeezes with a lot of grunts and wiggles. For a moment, it feels nice. My mother hugs me as well, though it feels obligatory, like she's still upset. Her arms are stiff. I can feel the tension in her jaw. Gabby just touches my shoulder, giving me another gloomy half smile.

"Call if you need anything!" Bill cries as I turn for the door.

As I shuffle up the front walk, I stumble a little—some of the slate slabs are loose. On the second floor, another window shutter has cracked. The garage door is busted and therefore permanently up, revealing the nonfunctional steampunk copper car hammered out to look like a snail I bartered the landlord for instead of making him fix the roof. There's a bill sitting on the welcome mat that reads *Final Notice* in red ink. It's not because I don't have the cash to pay it, I just keep forgetting. I'm not sure I should actually live on my own. For the first three months here, I neglected to activate the gas to power the oven. I twisted the oven's knobs, thinking the thing would work eventually. I called the landlord to say the oven was broken only to have him come out, check things, and ridicule me for not understanding how basic utilities worked. It's why I got roommates, I guess. Better to have other people handle those sorts of things.

I give my family a halfhearted wave as they turn off the street. It's a relief to be out of that car. If I had to sit in there with those unbelievers for another minute, I was afraid I'd scratch the skin off my arms.

Stop staring. It's that voice from the bar at the Tranquility again, and I cringe. I can't tell if it's male or female—it's more of an androgynous hiss. Who said it? The same person who pushed me? A shiver wriggles down my spine. I glance over my shoulder, realizing the risks I've taken by leaving the hospital. I am out in the world, and I have an assailant. Maybe I shouldn't be alone.

Something shifts in the shadows by my door, and I let out a yelp. A figure stands backlit in the sun, his features blotted out. I freeze. My fingers lose their elasticity, hardening to talons. The figure clears his throat and raises an assuring hand. "Eliza Fontaine? Desmond Wells."

Desmond Wells. See, there are certain moments where my memory slips away from me, evasive and taunting, but there are other times where it's as accurate as a photograph. Yesterday with Lance, despite the cocktail of drugs, despite my frustration, I remember perfectly. Every detail Lance gave me, every tiny shred of a clue I could cling to—it's all there. Desmond Wells was one of those clues. My rescuer. The person who pulled me out of the pool. His was a name in all caps in Lance's notebook. There was a phone number next to that name, its digits lining up so orderly in my brain.

My name is Eliza Fontaine, I'd texted to that phone number on my newly returned phone. *I think you helped me Saturday night at the Tranquility resort pool. Do you mind if I ask you a few questions?*

Sure, he responded. *I happen to be free today. I can meet you.*

Lance might not be looking into what happened to me, but I sure as hell am.

From The Dots

Dot didn't remember a lot about the start of her illness. There were the grinding headaches she complained of for weeks that made exploding nebulae flash in front of her face. She crumpled against walls, clutching her temples. There was also the blurred vision that doubled the number of Jack Skellingtons on the *Nightmare Before Christmas* DVD she couldn't stop watching. One evening, hopelessly dizzy, she tipped over while carrying her dinner plate to the table, carrots and chicken all over the floor in a vomitus mess. "There's something wrong with me," she said, finding herself on the floor, too.

Her mother looked startled. "Do you need to go to the ER?" But Dot shook her head. She just wanted to lie in bed. She just wanted the room to stop spinning. Her mother climbed in with her, stroking Dot's sweaty hair. But twenty minutes in, she checked her watch. "Honey, I've got to go to work now. I'm sorry." She worked as a dental assistant, peering all day at people's teeth and gums.

"You have to work *today?*" Dot groaned.

"That's how we eat. I'm your sole support." Long ago, Dot's father had passed away. Dot barely had any memory of him except for a kind-eyed man handing her a plastic egg from a grocery store gum machine and saying, "Dottie, there's a surprise inside." She couldn't recall what the surprise had been.

"How is it that Aunt Dorothy doesn't have to work, then?" Dot asked.

Her mother slid out from under the covers. Her expression hardened. "She's in a different boat than us."

"Can you see if she'll come over?"

"I guess," her mother said, reluctantly.

Dot told Dorothy about her mother always having to work. Dorothy sighed. "You know, your mother doesn't realize that time with a child is so fleeting. Money isn't everything. Work isn't everything. If I were to do it all over again with Thomas, I wouldn't have spent a moment on *Riders of Carrowae*. I would have devoted all my time to him. I would have watched him while he slept. I would have never taken my eyes off him. Maybe he would have lived. Maybe I didn't try hard enough."

Thomas. Dot always held her breath when her aunt mentioned her dead son. He had died a few years before Dot was born, so Dot had never known him. Dorothy carried around a photo of him, though, a little blond boy in a baseball cap clutching a toy train. Apparently Thomas was a peculiar, moody child, prone to wild fits and severe bouts of melancholy that no medication could fix. At ten years old, Thomas had found a handgun Dorothy kept in the house as protection after her husband died. Thomas figured out how to load it and turned it on himself.

Dot knew Dorothy still thought of Thomas constantly. Her aunt kept some of his clothes and toys in a closet in her bungalow—she showed Dot the box once, though she said never to look inside. Dot wondered if Thomas had said anything prophetic to Dorothy before he passed on. And where did children go when they died? Heaven? Was there a kid version? She wondered if Dorothy had *seen* him die, and if she'd sat with his body for some time afterward, soaking up its blood, watching it grow cold and stiff. Dot would have.

Dot didn't remember the epic seizure that had her knocking against the wall in the middle of the night, waking her mother in her room next door. Nor did she remember the ride to the hospital and the nurses whisking her back immediately. Nor did she remember the slide into the long tube that clanked and bonked, though she knew it must have been one of the first things that happened—it was the way the doctors searched for dark trouble. There must have been a conversation, too, where a doctor explained the mass they'd found in her head. The mass was pressing on a critical part of Dot's brain; they would have to operate immediately. Dot would likely survive, the doctor told Dot's mother, but the post-op recovery could be very hard on a child, so they had to be ready for that.

The next thing Dot remembered, she was waking up on a little bed with curtains pulled tightly around it. The air was cold, and she was alone. Her head was wrapped in bandages. Her body felt too heavy, like she'd gained a hundred pounds. Outside the curtain, she heard beeps. Someone was gagging. Her last memory had been going to sleep in her bed; she'd had a dream about Wednesday Addams, whom she idolized. Sometimes she wrote Wednesday Addams on the line for her name on tests. But where was she now? She stared in horror at a needle taped to the back of her hand. It fed into a tube, which led to a bag on a post. She wanted to pull the needle out, but something told her not to—that it would hurt even worse.

A figure parted the curtain. "Mommy?" Dot cried. It was a nurse in bear-print scrubs. "Your mother will be back," she said.

Tears spilled down Dot's cheeks. She felt scared. Why wasn't her mother here?

A few minutes later, the curtain to her little bed parted, and Dorothy burst through. She wore a beautiful silk wrap dress, but the ties of its belt trailed behind her, unfastened. A slash of lipstick sloppily decorated her mouth; her Chanel purse bumped against her hip, its clasp undone. She reached toward Dot and pulled her to her chest; Dot smelled her Dorothy scent, orange blossoms and Indian bunchgrass. "My girl," she said, cradling Dot's head close. "My sweet, sweet girl. I'm here now."

Dot nuzzled her nose against the soft, smooth skin of Dorothy's neck. Her aunt's pulse was so calm—usually, it chugged swiftly and industriously, like a giant nineteenth-century machine. She stroked Dot's hair. "We're going to beat this. I'll be here, always. I'll help."

And she was. And she did.

ELIZA

BLINDED BY THE sun, I am granted a few blissful seconds of imagining—daydreaming—what Desmond Wells must look like. Rugged, wavy hair, olive skin, and squinty eyes with baked-in crow's feet. A rough-looking sort of fellow; the human version of a pickup truck, but sensitive, too, the kind of man who shyly brags about the yield from the fig tree in his backyard. Big hands, big muscles, a man who is strong enough to pick up a girl and spin her around on his pinkie. Not normally the type of guy I go for, but definitely the sort of person fit to pull me out of a pool.

Then he steps out of the direct sun. "Eliza," he says in a tenor tone. "Hello."

He's no taller than I am, with thick black hair that's cut in a pageboy at his chin. His eyebrows are woolly, and his nose ends at a comical point. There is something oily about his complexion, and he has a puzzling configuration of facial hair on his upper lip and chin. He looks like Guy Fawkes. He's wearing an Oxford shirt and a tapestry vest. His shoes are very shiny and narrow. His arms look thin. I can't imagine this person skimming a pool for bugs, let alone pulling a person from it.

My shoulders droop. It isn't fair to be disappointed. Maybe I should have suspected this sort of person, since the text message response I'd gotten from him included a *Game of Thrones*–themed gif.

"H-hi," I say tentatively. "Thanks for coming."

Another awkward pause. I can feel him looking at me. I feel grimy and puffy from my hospital stay, and the Lakers shirt reeks of sweat.

"Anyway," I say, leading him toward the back of the house. I'm not sure I want to let him inside. I'm funny about letting in people I don't know, especially people who look like this guy. "Let's talk in the back."

The backyard has a natural water stream and a guesthouse so small it can barely fit a bed. There's also a shed out back that can hold two horses. When I moved in, I heard a cacophony of whinnies, and the air smelled like manure. Who knew people in Burbank kept horses? I don't have any, but there is one mare down the road that I like to visit—Beauty. She always pokes her nose out of her stall when she hears me coming, as if she knows my scent. Her eyes are so dark and limitless. She seems like she could keep a secret. There are times when I press my face to her muzzle and just stand there for a few moments, hoping no one will come around the bend and catch us.

The patio has a lot of dead plants and a nonworking fountain that's full of sticks and seedpods. I grab an empty Żywiec Porter beer bottle that was resting atop one of the lounge chairs and throw it into a spongy bush. Desmond narrows his eyes at the miniature carousel wedged between the guesthouse and the wall. I found it on eBay; it's a replica of an Allan Herschell from the 1950s, except it's got psychotic zebras, a pissed-off looking swan, and a lion without a head.

"That's quite a piece," he says with what seems like true admiration.

"Thanks. It works, if you want to ride on it. The song it plays sounds like 'In-A-Gadda-Da-Vida.' "

His chuckle is a half-avuncular, half-creepy *heh heh heh*. His gaze drifts to the papier-mâché rat sculpture I'd bought at a flea market. The rainbow rodent is smoking a joint and giving the finger. "Same to you, my friend," he says to it, elaborately bowing. I try not to grimace.

"So!" I say impatiently. "Thanks for coming."

I offer my hand to shake. His hand is calloused, and his grip is stronger than I expect. "Charmed," he says, holding my gaze. "I feel like I already know you."

"Well, you pulled me out of the water. So I guess you sort of do."

There's a flicker of something across his face. "Actually, milady, that's not what I mean."

My eyes narrow on the paisley brocade on his vest. He's got an amulet around his neck that looks like the same ones this shaman I once visited in the desert, post-tumor, was selling in his gift shop. There is a crawling feeling up my spine, and I recall the residual sense of fear I experienced just before dropping into the water at the Tranquility. Maybe it was a bad idea to invite him here. I glance around the high walls that surround my house from everyone else's. It's hard to know if anyone is home in this neighborhood. The houses are smashed together, but they're eerily quiet and sequestered.

"Um, explain?" I ask, trying not to let my voice shake.

He looks sheepish. "I happen to know you're an author. I even requested a copy of your book."

For a moment, I'm not sure what to say. "*The Dots*?" I bleat, finally. He nods. "H-how did you know I wrote that?"

"Forgive me, but after they took you away in the ambulance, I Googled you. I thought it would be important to know about the person whose life I just saved. And I read a press release about your book. It seemed right up my alley, so I requested a copy through the Amazon Vine program."

It strikes me as odd that a man like this thought *my* book would be right up his alley. Then again, I have no idea *who* my ideal reader is—except myself.

"But I didn't receive it." Desmond sounds disappointed. "Amazon said it wasn't available until publication."

"Yeah, we didn't end up going with the Vine promotion." I pick at a loose splinter on the table. "But how did you know my name at all? Did the cops read it off my ID or something?"

"*You* told me it. After I pulled you out. You were lucid. Talking. Once I got you breathing again, that is."

My cheeks burn. I'd forgotten about receiving mouth-to-mouth. I imagine Desmond's bristly facial hair scraping against my skin. On instinct, my chin starts to feel rashy.

"I don't remember that at all. What did I say, exactly?"

"Just your name, and something about a murder taking place at the resort in the sixties. And then your eyes got very big and you said, *It is I!*"

I wrinkle my nose. "Huh." That sounds like something Gloria Swanson would say in *Sunset Boulevard* as she swirled into the ballroom in all her jewels. I used to watch that movie at least once a month.

"Anyway, after that, the paramedics showed up—my companion had called 911."

"Your companion?" I picture an older, moneyed fellow leading this guy around on a studded leash.

"Paul. A work friend. I did all the rescuing, though." He smiles. "So how did you come up with your book idea? I find authors so intriguing. I'm hoping I might write a book someday."

"I'm not sure I'd call myself an *author,* per se."

His face falls. "Why not?"

"Because I've only written one book. And it's not even out."

He smiles at this, like I've told a joke. "Oh, I'm sure you'll write others."

I don't know about that. And I have no idea how we've gotten so off-topic. I clear my throat. "So on Saturday, you and your companion just happened to be strolling by the pool area when I fell in, or . . . ?"

"That's right. I was showing Paul around the grounds. It's a beautiful resort, isn't it? But then we heard thunder and started inside. We cut through next to the pool area, and that's when I heard the splash. I looked over the fence and saw there were no lifeguards. Then I noticed that whoever had jumped in wasn't coming up for air."

He says this boastfully, as though this is Sherlock Holmes–level sleuthing. "So you jumped in and fished me out?" I ask.

"Exactly." He smiles proudly. "I didn't waste a moment. You were easy to pull to the surface. So light! Like a hollow piece of wood!"

I'm not sure I've ever been compared to a piece of wood before. "But there was no one else in the pool area?"

"I believe everyone had been told to leave. Paul had to run for help. By the time a guard came, I'd already revived you." His eyes shine. "Do you remember?"

"I already told you. I don't remember *anything*."

"Ah." Desmond nods. "So! I suppose you want to know about me, then? Your dashing rescuer who brought you back to life?"

I blink. Maybe this is why normal people invite their rescuers over: To thank them. To stroke their egos. To promise them their firstborn. Or to find out what their rescuers are like, so they can *tell* said firstborn. I want to laugh, but I don't want to wound Desmond's pride. He might leave.

But before I can say anything, Desmond goes, "Oh, now, don't be shy. Let's see. My middle name is Lawrence. I was born in December—a Capricorn. I drink a lot of absinthe. The real kind, not the tripe they sell here in the States. I have a dealer in Nice." He leans back. "Have you ever tried it? The only true way to drink it is the way the *artistes* did, in Paris, poured over a sugar cube on a spoon."

"Sounds gross," I say absently, because I fear any enthusiasm might usher in an invitation to an absinthe-drinking event.

Desmond looks wounded. "It's not gross. It's transcendent. I got into it during my side job. I'm the lead Caesar at the Circus Maximus in San Fernando."

"The what?"

"The Circus Maximus! In the Valley? The celebration of ancient Roman and Greek culture? Among other things, we do a reenactment of the Pompeii volcano disaster and all five acts of *Julius Caesar*. It's quite well-attended." I must be looking at him with confusion, because he adds, "I can't believe you haven't heard of the Circus Maximus. I thought I read you were an English major."

I wonder what else he's read about me. "What does being an English major have to do with knowing about a Renaissance Faire in the Valley?"

He *harrumph*s. "It is *not* a Renaissance Faire. You should check it out. For two weeks in July, there are gladiator events, a soothsayer, a replication of the Oracle at Delphi, a reenactment of Homer's *Odyssey* . . ."

"That's from a completely different time period!"

He frowns. "Well, sure, but we take some creative liberties."

"And you're Caesar, huh?" I can so picture him in a toga and with a laurel in his hair. "You like it?"

He juts up his nose. "It's intense. I get assassinated twenty times in the two-week period. I try to really get into the character, which means every time I go down, it really and truly feels like a death." He looks at me meaningfully, and for a moment—a very, very brief one—I'm a little bit curious. I wonder if he could possibly think about death as much as I do. I wonder if he likes reading suicide notes as much as I do.

But then I fear I've let my gaze linger on him too long, and I avert my eyes. "So, um, what brought you to the Tranquility again?"

"Well, I'm a bit of a celebrity, too," Desmond says loftily. "*Besides* being Caesar, I mean. I'm also the second-in-command of marketing for the Los Angeles Comic-Con. I was meeting with my team to strategize for this year's event. We came up with very important initiatives, like how we're going to have members of the Umbrella Corp from *Resident Evil* protect the female cosplayers in case anyone harasses them. Those Umbrella people mean *business.*"

I have no idea what he's talking about. I also want to laugh, but I think he's actually serious. I can picture the poster in Tranquility's lobby: Comic-Con's logo, and then instructions directing the attendees to one of the conference rooms on the second floor. "So basically, your whole life is about conventions."

His eyes dance. "I love conventions. Hopefully, in the future, there will be conventions for everything you're into. People with the same interests could gather together and unite in their shared devotion to old-timey medicine balls, for instance. Or clock making. Or squirrels."

"Isn't that what social media's for?"

He sighs. "It saddens me how social media has changed the way we interact with one another."

"So you don't have an Instagram account, then? No Facebook for the convention?"

"Well, yes. Of course I do. But that's different. That's *useful.*"

"You didn't by any chance retire to the Shipstead bar after your strategizing?" I ask, deciding to change the subject again, hoping we've done enough getting-to-know-you bullshit.

He fiddles with the hair on his chin. "I don't know the name of the place we went to. What's it look like?"

"They're going for a yacht club feel, but it's more like a down-market cruise ship."

"Nope, we were in the one that looked like Easter Island."

I sigh. "I was hoping you could fill in a few blanks for me. Apparently *I* was at the Shipstead that night."

"But I thought you didn't drink."

"I don't. Normally." My brain catches. "How did you know I didn't drink?"

There's a small flicker across his lips, practically concealed under his curly mustache. "I think you told me. You were saying all kinds of things when you regained consciousness." Then he leans in. "So you can't remember *anything*?" I shake my head. "That sounds like what happened to our best chariot driver. He got trampled, had a concussion, and he forgot not only what happened that day but the whole two weeks of the *ludi circenses*. He never got any of it back, poor man." Desmond looks mournful.

I want to roll my eyes. I have a feeling the Circus Maximus is like what I've heard about athletes in the Olympic Village: they're crammed together in close quarters, dressed in questionable clothing, and they're all so excited about the pomp and circumstance that they celebrate by having lots and lots of sex. Except that in the Olympic Village, everyone is a hot Olympic athlete, and at the Circus Maximus, most people have day jobs at Best Buy. Still, I appreciate Desmond's acceptance of my botched memory. He's the first person I've come into contact with who isn't looking at me and this pool situation like it's all my doing.

"Well, I'm glad you were able to rescue me," I say.

"I'm glad, too." His eyes sparkle. "It's not every day someone like you falls to the bottom of a pool."

"I didn't mean to fall into that pool, you know," I blurt, before I can help myself.

"I am aware," he says, without missing a beat. But then he cocks his head and looks at me strangely. "Come again?"

There is a swoop in my stomach, but I decide to tell him. Desmond seems like he's a lot of things, but I doubt he'll judge. "I didn't jump in. And I didn't accidentally fall in, either."

Desmond's brow furrows. An expression slides across his face I can't quite discern. Alarm, perhaps. A sudden bolt to the brain. "So then you . . ." He trails off. His Adam's apple bobs.

My heart lurches. "I think someone pushed me. Do you know anything about that?"

He glances over his shoulder. "I don't . . . I'm not sure. It could have been nothing."

"Please." I step closer to him, the closest I've been to him all day. He smells like a greenhouse. Moss and algae. "Tell me what you know."

He glances behind him again. The silence seems to close in on us. The sun breaks from behind a cloud, slanting at us sideways, searing the part in my hair. Desmond's tongue darts from his mouth, pink and minnow-like.

"I think I saw someone running away."

From The Dots

Even after Dot's brain tumor was removed and she underwent radiation, her seizures still came weekly. The scariest were when she was at home, away from medical equipment and knowledgeable hands. Dorothy was always present and ready, her arms outstretched to catch Dot's falls. On their way to the hospital, Dorothy called Dot's mother. One time, she put her on speakerphone. "Wait, she had *another* one?" Dot's mother's voice squawked through the car. "What the fuck is going on here?"

Dorothy pressed her lips together and quickly disabled the speaker function. When she was done with the call, she glanced at Dot in the backseat. "I'm sure your mother didn't mean anything by that. She's just worried." But Dot felt alarmed. She'd never heard her mother use the word *fuck,* and certainly not in relation to *her.*

Her aunt spirited Dot to the hospital, though she chose a different one to bring her to than the place where Dot had had brain surgery: St. Mother Maria's, located west of the city. "It's the best of the best," she told Dot. Dorothy had an encyclopedic knowledge on the best of the best. She knew the best place to get a shoeshine, your spine adjusted, or the perfect banana split; she knew the best restaurants to pick up a fireman or a studio executive. She knew the best ways to fake a car accident—if, perchance, you were in the mood for defrauding your insurance company. She knew the best place to buy greeting cards for very specific occasions—sympathy for botched surgeries, congratulations on your sixth marriage—and where to get false eyelashes stitched into your biological eyelashes. She knew the best place to clean an upholstered couch covered in blood. "Not that I've ever had to use their services, but it's a good resource to have handy," she said. Dot's mother didn't even know the best place in their neighborhood to get pizza.

Dr. Koder, who was assigned Dot's case, came into Dot's hospital room one day to talk about her condition. "Look, we just can't pinpoint what could be causing these seizures. We'd like to keep her in the hospital until we can figure it out."

Dot's mother, who was sitting on the bed next to Dot's feet, bristled. "Correct me if I'm wrong, but isn't it her brain tumor that's causing the seizures?"

"Typically, with surgery and radiation, these types of tumors are completely obliterated, and usually patients are symptom-free. Dot has already gone through those steps, so we're thinking something else might be at play."

Dot's mother scratched a nonexistent stain on her scrubs. "I just don't understand how it could be something else. I just don't understand how this keeps *happening*."

Dorothy touched her arm. "There's no need to get worked up."

Dot's mother glanced at her. "This has been going on for too long. It's the twenty-first century. Medicine should be more advanced than this."

"It would be a much less complicated life if your little girl weren't sick, wouldn't it?" Dorothy simpered. Dot's mother gave her a furious look Dot didn't understand.

Dr. Koder coughed. "There are lots of avenues to try. We need to make sure it isn't an environmental issue, for example."

"An *environmental issue?*" Dot's mother repeated. "Are you suggesting our house is full of poison?"

"Of course not." Dr. Koder stared down at Dot's file in her hands. A metallic noise clanged in the hall. "I understand your frustration, but we *are* doing all we can. I promise. We'll get to the bottom of it."

Dorothy gave the doctor a sympathetic smile. "Of course you will." Her voice was like warm maple syrup.

While Dot was in the hospital, Dorothy rented a hotel room at the Sheraton down the street. She could have gone back to her suite at the Magnolia in Beverly Hills, where she'd been living ever since Dot could remember, but Dorothy said she liked to be close in case anything happened. She even bought a beeper and made the doctors page her before making any decisions. Dot appreciated her aunt's dedication and perseverance. Only once did Dot ask her if she needed to work on her novel, *The Riders of Carrowae,* instead of spending so much time by her side.

"Pshaw, work," Dorothy scoffed. "It can wait."

Meanwhile, Dot's mother went back to the dentist's office. She even resumed her regular full-time hours. "I need to keep my job so we keep our insurance," she explained. But it hurt all the same. Dot winced when she saw her mother walk into the room in the morning in her balloon-printed scrubs, knowing that soon she'd be gone. Sometimes, it seemed as though she left the hospital with a skip in her step. Once, when her mother was in the bathroom, Dorothy rooted through her purse and unearthed an envelope of freshly printed photos. By the looks of it, her mother had taken pictures of a birthday party at the dentist's office. "Oh, look, they're having chocolate cake." Dorothy slapped a rectangular image across Dot's legs. "And that's quite a *smile* your mother's got on her face, isn't it? Nice to see *someone* happy, anyway."

Dot decided to try her hardest not to need her mother. She turned away from her kisses and didn't answer her questions. "Oh, you shouldn't be so hard on her," Dorothy said. But then, not a half beat later: "Of course, you'll *always* have me."

That was right, Dot thought. Dorothy was more than enough.

There was a rotating cast of nurses, aides, doctors, and specialists in to see Dot, eager to figure out why her brain kept locking up. She had CAT scans, PET scans, bone density tests, blood plasma draws, a spinal tap. Dorothy lorded over every treatment, wanting to know about every aspect of Dot's care: what went into changing the sheets, why they took her blood so often, the types of needles they used for Dot's IV, what sorts of medications they gave Dot when she had a seizure, and the nutritional value of the smoothie they always gave Dot for lunch. She learned so much that she could probably have performed many of the minor procedures herself. In fact, one day while dozing, Dot felt the blood pressure cuff wrap around her arm and opened her eyes to find her aunt taking her vitals. "They let you do this now?" she asked, chuckling.

Dorothy blinked. "Sorry?"

It was a different voice—higher and less raspy. Dot looked again. The woman taking her blood pressure had dark hair and a finely boned face, just like Dorothy's. The only difference was that her eyes were green.

Dot told her aunt about the look-alike, and not much later, Dorothy got to experience her for herself. The woman, whose name was Stella, shuffled in to take Dot's blood pressure, not even noticing Dorothy in the chair, and Dorothy, for once, didn't make her presence known. When she left, Dorothy exhaled. "*That* was amazing. It was like I was in the presence of a paranormal event! I'd split in two! She should play a look-alike of me at parties."

"Or you could play a look-alike of her," Dot quipped.

Dorothy wrinkled her nose. "Why would I do *that*?"

The next time Stella came in, Dorothy invited her to sit on Dot's bed and chat. Stella was younger than Dorothy, and her nails were bitten to the quick. Dorothy moved close, lifted a lock of Stella's hair, and sniffed it.

"Do you get ovarian cysts from time to time?" she asked. "Is your eyesight just a *touch* myopic?"

Stella's eyes darted. "Pardon?"

Dorothy looked at Dot. "I want to see if her insides are the same as mine, too." Then she pressed her face close to Stella's. "Who's prettier?"

By this time, a nurse had entered the room and was giving Dorothy a skeptical look. Dot surreptitiously pointed in her aunt's direction, not wanting to offend Stella, though it was the truth. Stella was younger, but Dorothy was prettier.

"Do you need anything, dear?" Stella asked Dot as she stood and bunched her blood pressure cuff under her arm. Dot shook her head, and Stella was gone.

Dorothy chuckled after Stella left. "You'd think she would have enjoyed that. Not everyone has a doppelganger."

To gauge Dot's pain, one of the nurses suggested Dot grade her days, with A as perfectly healthy days and F as times where she felt close to death's door. Dot rated a lot of her days at the hospital a C-minus, sometimes even a D. On those days, the corners of the room warped into dragons and yetis. Her scalp itched tremendously, and every time she grappled for it, a clump of hair fell out. Dot's port, a gaping hole in her chest that fed medication straight to a vein, ached, and it became infected several times. The worst days were when she had seizures, because just before one started, she would feel the most nauseated she ever had in her life, and her vision would flip inward on itself, and she'd lose control of her limbs. She'd slip somewhere deep inside her body then—she witnessed everything, could see everything, but had no way of controlling what her body was doing. When she came out of it, her headaches were excruciating. Her skin felt like it was on fire. One time, the seizure was so violent that she almost bit through her tongue, and she had to have a giant bandage wrapped around the muscle for four days, lest she get another infection. She was so prone to infections. Bacteria adored her.

The only thing that got her through any of it was her aunt's presence. If Dot needed Dorothy to sit by her side all night, Dorothy would. If Dot needed her to shove her finger into Dot's mouth during a seizure so she'd bite Dorothy's skin straight down to the bone instead of her own tongue, she would—and did, having the indentations to prove it. Every day, Dorothy came into Dot's room with fat medical books she'd purchased from the UCLA Medical School bookstore, researching unusual brain, lymph, blood, metabolic, and autoimmune diseases that could be making Dot seize. She demanded private audiences with Dot's doctors and had even procured Dr. Koder's home phone number. She cornered her nurses in the hall and asked for "the real scoop" in case Dot's doctors were mincing words. One time, Dot saw her sneak into an unattended nurses' station and fiddle with the computer.

"What were you looking for?" Dot asked after Dorothy had scurried away just as a nurse came around the corner.

"Notes in your file, of course," Dorothy whispered. "Just in case there's anything I can look up. It's possible these doctors don't read all of the journals, you know. I'm filling in the gaps."

She sat by Dot's side for hours, reading her books, watching Dot's favorite programs on TV, making up stories. They fantasized about the food Dot would eat once she was out of here and able to eat a normal diet again—the hospital was keeping her on a very restrictive food regimen, thinking perhaps that she'd developed a bizarre allergy. She pointed to a restaurant called M&F Chop House across the street.

"We'll go there for burgers. I hear they make delicious ones."

Dot studied the restaurant out the window. It had golden light seeping from its core. The bar was full. A TV in the corner played the news. A group at a table in the front talked animatedly.

"Maybe I'll just live there," Dot mused. A week before, her mother had announced she was going to marry the man she was dating, a man Dot barely knew, and who had a child Dot had never met.

"Where would you sleep?" Dorothy asked. "On a banquette?"

"No, in the room where they chop up the meat." Dot had an unusual affinity for the smell of blood.

Dorothy chuckled. "You have *quite* the imagination."

"And every night, I could dine with interesting people—fortune tellers, witches, elves."

"Elves! Who else?"

It became a riff. Every day, they added to the tale of Dot at the Chop House. Dot would find a secret cave in the basement filled with crystals and stalagmites and gold doubloons. A dumbwaiter that led to a portal back to Gothic England, and she'd befriend Jack the Ripper. Dot of the Chop House had quite a few pets, but her favorites were her dog, Ko, and her bat, Tristan. Tristan had the power of speech, but he could only recite sonnets. Dorothy was impressed that such a little girl knew what a sonnet was.

"*For I have sworn thee fair, and thought thee bright, who art as black as hell, as dark as night,*" Dot recited gleefully.

"A genius!" Dorothy proclaimed.

"Your aunt's quite the firecracker, isn't she?" Dr. Koder said one day, popping into Dot's room unannounced when Dorothy had taken a coffee break.

Dot looked into the doctor's wet, Hershey-Kiss–colored eyes. She had a bit of an Anna Nicole Smith thing going, with the blonde hair and the huge boobs, but her glasses softened that, rendering her wise. Ish.

"Yes," Dot answered proudly. "Did you know she was once a model? And she got through half of medical school. In Tunisia, while she was taking a break from the CIA."

Dr. Koder's smile wavered a little. "Well, yes, but she's not a doctor *here*."

Dot frowned. "I know."

Dr. Koder leaned a little closer. "If you ever need some time alone, if it ever seems like too much, just tell us."

"If *what* is too much?"

"Well, sometimes family can be a little . . . suffocating. And it must be hard not being around kids your own age. You should check out our hangout area. We have a Ms. Pac-Man machine!"

Dot was confused. Maybe Dr. Koder didn't like the Halloween decorations Dorothy had brought in: doll parts popping out of coffins, decapitated bats, rotted eyeballs in cauldrons. Maybe they didn't like how Dorothy flirted with the male specialists. Maybe they didn't like the time she brought that bottle of Sauvignon Blanc and drank it in Dot's room. But it wasn't like she'd given Dot any.

And really, if the doctors should be mad at anyone, it should be Dot's mother. She barely showed up anymore. She just thrust all the responsibility on Dorothy while she attended office birthday parties and ate chocolate cake. Meanwhile, Dorothy helped Dot around the clock. Sometimes, Dorothy would come into Dot's room and collapse exhaustedly in a chair, even nodding off for a few moments, jolting awake if Dot so much as coughed.

"She probably *does* need a rest," Dot said. "She's trying so hard."

Dorothy swept in not fifteen minutes later wearing a Chanel suit and the Hermès scarf printed with prowling leopards, Dot's favorite.

"Did you see Doctor Koder in the hall?" Dot asked. "She said you might want a rest from here. You could go back to the Magnolia. I know how much you miss their eggs Benedict."

Dorothy paused from unraveling her scarf from her neck. "Why would she say I need a rest?"

"Well, I might have hinted that you were tired . . ."

"What else did you say about me?"

"I . . . I don't know," Dot said cautiously. Her aunt's voice had grown so loud and shrill. "Nothing, really."

Dorothy stomped around Dot's little room. "Jesus. Those jealous assholes. One of them gets an idea in her head, and it just infects everyone else. And meanwhile, it's you who suffers. My baby!" Then she whirled away from the window. "You don't really agree, do you? You don't want me gone?"

"I— Of course not." Dot had no idea what her aunt was talking about.

Dorothy collapsed to the chair and covered her face with her hands. "Oh God. You do, you do. This is how it starts. This is how I am abandoned."

"Aunt Dorothy," Dot whispered. "Please. Don't cry."

"Everyone leaves me," Dorothy said into her hands. "Thomas. Your mother. My mother. My husbands. Now you."

"Don't say that."

Her aunt kept her head down as she stumbled out of the room. "I can't be in here right now. I can't look at you."

"Wait!" Dot scrambled out of her bed, getting tangled in all the cords that fed into her body. "I'm sorry! Whatever I did, I'm sorry!"

She hobbled down the hall after Dorothy, dragging the IV pole behind her, but Dorothy was already through the exit's double doors. A nurse found Dot in the stairwell and walked her back to her room, saying that she couldn't leave the children's ward. Dot flopped back onto her horrid hospital bed and flipped through the TV channels. Everything on at that time of day was either terribly violent or a talk show featuring people yelling and sobbing. She turned the TV off and stared at the ceiling, listening to the soft murmurs of the intercom in the hall. After a while, she fell asleep, her scratchy, bleached pillow wet with tears.

That evening, Dot had another seizure. All she remembered was her head flapping back against the pillow; the next thing she knew, she was strapped down to the bed, some sort of metal bite plate in her mouth. Dorothy stood over her, tears in her eyes. Dot croaked out a note of joy, but her head pounded, and she writhed in pain.

"Honey, we have to get out of this place," Dorothy said hurriedly.

"W-what?" Dot asked blearily, her tongue thick. "Why?"

"This place is shit, that's why. I just found an article that this place has been written up for contamination three different times in the last ten years. I bet you it's contaminated again. I bet you *that's* what's making you sick!" She started throwing Dot's stuffed animals into her duffel. "Let's go. I have a car waiting. We're going to a new place across town."

"*Now?*" Dot tried to sit up.

"Yes." Dorothy extended her arm. "Do you think you can stand?"

Dot pointed to the restraints around her. Dorothy nodded and undid them. Dot stood, but her head throbbed. She thought she might throw up. She didn't want to leave, she wanted to lie down.

"I'm so tired," she murmured. "Let's go in the morning."

"We can't wait for the morning." Dorothy wrapped her arm around Dot's shoulders. "You can sleep in the car."

"Are the doctors okay with me going?"

"I signed all the papers to discharge you. It's our decision, not theirs. And anyway, screw them and their dirty hospital. I'm sorry I ever brought you here."

By now they were in the hall, which was eerily empty. Dot looked out the window. It was pitch-dark outside. A wall clock in the break room said it was 3:15 a.m. She took another awkward step. The bottoms of her feet felt like pins and needles.

"I wish I could say goodbye to Doctor Koder," Dot said. "I liked her."

Dorothy waved her hand. "She's not getting any answers."

"Can I call Mom?"

"After we get to the new place," Dorothy assured her. "After we settle in."

Around a corner, she caught a glimpse of a swish of fabric and dark hair. Dot did a double take—here was the other Dorothy, standing frozen next to a computer console. The real Dorothy straightened her spine and gripped Dot's arm. The other Dorothy—the nurse, Stella—stared, unblinking, for a full, long five seconds. Then, raising her chin, she turned away without a word. Dot and Dorothy scrambled down the stairwell quickly, their shoes echoing against the metal risers.

The walls of the new hospital's children's ward were painted a sunny yellow. Dot checked into a room and immediately fell asleep. When she awoke, her mother was standing in the hall, arguing with Dorothy.

"You had no right to move her in the middle of the night. The other place was fine."

"Didn't you *read* that article I found?"

"You should have called me about this. Instead, you just did it."

"I did it because I had to. It was her worst seizure yet. You weren't there. I was."

Dot opened one eye. Her mother had turned away. Her eyes had filled with tears. *You deserve that,* Dot thought.

A new doctor introduced himself a half hour later. He said he would be taking care of Dot's treatment. Dorothy beamed brightly. Dr. Osuri—young, twitchy, with too many pens stuffed in his pocket—fiddled with the stethoscope around his neck.

"It's lovely to meet you, Dot," he said, flipping through the medical file Dorothy had brought from St. Mother Maria's. "We'll get to the bottom of what's happening to you."

"Isn't that wonderful?" Dorothy cried, arms clasped at her throat.

What could Dot say but yes?

ELIZA

"YOU'VE GOT TO tell the police," I say to Desmond. I grab my phone and start to dial 911, then change my mind and look up the number for the Palm Springs PD on Google. "Right now."

"Okay," Desmond says, though he sounds uncertain.

I manage to punch in the digits. The phone starts to ring, and I thrust it at him. He holds it outstretched like a writhing snake.

"I'm not really versed in speaking with law enforcement," he says. "What do you want me to say?"

I snatch it back and listen as a receptionist answers in a peppy voice that I've reached Palm Springs PD, and how may she direct my call? "I'm looking for Lance," I bark.

"Lance . . . who?" the receptionist asks, all bubbles and sunshine.

As if there's more than one Lance working at Palm Springs PD? But I don't remember his last name. Had he even told me his last name? "Lance the forensic psychologist. Lance who visits patients in hospitals."

"Please hold."

They play Hall & Oates's "Maneater" while I wait. Who chose *that*?

"Can you describe the person you saw?" I ask Desmond. "Was it a girl? A guy?"

"I don't know." He looks sheepish. "I just remember . . . a dark flash. *Obsidian.*"

"Why didn't you tell the cops this when they interviewed you? They *did* interview you, right?"

"Well, sure, they came when the ambulance came, and they asked me what happened. But this is when I presumed you'd fallen in. I didn't know to be on the lookout for a criminal. And they didn't *ask* if I'd seen anything."

I curl my hand into a fist. Of course the cops didn't ask him. They'd probably already made up their minds I was drunk and suicidal.

"You have to tell them what you saw," I urge again. I realize how I sound. I picture Desmond later tonight, having absinthe with Paul, his comic-con buddy who'd been with him poolside, talking about his crazy run-in with the paranoid almost-drowned girl. But I'm also so relieved. There was a teeny, tiny part of me that did wonder if my family was right—maybe I *had* jumped into that pool, just like all the other times. Maybe I was having a psychological break. Or maybe my tumor was back. Maybe I was sick again. But no: I had an assailant. So there. I practically want to sing it from the rooftops. I'm *right.*

A voice breaks through "Maneater." "Hello, you've reached the Palm Springs PD tip line. If you have information about a crime, please leave your tip at the beep."

My heart sinks. Then again, I suppose what I have *is* a tip—it's better than nothing. After the beep, I say what I have to say, then hang up.

"Well, hopefully they'll call. And then I'll conference you in, if you're available. Or at least I'll give them your number."

"Of course," Desmond says. "I'll give you my address. I'm happy to help. *Very* happy."

And then he looks at me. I stand to go, but he remains seated.

His eyes soften. There's an expectant smile on his face, like he's waiting for the real party to start. Then something hits me. It's possible that I did something, poolside, when I woke up on the deck. I have a bad habit of having sex with strangers, despite how ridiculous I find them.

I can almost picture it. Desmond pulled me out of the pool, revived me, and I took off all my clothes in gratitude. I grabbed his crotch. Maybe we actually had sex there on the concrete before the EMTs came. And instead of being like every other guy and disappearing the moment the deed is done, Desmond actually has a conscience and has come over to see if I'm damaged and vulnerable. Or maybe he wants to have sex *again*. I weigh my options. He's a weird stranger who gets assassinated for fun, but he believes in me. And to be honest, his interest in me is flattering. I guess I don't have very high standards.

I take a breath and move closer to him. All at once, his greenhouse scent is appealing, and my nipples go hard. The moment my lips actually make contact with his cheek, he shoots away.

"Um," he says, fiddling with his vest. "Hello, nurse."

I fumble, too, jumping back so fast my calf slams against the table.

"I, um," Desmond is making a lot of noise with his keys. "I have a . . ." He checks his watch. "Work to do. A lot of vendors to visit. So, um . . ."

"Yep, lemme walk you out."

We get to the screen door at the same time and both reach for the handle, resulting in an awkward dance of him letting me go first, then me letting him go first, then both of us trying to stuff through the space together. We pass through my shiny kitchen, and I'm never so grateful for the pretty room in my life—it gives me credibility, sanity, even though if Desmond peeked in the pantry he'd notice an unhealthy amount of Kraft macaroni & cheese, which I eat by the truckload, even though I'm not supposed to.

We stop at the door, and I don't know what to do with my hands. Finally I just stick out my palm for him to shake.

"Thanks for coming by! Thanks for saving me!" Because what *else* do you say?

The door shuts. I spin around and survey my quiet house. My living room is filled with odd antique trunks and armoires I purchased from an antiques dealer in Santa Cruz. The pale pink couch has a mysterious stain on it that might be blood—it was like that when I bought it. In the corner is a dusty RCA Theremin from the 1920s. I've meant to take lessons, but I've never gotten around to it.

All of a sudden, the hair on the back of my neck stands. Someone is watching me. I sense a flicker in the corner of my eye and whip around, certain I'm going to discover a presence there. The curtains flutter as if someone has just jumped through the open window. Or maybe it's just the breeze.

"Hello?" I call out shakily.

No answer.

What if this isn't over? What if whoever tried to hurt me is still out there, hoping to hurt me *again*?

I rake my fingers down my face. My fingernails knead harder and harder until I know I'm close to drawing blood. But it isn't satisfying enough, so I twist a lock of hair around my fingers and pull hard. The pain is sharp, eye-numbing. I stifle a yelp. And then I run upstairs as fast as I can, eager for a closed door, eager for darkness, eager to get away from whatever this is.

■ ■ ■

My bedroom is long like a bowling lane and almost as thin. On the walls are animal skulls and posters of Wednesday Addams, who was my childhood idol. On my bureau are vitamin bottles, vitamin powders, a healing stone given to me by a shaman I visited in the desert, an iPod loaded with meditation tapes that I try to use but that don't really work, and the energy drawings I did with an art therapist that revealed my soul was a dark, twisted knot. I'm trying my hardest to prevent the tumor from invading my body again. But sometimes, I think the preventative shit is worse than the illness.

I think I saw someone running away.

I swallow hard. It's vindicating that Desmond has confirmed this, but it scares me that such violence actually exists. *Who could have pushed me?*

I picture my mother's face swirling above me yesterday in the hospital. And Bill's, and Gabby's. Who alerted them to come? How had they arrived so quickly? Then I remember it hadn't been *that* fast—I'd been sleeping for quite a few hours before I spoke to them. But still. Is it possible they'd already *been* in Palm Springs? But what am I presuming, that one of *them* pushed me? Why would they do that? Because I'm a drain on them? Because they're sick of my shenanigans? Because I'd *done* something to one of them? Something inside me rolls over with a ripple. Maybe. But why can't I remember what that is?

I stop on Gabby again. It's not as though we're close. After Bill made the introductions the first time she and I met, I went into the kitchen, and she followed. I didn't ask her to follow me. Nor did I really want her there.

"Um," Gabby said quietly once we were alone. "I heard your dad died. So did my mom."

I snorted. Like I was going to have *that* conversation. Straightening my spine, I pulled out a big bottle of vodka from the freezer. My fingers burned with cold as I unscrewed the cap, and I poured myself a tall glass.

"Want some?"

Gabby's eyes widened. "No way."

I tipped the glass to my lips like I was a pro. I'd never had vodka before, but I felt like I needed to establish myself with this girl early on so she knew the pecking order. I took the tiniest sip and tried not to wince. I watched Gabby stare at me in horror.

"Maybe you shouldn't do that," she whispered.

Then my mother and Bill walked in. My mother immediately saw the bottle on the counter. "What's that?"

Neither of us answered. Gabby pushed her glasses up her nose.

"Who got that out?" my mother said, staring at me.

Gabby cleared her throat. "Um, I did. I just wanted to try it."

Bill looked appalled. *"You?"*

"Oh, please." My mother rolled her eyes. "It was clearly Eliza."

"No," Gabby's voice was stronger now. "It was me."

I don't know why she took the blame. I wanted to believe it was because I was so crazy and unpredictable that she thought it would be better just to defuse my actions and not make waves. But I wasn't entirely sure. I needed to be sure. I needed her to fear me. Why I needed that so badly is something I can't remember now, but I distinctly wrote about it in my journal: *I don't need her feeling sorry for me. She doesn't know what I can do.*

Through the years, I proved to Gabby what I could do. I locked her in a closet and stood outside reading facts about body decomposition from a criminology textbook. I put preserved animals I found at pawnshops on her pillow at night. I was a fan of fake plastic spiders in cereal bowls, a rubber dismembered hand in her backpack, and once, shoving the old child-sized coffin I kept in my room into the front entrance of the house and squeezing myself into it just before she walked through the door. Gabby had fainted when she saw me—just crumpled bonelessly to the floor, thwacking her head on the doorjamb. She'd needed stitches on her eyebrow. And yet, when Bill asked Gabby what had happened, she said she'd tripped. She never told on me for anything I did to her. She just absorbed all of it silently, stoically, pretending like it never happened.

Why didn't she ever fight back? I heard her arguing with her friends on the phone. I hacked her email and uncovered quite a few heated debates on a *Harry Potter and the Half-Blood Prince* fan fiction message board. She lost her shit when a girl at school called her a "fuckface." I'd called her *far* worse. Was she doing it because she'd figured out not reacting was the path to victory? Or was she storing up each and every incident, cataloging it carefully and referring to it often, slowly growing angrier and angrier and then downright vengeful? Was she a volcano ready to blow?

Do you really think someone would want to hurt you? Lance had asked. Gabby might have wanted to, but I just couldn't imagine Gabby doing such a thing. She didn't have the chutzpah.

I open my eyes and look around. The light seems different in my room. For a moment, I've forgotten my train of thought. *I've had a stroke,* I think frantically. But the clock says it's only a few minutes later, and all of my limbs work. I reach for my cell phone, but I've received no new calls. I'm about to put the phone down when I hit the button for my saved photo gallery. There's a video I don't remember recording first in line in the preview window.

I press Play.

The camera pans over the hospital room I've just left: first the corner with the sink, then those ugly paisley drapes, then a slice of window, the view of the parking lot. I hear a small sigh. The camera shifts, then shows my body on the hospital bed: my arm, my fingers, my chin. My eyes are closed.

I look at the video's time stamp: 10:09 p.m., yesterday. The angle is such that I could have held the phone outstretched, selfie-style, but there was no way I'd taken it. I'd only found out my phone was in my room this morning.

Seized with an idea, I scroll back past the video to see if *I* had taken any pictures at the resort . . . but I hadn't. The last photo in my camera roll was an image of an antique cymbal-playing monkey toy; a customer had brought it to the store where I work in hopes of making a trade. The monkey was old and well loved, some of its fur rubbed off, the little battery compartment on its butt rusty and corroded.

I stare into the middle distance, prickles dancing up my spine.

When I purchased my phone, the setup prompts urged me to assign a security passcode, but I'd declined—I had a knack for forgetting numbers, and it seemed inevitable that I'd lock myself out again and again. I'd tried to set up fingerprint recognition, but the technology couldn't read my print right away, so I gave up. In other words, anyone could have accessed my phone without any trouble at all. Someone easily could have recorded the video . . . but *who*?

I click the Details button, but all it says is that the video was taken at the hospital. I stare at the little map of Palm Springs on the screen. I'd never realized the town was such a grid.

My throat is dry. My head is throbbing. But all of a sudden, it seems foolish of me to be just lying here, inactive. I have proof now. Someone was running away. Someone followed me to that pool. Someone could still be following me *now*.

I push off my covers and head down the stairs. I'm still in the acid-washed jeans from the hospital, but there's no time to change. I find my house keys at the bottom of my purse and ready them at the door. My car isn't here, so I'll have to take an Uber, but that won't be a problem. Where I'm going, I'm not sure. I just have to go *somewhere*. I have to figure this out.

Then a hand clamps on my shoulder. I squeal and jump back. "You're not going anywhere."

I turn around. It's my roommate, Kiki Ross. She slides around me, grabs my keys from my hands, and blocks the door. Her eyes are wide. Her mouth turns down with fear and possibly anger.

"Come here, Eliza," she says in a low voice. "We need to talk."

From The Dots

A few months later, Dot was in the hospital again. The doctors at the new hospital thought they'd fixed her with a new mixture of medications, but her seizures returned one spring day at home, shortly after lunch. The first one came on strong, with bright lights kaleidoscoping in her eyes. Her mind peeled away from her body and lay in flakes on the floor.

Dorothy hurried her back to the hospital. Back to Dr. Osuri and the children's ward with the cheerful yellow walls and hot-air-balloon mural. Back to the same room with the television remote that only worked sporadically. Dot waited for her mother to show up. Hours passed. Finally, she rushed in, still in scrubs.

"I'm sorry," Dot's mother said in a begging tone. "I came as soon as I could. There was an emergency patient. I didn't have my phone. And no one told me." She bit her lip. "Your aunt should have called the front office like I always *tell* her to."

"It's fine," Dot said, calmly, distantly. Dorothy was here, after all. She was off buying magazines at the gift shop.

More tests, a few days of feeling better, and then a relapse. Dot wondered what Stella, the look-alike from St. Mother Maria's, was up to. Now, a sad-eyed woman in a brown headscarf took her blood pressure most days. She had very cold hands and made a funny sniffing sound as she checked the gauge.

All the nurses were distant this visit. Unsmiling and serious, as if they were keeping a grave secret from Dot. Dot asked Dorothy what was going on. Dorothy sniffed.

"They're just snotty, jealous bitches. They can't stand that we're so pretty."

"But they're nice to the other kids. That one girl down the hall, Sarah? They give her lollipops, like, all the time."

"Yes, but that's because Sarah has a wealthy father. There's always an angle, Dot." Dorothy waved her finger. "Always an angle."

And then, a good-ish day—Dot could see straight, she could eat. At lunch, an aide wheeled in a cart from the children's lending library across the street. She must have been going to an adult ward next, because Dot noticed a *Los Angeles* magazine on the top of a stack on a lower shelf. When Dot saw her own face on the cover, she drew in a sharp breath. She looked shorn and dopey, her arms the circumference of pencils, her veins visible through translucent skin. Next to her was her aunt, her black hair sleek and straight, her skin flawless and her violet eyes wide. *Fighters,* read the big yellow caption. And then: *Dorothy Banks, Magnolia Hotel resident, puts her hopes and dreams on hold to save her dying niece's life.*

Dying. The word sliced through Dot's veins, hot as coffee. She'd certainly thought enough about death, even her own death, but she hadn't realized she was actually, literally, *dying.* It seemed impossible.

She thumbed through the pages. The story was embedded among slick pieces about Beverly Hills home renovations and ads for plastic surgeons. Dot read every word of the piece, focusing on words like *cancerous* and *inoperable* and *terminal.* She'd never heard the doctors describe her illness in those terms before.

She ran to the bathroom and threw up pinkish, gummy chunks in the sink. When she returned to her room, Dorothy had reappeared. She was fluffing up the pillows and humming. A nurse named Lisa stood in the corner, pretending to busy herself with Dot's medications. Then Dorothy noticed the magazine on the bed.

"Ah," she said to Dot. "So you've seen it."

"When was this picture taken?" Dot demanded, so angry her teeth were chattering.

Dorothy lowered her eyes. "A few months ago, dear. When you were at the other hospital. Don't you remember?"

"No." Dot tore through her memories. She tossed useless visions aside like limp T-shirts she had no interest in wearing. There was nothing in her brain about a photo shoot. She would have never allowed a photographer to take a picture of her when she looked so grotesque. But that was the trouble with her brain: sometimes, memories dropped out of her entirely, like water through a sieve.

She grabbed the magazine and stuffed it into the trash can, though not before checking out her picture one last time.

"I look *awful*."

"Oh, darling. The article brings awareness to your case. Everyone will see now how sick you are. I'm thinking of starting a foundation for donations. That article is all about you!"

Lisa cleared her throat. Dorothy glanced at her and set her mouth in a line.

"The article hardly mentioned me except to say I was dying," Dot said. It was difficult to even say the word out loud. "It said my tumor was cancerous and inoperable. I thought my tumor was *gone*. And no one told me I have cancer!"

"You don't," Lisa answered loudly.

"It says that?" Dorothy glanced at the trash can. Dot was afraid she was going to fish the magazine out, but instead she folded her hands in her lap and remained seated. "Honestly, darling, sometimes reporters—well, they exaggerate things. Look—it doesn't matter. People probably won't read the article. They'll just look at the picture and the headline. That's what's important."

"They'll still see the picture of *me*, then."

"You don't look so bad."

Dot wasn't in the mood for lies. "Has Mom seen this?"

Her aunt's head shot up. Her skin seemed to visibly gray. "You know, I was doing this as a *favor* to you. I was just trying to make sure you didn't end up like Thomas—I'm certain there was something wrong with his brain, but no doctor would listen. It's articles like this that get doctors to sit up and notice. But I'll leave you *alone*, since that's what you crave." She walked out and shut the door, hard.

Dot stared at the door, shocked. Across the room, Lisa sighed.

Dot's gaze fell numbly to the tiles on the floor. They were a faded avocado-green color and covered in scuff marks. She pushed the beaded bracelet Dorothy had given her when she first got sick around her wrist. It had a bunch of skeleton charms on it. Charm bracelets were out of favor this year at her school, but she didn't want to take it off. That would hurt her aunt's feelings.

Lisa glided over and touched her shoulder. "Hey there, hon. Want me to stay for a little bit? We could play Uno."

Dot shook her head yes, then felt the ever-present tug. "Maybe bring my aunt back in, if she's still here."

Lisa's face fell. "Are you sure?"

"See if she's out there. Please?"

It took two more *pleases*, but Lisa did as Dot asked. Dorothy walked in with a sour look on her face.

"You must hate me," Dot blurted.

"You're lucky the elevator was taking a long time," Dorothy said at the same time.

They looked up at each other. Dorothy bent down and pressed her chest to Dot's. "Why, I could never hate you, darling," she said, looking into Dot's eyes, as honest as she'd ever been. "I'm your biggest fan."

A few days after the *Los Angeles* incident, Dorothy came into Dot's room excitedly. Dot looked at her through a curtain of exhaustion. She'd been having so many seizures lately. They pounded her hard, huge waves rolling onto a rocky shore. Her brain actually felt tired from so much quaking. Sometimes, in quiet moments, she thought death might be kind of nice. Not nearly as chaotic, anyway.

"The doctors are having a meeting about your condition," Dorothy crowed. "Apparently, you're a bit of a medical mystery. And guess what? They're letting *me* sit in on it! Isn't that wonderful?"

Dot blinked at her. She lingered on the *medical mystery* part.

Dorothy preened about the room. "Thank God they finally respect me. Now we'll be sure they aren't lying to us. I'll get the real dirt."

"You think the doctors are lying?" Dot asked. Dorothy didn't answer.

Dorothy wore a silk caftan and Chanel pumps for the meeting. She hired a makeup artist to do her face. "Wish me luck," she said before she went into the conference room. The meeting was at ten a.m.; the clock crawled to eleven, and then twelve, and still no Dorothy. At 12:30, Dorothy finally returned. She'd eaten off all her lipstick, and she was muttering.

"What happened?" Dot asked, turning off *Days of Our Lives*.

"The doctors are wrong," Dorothy said. "It's asinine. Irresponsible."

Dot felt a pull in her chest. "What did they say?"

Had the tumor returned? Would she have to endure radiation again, that hot line turning her insides to liquid, reducing her to molten piles of stones? It was bizarre—despite all the seizures, her MRIs kept coming back clean. But maybe the scans weren't catching everything.

"They're going to transfer you. They want you in the ICU, without visitors. They're saying it's so they can rule out anything environmental that might be causing your seizures. But I think that's bullshit. I think it's a conspiracy."

"They're putting me in a room without visitors?"

"I'm filing a complaint, don't you worry, but I'm not sure it's up to me anymore." Dorothy's gaze shot to Dot. Her pupils were hard, black pins. "What have you been saying about me?"

Dot grabbed a handful of sheets. "Nothing."

"They trick you. They pretend they're your friends, they get all buddy-buddy—darling, you *had* to have said something. I believe they're putting you—*us*—in the ICU as punishment."

Punishment? For what? Had Dot somehow slipped to them that she'd had a sip of Dorothy's wine a few days before, when Dorothy had turned her back? Or did she tell them she'd stolen the M&M's packet off the desk at the nurses' station? Dot had moved during a recent MRI, too. The tech hadn't commented, but he also hadn't said they needed to repeat the procedure. She'd just been so *itchy*.

"I'm sorry," Dot whispered, her bottom lip wobbling. "I don't know why they'd do this."

Dorothy took off her left shoe, rubbed her ankle, then put it on again. "Just know you can't trust them. Ever."

"Can't we just move to another hospital?"

"It's not so easy, honey. Not anymore. They called your mother."

"Surely *she* doesn't want me in there all alone!"

Her aunt made a strange coughing sound. "Look, I'm not trying to make her out as the bad guy, but I think she was in on this decision, too." She set her jaw. "Anyway, I have to go."

"What?" Dot sat up straight. "You can't *leave*!"

"I have an appointment." She stroked Dot's arm. "I'll be back, don't worry. Just be good, okay? As long as you're good, it will all work out fine."

She sauntered out of the room in a heady scent of orange blossoms. Dot couldn't control her tears; she sobbed uncontrollably for at least ten minutes. She was surprised the crying didn't propel her into a new seizure. She didn't know what to make of any of it—had her mother been in on the decision? What if she'd *proposed* the idea? What if this was some way to get her away from Dorothy? She was jealous, maybe, because clearly Dorothy had taken her place.

But why did Dorothy leave? Why wasn't she fighting this? She'd fought so hard for everything else.

A few minutes later, Nurse Lisa swept in and pulled out Dot's IV tubes. Then she ordered her out of bed so she could strip her sheets. She dressed Dot in another gown and took her to X-ray and to draw blood.

"But you already drew blood today," Dot whined.

"We just want to make some comparisons," Lisa said cheerfully.

Dot had yet another MRI and CAT scan that day, too. And after all that, with no explanation, they wheeled her into the ICU.

It was deathly quiet in the ward. Dot's room was tiny and had a strange smell she didn't recognize. She was old enough to understand that all around her were other children who were very, very sick; probably some of them would die soon. Feeble wails from babies woke her up in the night. Sounds of vomiting. A woman, standing outside her door, crying uncontrollably. What on earth could Dot have done to land her in here? Had she said something disparaging in her sleep? Did the nurses know that she and Dorothy made fun of some of them when it wasn't their shifts? Maybe the rooms had little microphones hidden in them, like in the movies, and the nurses heard everything. If Dot just apologized, could she go back to the normal ward?

Or was she really this sick?

And then, in the morning, she heard Dr. Osuri's voice: *I said you couldn't be here! What part of that don't you understand?*

Dot strained to hear whom the doctor was talking to. Had some madman broken into the ICU? She hallucinated axe-wielders, orange storm clouds, pointy-horned ibexes. The drugs she was taking to quell the seizures made her so drowsy, and she dropped back into sleep. Just before she slipped into unconsciousness, she saw her mother standing in the doorway, her arms crossed over her chest, a tight, worried look on her face. Dot probably could have struggled to stay awake to say hello to her, but she didn't want to.

A few hours later, Dr. Osuri came in to check on her, praising her for having no new seizures in the night.

"See, I'm better!" Dot crowed. "So get me out of here!"

Dr. Osuri chuckled. "Soon, I promise." There was a sad, kind look on his face. Dot was sure this hadn't been the same doctor who'd been yelling at someone earlier in the day.

Three days in the ICU, no new seizures. Dot played Solitaire on an iPad; a nurse gave her the wireless password and she watched toy reviews on YouTube. Her mother appeared in the doorway, but every time, Dot pretended to be sleeping. Patients around her moaned. An alarm went off in the middle of the night; nurses and doctors hurried into an adjoining room, and there was a flurry of tense instructions and *bleeps* of machinery. Dot was astonished to fall asleep amid the cacophony. In the morning, when she woke up, she had no idea if the person who'd had the episode so late at night had lived or died. Her brand-new cell phone, which Dorothy had bought for her but which Dot didn't quite know how to work yet, received text messages, a very new thing.

Are you being good? Dorothy had texted her. Dot answered yes. *Not talking to anyone?* Dot answered no. *Good, and don't think anything, either,* she said. *Because they can read your thoughts.* Who? Dot always asked. Dorothy never answered.

ELIZA

KIKI LEADS ME into the kitchen. I am silent. My heart is banging. Her brother, Steadman, who's my other roommate, stands at the island, hip thrust out, an I Heart Zombies coffee cup in hand. He's glaring at me.

"Uh, hi?" I say uncertainly. "What's going on?"

Steadman snorts, the very action making his blond, feathery bangs lift from his forehead. His eyes are dark-rimmed, as if he has applied eyeliner. He's pear-shaped, with a big ass, a lot to grab on to. Today he's got on a gray sweatshirt that's too tight as well as fitted black jeans and shiny high-top leather sneakers. By the smell of it, there's bone broth in that mug—I have some in the house, as it's supposed to annihilate all bad cells in the body, and though I can't take the flavor, he finds it delicious.

Kiki stands at the island with a meek look on her face. The only similarity between her and Steadman are their striking, ice-blue eyes. I met Kiki at the writing group I joined earlier this year. I'd been working on *The Dots,* and I needed someone to read a draft, but I didn't want that someone to be anyone I knew—I couldn't imagine letting my *mother* look at it, and all of my college friends were majoring in business or some sort of useless science-like mumbo-jumbo having to do with quarks; I doubted they'd be useful in offering critique. When I saw the poster for a writers' group advertised on a bulletin board at Trader Joe's, I'd thought, *Why not?*

The woman who started the group, Sasha, held the meeting in her apartment, which overlooked the very Trader Joe's parking lot where I found the ad. The apartment was filled with a lot of Native American décor—masks, beaded things, feathers, a wooden canoe mounted on the wall—and smelled like tobacco. Low, atonal, rhythmic chants played over the stereo. There was a bowl filled with small, smooth stones on her coffee table; I worried them between my fingers, terrified to pull the six sets of eight stapled pages I had made for the group out of my bag. It was the first two chapters of *The Dots*. I was terrified for anyone to read it. Then it would be real.

Kiki sat next to me that first day. She had threads of gray through her hair and carried herself with the air of a much older, wiser woman, so I was surprised to find out later she is only twenty-seven. She wore a flowing skirt sewn together with rainbow-colored quilted strips, and she smelled like Strawberry Shortcake's little plastic head. When she noticed me, I must have been putting off a serious fear vibe, because she gave me a comforting pat on the hand.

The others in the group sat on the wicker chairs and beanbags Sasha had piled together in the room. Sasha cleared her throat and looked at me. "Eliza? Ready to pass around?"

My fingers crimped around my pages. I wasn't sure I could let go of them. They were so unvarnished and inadequate. All at once I desperately had to pee. That always happened when I got nervous.

"How about I go?" Kiki piped up. "I have some new poems."

Sasha looked at her evenly. Someone near the door groaned.

Kiki passed out her poems. Pages riffled. The room went silent.

As I read, I began to relax. Her poems were about astrology and vaginas. They were written in iambic pentameter and couplets. She'd rhymed *uterus* and *Oedipus*.

The critique began. As everyone tactfully pulled Kiki's pieces apart, she sat quietly on the couch, her posture perfect, her expression serene and pensive. By the end of the session, I finally felt ready to show my work, but Sasha deemed that the group was over for the night. Everyone stood to leave. Kiki turned to me and smiled. "Well. I think I need a drink after *that*."

I went with her out of guilt—I'd sent her lousy writing to slaughter in place of mine. But Kiki didn't see it that way. "I appreciate everyone's feedback, but I'm submitting those pieces to *Poetry* just as they are," she announced, smoking a joint as she walked.

At the bar, Kiki Germ-X'd the tabletop while we waited for the bartender to get the drinks. "Bar counters are worse than public bathrooms," she said in that same placid tone that never seemed to leave her voice. She told a long, convoluted story about various relationships and breakups with seamy-sounding men at least thirty years her senior. Her parents had owned a dandelion farm when she was young, and they made special tea that hippies bought through mail order. But now the dandelion industry has dried up, and they live in a subdivision near Pasadena, where Kiki lived as well. At one point, Kiki sipped her vodka, made a face, and plucked an extra lime out of the cubby behind the bar that contained maraschino cherries, olives, and cut-up fruit. I liked how she looked right at the bartender when she did it, daring him to say something to her about presumptuousness and personal hygiene.

A few months later, when my book sold and I collected some cash, I asked Kiki if she wanted to be my roommate. I didn't enjoy bumping around in the new, free-from-my-parents' house by myself. I kind of wished I were still in the dorm at UCLA—I liked the idea of having fifty-five sleeping coeds just a knock away. Kiki was happy to leave her parents' dumpy tract home. Her deal, though, was that if she moved in, her brother, Steadman, who was also living at home, had to come, too.

"Otherwise he's *never* going to leave my parents, and they're so sick of him," she said. I knew the feeling.

I asked what Steadman did, and Kiki said he managed a curiosities shop in Venice. "Does he need extra employees?" I asked immediately. I'd pulled eighteen-hour days working on my book, but once I'd finished, I needed something else to occupy my time. I was up to taking four baths a day. Many hours passed where all I did was thumb through a big Edward Gorey anthology.

Now, I pad to the fridge, open it, and grab a bottle of water. The shelves are stuffed with Trader Joe's fare. Steadman's name is written on the soy milk and individual pots of Greek yogurt. He pens *S.R.* across the skin of each individual clementine in the bag. This is why I moved my vitamins upstairs. I don't want to have to put my name on them.

I can feel Kiki and Steadman staring at me.

"So is it true?" Steadman asks.

"What's that?" I ask after taking a long drink.

"The *pool,* Eliza!" Kiki holds up her phone. "Did you almost drown?"

I swallow hard. "How do you know that?" Could Desmond have told them on his way out?

"A website in Palm Springs wrote a piece about you. I just read it. I thought it was for your book, but it's about someone pulling you out of a swimming pool."

"So it *is* in the news?"

I snatch the phone from her. *Woman Rescued from Near-Drowning* reads the headline on the screen. The story posted twenty minutes ago—my Google Alert, which I'd set to ping whenever a mention of me popped up online, must have missed it. The article says a young woman, twenty-three, fell in the pool and that the police were called. They mention my name, but there's no picture of me. No mention of foul play, either.

I hand it back quickly, feeling queasy. "This doesn't tell the whole story."

"Okay, what's the whole story?"

"What happened in Palm Springs is her business, Kiki," Steadman interrupts. He looks at me. "*But,* if you're going through something, maybe you should talk to us. I mean, I have a business to run. And when you show up on your off days acting erratic, the business loses money."

I squint. "Huh?"

"What happened on Friday, Eliza. You showed up all . . . I don't know. Weird." He wiggles his arms and shoulders, octopus-style, to demonstrate *weird.*

I squint, trying to remember Friday. As far as I know, I hadn't left the house. My big excursion to Palm Springs had happened the following day.

"What are you talking about?" I ask.

Steadman sips from his mug and swallows noisily. "Herb said you came in all dazed, but when he tried to talk to you, you clammed up and left. You freaked him out, which says a lot, you know?"

"Herb was wrong. That wasn't me."

He slaps his arms to his sides. "Eliza, come on. It was *you.* So what are we dealing with here? Drugs? Alcohol? Do you need to go to rehab?"

"Look, I'm fine. And if I did do that, I'm really sorry," I try, adding a little laugh. "How about we just forget this?"

Kiki grips a Bakelite napkin ring in the shape of a tarantula. Over Steadman's head is a squirrel skeleton. The moment Steadman moved in he brought tons of knickknacks from the curiosity shop with him, and though I don't mind most of it, the raccoon penis he fashioned into the centerpiece of a dream catcher that hangs over the sink doesn't exactly put me in the mood to do dishes.

"This is all so worrying," Kiki says quietly. "All your memory lapses, and now the drowning thing . . ."

"I didn't drown. I'm still here."

"But you *tried* to drown," Kiki points out.

"No I didn't!" I consider mentioning the murder angle, but this is definitely the wrong audience. "It was an accident."

Silence. Steadman taps his long nails against the mug. Kiki stares out the window and looks like she wants to cry. I've still got "Maneater" in my head. *Oh-oh here she comes . . .*

"When you say *all* my memory lapses . . ." I say. "Can you give me another example?"

"Well, there was that time two weeks ago when I saw you at yoga," Kiki says. "You were leaving, I was coming? I waved, and I swear you saw me. But then I bring it up later and you look through me like I'm nuts."

I try to laugh. "I remember that—or, I remember you telling me you'd seen me at yoga. But I wasn't *there*. I haven't been to your studio in months." I tried to like yoga, I really did, but I kept laughing through the instructor's chants. I kept rolling my eyes at the Sanskrit names for the poses.

"But I saw you," Kiki asserts. "You looked right at me!"

My gaze shifts down. Could I have been there? Why don't I remember? "I think you were confused," I insist.

The siblings exchange another look. Steadman starts to pace. "It's other things, too. Not keeping up with the household responsibilities when you say you're going to. Not cleaning like the schedule dictates."

I blink hard. "Wait, that thing was real?"

Steadman put up a chore schedule on a white marker board in the mudroom. I'd actually made fun of it to Kiki. Maybe even in front of Steadman.

"Plus you sometimes eat our food, and you use the toilet paper you didn't buy, and you never paid cable last month, and we basically had to go *without* cable until the two of us coughed up some funds," Steadman adds. "And you *said* you were going to get cable. You *said* you called the cable company."

"It's my house!" I exclaim. "If I don't want to have cable, then we're not going to have cable."

But as soon as I see the rage in his expression, I realize my mistake. If Steadman leaves, Kiki might, too.

I mumble a halfhearted apology and head out the door. I don't slam it—that might qualify as erratic, unstable behavior, the kind of behavior defined by people who drink too much and don't own up to skipping yoga and who throw themselves into swimming pools. I walk the whole way to the edge of the property line before I turn around and give the house the finger. Chore charts? Cable? Really?

It's mild outside, and the sun has sunk below the trees. I start to walk, hoping movement will settle me down. Halfway to Riverside Drive, I hear footsteps and turn around. It's Kiki. She's barefoot, and her eyes are red, and her golden hair is flying behind her like the tail of a kite.

"Eliza," she calls.

I consider running, but she'd catch me by the end of the block. So I stop. My arms hang heavily at my sides.

"I'm sorry." She's breathing hard. "I didn't know my brother was going to say all those things."

"You could have stood up for me."

Kiki twists her mouth. "I know. But Steadman, he . . . well, whatever." She smiles sheepishly. "And it's kind of true, honey. Lately you've seemed barely aware of your life." She puts her hand on my arm. "Are you *sure* there's nothing you want to talk about?"

I stare down at Kiki's pale, freckled hand. She's got a thick plastic ring with a plastic roach trapped inside of it. She got it at Steadman's shop, but she doesn't work there. Part-time, she plays an Elsa from *Frozen* for birthday parties, company meetings, ribbon-cutting ceremonies, and for hungover fraternity brothers. It's weird who requests an Elsa. You never know. Anyway, she wears the ring while princessing it up, the bug spun toward her palm. She says it gives her power.

Everything I need to tell weighs on me with the dull, pressing force of a dentist's X-ray bib. Not just the drowning, not just the person Desmond saw running away, but everything else, too. I never told Kiki about the suicide attempts. I never told her about my tumor. I don't want her looking at me differently, and I know she would. I don't want her pitying me, though it seems like she is anyway.

Maybe, though, it would be okay to have a friend to worry with. It's one thing for my family not to believe me about jumping into the pool; it's another for Kiki to say, unprompted, that I'm having memory problems. What if I *am* still sick? What if the tumor has come back? Some people are good at crossword puzzles or jujitsu. Maybe I'm good at making tumors nestle inside my skull.

Only, what about that person running away? What is *that,* then?

I can't tell Kiki. Just uttering those words, just giving my condition shape and air, means that this sudden and sharply defined worry might be the truth.

"I'm fine," I say quietly. "I'm just . . . tired. Freaked out about the book, maybe. Afraid people aren't going to like it."

"Of course," Kiki says. "It's got to be a lot of pressure. But you should be happy about it, Eliza. You're getting published in what, a month? It's going to be amazing." She slaps the sides of her thighs. "Want to get dinner somewhere? I'm up for anything."

There's a lump in my throat. "I just want to take a walk by myself."

"Of course, of course." She pulls me in one more time for a hug. She smells like weed, and her weight against mine makes my throat-lump six sizes bigger. "Get some Baked Alaska at Bob's Big Boy," she murmurs in my ear. "And a big glass of milk."

I start walking.

It is after five, and Burbank is dead. The roads are wide and empty, perfect for drag races. A girl wipes off the tables of the greasy Mexican joint, and tinkling mariachi music escapes out of speakers. A high-end Mercedes slips silently out of the gates of Warner at the end of the road, then makes a slithery turn onto Olive, escaping for the highway. Its stealthy, amphibious motion triggers memory upon memory of all the weird, unexplainable things I'd recently done.

Like jumping the fence of a chain hotel and plunging into the first body of water I could find—which happened to be a large, outdoor hot tub. I forced my face into the hot water. Only when I couldn't breathe did I feel relief. *It's going to end. I'll be free.*

Or the memory of riding a bike down the path that cuts through Santa Monica and Venice beaches and suddenly, arrestingly, having a palpable fear that someone was chasing me. I turned around, and I *did* see someone. Maybe lots of someones, all with angry, vengeful eyes. The only way I could fathom getting away was plunging into the Pacific, so I'd made a madcap run across the sand. A wave had taken me down immediately. A father and son dragged me out after the breath had left my body. *Why is she coughing?* the little boy kept asking. *Is she going to be okay?*

And the memory of two nights ago, when I'd crashed into the pool at the Tranquility. The cold water had been so shocking, but once again, I'd felt safe. I flailed onto my back and, for a moment, opened my eyes.

I stop short just before the curb cut. There *was* someone on the pool deck, just like Desmond said. The glare from a spotlight blotted out any discernible features, but whoever it was stood above me, chest puffed triumphantly, as I sank.

I grab my phone and dial the police station again. The same receptionist picks up, and I can't remember Lance's last name *again*, and I can't bear to go through the spiel of the message one more time. I hang up and demand my phone's automated assistant give me the number to the Tranquility. "Can I be connected to the Shipstead bar?" I ask after the front desk answers.

There's a pause, and then someone else picks up. "Shipstead." It's a man with an Australian accent—*Sheepstid.*

"G'day," I say. Whenever I hear an accent I have the urge to speak with one, too. "Uh, I'm a private detective, and I'm checking in on my client's wife. She says she was at your bar a few nights back, and I want to see if she was there the whole time or if she left and went somewhere else."

"Okaay." He sounds circumspect. "Which day was this?" I tell him. "I wasn't here Saturday. That was Richie."

"Is he working today?"

"Nope."

"When will he next be in?"

"Uh . . . tomorrow, I think. Or the next day."

"I might be dead by then!" My accent is gone. "Can you give me his cell number?"

The bartender bursts out laughing. "Uh, *no.*"

And then he hangs up.

There's a blare of a horn, and I jump. I've wandered into the crosswalk. I scamper to the curb, my heart in my throat. The image I've just seen of someone standing above me as I sink into the pool in Palm Springs skulks around me like a sullen cat. There had definitely been a shadow standing motionless over me, making sure I was floundering to the bottom.

On my phone, I Google *Tranquility resort pool accident.* The article Kiki showed me is the only one listed. There were no reported accidents at the resort's pool besides mine.

Then I Google *Palm Springs stalkers.* A twenty-four-year-old girl was stalked by an ex-boyfriend. A forty-five-year-old nurse posted sexy pictures of herself in Palm Springs on Facebook and some crackpot stalked her to the Elvis Honeymoon Hideaway. Neither situation has much in common with what happened to me.

I Google *Los Angeles stalkers,* but that brings up too many hits to wade through. Next I search *Can the police lie to you.* And *Police cover-ups*. And finally, *How to get a memory back from your brain*. This leads me to an article about Post-Traumatic Stress Disorder, which tells me something I already know: memories, especially powerful and emotional ones, are stored in the amygdala, where my tumor resided. These same memories are fragile and easily destroyed when they aren't given time and space to form—there's a whole biochemical and electrical process that fixes a memory in place. Also, just because you think you remember something happening doesn't mean it actually occurred the way you remember it. Brains have a tendency to rewrite memories based on what you'd *like* to remember, or what someone has *told* you to remember. Or your mind might conflate two memories into one, the synapses in the brains getting tangled and confused.

Is that it? Am I confusing the pool incident with an earlier plunge? I want to think so . . . but no. That face standing over me is so crisp in my mind. I have to believe in it. Once I start doubting myself, the memory will slip away forever.

I need to lie down somewhere. I gaze at the sidewalk, considering it—this street is clean enough to eat off. Then I spot an even more tempting option: a corner bar across from Warner's that used to be a whorehouse. There's a winking floozy painted onto the window, a neon wine bottle above the bar. I wonder if a certain someone is inside. My mouth starts to water. My body actually lunges toward the place like a plant leaning toward a ray of light.

I push through the door and am greeted by twilit gloom. It's a bar with multiple personalities: the jukebox, bad lighting, and bathroom of questionable cleanliness suggest dive, but then there's this whole wine cellar corner thing going on, the menu features beef cheeks, and there's a PBS news broadcast on TV.

I settle into a stool and gaze down the sparse line of patrons. Most of them, like everyone hanging out in Burbank at this time of day, are either studio people who don't want to be bothered or screenplay hopefuls who are hoping to rub elbows with someone who will listen to their pitch. The bartender, Brian, tosses a coaster my way with a grumble. He's always muttering to some guy about what cunts women are, how they're liars, how they make no sense, how they're whorish and opportunistic and way more superficial than men. I also can't stand his hipster beard.

"Gin and tonic," I shout to him. He begrudgingly makes it, silently plops it in front of me, and sticks the paper bill in an empty glass.

Then I feel a sort of magnetic pull, and I know the person I've come for is here before I actually see him. There he is: denim jacket, stubble, floppy hair, square jaw. He's sitting at the other end of the bar, reading a magazine. As if suddenly aware of my presence, he looks up and stares at me, too. His lips twitch. He stands and walks over with a bearlike lope. I stretch off the stool and roll on the insteps of my feet, heart pounding, seething at the sight of him, but also relaxing, knowing exactly how this will play out.

"Liza," he says, when he's close. "Long time no see."

I don't know if he gets my name wrong on purpose or if he really doesn't know it. It's also possible I've given him this name instead of my real one.

"I've been busy," I answer.

He takes a long sip of his drink—it's something brownish with clinking ice cubes—and passes it to me. He knows I'm not picky. He knows I'll drink it, which I do. It's whiskey, the cheap kind. My throat feels gouged.

He looks me up and down, his eyes twinkling. "You busy now?"

I raise my eyebrows at him. "Not really."

There may be a little more talk than this, maybe even a gin and tonic or two, probably more glares from Brian. But what matters is that after not very much time, Andrew grabs my hand with urgency, and there we are in that horrid bathroom with its crumbling grout and the shit-stained toilet and the foul-smelling urinal cake, my body pressed up against the wall, his fingers rushing to unzip, me feverishly pulling the grungy hospital T-shirt over my head. I shut my eyes and sink into this as best I can. There is acid in my throat. I may vomit soon. But for a few seconds, I can forget everything about who I am and be some girl I don't know, some waste, a putrid, repulsive Liza a man wants to ravage. That's all I am worth, deep down. I don't know why this sort of depravity feels necessary, but it does. Maybe it's another trick of my amygdala.

It's over fast. Andrew hands me a cigarette; he's always got a pack. He smokes one, too. We blow the smoke out the bathroom window into the alleyway. A limp hank of hair falls across Andrew's forehead.

I tap his arm. "Is that a studio pass around your neck?"

He flicks the ashes from his cigarette into the toilet; the water fizzles. "Maybe."

"You working on a writing team?"

"Maybe."

When we first met, he admitted that he hoped to work on a TV drama, maybe a police procedural. This was when we'd had a normal, flirty bar conversation, before he understood I was easy and desperate and didn't need verbal foreplay to strip naked. But I didn't play the game entirely—I told him nothing about myself. But now, I kind of want to tell him something. I just don't know what.

I think of it as he's zipping up. "I was almost killed two nights ago."

He looks at me, really looks at me, and raises an eyebrow. Then he snorts and rolls his eyes. "Yeah, right."

"It's true!" An additional thought appears in my mind with astonishing force. *And I could kill you, too.* I almost gasp out loud, shocked my mind coughed that up.

He licks his finger and uses it to stub out the cigarette. It makes a dangerous sizzle, and he drops it in the toilet. Another sideways glance, and then he finally buttons his pants. "We've all got our stories, Liza. We've all got our stories."

From The Dots

After Dot was banished to the ICU, Dorothy's schedule got very busy. She wrote Dot cards that the nurses passed through that explained she was in "meetings." Maybe *Riders of Carrowae* was finally getting published. Maybe she'd met a man—husband number three. Dot had gotten over the *Los Angeles* magazine thing, mostly because it had had the reverse effect of what she'd feared. Recently, the doctors had decided to allow her fifteen minutes of visiting time a day, and seven kids from school had come to see her. They'd brought candy, DVDs, and paperback books she hadn't read yet. A pale girl named Matilda who Dot had always admired sat at the side of her bed and marveled at the needle marks on Dot's arms.

Two days later, another card from Dorothy came; she was going on a three-month trip for research. Dot was horrified. She called Dorothy's cell phone.

"How can you leave me in here?" Dot cried.

"I know, I know," Dorothy said. "But you're strong. You can handle this. And I've let work go for a very long time, dear. An agent is finally interested, and they've given me a deadline. I've got to get back to it."

"But I thought the book was done," Dot said.

"That's the thing," Dorothy said. "People aren't into barbarian novels right now. My agent wants me to restructure it and make it about the Holy Grail. So it's essential, you see, that I go to southern France. This new direction won't work unless I see the region firsthand."

Dot seemed to sense a distance in her, like her aunt was angry at something Dot had done. Did she think Dot *had* said something to the nurses to banish her to the ICU? But what was it Dot shouldn't have said?

She was feeling better, though. Clearer, with no new seizures. The next day, friends from school stopped in again, and Dot was able to have a whole conversation with them without feeling dizzy and nauseated. Then her mother appeared in the doorway wearing jeans and a T-shirt instead of work scrubs. Dot didn't have time to pretend she was sleeping. Her mother's face broke when she saw Dot awake. She made a big deal out of placing her car keys in a pocket of her purse. When she looked up again, there were tears in her eyes.

"Aren't you supposed to be at work?" Dot said coldly.

Her mother settled on her bed. "I took the day off." She inspected her carefully, sort of hesitantly. "I'm really sorry, Dot."

"Sorry about what?" Dot asked.

Dot's mother's eyes filled. "*Everything.*"

Then she pulled a box out of her purse. Inside was a music box with a spinning ballerina on the top. When she turned the crank, the box played "Somewhere Over the Rainbow."

"Ballerinas?" Dot said, making a face.

Her mother's smile twitched. "I know it's not your thing. I just thought . . ." She made the ballerina spin again. They watched her dance in silence.

Not long after, the fog that had hung in Dot's head was completely gone. The doctors announced that her blood work numbers were perfect, and there was no more suspicious brain swelling. They even did a trial day without seizure medication, and even *then* the seizures didn't return. Dot's mother, her soon-to-be stepfather, and her stepsister met with the doctors, and though it was a happy meeting, Dot couldn't stop thinking that there was something wrong with the family picture. It was supposed to be Dorothy in here with her, finally seeing the light at the end of the tunnel.

"When will Dorothy come back?" Dot asked her mother.

Dot's mother industriously packed her things into a new plaid suitcase. "You're going to love our new house. Almost all the renovations are done."

"Has Dorothy seen it?"

"And your room! It's very big, Dot. And it has a window seat. You've always wanted one."

"Is Dorothy out of town?"

Finally her mother looked at her squarely. "I have no idea," she admitted offhandedly, as though the question were a little absurd. As though Dot had just asked the whereabouts of a certain squirrel they saw at the park, or whatever happened to that ladybug who frequented their upstairs bathroom.

"Do you know why she left?"

One shoulder rose. "She's like this, Dot. She's always been like this. She comes and goes. You can't rely on her." Something in her face shifted, and her throat bobbed. And then: "Your room's a little oblong and unconventional, but I think you can make it work."

Despair and anger rattled through Dot. Clearly her mother was still jealous of Dot and Dorothy's special bond. What if her mother hadn't told Dorothy their new address? What if she was never able to find them? What was *wrong* with her mother? Then she realized: she had a cell phone; she could text Dorothy the address herself. Take *that*.

Buoyed once more, she asked, "Can I pick the color for my walls?"

Her mother paused from packing. "What were you thinking?"

"Black." Dot grinned nastily.

Her mother zipped up the suitcase efficiently and then grinned right back. "Perhaps yellow would be more cheerful. I was thinking yellow and gray."

Nurse Lisa, on the prowl by Dot's door, beamed. "Yellow and gray is a lovely combination." She went to hug Dot goodbye, but Dot ducked away from her arms. Could Lisa also have had something to do with Dorothy's leaving?

They're jealous bitches, Dot thought, remembering what Dorothy had said about the nurses. Even if it was just in her head, swearing made her feel embarrassed and ashamed. But it also made her feel kind of better, too.

ELIZA

MY AGENT, LAURA, calls the next morning while I'm still in bed. I should be up, of course, doing sun salutations or jogging or greeting the day with a barbaric, disease-free yawp, but instead I'm under a thick mink blanket, drooling.

"You sure came up with a creative way to drum up attention for this book," Laura crows after her assistant patches me through.

"Huh?" I sit up creakily and look at the clock. It's 6:14 a.m.

"This stunt in the pool! The press is amazing—it was picked up off that little Palm Springs website, and now it's gone viral. *The Dots* is on the map! There have been three articles about you on publishing blogs. Even more people are clamoring for an advance copy than before, and your pre-order sales got a bump. Good going, girl!"

I start to say something, but she talks over me. "There are even rumors that you think someone's trying to kill you." She lets out a short little *ha* of breath. "You really *are* like Dot from the book. It's a performance piece, really. Life imitating art. Keep it up!"

I've never met my agent because she lives in New York and I have a fear of flying, but I have concocted a mental picture of her that I envision every time we talk. I see her as a tall, stalk-like, tornado of a woman with sleek, perfectly highlighted hair and a large, square diamond ring on her right hand. I bet she has wide, frantic eyes that rarely blink. I bet she's one of those people who makes constant eye contact. I bet she screams at her assistants but they are still devoted to her, like tortured but pampered little lapdogs.

I still can't believe she even *likes* my book. A week after I'd mailed the first draft to Laura, she'd called me in hysterics. "This is great! Chilling!"

"Wait, really?" It seemed so unfathomable. I was proud of the book, but also embarrassed by it. Maybe the story was silly. Maybe it was the most ridiculous thing ever written. I'm not a very good judge of good fiction versus bad, considering all I've read my whole life was epic poetry and trashy horror. I wondered if every so-called writer went through such a roller coaster of ambivalence or if it was just me.

Now, I wriggle my feet out from under the covers and gasp. I have forgotten that I painted my toenails black last night, in a post-sex-with-Andrew sloppy drunken flurry, and for a moment I think I have gangrene.

"I didn't try to kill myself," I tell Laura. "We need to issue some kind of statement."

"It's not like anyone believes what they read on the Internet," Laura scoffs. "The point is you're officially interesting. I've gotten a few requests for interviews. Your publisher wants to send out more galleys to bigger reviewers. Do you have anyone you'd like me to send it to?"

"Just don't send it to my family!" I say haltingly, almost in a shout. I swallow hard, embarrassed by my flurry of emotion.

"I didn't mean family," Laura says. "Unless they work for *Entertainment Weekly* or *People*. Do you know anyone from there? Do you know any BookTubers? Any Bookstagrammers?"

"I don't even know what those words mean," I admit.

"Oh. Okay. No matter! Oh, but also? I haven't given out your phone number yet, but don't be surprised if reporters figure it out and start calling you."

"How are they going to figure it out?" I cry, feeling a clutch in my chest. "Do I have to *talk* to them?"

"Absolutely not. I don't want you giving away anything about the book before it comes out. I think it should be a huge mystery—who is this Eliza person? Is her book true or false?"

"The book is false!" I almost scream.

"I know that. I'm just saying, people will *wonder* now. You officially have mystique. The marketing and publicity teams are over the moon. And then, once the book drops in stores, you'll go on a tour."

"A tour?" I repeat, ludicrously, as if I've never heard the term.

"Signings. Readings. Q and As." She clucks her tongue. "Most debut authors don't even get an offer to do a tour. This is a big deal. Be happy!"

I can already feel the panic coming on. "But what if people start asking me crazy questions during the events? Like, personal things? Things I don't want to answer?"

Laura chuckles. "Then don't answer them. It's not like this is some sort of test where you have to fill in all the blanks. But you really should do a tour, Eliza. The book business is about building relationships. You can't operate in a vacuum."

"Thomas Pynchon does," I babble. It's the only thing I know about the author. I haven't even read any of his books. I started *V.*, but I read the same page about twenty times, thinking there was some sort of major printing-press mistake and all the sentences had been rearranged. The second page was just the same.

Laura has been saying something about Thomas Pynchon that I haven't heard. I catch up with the conversation as she's going "—at least drum up some social media presence, okay? Instagram. Facebook. Snapchat. I don't care. Say something about Dorothy and Dot, your inspiration for the characters. I bet after your pool fiasco you have a lot of new friend requests. And look, I hate to drop this on you, but you know your editor, Posey? She's in LA right now. She wants to have lunch with you at the Ruby Slipper Café—I think it's in Beverly Hills. It's probably to talk strategy about the pool thing and how you can drum up even more buzz for the book. Can you do today at 12:30? She'll be expecting you."

"I didn't fall into that pool to drum up buzz for the book," I say quietly. "I need you to understand that."

"Of course you didn't," Laura assures me. "But I'll take that as a yes about meeting Posey. Now, listen, please be on time, because Posey is very busy." I hear her other line ringing. "Good luck, darling! She's going to love you."

Before I can respond, she bids me adieu and hangs up. And I stare at the phone and then at the gray morning sky out the window, trying to figure out what the hell just happened.

My gaze falls to the four large boxes on the floor. I'd received them on Saturday, the day I left for the Tranquility. Each bears my publisher's logo on the side; just beneath that, in joyless font, it reads: *The Dots, Eliza Fontaine.* I sit up, lean forward, and pull one box toward me. It doesn't take much of an effort to pry the cardboard flap open with my fingernails and wrench the top copy free.

The book feels heavy in my hands. The pages, deckle-edged, are pleasing to touch with the tips of my fingers, and the paper gives off a heavenly smell. The cover is slick and pink, like the inside of a mouth, with two dark-haired women, one taller, one smaller, standing side by side. Dot and Dorothy. My two main characters.

I think about something I can write about them on social media. Something innocuous. Most of what I've posted on Instagram are pictures of scary dolls and figurines I've seen at junk shops. But today, I hold a copy of my book up to my face, snap a picture, and post it on Instagram. *T minus four weeks,* I write as the caption. I don't know what else to say.

But just as Laura has predicted, an account whose name is a jumble of letters and numbers gives me a like. So do three others. And then up pops a comment: *Why'd you jump into that pool?*

I swallow hard and look at my book again. I turn to my author photo on the back flap. It's my face—pale, red-lipped, and saucy—and it's my hair, wild and black—but it doesn't really look like me. It looks like someone with confidence, panache. Someone who knows what the hell she's doing. Someone who wouldn't get shoved into a pool.

I don't know what happened, I mentally compose as a response to the post. *But hopefully, soon, I will.*

■ ■ ■

On my way to the Ruby Slipper Café, which is on the most touristy stretch of Beverly Drive, I text Desmond Wells to ask if he got a response from the Palm Springs PD yet. It's been enough time. Most people would get a call back already. But Desmond doesn't reply. I feel snubbed. What's that guy got to do right now that's better than talking to me?

My phone rings again, startling me. I look at the screen. It's Gabby.

"What's up?" she says cheerfully when I say a cautious hello.

I stop in front of a soap store that has a chubby cherub as its logo. "Not much. You?"

"Oh, just working. Lots to catch up on from what I missed yesterday."

I can hear Gabby's keyboard clacking in the background. I bet she's talking to me on a headset. "So I'm just making sure you're . . . okay. Are you at home right now?"

"Gabby . . ." I clear my throat, realizing that perhaps this is an opportunity. "I really, *really* didn't try to commit suicide that other night. You believe me, right?"

"Um . . ."

I hear her breathe in to say something—probably that she doesn't—and I cut her off. I can't bear another announcement of mistrust in my mental stability. "But also, how did you guys know I was in the hospital?"

". . . What?" Gabby's voice sounds far away.

"Well, when I woke up, you were there. All of you. How did that happen, exactly? Did a doctor call you? Someone from the hotel?"

Gabby coughs. More typing. "They found your driver's license in your purse. And somehow that connected you to Mom. You should ask her—she's the one who got the call. But then she called me, and we rode to Palm Springs together."

"So you got there the morning I woke up? Or the night before?"

"That morning. When we got there, you were still sleeping. The doctor filled us in on what happened, officially."

Officially. I roll my jaw. Her story seems believable. I'm not sure what I'm trying to catch her in, exactly. I just feel like there's a big hole in my brain when it comes to that night. Something major I'm not remembering.

"Why did you take the blame for the vodka the first time we met?" I blurt out.

". . . Huh?"

Across the street, a toddler throws herself down on the ground and starts to wail. Her mother crosses her arms over her chest and stares up at the cloudless sky.

"You should have said I got it out," I say. "You should have made my mother smell my big glass of vodka. Why didn't you? I'm sorry about that, by the way. I was a huge asshole."

There's a strange noise at the back of Gabby's throat. "I don't remember a big glass of vodka, Eliza. Are you sure it happened?"

"It happened. I wrote about it in the journal I kept at the time."

"Well, you were always good at telling stories."

Clearly this is some sort of ruse. Gabby *has* to remember. "And why did you never get angry when I took that cashmere sweater Bill got you for Christmas and wore it to that party and got beer all over it? Why didn't you ever tell me to stop putting weird shit in your bed? Why didn't you say what really happened when I scared you in that coffin?"

"Where is this coming from? Why does this matter?"

The toddler has now stood up and is clinging to her mother's leg. I watch as they hobble along together toward the crosswalk. "I just thought of it," I say weakly. "I just want to know."

"You sound strange," Gabby says. "Should I call Mom?"

"Jesus. I'm fine."

I hang up, fuming. I stare into the soap-store window. All the sales associates are wearing angel wings and body glitter and walk in mincing little steps. I will never go into that store, I decide. No matter how great the soap is.

How could Gabby not remember that vodka incident? It's so significant. I can still picture every detail: the fury on my mother's face, the thrill I felt at how easily I could manipulate Gabby, and the hitch in her voice, too, when she said, *Maybe you shouldn't be doing this.* And then how, once Gabby took the blame for the vodka, it was all put away so quickly, as if it was best left unexplored.

Could I have made something like that up? But if I had, what was the real thing that happened instead? Had Gabby and I met and played Uno on the couch? Watched the Disney Channel? Traded Pokémon cards? That wasn't me. That was never me. The only other option, then, is that she's lying—she *does* remember, but she doesn't want to talk about it. But why wouldn't she want to talk about it? Especially considering I apologized.

It occurs to me I never found out why Gabby called. Not that I'm calling her back now.

Ruby Slipper Café, the restaurant where I am to meet Posey, is bare bones and unpretentious for Beverly Hills, a dark little place with crowded, wobbly tables and loud Brazilian music playing. As I step inside, every table is full. I look around. I've only met Posey on a blurry Skype screen, which means a large percentage of people in this place could potentially be her. I stand at the back of the line for food, every so often getting jostled by other customers.

Every time someone bumps me, my whole body ripples with discomfort. The buzz of voices, the smell of coffee, the low bass line of music . . . I feel too exposed. Unsafe. Too many people are staring. Just as I'm thinking this, a man at the far end of the room glances up at me and holds my gaze. He's wearing tinted glasses and has a long, thin nose and a square chin. A Yankees cap is squashed on top of his head, tamping down frizzy, graying hair. I stiffen. A long time ago, before I was afraid of airplanes, I was in New York City with my mother and a man in a raincoat snickered at us from a nook between buildings, opened his coat, and flashed his penis and wrinkled testicles. I've never forgotten his face.

That's it. I can't be here. I'm not ready to be out in the world—or maybe someone *is* watching me. Folding in my shoulders, I squeeze past two men ogling the pastries and step out to the front porch. Traffic whizzes past. Knots of pretty girls in high shoes sashay down the sidewalk. My lungs have hardened in my chest. My fingers shake as I fumble for my phone in my pocket—I need a ride home, *now.*

"Eliza?"

A tall woman with kind eyes stands at the little gate that separates the café from the street. She has at least a foot on me. Her arms and legs hang apishly low. Even her fingers are spindly. She's got a candy floss fluff of black hair around her head, she's wearing a strappy sundress despite the fact that it's only 60 degrees and gloomy, and the sundress's fabric pulls tightly against her swollen, pregnant stomach.

"Posey?" I say almost inaudibly.

"Yes!" She sandwiches my hand between hers. "Did you just get here? Shall we go in?"

The fingers on my other hand are still wrapped around my phone. "I, um—"

But she's already pulling me into the restaurant. "It's hideous of me that I've waited so long to come and see you. I mean, your book is practically out in the world! But I had to go through the IVF procedures for these"—she gestures to her belly—"and that seemed to take for*ever*. Do you realize they have a vaginal wand in you every day? You can't have a life. And then there was the morning sickness—I practically couldn't leave the house." She leans over herself and speaks to her stomach. "Why have you made it so hard on me? Couldn't you have given me a break?" She uses a barking, militant voice.

"How many are in there?" I ask nervously as we walk up the stairs.

"Three." Posey grins. "Three little boys."

"Whoa."

Posey grabs a menu and walks to the back of the restaurant like she's a regular. She gestures for me to sit at a booth, and I don't know what else to do but comply. I will talk to her for a few minutes, I reason. Then make an excuse and go. Surreptitiously, I peek at my phone and cancel my Uber request. I glance around the room. No one is staring at me anymore. Maybe I'm okay. I feel safer now that I'm not alone.

Soon enough, there are three sandwiches, a big bottle of juice, and an enormous slice of carrot cake I'd seen behind the glass in front of Posey. I order a smoothie with acai berries, but I can't fathom drinking it. "Now," she says, lacing her hands under her chin and peering at me. "Tell me everything. Tell me about you."

I shrug and place my smoothie down without spilling it, which is a wonder, because my hands are still trembling quite badly. "Oh, well, you know. I'm nothing special."

"The world is fascinated with you right now. You're the mysterious author who flung herself into a pool."

"I didn't fling myself," I say quickly, and then I cock my head. "The *world*?"

"Well, maybe not the *world,* but a lot of people. I have to admit we added a little fuel to the fire—we said the woman in the novel goes through quite an ordeal, and perhaps creating that character was too much for you. Perhaps you were exorcising your own demons, which led to the incident."

"But . . ." I'm astonished. "That's not *true!*"

"All the more reason for you to explain that in interviews after the book is published," Posey chirps happily. And before I can protest *that,* she goes, "So. How did you come to write *The Dots*? Just so we have our stories straight."

This is just Posey's job, of course, and it's natural she's curious. She bought my novel, gave me an advance that equaled probably ten years of a typical twenty-something's salary, and now she wants it to succeed. I can't hold these questions against her, though the whole rise-to-infamy thing makes me feel . . . dirty. Like I've sold out—and I haven't even sold anything yet. Successful books should be judged by literary merit and literary merit alone, shouldn't they?

There's another thing. None of my other drowning incidents were publicized—there was no reason to publicize them, as I wasn't anyone of note. But if someone wanted to dig, they'd find some records about me. The guy and his son who'd lugged me out of the Pacific Ocean in Santa Monica might come forward with a report. Or the janitor who came in to clean the Days Inn hot tub and saw me lying facedown in the bubbles. I could just see that story in print: *She wasn't even staying with us,* the janitor would say. *Didn't have a key card or anything. I don't know how she got into the Jacuzzi area, either, as it's usually locked tight. And she said there was someone after her, except I didn't see anybody . . .*

I feel Posey waiting for my answer. I don't know what propels me to say what I say next, I don't know what drives me to make the leap. It just comes out. "Halfway through my junior year at UCLA, I got a brain tumor."

"Like Dot?" Posey asks, hand on the side of her face. "Good Lord!"

"Kind of like her. A similar tumor—I stole that detail because I knew how it worked and could guess what the treatment for it was."

Posey narrows her eyes. She has somehow gotten a piece of lettuce on her cheek, but I don't want to embarrass her by calling attention to it. "What do you mean you could *guess* the treatment?"

"My treatment was kind of a blur. They operated immediately, and then I was in a sort of . . . haze."

"Really?" Posey leans forward and scrutinizes my scalp. "You must have had a good plastic surgeon. I don't see any scars."

"LA, right?" I laugh, a little mirthlessly, a lot awkwardly. "They used a new technology where they didn't have to do much cutting. Anyway, I guess I'm okay now. Amazingly. Everyone says it's a miracle."

Posey shuts her eyes. "And here I've been whining to everyone about IVF and carrying three watermelons. That must have been horrible for you. I'm so sorry."

"It was, mostly because I've always been afraid I was going to get a brain tumor," I admit, hating that I'm practically echoing my mother's words. "It was a self-fulfilling prophecy. Anyway, after I recovered, I went back to my parents' house. I was stuck in my room, feeling out of it, and I needed something to do, so this is what I wrote."

Posey's eyes gleam. "And you wrote this book in just days, didn't you?"

"Well, not days, but it only took a few weeks. I couldn't stop. I had to keep going until I was done."

"You were in a fugue state." Posey sounds delighted. "I've always wanted to meet someone who's gone through it. What was it like? Did you take on a different personality?"

"Uh . . ." I wish I had. That sounds so interesting. "No. Not really.

I just had this idea, suddenly, and I wanted to make sure I wrote it before I forgot it."

Posey laces her fingers over her belly. "You authors and your processes. Do you know that I work with a man who wrote his entire novel on the subway to and from his shitty job at some doctor's office on the Upper East Side? He did the whole thing on his BlackBerry. Poor thing didn't even have a *new* phone. He had to use that awful keyboard." She leans forward. "So why did you write *this* particular story? What led you down this path?"

"I just started writing. First it was to try and put words to my experience—you know, being sick. So I wrote about a girl who was stuck in a hospital room looking at the steak house across the street. She imagined herself there, with a cast of interesting characters. I gave her someone to talk to. And then it just . . . morphed."

"Did you have to do a lot of rewriting? Did you outline?"

Maybe I *had* been in a fugue state, because I don't exactly remember my process or how ideas came to me, only that when they did I wrote them down. Maybe there was some invisible beast perched next to me, whispering in my ear. A Roman goddess of fiction. Desmond would probably appreciate that.

I feel insecure not having easy answers; older, wiser authors probably do. Eliza the dilettante, fiddling around at her keyboard, hammering out some words, forming them into sentences, the words rolling their eyes and doing the job for her, somersaulting and catapulting around until they form a story. That's how writing my book felt. Like something else took over. Like I'd just been along for the ride. "My best thoughts came in the middle of the night," I dredge up, even though it isn't true. "From a dead sleep."

"Marvelous. And do you think we'll read another book about Dot?"

I make a face. Why would I write another book about Dot? She has nowhere to go in the end. She seals her fate.

"Excuse me."

The New York City Flasher stands over us. Up close, he smells like Head & Shoulders shampoo. His eyes aren't as wild as I expect, but still my heart thunders in my chest. He is standing so close we are almost touching.

"Yes?" Posey touches her belly territorially.

The man looks at me. "We've met, right?"

I blink. The berry seeds in the few sips of smoothie I drank feel gritty on my tongue. All at once, my heart is throbbing in my throat. Should I know the answer?

A furrowed frown invades his craggy face. "Well. Maybe not. My apologies. Sorry for bothering you." And then, giving me another nod, he walks off.

Posey wrinkles her nose at him. "Los Angeles is just as weird as New York." She says this joyfully. The world, I realize, is a funny place to most people. A fascinating place. Nothing to be afraid of. If only I was like everyone else.

Posey takes my hand. "So listen. We just got a really exciting media request for you. It'll air the day your book comes out. Are you ready? *Dr. Roxanne*."

I frown. "A *medical* show?"

She smacks her temple in an *oh, silly me* sort of way. "You're the type who doesn't watch TV, aren't you? Of course you are. *Dr. Roxanne* is a talk show. She's almost as big as Oprah. Took over the book club thing when Oprah went off the air!"

"Wait, you want me to be on TV?"

"Laura said you'd be okay with it. Please, Eliza? We'll preview all the questions before you're on the air. You don't have to get into your medical history if you don't want to. Think of it as a spa day—you'll get your hair and makeup done, you'll get dressed up in wardrobe, everyone will adore you." She pops a bite of cake in her mouth. "Besides, you *deserve* it. Especially after your ordeal in the hospital, you know?"

The door to the café opens; Flasher has gone. Ushered in is a tall, beautiful man who smiles at me. It's a refreshing trade.

I press my fingers against my knees and then nod at Posey. "Okay," I say. Because I want her to like me. I don't want to let her down.

Besides, how bad could it be?

From The Dots

When Dot was in junior high, she became good friends with Matilda. Like Dot, Matilda enjoyed hacking off her hair and dressing in postmodern outfits involving tinfoil. The two of them sat on a sweaty-smelling beanbag in Matilda's brother Kyle's bedroom and listened to punk rock on vinyl: The Dead Kennedys, Descendants, Alice Donut. Matilda pierced Dot's belly button with a needle and rubbing alcohol. Dot shaved Matilda's head with her dad's clippers. They made out some. They read Shakespeare's Dark Lady sonnets over and over, wishing they could inspire such fitful and frenzied feelings in a person.

One day, when they were creating a diorama called Barbie Gets Into an Auto Accident, Matilda's mother came in the room and said that Matilda needed to see her grandma that day. She was very sick, and she would likely die within a few hours.

Dot asked if she could go along. Matilda's mother looked at her strangely. "Are you sure?"

"Yes," Dot answered, glaring at Matilda's mother from behind nearly a whole tube of mascara and stick of eyeliner. Matilda's mother reluctantly agreed. Maybe she was just afraid of her spooky daughter and her spooky daughter's friend, or maybe she was giving Dot a little extra forbearance. Dot might not have had any relapses since she was nine, but that *Los Angeles* article had proclaimed she was going to die, after all.

They got into her mother's Mercedes. Dot was expecting to pull up to a hospital, but instead they wound through Mulholland Drive and came upon a bungalow that overlooked the canyon. "Your grandma's in the back bedroom," Matilda's mother said. *Duh*, Dot wanted to snark. Where did they think she'd be, swimming in the pool?

Then she turned to Dot. "You can sit in the kitchen and wait."

"No, I'll go in, too," Dot insisted. She hadn't come all this way for nothing.

Grandma was sitting on a rocking chair, an afghan thrown over her legs. Her eyes were bright, but there were all sorts of tubes running into her. A silver machine pumped oxygen. The people gathered around her freaked out at her every move, asking if she was comfortable, if she needed anything to drink, if she was getting enough oxygen, if she was cold, hot, bored, scared. Dot felt nonplussed by the tableau; something was wrong. Then she understood: normally, *she* was Matilda's grandmother. Today she was the healthy one. The one nobody was worried about.

She looked down at herself, astonished. How was it that she'd had seizure after seizure and now . . . nothing? When would the demons wriggle back into her brain? Could her scans really still be clean?

She wished her aunt knew how healthy she was, but Dorothy had never returned from her book research. Five years had gone by with no sign of her—or any signs of the book. Upon leaving the hospital, Dot had tried to text Dorothy her new home address, but Dorothy never replied. Dot sent letters to the Magnolia Hotel, but they were always returned to her, saying Dorothy had given no forwarding information. Regularly, Dot scoured the Internet for news of her, but there was never anything. She looked through magazines, thinking Dorothy might pop up in a society photo—after all, hadn't she been society herself, once upon a time? She typed her aunt's full-name-comma-Alabama, her aunt's full-name-comma-Alaska, and so on down the list of states, canvassing each Dorothy Banks to see if she was a match. She did the same for towns in England and Italy, in Japan and Eastern Europe. She tried to remember aliases Dorothy enjoyed when they played Funeral and Oscar Night: *Teresa di Vicenzo. Honey Ryder. Kissy Suzuki.* It astonished Dot that they were Bond girls—she'd never known. She watched the Bond movies, thinking they might provide a clue. She wanted to search for Mr. Contact Lens or the government man Dorothy had dated, but come to think of it, she didn't know their first or last names. Even *Milton Banks, dead filmmaker,* a link to her ex-husband, didn't yield any results.

Dot wandered through cemeteries, searching for Dorothy's son Thomas's grave, but never found it. She even searched her own cache of memorabilia, poring over the few photos of Dorothy she'd kept. One was a photo of Dorothy and herself poolside at the Magnolia—it was the day, Dot remembered, Dorothy told her about the River Styx. From that day forward, Dot had avoided water. Another photo was Dorothy and Dot in matching fur stoles; Dorothy held a real cigarette on a long holder, Dot smoked one made out of candy.

This person was once here, Dot thought, turning the photo in her hands. *But now she's gone.* Was it possible to literally drop out of the world?

A few times, she thought she saw Dorothy around town. She'd see a slender, dark-haired woman waiting for a bus or standing in line at the pharmacy, and her breath would catch. Once, after a miserable lunch with her parents at Terranea in Rancho Palos Verdes, Dot came out of the ladies' room and saw Dorothy pushing a cleaning cart down the hallway toward the guest rooms.

"*Dorothy!*" Dot screamed, grabbing her arm. When her aunt turned, she was wearing her signature Hermès scarf printed with prowling leopards tied around her neck. Dot flung her arms around Dorothy in joy, forgetting all feelings of anger or abandonment. Dorothy had been found! Huzzah!

But Dorothy reared back. "What? Who? No!"

Her voice was higher, choppier. When she raised her head, her eyes were green. She looked at Dot with fear, probably because Dot was just inches away from her face.

Dot shot away. Something about the woman's voice clicked a cog into place in her brain. A fuzzy memory came back of her aunt pestering a nurse from the hospital because she was her doppelganger. Could this be the same person? Dot knew she'd learned her name, but she couldn't conjure it forth.

"Sorry," she said quickly, and then turned away. She ran all the way back to the dining room, nearly knocking over a bellboy pushing a cart piled with Louis Vuitton train cases.

Every once in a while she asked her mother about Dorothy. Dot had stiffened into resentment for her mother—she'd definitely had a hand in sending Dorothy away. Her mother seemed to sense the resentment, but instead of trying to win back her love, like some people's parents' might, she was a hard-ass with Dot, constantly riding her to straighten up and brush her hair and do her homework and, goddamn it, don't wear eyeliner all the way out to your temples, you look insane. Dot would fight back, and their arguments would escalate to screaming matches, and Dot's mother would finally turn to her new husband and say, "I can't handle her anymore. I don't care what she does," as if Dot wasn't in the room.

Dot would have thought asking her mother about Dorothy would spark a new argument, but usually her mother was cavalier about Dorothy questions. "The thing about Dorothy is that she could be anywhere," Dot's mother mused recently. "Selling rugs in Monaco. Taking a writing course at the Sorbonne."

"Where's that?" Dot asked with interest.

"Paris," her mother answered.

Dot's eyes lit up. France! She did say she was going there! "But how is it that she's been there for so long?" Dot asked her mother. "Isn't France expensive?"

Her mother shrugged. "Money is no object for good old Dorothy."

Dot placed her hands on her hips. "If she's so rich, why did you never ask her for money when I was in the hospital?" Her mother stared at her in confusion. "You wouldn't have had to work so hard. She could have paid some of the bills. You could have *visited* me more often," Dot explained. She hated that she had to explain. She felt so weak, so exposed. Her mother should have worked this out years ago.

Her mother shook her head. "No, no. Dorothy's money is for Dorothy. She doesn't spend it on anyone else. Well, except for Thomas, when he was alive."

Dot perked up. "What was Thomas like?"

"He was . . . odd." Her mother averted her eyes. "Look, I'm not saying Dorothy didn't have her fair share of pain. However, that doesn't mean we should overlook her shortcomings."

Dot snorted. "Which are what, exactly?"

"Dot, it's time you understand. Your aunt . . . she's not what you think."

"What do you mean by that?"

"I mean . . . mentally. She's . . ." Her mother turned away.

"Are you saying she's crazy?" Dot demanded. "How can you say that about your sister?"

Her mother shrugged. "I know you love her. But I know this because she's *my sister*. I grew up with her. She's always been this way."

Dot considered this. The details she knew about her mother and Dorothy growing up together were shaky: they were the daughters of a New York banker father who was always away on business and a mother who dabbled in modeling but mostly just took pills, drank, and entertained friends. They lived on acreage in Long Island; they had a driver and went to Manhattan private schools. They had a day nanny and a night nanny. There were elaborate birthday parties, though Dot's mother doesn't recall her parents ever attending. Later, the girls went to boarding school, though not the same ones. So how did Dot's mother even *know* what her sister was like if they were sent to different schools? Her mother had to be jealous: her sister had gotten all the looks, talent, and *panache*. Dot's mother, on the other hand, turned away the family cash, fixed teeth for a living, and had thin, stringy hair.

"You used to like her," Dot said miserably.

"This isn't a matter of me liking her or not liking her. It's a matter of what's true and what's false."

"Well, she seemed perfectly healthy to *me*." To which her mother exchanged a loaded look with her stepfather. Dot rolled her eyes.

Her aunt's absence had carved a hole in Dot's chest. Once, she had even gone to the school therapist of her own accord, walking into the office and sitting down at his desk and demanding he stop whatever he was doing and talk to her. Dot had known the therapist had wanted to talk to her for quite some time. She'd seen him watching her lurk in the hallways as she tried to melt the popular crowd with her mind. Several days a week, she wore six-foot wings across her shoulder blades, and she'd heard the therapist whisper to another teacher, "Are those made of human skin?"

In his office, Dot told the therapist how her beloved aunt must have abandoned her because of something she had done. "Why would you say that?" the therapist asked. "What do you think you did?"

Dot considered this. She'd gotten sick? She'd said the wrong thing at the hospital? She hadn't seemed grateful enough? She'd thrown that fit about the magazine, even though it was justified?

"I think you may have to just pretend that she's passed on," the therapist said. (He wasn't, Dot would learn later, an *actual* therapist, but a school counselor with a teaching degree.) "Talk to her, and she will listen, but you have to make peace with her leaving. We have to believe she's in a better place, and you have to try to get yourself to a better place, too."

Dot had never heard such bullshit in her life. But she did follow a bit of the counselor's advice: every night, she wrote letters to Dorothy in her journal. They mostly listed details of her day. *Had another MRI, and I'm still clean. I made out with Brody Fish in the dissection room. He seemed scared because we were sitting next to twenty half-opened cats. Matilda and I set our hair on fire after school. It smelled awful.*

She penned Dorothy's responses, too. Each told of the amazing things Dorothy was up to in Paris. Living in an apartment with a view of the Arc de Triomphe, shacking up with the president of France, busking on the streets of Cannes with a ukulele and a Standard Poodle. Dorothy was always good at belting out The Who. But the responses never filled the hole. They barely helped at all.

At Matilda's grandmother's deathbed, surrounded by all that medical equipment, Dot watched an old woman who definitely *was* going to die hug Matilda fiercely. There was this brave look in her eye that puzzled her. Was it true bravery, or was she putting on a facade because she didn't want her family to worry? That, Dot reasoned, was the ultimate show of love, a love she'd been deprived of for so long. She felt a pang inside her, wishing for Dorothy so desperately she could practically taste it, metallic, cold, addictive, on the back of her tongue.

ELIZA

ON WEDNESDAY, I make a list of people who might hate me. Friends from childhood, old neighbors, my parents, Steadman, people from the writing group Kiki and I belong to whose fiction I critiqued the teensiest bit too harshly, customers from Steadman's curiosities shop I snubbed, that man I rear-ended earlier this year and, instead of giving him my insurance details, I fled the scene. Any of them could be the right answer, but they all feel wrong. I have done worse things. I know it. I just don't know what they *are*.

So how can I get more information on what happened? I try the Shipstead several more times to no avail. I listen to my self-hypnosis tapes in hopes that I'll put myself into a trance that will conjure back the memory. I look up *Amygdala tumors* to see if they regularly recur. They can. I look at pictures of some amygdala tumors for a while. They are ugly, white splotches against a dark, spongy mass.

Then I type in Eliza Fontaine-comma-amygdala-tumor, in hopes of . . . well, I'm not sure what. It's not like the hospital would list my medical records on a public forum. It would be nice, though, to see a scan of *my* tumor; it would make it easier to picture it in my head again now. But the only stories about me are about my pool plunge and links to the book, which I peruse quickly, then click out of because they all suggest that I'm either suicidal or extremely attention seeking.

I stalk old friends online to see if any of them were in Palm Springs the night I fell into the pool. None of them were. I look up Desmond Wells, too. His picture is front-and-center on the official site of the *Ludi Circensus* festival in San Fernando. There is Desmond with an ivy wreath in his hair and wearing a toga with a rope for a belt. His legs, I note, are oddly hairless. I wonder why the hell I'm looking at his legs.

I also need to prove to Kiki that I've got my shit together and don't require her concern. It all dovetails nicely into an invitation to her to the Greater Los Angeles Kitty Splendor Cat Show this afternoon. When Kiki was young, so the story goes, she and her family paraded a chubby Maine Coon named Buster around the country in hopes that they'd make the national finals. She still has pictures of Buster all over her bedroom, and rumor has it her parents keep him, stuffed, on their mantel. We don't have a cat now—her brother hated the experience as much as she loved it, and clearly he makes all the rules—but Kiki says just being in the presence of feline excellence helps fill the void.

The show is in the ballroom of a Westin hotel one block away from the Chinese Theatre and the Hollywood Walk of Fame. All the tables in the space are against the walls, and the room is full of meowing. Most of the cats are in cages, and it's hard to know who the judges are because everyone's kind of a clone, male and female alike—dumpy, frizzy-haired, bespectacled, talky. I see about a hundred puffy-paint cat sweatshirts. Men with beer guts wear message tees that say *Meow Power*. We pass a group of cat dorks telling a joke; the punch line has something to do with a Siamese. "Mister Mistoffelees" from *Cats* blares over the PA. Admittedly, the cats are gorgeous—most of them look like completely different species than the mangy messes I'm used to dealing with. A Persian looks at me with such intelligence I'm pretty sure he's reading my mind. I shake a feather I plucked from a drawer at home at a Sphinx, and I swear he rolls his eyes, like I've got to be fucking kidding.

I nudge Kiki's side. "You really used to love this as a kid?"

"Oh, it was wonderful. I had my first kiss during a kitten judging." Kiki gives me a smirk. "I guess you're too good for me now that you're going to be on *Dr. Roxanne*?"

I couldn't resist telling Kiki about *Dr. Roxanne*; she watches a lot of daytime TV, so I figured she'd know who Dr. Roxanne was. Sure enough, when I broke the news, she screamed. "That woman is amaze-balls! Your book is going to be everywhere because of her." She took my hands and jumped up and down. "We should have a party when it airs!"

Still, I dread Roxanne's questions. I'm positive one of them will have to do with my illness. I don't want to talk about it. I don't want it to define me. I should have never told Posey about it, but I'd felt like I needed to set the record straight. Only, what if she's already told everyone? What if *that's* what the marketing team is concentrating on now?

I don't want to be known as the phenom who had her skull cracked open by some sort of new brain-surgery technology and then two weeks later starts—and finishes!—a novel. People will see me as a Rain Man. A spooky savant, possibly with robot parts. Sufferers are more than the sum of their suffering, but the rest of the world doesn't see that. If Dr. Roxanne prods me to talk about my illness, I'll never know if my audience buys my book because I am the girl who overcame the brain tumor or because my book actually sounds interesting. Maybe I shouldn't care. Maybe I should just be happy they buy it, period. But I want them to *like* it. I want them to like *me*.

Kiki's eyes are dreamy as she walks toward a crate of Russian Blues. "Are these descendants of Mr. Azure Enchantress?" she asks the owner, a pale, balding man who is most definitely a serial killer. He nods, and Kiki is off and chatting.

I wander away from the booth. The cages to my right and left are exactly the same. Next are booths of cat toys, organic food, feline vitamins. The ribbons and trophies, not yet awarded, are displayed on a table covered with a blue velvet cloth. I've been in here for five minutes, and I've had enough of cats. I duck into the hallway that leads to the lobby and suck in cool, hypoallergenic air.

The lobby is sparse this time of day. Sounds echo off the high ceiling. I close my eyes, enjoying the public bustle. I like that workers at a hotel have to be friendly and accommodating at all times. Like, if you have a meltdown in the lobby, someone at the front desk will hurry to your side and give you a glass of wine. A little kid plunges her hand into a basket of potpourri at the desk, and no one says anything. A man in a suit, perhaps a manager, notices me and gives me a wink. There's something about his expression—or maybe being in a hotel, period, with its clean smell and sexy lighting scheme—that gives me a flutter of déjà vu, and then a bolt of terror. I look at this man again, certain he's someone nefarious. He has already turned away.

Then I hear a voice. It's golden-toned and snarky as it snakes across the lobby. I turn in the direction of the sound as someone stands. He's got a shock of red hair, a large head, and a long, skinny body. The voice belongs to a boy-man on his cell phone. His walk is loping and bobbing, like a goose—but it's a walk I've seen before. If my brain could vibrate, it would right now.

I know him. I just don't know why.

I'm so startled I lurch back, banging hard into a table containing pamphlets for things to do in LA.

"Are you all *right*?" an older lady in a puffy-paint cat sweatshirt cries behind me.

I give her a distracted smile. My gaze returns to the redhead by the couch. Part of me wants to walk over there so he can see me, but being that I can't place how I know him, maybe that's a bad idea. I slink along the wall and settle into a chair that's significantly closer to him. I tuck my head into my neck like a pigeon and ball up my body so he'll pay me no mind. My hope is that proximity will spark something in my memory.

"Hey, it's okay," he murmurs into the phone. "It's going to be fine."

He plops back on the couch and puts his feet up on the coffee table. *Rude,* I think. I used to know someone who did that: *Who?* He has a mildewed laundry/male hormone smell billowing around him: unwashed clothes, dorm rooms, sex. My stomach twists.

"I don't think the cops will ask anything," he goes on. "I mean, why would they ask *you*? And you don't need to bring up Eliza or Palm Springs."

What?

A cold blast of air from the AC wafts up my shirt, only adding to my chill. The guy stands up again, and I look away, feeling caught, feeling visible. Amazingly, though, he doesn't seem to see me. "Don't stress about it, then. Anyway, it might blow over. They haven't called you yet, right? They might *not* call." A long pause. "Well, I can talk you through things to say, things that won't make them ask more questions."

Abruptly, he walks away from the couch nook and heads for the revolving doors to the street. I sit up straighter in my chair. Fumble for my phone. Still puzzled as to who he is, I snap a picture of his profile. As I slip it back into my pocket, he's gone. How has he moved so quickly?

I spring up. The revolving doors are just ahead, but there are a bunch of tourists in front of me, some going in, some going out, and I have to let all of them go first. After a lot of bumbling suitcases and shopping bags and a fold-up stroller that comes unfolded inside the revolving door, after two teenagers chewing sugary-scented gum and a woman who literally stands right in front of me but doesn't push the door to move, I step outside. The air smells like exhaust and Chanel perfume. The Walk of Fame, visible to my right, is madness: church groups in matching T-shirts, dirty college kids, pretty girls in short skirts and big sunglasses, mothers with babies strapped to their chests. I don't see a redhead anywhere. I stand on my tiptoes. He can't have gone *far*. If I could even see the top of his head, I'd know which direction to go. But it's like he's disappeared into a hole in the ground. My ears are still ringing. My body is slick with sweat. What did I just hear? How can I just be standing here, doing nothing?

The revolving door spins again, and three kids scurry out, knocking into me. I wheel back, and my bag upends, spilling onto the ground. "Oh," their mother says, hurrying behind them as they run toward the street. "God, I'm sorry. They're animals."

She crouches to help me to pick up the Kleenex, wallet, and mascara that have tumbled out of the bag. "I'm fine. It's fine," I say, and she leaves. A copy of *The Dots* has fallen out, too; I placed it in my bag before I left today. The book has fallen onto a stack of rental property leaflets, upside down as compared to the rest of the titles. It reminds me of when a tarot card reader lays down a card inverted. I pick it up, wondering if, like a tarot card, the pages inside reflect the opposite message of what I originally wrote. I crack the spine and read a few sentences toward the end. And actually, it does seem to have worked. It's Dot who's acting like a monster, Dorothy the martyr. It's incredible how language can turn in on itself so easily, containing so many different meanings.

"*There* you are."

Kiki blusters through the double doors, now clad in a puffy-paint cat sweatshirt, too. She stops when she sees my face, her cheeks going pale. "What's the matter?"

I look at her blankly, my throat dry. I call up the picture I just took on my phone. It shows the redhead, his chin jutting, his hair in his face, his eyes wide, two dirty skater shoes splayed out pigeon-toed. "Do we know this person?"

Kiki studies the screen, then searches my face. Her throat bobs as she swallows. "Eliza." She speaks very carefully. "Eliza, that's Leonidas. I'm pretty sure he used to be your boyfriend."

From **The Dots**

D ot met her boyfriend her junior year in college. Marlon sat in the back row of her Introduction to Art History class, which every undergrad was required to take, no matter your intended major. The rumor swept through the class that in high school, her soon-to-be boyfriend was a performance art ingénue; at the beginning of the year, he stole rats from a local pet store and released them in the school hallways, and then he videotaped the whole thing. Apparently, it was so amazing some art gallery in Silver Lake was giving him his own show.

Marlon always seemed to be holding court at the back of the lecture room, telling some fantastical story, getting a lot of laughs. Whenever the teacher called on him, he had interesting interpretations of the artists' motivations. Puzzlingly, though, Dot overheard someone saying he was a physics major and wanted to study quarks after graduation. Dot had no idea what a quark even was. So he *wasn't* an artist, then?

One day, Dot noticed him embracing a very short girl in the quad, and she'd seethed with jealousy—what did she have that Dot didn't? But later, she found out the girl was his neighbor from when he was in kindergarten. Dot was surprised at her relief; by that point, she realized she couldn't deny her crush. She was good at making the first moves with guys, and so, when she came upon him at a holiday party in her dorm, that's just what she did.

Apparently, Marlon knew about Dot, too. "You're famous," he said, after they'd kissed.

Dot lowered her eyes. She thought he was going to mention her tumor. Her illness had garnered unexpected attention through the years: In junior high, older girls doted on her like a baby doll. In high school, angst-ridden boys found her intriguing because she'd walked the thin line between life and death. In the high school locker room, changing for gym, she noticed girls sneaking looks at her head. She heard the name *Frankenstein* directed at her more than once. Along with getting a lecture on how Frankenstein was actually the creator and his brain-stitched creation was called "the monster," those girls also received dead mice in their lockers. Matilda would giggle as she played lookout as Dot placed them there, atop lacy pairs of underwear and love letters and unopened pregnancy tests. But for the past three years in college, she hadn't bothered to mention it to people. She didn't want it following her anymore. She wanted to start over. Still, she wasn't surprised someone had found out.

But no, Marlon said she was famous because she was Dorothy Banks's niece. "My grandparents live near the Magnolia Hotel," he said excitedly. "She's, like, an institution there."

"She doesn't live at the Magnolia anymore," Dot said quietly.

"She doesn't?"

"Nope. She moved out years ago."

He looked confused. "Oh. Huh. I swear they said they just saw her."

"She has this doppelganger, sort of," Dot said. "Maybe that's who you saw. *She* still lives in town, I think. But I haven't seen my aunt in twelve years."

"Where'd she go?" he asked.

"She might be at the Sorbonne. In Paris."

"Really? You should visit her. Paris is awesome."

Dot started up. Why *hadn't* she? Just because her mother said that bullshit about Dorothy being troubled didn't mean she had to buy into it. And she was old enough now. She could find the Sorbonne and track Dorothy down.

That weekend, home with her family for dinner, she mentioned to her mother she was going to buy a ticket. "Paris?" Her mother wrinkled her nose. "What's in Paris?"

Dot couldn't believe her mother had forgotten. "*Dorothy*," she said haughtily. "At the Sorbonne? That ringing a bell?"

Her mother looked shocked. "Oh, Dot, I don't think that's actually true."

"What are you talking about?"

"I said she *might* be there. But she's probably somewhere else."

"No, you said she *was* there." But as soon as Dot said this, she was sure her mother was right. She'd never definitively said anything. This angered her. She'd hitched her star to Paris. All the fictitious letters she'd written from Dorothy were from Paris. She'd bought coffee table books of Parisian photography so she could imagine Dorothy sitting at the Tuileries Garden or hunting around the Catacombs.

"Do you know where she is at all?" she demanded.

Her mother shook her head. "I haven't heard from her since you were in the hospital."

Dot fumed. "If I had a sister, I would cherish her. I would look for her if she went missing."

"You have a stepsister," Dot's mother pointed out, gesturing to her stepsister's empty chair. The stepsister was at college marching band practice. "And honestly, Dot? I used to hear you talk about her behind her back to that weird girl you were friends with in high school in a voice that says to me perhaps you weren't cherishing her. People who live in glass houses shouldn't throw stones."

When Dot made some calls, she found out no one at the Sorbonne had heard of Dorothy Banks. She slammed down the phone, staring at the globe that sat on her stepfather's home office desk. Dorothy could be anywhere on that spherical map. On one of the bumpy mountain ranges, in the middle of the turquoise ocean.

But then, two days later, while Dot was in an American literature lecture, a grad student called for her in the doorway. "There's someone here for you downstairs, and they say it's urgent," he said in a stoned voice. Dot walked out of the school slowly, afraid it would be her stepfather. Maybe her mother was sick, or even had died. But when her vision adjusted, she gasped.

It was Dorothy. *Really* her. She was home.

ELIZA

WEDNESDAY AFTERNOON, I get a text from Bill that says, simply, *We need to see you. Can you come for dinner?* Hours ago, I would have blown it off. They're just going to shove the Oaks Wellness Center idea down my throat some more. But after what happened just outside the Cat Show, maybe I need to go to the Oaks. I certainly need *something*.

Because I am too shaky to drive, a Hyundai with an Uber sticker in the window drops me off at my mother's place. The house is on North Beachwood Drive, a snake of a street in the Hollywood Hills. It's a circular, shell-pink bungalow that, when we moved in, reminded me of a cupcake; apparently, in the 1930s, it belonged to a magician who'd died attempting an underwater lock-breaking stunt. I'd heard that the magician had installed a secret door that led to a private lair, but though I'd spent days knocking on the walls, looking for openings, I never found it.

I loved the place when I first moved in with my mother—we'd bought it for a steal at a sheriff's sale; it was haunted, apparently, which is why no one else wanted it. The building was carved up into lots of small, stucco-walled, womb-like rooms, each crisscrossed with cobwebs and stinking of mold. Dusty, ghost-shaped slipcovers were draped over the sofas, which apparently came with the place, though they were so filthy we immediately put them on the curb for the garbageman. A giant brass candelabrum stood in the middle of the dining room table, each red candle melted into pools of bloody wax. There were gory, dark-red stains on the upstairs Oriental rug that I prayed were blood. A pergola in the backyard looked like it had been chopped up with a dull axe. There was a little cemetery out back filled with little stones marked *secrets;* I dug them up and found no graves. Shaky script was on the inside of the closet walls in the bedroom that became mine. All of the handwritten messages were facts about death: *within three days of dying, the enzymes that digested your dinner begin to eat you.* What a remarkable person who lived here before us, I'd thought with glee. We could have been best friends.

A friend I would have *remembered.* Because you remember friends, don't you, even ones from long ago? And you remember *boyfriends,* no matter how inconsequential? How could I have forgotten an entire boyfriend? I remembered random boys I pulled into the dissection room to make out with in high school. I remembered a sickly boy named Darius who felt me up on a school bus trip to the La Brea Tar Pits. And yet a whole boyfriend has been wiped from my hard drive. Was this possible?

"Oh, *him,*" I'd said to Kiki at the Cat Show, quickly, urgently, to cover up my distress. "Sorry, he just looks so different these days." I'd dramatically slapped the side of my head. "Brain fart!"

Inside, though, I was panicking. I'd already forgotten the name Kiki had told me. All I remembered was that it was long, complicated, and pretentious. My tumor was definitely back. That had to be it. The doctors hadn't dug the whole thing out. After the procedure, I was told I might forget moments, names, faces, details . . . but this seemed bigger than anything like that. This was an entire person.

Kiki had looked at me with concern. "I actually never met him, you know. I only recognized him from your Facebook page."

I frowned. "I don't have a Facebook page."

"Sure you do. I looked at it after we went to the bar that first time after workshop. There were pictures of you and Leonidas on it. You were both wearing UCLA sweatshirts. You looked really happy."

I didn't know whether to continue to rebuke this claim or go along with what she was saying in an attempt to appear in control of my reality. I decided on the latter. "Oh. Uh, yeah. Well, I've been trying to put him out of my mind."

She cleared her throat. "He wasn't . . . *abusive,* was he?"

Her guess was as good as mine, but because I didn't want her to worry, I smiled confidently. "No, no, nothing like that. It's just alarming when you hear someone talking about you across a room."

She frowned. "What was he saying?"

"Forget it," I said. There was no way I could mention that stuff about Palm Springs and the cops. Then I touched the hem of her sweatshirt. "*That's* quite a fashion statement."

Kiki stroked the cat's puffy face. "Yeah. I ran into this breeder my parents used to be friends with, and we got to talking. She sells these on Etsy for eighty dollars. I couldn't say no."

And then she'd blathered on about the MacDonalds' latest Abyssinian and how the winning Maine Coon looked like an asshole and had let out some putrid gas. I thought the Leonidas thing had blown over, but she gave me nervous glances when we got in the car and headed for home. When I went to my bedroom, I heard her whispering downstairs to Steadman. I can only imagine what she said. *Eliza forgot her ex! Is that normal?*

As soon as I bolted the door to my bedroom, I pulled up Facebook and typed in my name. I have a fan page for *The Dots*; it has 834 likes. There are no pictures on the page besides the cover art and my headshot—certainly none of this Leonidas person and me in UCLA sweatshirts. But if Kiki really did look me up on Facebook shortly after we met, I wouldn't have had the *Dots* page yet—I hadn't even finished the novel.

I keep searching, but I can't find a separate personal page for Eliza Fontaine, the Girl. So am I crazy, or is Kiki? Maybe someone took my personal page down? But how could someone remove an account I don't even *remember*?

Then I pounced on my directory from my dorm at UCLA from last year. There was no one named Leonidas in it, not that that really proved anything—he could have lived somewhere else. Was he like the boyfriend I'd written about in *The Dots*? Had I met him in art history class? But I remembered art history. I remembered the teacher with her shelf of dark hair and how she always wore saris even though she wasn't Indian. I remembered Mariel, the girl I sat next to in each class—she told me once that if Pablo Picasso was still alive, she'd definitely give him a blow job. I don't remember a boy in the back of the room holding court, or a boy giving astute answers about Mondrian, or a boy I became slowly obsessed with almost against my will.

So how had we met, then? Why had we broken up? Why was he talking about me and Palm Springs and the police? Who was he talking to? And then, as I was lying there in my bed, a memory struck me, a hard soccer ball kicked to the side of my head. I saw myself lying on the tiled floor in a back hallway. I smelled mozzarella and grease, and I heard loud '90s glam rock on a tinny radio. I saw that same redhead from the hotel lobby standing over me.

Leonidas—I assumed it was him, though this memory played for me like a television show I'd never seen and I had to scramble to figure out the characters—glared at me, the blood drained from his cheeks. "You *promised*," he said through clenched teeth. "I can't believe you."

"I'm sorry," I heard myself saying. In the memory, I was covered in blood. Was it *my* blood? Was my brain just conjuring up blood for dramatic effect? I looked back at him, and he lurched toward me, and I let out a squeal. "I'm so sorry!"

And then, *poof,* no more. If there's anything true about the memory, why was he so angry with me? What sort of crime had I committed? Had I had an affair? I wouldn't put that past me—in high school, I cheated on every boyfriend I had. It was like I couldn't help myself.

Maybe this is why I blocked Leonidas out—I'm ashamed of what I did to him. Maybe I *am* scared of him and what he might do in revenge. Could he have been in Palm Springs, wanting to hurt me?

It kills me that I don't have an available answer. I think my brain knows, but it isn't able to tell me, possibly because of a new tumorous invasion choking vital pathways. Why have I taken all those vitamins, then? Why have I eaten so many fucking blueberries? I should have been gorging on pizza and cigarettes all this time. I could have avoided the shaman in the desert and all that exercise I struggled through. Maybe this is why I drank those bottles of Stoli at the Tranquility. Maybe it's why I've been groping for liquor whenever I can find it these days—I still feel buzzed, in fact, from a shot of whiskey I drank before leaving my house to come to my parents'. I'm digging my own grave instead of letting my faulty brain dig it for me. There's comfort in what I can control.

I pull out my phone and type in the address for Dr. Forney, the neurologist I recall being somehow related to my tumor diagnosis. The office picks up when I call and ask to speak to the doctor.

"Is this an emergency?" the nurse asks.

"I'm not sure," I whisper, but then I get myself together and say I just want to schedule an MRI. Just to check. Off the record. It's not like anyone has to know.

"You'll need to get a referral for that," she says. "I can make you an appointment with Dr. Forney here in the office. He has an opening next week."

On second thought, maybe I don't want to talk to the doctor. Dr. Forney might be able to tell I've been drinking, and he'll scold me. Dr. Forney might know about my fall into the pool and assume

I did it on purpose. He might recommend I recover in a place like the Oaks. But what I want is empirical evidence only. A picture on a scan. An amorphous, ruinous blob.

"Thanks, I'll call back," I tell the nurse, and hang up.

I start up the walk to the house. This is the street tourists use to enter Griffith Park to hike to the Hollywood sign and today, like always, the street is jammed with parallel-parked rental vehicles. Giddy tourists armed with cameras and water bottles leisurely saunter in the middle of the road as though heading to a large outdoor concert. All of them have winsome, eager smiles of people who don't have to stay in LA for any length of time. When I was a teenager, I used to hang out an upstairs window and throw water balloons at them. "*Stop*," Gabby would hiss when she caught me. "That's not nice." I always rolled my eyes. She was always so obsessed with being nice.

On the porch, I stop. I suddenly smell a perfume I recognize but cannot place. It actually stuns me for a moment, rendering me stupid. I hear screeching in my head.

The door whips open. "Eliza!" Bill's arms are outstretched in a T. "How are you? Doesn't it smell *good* out here?"

I smile dazedly. "Yes. What is it?"

He gestures to a tree I've never noticed before. The thing has big orange fruits hanging low and breast-like from branches. "When did you plant that?" I ask.

He shrugs. "It was here when we moved in." He looks at me curiously. "You all right?"

Part of me wants to collapse at his feet and tell him the opposite, but I'm afraid of what this will usher in. Better that I handle this myself, quietly, without panicking anyone else. "Fine," I say in a clipped voice. "Just great."

Bill lets me through the door. Once Bill and Gabby moved in with us, the spooky old house was gutted and transformed into an airy, open rectangle with spare furniture and high-end electronics. The moldy furniture that had been here when we arrived was moved out, the *secret* graves were bulldozed over, the stained-glass windows of hollow-eyed saints and sinners were carefully removed and replaced. I got to keep the creepy death words in my closet for a while, but one day, apropos of nothing, my mother said she'd painted over them. "They were just too morbid," she said. I cried for days. I mourned the loss of those words. I rewrote the facts I could remember in pencil, but it wasn't the same. I didn't have the same shaky script. I couldn't get the backward slant of the letters just right.

How do I remember *that* so well, but not Leonidas?

"Well, I gotta say, you look great."

I jump and turn around. Bill's in the doorway, rubbing his hands together.

"Thanks," I say, though I know I don't look great, not at all. I appreciate Bill's practiced cheerfulness, though. The day the father and son pulled me out of the ocean, Bill drove me to the hospital for treatment. He acted as though we were driving to somewhere innocuous, like Home Depot.

"Oh, look, a farm stand," I remember him saying halfway there, pulling over. "Eliza, you want a peach?" I often think my mother doesn't deserve him, though perhaps they work in a yin and yang way, his kindness balancing out her prickliness.

"Want anything to drink?" Bill asks now. "We've got water, soda, orange juice . . ."

"Uh, water is fine," I lie. I'd kill for a shot of bourbon.

He makes a little nicker sound and disappears into the kitchen. I pad toward the built-in bookshelves, also a new addition after he moved in. They've got a lot of titles lined up, though most of them are about the Civil War, Bill's forte. Also on the shelf are southern romances, the pastel-covered kinds, and a gritty memoir about a woman who grew up in a one-room shack and had psychos for parents. They must be my mother's, though I've rarely seen her reading.

But then there's this thin book, really just a pamphlet, lying on the sleek, Lucite side table. *On the Meditation of the Mind.* On the back is a picture of a man with bulging eyes and frizzy, Einstein hair.

I stop short, a chill running through me. It looks like the guy who said hello to me in the café with Posey. His name is Herman Lavinsky. Goose bumps rise on my skin. Why do I know that name?

I grab my phone and find Google. Herman Lavinsky is a "healer" in Los Angeles. He leads people on "spiritual journeys" through Death Valley. I'm about to call up his website when the floor behind me creaks.

"Here you go!" Bill appears with a Perrier. A lime bobs cheerfully on top.

I show him the book. "Who is this guy?"

Bill shrugs. "No idea. Must be one of your mom's." He takes the book from me and puts it back on the shelf. He takes my arm. "Come on, honey. We need to talk to you."

I give the spine of the book one more glance. On second thought, maybe the writer isn't the guy from the café—that guy didn't look capable of writing anything. Still, there is something about this book that starts an itch in my brain. I get a flash—brief, foggy, more a smell and a sound than an actual image—of being in an antiseptic room, someone's clogs slapping quietly on the floor, and a voice saying, *Okay, count backward from ten.*

It makes me shiver. What is it from? A nurse giving me anesthesia, maybe, when I had the tumor? Some crackpot I visited post-tumor to ensure I didn't get sick again?

"Okay," I say, turning to Bill. "I want to talk to you guys, too." I want to tell them about Leonidas. If they see him around, they need to tell me. If he knocks on their door, they can't let him in. Maybe they can fill me in on who he is, too.

Bill might have renovated most of the house with exotic woods and high-end blinds and robotic pneumatic systems that sucked up dust before it has time to settle, but my mother kept the kitchen almost as it was when we moved in. The cabinets were repainted in clean white, but the knobs remained the same round, bland brass buttons. The stove has four burners, the countertops are not marble but made out of some spongy material with little flecks of what they want you to think is stone smashed into the surface. Our old kitchen table, the one I used to impale with the tines of my fork, is still in the corner, as are the wooden chairs with the wobbly legs.

My mother and Gabby stand together at the kitchen table, though when I walk in they jolt apart, as though I'm a big electromagnet reversing their polarization. "Uh, hi," I say to my mother. And to Gabby, "I didn't know you were coming."

They hem and haw. Then, something on the table catches my attention. It's my book. Just sitting there, spine closed, cover glossy. My heart is in my throat. I point at it. "Where did you get that?"

Gabby's eyes grow wide. My mother doesn't answer.

I start to tremble. "I'm serious. Why is it here?"

"We got it in the mail today," my mother says in a low voice. "There was no return address."

My mind is racing. *Damn it, Posey.* I specifically told her I didn't want my family to receive it. I'd been *so clear*. She wouldn't have gone against my wishes. Only, does that mean someone *else* did? Not Laura, either—so who?

The person who wants to hurt me? I swallow hard. Is that insane?

My mother lets out a breath. "And we have a problem."

There is suddenly a surplus of saliva in my mouth. It takes three swallows to get it all down. "What do you mean?"

My mother points to the book. Her eyes are blazing. "You can't actually publish this, Eliza."

Sweat dots my back. I think, for a moment, I've heard her wrong, but then Bill adds, "We've tried calling your editor already, but she hasn't called back."

"Wait a minute," I say slowly. "So . . . you read it?"

My mother looks exasperated. "Yes. We read it."

"And . . . you didn't like it, I guess." I laugh self-consciously, though it comes out choked.

My mother's eyes bulge, as if this is the most asinine question I could have asked. I am burning with shame. Maybe what I've worried about all this time is true: my book is literally the stupidest, pettiest, most ridiculous piece of writing ever to be put down on paper. Only, if it is, why did my agent applaud it? Why did my editor buy it? What the fuck is going on here? I review what my mother just said and feel a ball of anger knot in my chest. "And you called my *editor*?"

"Yes, and *you* have to call her, too," my mother says forcefully.

I grab my book and press it to my chest. "I didn't *ask* for you to read it. I never told you about it because I knew you wouldn't like it. Just like you don't like anything I do."

"Eliza," Bill starts. "That's not—"

"No, forget it." My cheeks are blazing. "I have to go. I'll see you later."

"Wait!" Bill catches my arm. "It's just that . . . the story you wrote . . . are you sure? Maybe you should pull back, have a think. You're a lovely writer. You must have other stories in you."

I wrench away. "Everyone else thinks it's great. My agent tells me it's getting a lot of good buzz."

My mother looks at Bill in horror. "*Others* have read it?"

"No one but my editor and agent, and maybe some others at the publishing house, but reviewers are looking at it now." For a split second, I wonder if Laura has recruited my mother in a twisted reverse psychology initiative, because now I *want* it to go to reviewers. I want the whole world to review it. I want to show her that others think it's decent. Why does she get to deem something unpublishable? It's like she's taking it personally!

Then I get it. I step back and laugh. "You're pissed about the mother character, aren't you? Because I made her nice at first, but then she's totally unsympathetic. You think it's you."

My mother bites hard on her bottom lip and says nothing.

It's so telling. Of course it's the only thing she noticed, and she isn't able to see past it, and she decided, based upon that fact and that fact alone, that my book is shit. Her disapproval of the one true thing I've done with my life so far falls in line with everything else she's ever felt about me, so I shouldn't be surprised.

So why *am* I surprised? Why do I care so much? Why does it physically hurt?

My mother strides forward, yanks the home phone from the wall, and hands it to me. "Please. Call your publisher right now. Tell them you've changed your mind."

I bark out a laugh. "Just because you think it's a bad book doesn't mean you get to cancel its existence."

"Eliza!" Her eyes are wild. She looks like she might cry. *"Please!"*

I take the receiver from her and slam it back into its cradle. "No," I say. "You're not being fair."

Bill places his hands on the table. "Eliza, *why* did you write this book?"

It feels like a trick question. "I don't know. Because . . . I've always wanted to write a book."

There's a bubbling sound at the stove, and a charred scent to the air. My mother glares at Bill. He holds his palms up in the air. No one moves.

My skin prickles. "Does this have something to do with someone pushing me into the pool?"

My mother shuts her eyes. "No one pushed you into that pool, Eliza."

"But the guy who pulled me out of the water saw someone running away from the scene."

"No, he didn't."

I scoff. "How do you know? Why would the guy lie? I think the person who pushed me was Leonidas."

My mother, to Bill: "Her college boyfriend?" Then to me: "He wouldn't do that."

"How do *you* know?"

Finally, Bill seems to notice the burning sauce. He sidles to the stove to save it. "I mean, isn't Leonidas a hundred pounds soaking wet?"

"He's still capable of *pushing*," I say through clenched teeth. "He could be dangerous. He hurt me when we were dating."

"He *did*?" My mother looks astonished.

I duck my head. I really have no clue.

"I don't think it was Leonidas," Gabby says in her small, meek way.

I turn to her, eager for more. "Why do you say that?"

One shoulder lifts. "He . . ." She trails off. "He always seemed nice."

"Didn't he rescue rats from a pet store?" My mother's voice cracks. "Wasn't that his big claim to fame?"

"No, that was Dot's boyfriend you're thinking of. You're getting us confused." I'm astonished she retained anything from the novel, considering how vehemently she loathed it. "Look, I overheard him talking to someone on the phone today. About *Palm Springs*. And about calling the police."

"But couldn't it be a coincidence?" Gabby says carefully.

"That's ridiculous," my mother says at the same time.

My head swivels between them. "It's not ridiculous. Someone is *after* me. Someone wants to *hurt* me."

"Eliza. Honey." Bill presses his hand on my shoulder. It's warm and large, and his fingers clamp down on bone. "No one's going to hurt you. We're right here. We'll make sure. We want you to get better."

Across the table, Gabby nods. When I look at my mother, her eyes have softened. The atmosphere distorts. They look so earnest, suddenly. Like my well-being really is the only thing on their minds. And it seems possible, in this moment, that if I just give in, if I tell them that I'm lying and that what happened in Palm Springs was just like all the other times, their love for me will blossom, and they *will* keep me safe. I mean, it's partly what I'm worried about anyway, right? That I'm sick again? So why can't I let them help me? I picture a fantasy: I'm whisked upstairs and taken to my old bed. Bill wheels in the TV and brings me soup. Gabby reads to me from a magazine. My mother cries quietly into a handkerchief.

But as I open my mouth, I realize that in order to attain this sort of care, I'll have to tell them something that isn't true. And I can't do that. "There was someone at the pool that night," I say instead, feeling so weary. "There really, really was."

Bill's shoulders slump. Gabby's head drops on her neck. My mother presses her hands over her eyes and lets out a long breath. Then, shaking her head, she turns and walks out of the room. Just like that.

"Please call your editor," she says over her shoulder. "I'm serious."

I watch her back disappear through the door. Upstairs, a door shuts. The AC, another addition after Bill and Gabby's arrival, kicks on.

I whip around to Bill and Gabby. "What the hell is going on?"

"We're worried about you," Bill says softly. "We're not sure what you remem—"

A movement to my left distracts me. I shoot up. A dark, shadowy face is in the courtyard, looking in. I rush to the window. "There's someone in the . . ." The shadow shifts. I blink, and it's *me* out there. I blink, and everything mutates again. It's just my reflection.

I rub my hands over my eyes. The yard is empty; even my reflection in the glass is gone. I press my nose to the window, craning my neck far to the right. There are petals strewn across the brick patio. Leaves have fallen into the pool. The palms are still. The chrome hood over the bricked-in grill is immaculately shiny.

I turn back to Bill and Gabby. They're both pinned against the island as if a blast has pushed them there. I've caught them in strange poses: Gabby's shoulders are turned in and her hands are limp claws by her chest. Bill's got one arm slung across her waist, and his feet seem planted. It's like our own little Pompeii has happened, freezing and hardening them in ash.

"Did you see it, too?" I whisper.

Bill's throat bobs as he swallows. "I didn't see anything." He glances at Gabby, and a silent conversation flows between the two of them. Together, they peel away from the island and sit back down at the table.

"Sorry. I just thought . . ." I clear my throat, still feeling the prickly sensation that someone's watching me. Then I turn to Bill. "What were you saying?"

Bill shakes his head. "Forget it." He pushes a plate at me. "Fill it up. You're getting so skinny you're disappearing."

From The Dots

Dorothy was waiting in the school parking lot in a black-on-black Mustang convertible. She wore a large floppy hat that tied under her chin and big sunglasses over her eyes. Dot's heart swelled and nearly burst. This had to be a mirage. There was no way her aunt had come back to her after all this time. She'd given up hoping.

"Darling," Dorothy said, stepping away from the car and opening her arms. It was her voice, exactly as Dot remembered it. And when she pulled Dot to her chest, everything felt just the same as all those hugs from years ago. "Oh, darling, I've missed you so much."

Dot was too stunned to speak, but when she did, the questions came out like a geyser: "Where have you been? What have you been doing? Were you in Paris? Were you writing? Did you have a ukulele and a poodle?" The only thing she didn't ask was the most important question: *Why did you go? Why did you leave me?*

"Come, come," Dorothy said, opening the car door. "I'll tell you everything. Best not to tell your mother about this, though."

Dot snorted. "Don't worry about *that*."

They drove around LA for a while. Dot didn't say much—she was too overwhelmed and intimidated and didn't want to say the wrong thing. They pulled into a familiar neighborhood to the west of town. "I thought we could go here for old time's sake, since we made up so many stories about the place," Dorothy said. She pointed to a restaurant in the distance. *M&F Chop House,* read the neon sign. Across the street, St. Mother Maria's, Dot's second hospital, loomed gray and institutional in the dull, midday light.

Dot didn't really want to be here—she hadn't returned to this part of town since she was sick, but there was no way she was disappointing her aunt, so she said nothing. Instead of going through the front double doors, Dorothy parked in the back and led them around to a side entrance, down a set of stairs, and to a door where she knocked three times. "Like a speakeasy," she said cheerfully. "This entrance is for the important people."

A man with a round, smiling face, pig-pink skin, and a Winnie-the-Pooh voice opened the door, welcomed Dorothy with a hug, and led them up a set of indoor stairs lined with framed restaurant reviews. In the dining room, the walls were paneled in warm-colored wood, and the air smelled like meat. The man introduced himself to Dot as Bernie. He sat them in a booth that was so far in the back of the room Dot was pretty sure no one knew they were there. It struck Dot as odd; when she was young, Dorothy used to grouse whenever she wasn't given an establishment's best table. When she called this to Dorothy's attention, her aunt's eyes sparkled. "Honey, this *is* the best table. People are going to leave us alone. Now, look at this place. Remember all those stories?"

Dot beamed shyly. Of course she remembered. She was thrilled *Dorothy* remembered. She hadn't been sure, over the twelve-year gap, what she'd meant to Dorothy.

Dorothy ordered champagne, then took off her sunglasses and removed the hat from her head. Dot gasped. In the ten years that had passed, she'd pictured Dorothy aging and growing lumpier, but the woman who stared back at her had smooth, lineless skin. There wasn't a single gray hair in her black mane. Her eye makeup was dark lines and dramatic sparkles, and when she smiled, her teeth were whiter than Dot's. Dot could plop her down on her college campus and half the guys would hit on her. Only her hands, with their protruding veins and smattering of freckles and the slightest beginning of gnarl, gave her age away.

Dorothy looked carefully at Dot, too. So long, in fact, that Dot began to feel self-conscious. She ran her hand over her hair and straightened her sweater. She was wearing a black cashmere boatneck sweater she'd found at a consignment store; it smelled slightly of mothballs and smoke. On her head was a small, netted hat. The netting kept getting in her eyes.

"You've grown into a remarkable young lady," Dorothy decreed.

Dot was so overcome she thought she might cry. "Thank you."

"It's quite uncanny how much we look alike, isn't it? We could be twins!" Dorothy pressed her hands to her bosom and sighed. "If only I'd been here to see you transform."

"Why weren't you?" Dot asked, before she could stop herself.

Dorothy sighed. "It wasn't possible."

The waiter delivered drinks. Dot was surprised she'd been given champagne, too. She stared at the bubbles rising to the top of the flute, feeling uncertain. Through the years, kids thought she was fucked up on seizure drugs and party drugs alike, but she'd taken the doctors' suggestions to heart. She drank a little from time to time, but only beer. Anything harder frightened her. She feared excess would shepherd the lesions back into her brain like loser teenagers squeezing through a cracked-open back door at a VIP club.

"Are you sure this is okay?" Dot pointed at her drink.

"What, because of your illness?" Dorothy waved her hand. "It's perfectly fine. Besides, you're almost twenty-one, aren't you?" She sighed with pleasure. "My little lady."

Dot put the drink to her lips. It tasted fruity and sour at the same time. The bubbles exploded on her tongue. She felt surprising heat as the liquid went down her throat, but it warmed her stomach pleasantly. She smiled at her aunt across the table, and Dorothy smiled back.

"Two lovely ladies having a cocktail," Dorothy proclaimed, giving Dot a wink. Dot beamed and took another sip. They were back together. It felt so right.

Dorothy was staying once again in her same bungalow at the Magnolia. "They held the old suite for me," she trilled. She'd come back a few days ago.

"Back from where?" Dot asked.

"Oh, so many places," Dorothy sighed, finishing her drink quickly.

First, she really *had* been working on a section for her book, she said, one whose research took her to French and Austrian castles, then to Morocco, then even other parts of Africa. In Somalia, she met a tribal leader named Otufu, and they'd begun an affair. Dorothy couldn't quite picture a life with him—the African way of life was so different from anything she was used to—but she thought it would be interesting research for a book, so she remained. Only, then she found out that Otufu was involved with warlords in the area, running guns or some such—"a real baddie," she explained. "I had to get away from him. I had to get to the U.S. embassy, but it was a risk to leave his compound. The place was rife with armed guards. A maid helped me sneak out in the middle of the night. I ran barefoot to the embassy; some of Otufu's men were chasing me. They had to helicopter me to Italy for safety, but they suggested I remain in hiding for a while. Otufu knew people everywhere. He thought I was going to talk. There was a price on my head."

"Holy shit," Dot gasped.

"I stayed in Rome for a while, in this ramshackle apartment that barely had any heat. I wrote a little, but mostly I just ate, read books, and took lovers." She gave Dot a saucy look. "It was a heady time, and time passed so quickly—before I realized it, really. After a while, the embassy told me that it was probably safe for me to return to the States. I missed you so much—I wanted to see you. So here I am."

Dot blinked at her. "That's amazing."

"Oh, well, you know." Dorothy signaled the bartender for another cocktail. But then her eyes widened at something across the bar. Dot turned to follow her gaze. A woman in a black suit was sitting at a table near the window. Her hair was slightly less blonde than before, and there were crow's-feet at the corners of her eyes, but Dot recognized her immediately.

"Doctor Koder," she said, half standing. And then her heart dropped to her stomach. Dr. Koder was in a wheelchair—the motorized kind, bulky and huge. Her twisted fingers fumbled to eat a salad. A strap around her waist held her body upright.

Dot pressed her hand to her mouth. "What *happened* to her?"

"Stop that." Dorothy pulled her back down to sit. "It's rude to stare."

Her nails dug into Dot's arm. Dot stared at them; they looked, for a moment, like talons. Her gaze fell to her plate. The steak juices were thick and red, marbling her potatoes.

"That was my only reservation in coming here," Dorothy said quietly. "I worried we'd run into someone from that time. I mean, I know it was hard for you, too, dear. So hard. But you can't imagine what I went through, day in and day out, not knowing if you'd live."

Dot nodded. She glanced back at Dr. Koder, surreptitiously watching as the woman scooped up a bite of creamed spinach. A splotch fell to her shirt, and the man she was with, a kindly fellow in a tweed jacket, leaned across the table to dab it off. Dr. Koder gave him a bright, beautiful smile.

After that, Dot looked away, deciding she wouldn't give Dr. Koder another thought. Whatever Dorothy wanted, Dorothy would get. Dorothy smiled, seeming to register this.

"So," she said smoothly, tipping her drink to her lips. "Tell me about *you*. You're in college now! I can't believe it!"

"Well, I'm thinking of majoring in English," Dot said.

Dorothy clapped her hands in delight. "How lovely! The world needs more literature professors."

"Actually, I was thinking of becoming a writer," Dot said quietly.

Dorothy didn't seem to hear her. "And maybe you'll read my book for your course!" she crowed. "I'm sure it'll be on the syllabus once it's published. I mean, I'm no Henry James, but they have lots of modern fiction on course lists these days, don't they? I'm much better than those dreadful modernists for sure. And Stephen Crane?" She made a gagging sound. "They could definitely bump *him*."

Dot reached for her champagne glass again, trying not to feel overlooked. Dorothy had been out of practice talking to people for a while, that was all. Dot should just let her prattle on. She didn't want anything to be wrong with this evening. She wanted it to go exactly as her aunt desired.

ELIZA

IT IS A BITCH to get to Steadman's curiosities shop in Venice—so many highways, so many traffic lights, idiots on cruiser bicycles, homeless crackheads lying in the middle of the street. It's even worse because I still haven't picked up my car from Palm Springs, which means I have to rely on a cabdriver to take me, and the stopping and starting traffic makes me carsick. When I finally get there to start my shift that Friday, two days after the Cat Show, I feel my usual disappointment with my surroundings; the place always looks a lot better in my mind's eye. The shop is one notch above a hovel, shoved onto a side street near the canals and lit by a single orange bulb. The single room seems to get smaller and narrower as the hours pass, closing the taxidermied heads and ancient medical equipment and necklaces made of bones over me like a cask. Sometimes, I'm not sure working here is worth the eight dollars and fifty cents an hour Steadman pays, which isn't even California's minimum wage.

I sit on a tufted stool behind the antique cash register, jiggling my foot to the classical station on the radio. Though a meditative coach told me that classical music dissolves harmful pathways in the brain, it's still like nails on a chalkboard. I want to change the station, but Steadman has taped up so many rules about appropriate music for this place. *No Pop, No Country, No Rap, No Halloween.* I think he wrote that last one just for my benefit. What does he think I'm going to do, listen to "Monster Mash" all day?

Long shadows slope off the animal heads hanging on the walls. Several baby coffins balance atop a tall pile of boxes marked things like *Alligator Teeth* and *Freeze-Dried Turtles* and *Victorian Human Hair Wreaths.* There is a jewelry case bearing things like earrings made out of miniature doll legs, cicada wings, and voodoo chicken feet. Across the room, which is little more than an arm's length away, is a flyer that reads, *Interested in Taxidermy? Come to our class May 12!* Guess who's teaching it? Me.

Because, clearly, that's all I'm qualified to do. Not write books.

The Dvořák piece ends, and the DJ sleepily tells us what we're to hear next. I refresh my phone screen again and again, thinking I might have missed a call from Lance the detective or the bartender who may or may not be named Richie. This store has spotty service—the high concentration of human bone seems to interfere with a cell signal.

I hear a jingle and nearly drop the phone—it's *ringing.* But then I realize it's the front door, which is almost as unlikely—most of our customers are creeps who order online. A figure stoops to get through the narrow door and stands for a moment next to the life-size, bisque-faced man doll. As his features organize themselves, I cough out a laugh. Today he's got on a wine-colored hooded cape. "*Desmond!*"

He shades his eyes and squints all ten feet to where I am behind the register. "Eliza. It *is* you."

He sidesteps a few open boxes and approaches me. There's a big smile on his face, though it fades to disappointment when he sees my expression. "How did you know I work here?" I demand.

"I looked you up online. There was a picture of a cat skeleton on your Twitter, and your location finder was on, so it was easy for me to pinpoint where you were." He grinned triumphantly.

My heart is thrumming in my ears. Location finder? What if Leonidas is stalking my Twitter, too? "You should have just called me. I've been sending you texts all week."

"Ah, but calling you lacked the mystery. I wanted to *find* you." Then Desmond glances around the room. There's a strong odor of charred hair. Wind-up teeth chatter on a shelf.

"This place is magnificent," he decides. He spins on his heel and surveys the other side of the room. "There's a convention for people who like Ouija boards?" He points to a flyer next to some antique wigs.

"In Baltimore," I say sulkily. "It's Ouija's birthplace."

He looks at me excitedly. "I'll go if you go!"

I give him a sour frown. "No, thank you."

He points at a metal tool that looks like an oversized corkscrew. It's nestled in a rosewood box and is on sale for $930. "A trephine," he says, with adulation.

I chuckle despite myself. I can't help but be impressed. "You are one of the few people who actually know what it's called."

"These are fascinating. Physicians thought that if they drilled holes in the skulls of patients who had brain disorders, they'd let out the bad spirits."

"*I* know that."

"One of my favorite paintings is by Hieronymus Bosch of a guy laying on a chair and a doctor drilling into his head."

"I have a print of that, if you're interested," I grab a binder underneath the counter of laminated images we can order as posters. When I find the Bosch, Desmond taps the page with his pinkie finger. He's wearing a signet ring. "He looks like the Tin Man," he says, pointing to the doctor with the drill. There's a metal funnel on his head.

"Art experts say that's his hint that he's a quack," I say, enjoying showing off the only thing I can remember from the one art history class I took my first semester of college.

"Well of *course* he's a quack. He's drilling into the guy's *head*. Who wants to do that?"

I shut the binder. "Why are you here? Did the police get in touch with you finally?"

Desmond pauses. "Well, no. I haven't heard a thing. I just wanted to see how you were doing, my fairest." He wiggles his eyebrows.

All at once, I flash back on my humiliating lunge toward him the day he came to my house. What had possessed me to do such a thing? It's kind of a relief that he's shown up today. I'd conjured that absinthe-with-Paul, holy-shit-you-won't-believe-what-this-weird-girl-did-to-me scene in my mind too many times over the past several days.

I fold my hands and try to look proper and sober, though it's difficult when surrounded by stuffed parrots in antique birdcages and a huge sign over my head that reads *Just in! Whale Penises!*

"I'm hanging in there," I admit, though I sound so miserable it can hardly be accepted as the truth.

Desmond's brow furrows. Then his voice drops an octave, as though he doesn't want the taxidermy animals to overhear. "So I might as well get to my point and let you go on with your work. Would you like to partake in a beverage with me sometime?"

I stare at him. "Do you mean go out for a drink?"

"In layman's terms, exactly."

A date. I'm unequipped for one of those; I feel I've never really gone on one. Then again, I must have: there was Leonidas. If only I remembered what sorts of dates we went on.

Desmond leans his elbows on the counter. "I'll take you anywhere you want. I'll do whatever." He smiles kinkily, which is not unattractive, exactly.

"I'm kind of busy," I say automatically.

"Are you sure? You can't even spare time for an aperitif?"

"I don't know what that is."

"What about coffee? Even for ten minutes. Whenever you're done with work today." He tilts his head, and his woolly eyebrows hood over his lashes. "We parted so inelegantly last time. And far too abruptly for my liking."

Maybe he *had* wanted to have sex with me; maybe he'd spent the last four days ruing how he'd chickened out. I fiddle with a rabbit's foot Steadman keeps next to one of the brass register keys. The thing is, I am awfully lonely. I crave sex, but I can get sex. It's closeness that's more elusive. Sometimes, I get the urge to walk through a parking lot next to someone. To hold someone's hand. To have someone make me a sandwich or place a washcloth on my head when I'm sick. I don't know if that person is Desmond—I still can't quite imagine kissing him without bursting out laughing—but a little companionship would be nice.

Then I think of Leonidas again. I have *that* to figure out, and I've decided on what I'm going to do. "Uh, there's something I need to take care of after work."

"I'll join you!" He instantly looks sheepish. "Sorry, it's just that I so rarely get days off when the convention is in full swing, and I'd love to see you, but if I'm being outré you can tell me to cease and desist."

"It's okay," I say slowly, considering. I shouldn't rope Desmond into this, but it might not be a bad idea to bring him along.

I take a breath. "I'm actually looking into my killer. Or, well, *almost* killer."

"You mean from the pool?" He puffs out his narrow rib cage. "I'll definitely accompany. You need protection."

"Are you sure? Because I have this idea of what I need to do, and you might not like it."

Desmond pretends to peel back his wrist and toss something in front of me. "The gauntlet has been thrown." It's a wonder he doesn't have a *real* gauntlet. "When are you off? I'll meet you here anon."

I tell him, and he swoops his cape and exits with Edwardian flair. I am left with a symphony of strings and a whole bunch of lifeless, staring animals. I look around at them, wishing I could ask them if that actually just happened. I feel excited, kind of. In an eye-rolling sort of way. But before I can really dwell on it, a busload pulls up and out pour the other sort of people who buy from this store—busloads from God-knows-where, with their huge empty boxes. They look so normal, lumpy, suburban, and neighborly, but they come in here and fight over the weird objects rescued from babies' stomachs and archaic tools of horrible things we used to do to one another before we knew any better. It's a phenomenon, really.

Two hours later, Steadman arrives, relieving me from my shift. "We had great sales today!" I crow. I am trying not to walk too unsteadily or slur my speech, but I actually had three shots of meade, the only liquor I could find under a two-foot-high pile of papers in the cramped back room, in order to quell my buzzing nerves for my big Leonidas investigation. "We got a bus of tourists from Pasadena!"

Steadman slams his briefcase down on the counter and juts a thumb out the front door. "Someone's waiting for you outside." At first, I think he's pissed because he knows I've been drinking. But then he adds, "He's driving a Batmobile, and it's taking up all the good parking."

"He's driving a what?" I scurry out from behind the counter. It takes me only a second and a half to cross the store and open the front door. Sure enough, Desmond is standing at the curb, and I'll be damned, he's stolen Batman's car.

From The Dots

I have something to tell you," Dot said softly to Marlon during art history. They were talking about the Impressionists that day, paintings of ethereal flowers and rain-speckled streets. It was exactly the sort of art Dot wasn't into—when she was young, if she walked into a doctor's office with a Monet print on the walls, she would turn and walk right out. Dorothy would indulge this, saying Monet made her want to kill herself, too.

Marlon gazed at her with interest, putting down his pen. But then, because Dot was afraid of anyone overhearing, she wrote it down on a piece of paper and slid it toward him: *My aunt is back. You know who.* And of course he knew. They were together by then. Dorothy was all Dot talked about.

I'm secretly meeting with her every Wednesday, Dot wrote after he read this first part and widened his eyes. *She wants to meet you.*

She slipped the paper to him again. He read it, nodded, and then wrote something down. *Sure. I'm in.*

Dot made him eat the paper so no one would see.

On Wednesday, they got in Marlon's car. "Where are we going to meet her?" he said excitedly. "The Ivy? That new Korean place on

Melrose? An S&M club? I mean, she's fabulous and up for anything, right?"

"Actually, she really likes this steak house in Alhambra," Dot said. Her boyfriend made a face. She squeezed his hand. "It's cool, I promise. Wait until she tells you her stories. You'll be blown away."

Marlon's brow creased anyway when he saw M&F, which looked, Dot suddenly noticed, only a notch better than the Texas Roadhouse chain. "It's really nice inside," she said, gesturing to the valet line. Of course, *they* didn't use the valet: as usual, Dot went for the back entrance, rapping on the door like a pro.

"What's with the speakeasy thing?" Marlon grumbled uncertainly.

Dot beamed. "That's exactly what Dorothy said!" There, it was kismet: he and Dorothy were going to hit it off for sure.

Dorothy hadn't arrived yet. Dot settled into her regular chair, and Marlon sat across from her.

"Shouldn't we be at a better table?" he asked. "We're next to a utility closet. Our food is going to taste like bleach."

"Oh, stop," Dot said. "No one bugs us here. We can talk."

The bartender Dot now knew well was mopping the bar; he looked up and smiled. "Champagne?" he said, and it materialized immediately. Bernie the waiter set down three glasses: one for Dot, one for her boyfriend, and one at Dorothy's empty seat.

Marlon looked at Dot nervously. "I thought you only liked beer."

Dot shot him a look. "Don't be such a prude."

Dorothy appeared in the back hall in a flurry of mink and silk. Dot shot to her feet; Marlon lingered shyly behind her. Dorothy hugged both of them, exclaiming over and over how *nice* it was to meet Dot's boyfriend, what a *specimen* he was. "So tall!" she cried, touching the top of his head. "And that hair! You should bottle it! And what do you do to remain so slender!"

Marlon blushed. "Genetics, I guess."

"Lucky," Dorothy said, winking at him flirtatiously.

They sat down. Marlon was still nervous and twitchy. Dorothy took a big gulp of champagne and made a face. "No wonder you're not drinking this." She pulled a flask out of her bag and snapped her fingers; two lowball glasses appeared. "From my special vault." She poured brown liquid for both of them.

"What is it?" Marlon asked.

"Whiskey, darling." Dorothy grinned.

Marlon gave Dot a skeptical look. "I'm not really into whiskey."

Dot kicked him under the table. *So don't drink it,* she thought angrily. *Just don't be a killjoy.* She drank the whiskey heartily, with big swallows, ignoring the burning sensation in her belly.

Dorothy began to tell Marlon the tale of her African tribesman lover, Otufu. She included details she hadn't told Dot—hiding in a whorehouse in some Somali village, having an assault rifle thrust into her hands in case she needed to defend herself, watching Otufu's henchmen murder a man inside Otufu's compound. Marlon blinked rapidly. Dorothy finally waved her hand in front of his face. "Hel-*lo*? You still in there?"

"I feel like I'm in a movie," Marlon murmured.

Dorothy slung her arm around him. "Love this one, darling," she said to Dot. "He's a keeper."

Steaks, then, and a limo to a club Dorothy knew about for dancing. The club was through an entrance down a dingy set of steps; halfway to the door, Dorothy paused and glared at the sidewalk. "I think it was a paparazzo," she whispered, pointing to someone with a camera. She pulled her scarf over her head and ducked out of sight.

Inside the club: foreign types, emaciated models, drunk bodybuilders. Dorothy kept her scarf over her head the whole time, a makeshift hijab. Dot danced wildly, feeling unhinged and free. At two a.m., Marlon gently pushed Dot away when she tried to put her hands down his pants.

"Babe, you seem really drunk," he said gently.

Dot peppered him with kisses. "Nah, I'm great!"

"I'm worried about you. I want to make sure this isn't hurting your brain, you know?"

"I've hardly had anything to drink," Dot assured him. And it was true: just a few sips of the whiskey at the restaurant and maybe one drink here over the course of several hours. She was just high on life! Euphoria flooded into her, ripening her valleys, turning her leaves green.

But then she dropped to the floor as though her knees had been chopped off. People laughed and scattered. She tried to stand, but her head lolled on her neck. Vomit rose in her throat. Her legs wobbled, then went out from under her. The last thing she remembered was hearing the bass thudding against the club's floor and noticing feet around her, and a dropped plastic cup, and someone's chewed-up gum.

She woke up in a white bed in a quiet room. Something was beeping next to her, and she could feel a dull ache in her arm. Her first thought was that she'd fallen through a wormhole and was nine years old again and in the hospital. The room began to take shape. She saw green-and-white-striped curtains. A flat-screen TV on the wall. Out the window, a glimmering pool, palm trees.

A man in a white doctor's coat appeared over her. He had a broad nose, wild eyebrows, intense, dark eyes. He smelled strongly of aftershave, which turned Dot's stomach. "Feeling better, Miss Dot?" he asked in an Indian accent.

Dot looked around. "What happened? Where's my boyfriend?"

"Just rest, all right?"

"Where's my mother?"

The door opened, and Dorothy rushed in. "Darling, you're up." She touched the man's arm, just below his elbow. "This is Doctor Singh. I had him pop in to check you out."

Dot blinked. She must have fainted last night. From a seizure, surely. Another tumor. She bit down hard on her tongue.

Dorothy fluffed a pillow next to Dot. "You're in my suite. At the Magnolia."

"Is it . . . bad?" Dot whispered.

"Is what bad?"

"The tumor. It's back, right?"

Her aunt's shoulders sank, and she smiled. "Oh, *honey*." She pressed her cool hands on Dot's forehead. "You just had too much to drink last night. That's all."

Dot tried to sit up. "Are you sure? Maybe we should have me tested. Maybe we should call someone."

Dorothy waved her hand dismissively. "Just rest. You're dehydrated, that's all. Too much alcohol does that to you. You should be thanking me. Doctor Singh was very kind to come here with all this equipment." She leaned closer. "That IV will make you feel much better."

"Thank you," Dot said, robotically. Something felt off. Maybe it was just that she was exhausted, and there was still the residue of fear clinging to her. That tumor pulsed inside her, she knew, still hiding; those nasty little cells were rearranging, mutating, poisoning her. She still very much believed that.

"And incidentally." Dorothy turned away from her and peered at herself in the mirror, fluffing her curls. Dot thought she saw her snake an arm around Dr. Singh's waist, but when she wriggled up higher in the bed, her arms were by her sides. "Don't mention it to your mother. She was never really one for partying." She met Dot's eyes in the glass. "It'll be our little secret."

ELIZA

"WHAT THE HELL is that?" I ask as I step onto the sidewalk.

Desmond, who has changed from his cape into a shiny-looking button-down, jeans that show exactly how thin his hips are, and a red beret, stands at the passenger door. "The Batmobile. And you are my Vicki Vale."

"I look nothing like Vicki Vale." The garish vehicle is all angles and wings and covered in a cheap-looking matte paint. It has a long front end with a launcher. There are vents on the sides and exaggerated wings at the back and some sort of rocket booster where a tailpipe should be.

"Does it drive?" I ask.

"Naturally."

"And it's *yours*?"

Desmond opens the passenger door, which flips up like a DeLorean. "Naturally."

"Why didn't I see this at my house the other day?"

"It was in the shop, getting new paint," Desmond says. "That day, I came on a bike."

The car uses a normal key and has a Buick logo on the steering wheel. The dials and readouts are less techie than I thought they'd be; the speedometer's top speed is a tame one hundred thirty miles an hour. As we pull away from the curb, people barely give us a glance. It's Venice, though. We could be octopus people in a penis-shaped spaceship and no one would care.

"Where to?" Desmond asks.

"This office in Westwood. Not far."

This morning, I found Leonidas on Facebook. It took some doing. His is a fan page, for one thing, and he lists himself as "The Only Leonidas You'll Ever Need to Know." He isn't my friend on my fan page, but perhaps he had been on that other page I used to have that disappeared into the ether, if I'm to believe that it existed. He's the only twenty-two-year-old Leonidas Lorre in Los Angeles—the only one you'll ever need to know, clearly—and thank God his page is public. Naturally, I carefully scrolled back to see if there were phantom pictures of him and me together. The guy has a thing for taking pictures of sunsets, really bad tattoos he spots around town, and his breakfast every morning, but there are none of me.

The page says Leonidas works part-time in reception at his father's plastic surgery office in Westwood. It's the same block of office buildings where my mother works, too, as an assistant to a podiatrist. I can picture the Whole Foods down the block with its parking garage and bike racks. I looked up the office number, called it, and heard his voice answer. It jingled bells in my head. That voice had spoken to me. It had said nice things. But had it yelled, too, like in my one memory of him? Had it yelled a lot?

I touch my temple. An MRI is in the books at a walk-in clinic in Los Feliz that doesn't ask any questions and doesn't take insurance. The schedule was so jam-packed with other people wanting mammograms and bone scans and whatever else that I have to wait three weeks. The tumor feels like a foregone conclusion, really; maybe I don't even *need* an MRI. After all, what else could have stolen my memories so effectively? I picture the tumor as the Grinch who stole Christmas, chuckling as he stuffed my life experiences in a Santa sack and climbed up the chimney.

We drive several mural-riddled Venice blocks in silence, Desmond cruising in his Batmobile with only one hand on the wheel. *This American Life* on NPR plays scratchily through the car's speakers. Ira Glass's nasal voice is incongruous in such a vessel.

"Tell me seriously," I ask Desmond. "Did you steal this thing from a museum?"

"Not at all. I got it at an auction a few years ago."

"Didn't it cost a fortune?"

He gives me a saucy smile. "I had a small inheritance."

What a stupid thing to spend money on, I almost say, but I catch myself. When I got my book advance, I went through this phase of special-ordering my produce from a company who swore all their crops had been blessed by the Dalai Lama.

We drive through astoundingly light traffic on Santa Monica, managing to make almost every traffic light. As we're gliding toward Westwood, Desmond gestures at an apartment complex down Camden Avenue. "That's my building. Camden Arms, apartment 105," he answers, glancing at me with a grin. "It has Tesla EV parking, in case you've got one of those."

I stare at the large, gleaming building. A Porsche has just pulled into the roundabout. "Can most convention marketers afford such a nice place?"

"Well, technically, it's my parents' apartment. But they're rarely there. My brother lives there, too. Stefan. He's a dabbler."

"A what?"

"He dabbles. In many things. You'll see when you meet him."

I slide closer to the window. There's no way I'm meeting Desmond's creepy brother, Stefan the Dabbler.

Stoplights, pedestrians, strip malls. I fill Desmond in about Leonidas and what I'd overheard at the hotel, trying hard not to give away the fact that I'd only recently relearned about Leonidas's existence. "He seemed to be in cahoots with someone. Apparently, the police have been asking questions." This buoys me—perhaps the cops had taken me seriously after all. "I want to know if Leonidas was in Palm Springs that night. If he was, he could have done it." I bite down hard on my lip. "I just don't know why."

"Was it a bad breakup?" Desmond asks.

"Yes," I say with near certainty, thinking of the memory of myself on the floor of the greasy-smelling pizza place and Leonidas lording over me, telling me I'd done something awful that couldn't be fixed.

"Did you tell your police contact about Leonidas?"

I explain that I've left a lot of messages on the tip line, but there's been no call back. "Are you sure Lance is even a detective?" Desmond asks. "He could be a gossip hound. People pay big money for a scoop on an interesting person."

"Why would anyone want to gossip about *me*?" Then I set my mouth in a line. I think about what Posey said: *The whole world knows your story.* On the other hand, Lance had shown up just thirteen hours after the pool thing. *He* didn't know I was interesting yet. Could news travel that fast?

Desmond adjusts his beret so that it sits on his head at a jaunty angle. "I mean, did this Lance guy show you a badge, something that connected him to the police department?"

I scratch my nose. "Well, no . . ."

"So you just took him at his word?"

"I guess. Although actually, Lance isn't a detective, per se. He's a forensic psychologist."

Now Desmond looks confused. "Why would they send *him* to talk to you?"

"I guess he thought . . ." I breathe out. "He had this idea that maybe I had been trying to kill myself."

Desmond doesn't react right away. "I guess I can see how people would assume that. Being that you were at the bottom of the pool."

"I was at the bottom of the pool because someone pushed me in and I can't swim."

"*I* know that. But why doesn't he?"

I sigh. "Lance knew things about me before he even came into the room. And then my mother filled in the rest."

"The rest of what?"

There's no way I can get out of explaining this. I'm already in too deep. "I had a brain tumor about a year ago."

Desmond frowns. "I'm sorry?"

"A year ago. I had surgery. I'm better, but . . ."

He looks like he's about to cry. "Oh, my sweet girl."

I explain my tumor and the suicide attempts that led up to it. "So my mother thinks the fall into the pool is just another one of those attempts. I guess she doesn't think I'm better." I make a face. "Sometimes it feels like she almost *wants* me to be sick. Or maybe not sick. Maybe just . . . contained."

"How so?"

I think for a moment. "When I first attempted suicide, she did the normal stuff a mother would do. She cried, she paced, she was really concerned. But after each subsequent attempt, she started to disassociate. It was almost like she was *annoyed* that it kept happening, that I should just snap out of it already. She kept putting me in the hospital, and she acted pissed when I got out, and she had this whole *I told you so* thing going whenever I tried to drown myself again."

"How did she react when you were diagnosed with a tumor?"

"I remember her marching in to the nurse one day and being like, *Well? Is she better yet? Is she cured?*"

"That sounds like she wanted you out of the hospital, not in."

"It was more like she was impatient. She's just so annoyed at me all the time anyway—it was like this even before the suicide stuff. She never understood me. Everything I was into, everything I said, she just . . . recoiled."

"Mothers and daughters," Desmond sighs. "I've always heard that's a tricky bond." Then he glances at me. "Thank you for telling me that. You're very brave."

I squirm in my seat. There's no need for him to memorize the moment. Then again, Desmond has a point. I haven't told anyone this much about myself or my family in a long time. Not even Kiki. Maybe it's because Desmond has no preconceived notions of me, and because I don't expect to know him after today. Or maybe it's because he sits so quietly and listens without immediately interjecting an opinion.

The streets whip by. I count three black cars, six silver. Several people gawk at the Batmobile. "What was the hospital like during your tumor?" Desmond asks.

"Well, like I said, I can barely remember it. I felt drunk the whole time, probably pumped up with morphine and other meds. All I wanted to do was sleep. I remember talking a lot, but it must have just been in dreams. When I was awake, I had no attention span, and I had splitting headaches if I didn't take my painkillers."

"Gracious me," Desmond murmurs.

"There were silent moments in my room when I was alone, and I recall staring at my hands as though I'd never seen them before. I whispered certain words to make sure I was saying them correctly. *Milk. Balloon. Dog.* They'd sounded foreign. It also felt like something had been taken from me, a big hole scooped in my brain."

"The tumor?"

"I don't know. I never saw a brain scan of it."

"Why can't you swim?" Desmond asks, after a long silence. "I thought every kid in California knew how to swim."

"Do *you* know how to swim?"

"Indeed. I can even do the butterfly."

Show off. "I probably swam a little as a kid, but after a while, I started thinking that all pools of water—or lakes, or oceans—were the River Styx. I read a lot of Greek mythology. My mom had me taking swimming lessons, but I backed away from the pool every time, imagining Doré etchings of a creature rising out of the waves and pulling me down to hell. I never wanted to go in. I would start crying."

Desmond clucks his tongue.

"After a while, my mother canceled the lessons. I'm sure she was embarrassed."

"You could take lessons now," Desmond says. "Unless you *still* think all water leads to hell?"

"I don't. But now, water has this . . . association. I jumped in it or ran into it or ducked under it hoping to die. It carries too much baggage. I'd rather just stay on dry land."

"Gotcha." Desmond taps his forehead. "Mental note: Do not take Eliza to any beach resorts anytime soon." He holds up a pale arm. "Not that I'm partial to the beach myself."

Leonidas's father's office is several blocks away. We park in the lot of the Whole Foods I'd pictured so easily—I used to stop here after school, sometimes, when my mother was finishing up work. I got a kick out of shoplifting fresh produce—plums, nectarines, single cherry tomatoes.

We walk along the street reading the building numbers. When we get to 1104, Desmond studies the sign for Dr. Lorre and scrunches up his face. "Your ex-lover is a plastic surgeon?"

"Uh . . ." I hate how I'm not sure. "His father is. Leonidas works in reception."

"So what's your plan of attack? You want access to his phone, right? See who he was talking to? Where he's been?"

"Yeah."

"And how are you going to do that?"

"Well, I'm not sure. But I'm hoping you'll provide a subterfuge while I figure that out."

Desmond removes his beret and runs his hand over his slick hair. "Give me my instructions," he says gallantly.

"Say you've got an appointment. Get into the waiting room, then fake a leg injury in the hall. He'll run to your rescue, and while he's away from the desk, I'll grab his phone and look through it. Take pictures if I have to."

Desmond is blinking rapidly. "You want me to pretend I want plastic surgery?" He looks chagrined. "That's pretty much against every principle I stand for."

"It's not like you're going to actually *get* the surgery."

"What if someone I know sees me?"

I snort. "You really think your gladiator cronies are going to be hanging out at a plastic surgery office? Get a grip. You'll be fine. Go in there, and say you're getting calf implants."

He stares at a raised leg. "But my calves are fine! I've been told by quite a few ladies I have lovely calves, in fact."

I shut my eyes. "You know what? It's cool. We don't have to do this. I don't even know you. It was nice of you to drive me here."

Desmond places his beret back on his head. "No, no. I'll do it. I shall cast aside my preconceptions and do it for you."

"Seriously, Desmond. It's fine."

"I *want* to do it. It's my quest!"

"If you're sure . . ."

"I am beyond sure. But what if a man doesn't have an appointment around now? He'll know I'm up to something."

"You'll be faking that injury within a few seconds of getting in there, so you won't need to explain much."

The front door to the building is unlocked, and I march through, holding the door for Desmond. My muscles seem to remember the way to the suite—perhaps I've been here before.

We stop at the glass-paneled door with Dr. Lorre's name on it. I peek through and see Leonidas's wobbly, freakishly tall shape at the front desk. He's leaning over a cell phone, probably the very same phone I'm going to have to intercept. I feel a pinch at the sight of him, head bent down, earbuds in. I can just imagine what he's listening to: My Chemical Romance. 311. Old, curmudgeonly country. I know this without knowing *how* I know it.

I glance at Desmond. "You still okay?" I ask. He gives a wobbly nod. "So just go in there, say you need to use the bathroom, and do the leg thing."

"Which leg?"

I point to the right one, then change my mind and pick the left. Then I twist the doorknob for him and point into the waiting room, gesturing that he go inside.

A *whoosh* of cold air sweeps out as Desmond pushes the door open farther. The door swishes shut again, and I press my ear to the jamb, praying another client doesn't walk in the front door for an appointment and witness this. Then I peer through the window, my heart hammering fast. A mottled-glass version of Desmond strides to the desk, and a mottled-glass version of Leonidas says something. There are murmurs I can't make out, and now Desmond is going toward the waiting room. In seconds, I hear a sharp, completely overdramatized shout from the hallway. Still, I want to kiss him for actually following through with it.

Leonidas practically vaults from the front desk at the sound of Desmond's cry. He disappears from view. I count to five, then twist the handle to the door. Cool, lilac-scented air rushes in. I look to the right and left, but the waiting area is empty. Pictures of vapid-eyed women with flawless skin and enormous breasts stare at me from the walls, and across the room is a slightly pornographic shot of a woman's thighs. A few silicone breast implant samples sit on the coffee table next to a vase full of flowers.

Desmond moans in the hallway. "Are you okay?" comes Leonidas's voice.

"Oh, the pain!" Desmond wails.

My gaze darts to the desk. There is a computer monitor, an appointment book, a bodybuilding magazine, some forms. I spy an Android phone sitting near a dirty black messenger bag that's covered with patches for a bunch of eco-conscious action groups. I reach over the desk and grab it.

The screen is still lit up from Leonidas's use, which is a boon because that means I don't have to guess at a passcode. I stare at a line of apps. Fingers shaking, I press the phone icon and navigate to Received calls. Names pop up on the screen with corresponding dates and times. First I look at his calls made and received on Saturday night, when I was in Palm Springs, and even on Sunday, when I was in the hospital. There are a few of them, but it's hard to know where *Leonidas* was when they were made. It's something I hadn't quite worked out in my head when making this plan. This phone isn't going to just give up the information. I'd need access to wireless towers, and I had no idea how the hell to get that sort of data.

"You tripped over your shoe?" Leonidas is saying in the hallway.

Then I try to remember the exact time I'd seen Leonidas at the Cat Show on Wednesday. Morning? Early afternoon? I scroll back. Numbers swim before my eyes. Some of Leonidas's callers are names he'd keyed into his contacts—Mom, Dad, someone named Burt. Other entries are just numbers. I fumble for my own phone and take a picture of the whole screen of numbers, cringing at the fake "click" sound when the camera snaps. I do the same thing with his Outgoing calls—he'd made quite a few of those, too.

"Let's see if you can stand on it," Leonidas is bellowing to Desmond.

"I'll never walk again," Desmond is saying. "I'm done for."

There's scuffling in the hallway. Grunts. "Up we go," Leonidas says.

I drop his phone and hurry out from behind the desk. I'm out of the office by the time he and Desmond emerge around the corner. In the silent hall, my heart is a loud drumbeat in my ears. I breathe slowly, willing it to settle down, but it rockets on and on and on.

A few moments later, the door opens. "I can call an ambulance," Leonidas is saying.

"Oh, I'll make do," Desmond says weakly.

"Really. It's no troub—" Leonidas starts to say, but Desmond shuts the door in his face.

He turns to me with an expression I can't quite decipher; it almost seems like he might throw up. "Let's go." He grabs my hand and we hurry down the hall into the stairwell. Our shoes clonk noisily down the metal stairs. In the landing, we cock our heads to listen for the door above to make sure Leonidas isn't following us. All I hear is a small dog barking somewhere in the distance.

In the parking lot, Desmond bends at the waist. "I just can't believe I did that. That poor kid. I lied to him. He's probably worried about me now. He's probably going to call an ambulance."

"It's fine. You're fine."

"And I said I was getting calf implants." His voice is rising. "What if something happens to my calves as a sort of karmic revenge?"

"What, like you get calf cancer?" I ask. Desmond looks horrified. I pet his arm. "Don't worry. Calf cancer isn't actually a thing."

Sweat is pouring down his face. "That just felt so wrong."

"Get a grip. You're the one who wanted to come, and I gave you an out. I thought you'd be braver about all of this, considering you're a knight or whatever."

"A Caesar." Desmond sounds miserable. And then, to himself: "I can't believe I *lied*!"

We walk back to the Whole Foods parking lot in silence. I'm such an asshole for dragging him into this. Desmond unlocks the Batmobile with a shaky hand. "You don't have to drive me home," I tell him.

His head sweeps up. "But how will you get where you need to go?"

I show him the Uber app. "I'll be okay."

Desmond places his hands in his pockets. An ambulance siren whoops in the distance, and I can tell he's getting worried that Leonidas is the one who's called for it.

He laughs, wearily. "I guess I'm just not cut out for undercover work, huh?"

"Nah, you did great."

"You think so?"

"Yes. I got what I needed."

"Ah. Well, that's what I was here for."

We look at each other. With a hopeful smile on his face, he almost looks cute. If he shaved and had a haircut and plucked those eyebrows, the raw material is there. I don't even mind his shortness, really. And his hands, though little, are well made. Pretty, even. There's something sort of endearing about his extreme worry about calf cancer. It's the sort of thing I'd worry about, too.

I'm keenly aware, suddenly, of the hair whipping in my face, of how it feels like my nostrils are flaring like a bull's, and that my bra can be seen through my sweater. I can almost imagine walking over to him and wrapping my arms around his shoulders. Maybe I should.

A honk cuts through the air, and we jump. "Anyway," I say quietly, lowering my eyes. "Thank you."

"My pleasure." Desmond bows. "Let me know if you uncover any interesting information from the phone calls."

I pivot, give him a half wave, and turn toward Whole Foods as though my car will be there, though you never know where Uber cars will park and how quickly they'll show up. It feels cinematic to be walking away from him; I hope that he's checking me out from behind. The air seems crisper, cleaner. I even whistle half a refrain.

When I hear footsteps behind me, I assume it's Desmond, coming to spin me around and dip me into a kiss, just like Caesar and Cleopatra. I can't believe how much I want him to do this, suddenly, nor can I believe how inevitable it feels. There's a hand between my shoulder blades. I twist around, ready to grin at Desmond, but the sun is in my eyes, and all I can see is a hazy silhouette that definitely isn't his. Something about the bright sun and the adrenaline and the influx of alcohol in my system makes me abruptly woozy, and as I blink at the figure in front of me—a figure still obscured by the sunlight, looming though, maybe menacing—my field of vision narrows, and my legs crumple.

"Oh shit," a voice whispers as I hit the ground. And then: "No! What the hell? Get up! Please! Get *up!*"

I roll onto my back, desperate to keep my eyes open. Someone is trying to pull me up. He or she has skinny fingers. Capable arm muscles, though not particularly strong. Minty breath. Maybe hair, long hair, tickles my neck. Only, before I can register what happened, my eyes flutter closed, and I pass out right there in a dingy alleyway, just out of sight of every pedestrian on Weyburn Avenue.

From The Dots

After waking up to the IV in her arm, Dot knew she should tone down the drinking, lest she end up addicted. The real addiction, though, was Dorothy. Dot couldn't stop seeing her. Every Wednesday, she met with her. Their evenings out were relegated to M&F, that dark little club in West Hollywood, or long limo rides around the city, taking in its glamour from behind tinted windows. Champagne flowed in the backseat of the car. Dorothy always had a flask of something. Bernie at M&F presented them with his best wine, and the bartender at the dark nook of a club fed them neon-blue liquid straight from the bottle.

Dot lapped up Dorothy's stories and attention. She beamed as Dorothy slung her arm around Dot and told her she was beautiful, amazing, funny, fantastic, the best niece a woman could ever want. But at the end of each evening, Dot blacked out, only to emerge the following day sticky-mouthed and slumped on the green-and-white-striped divan of Dorothy's Magnolia bungalow. Dr. Singh never returned, but Dot was haunted by the same headaches, the same disorientation, the same dread. She must just be one of those people who can't hold their liquor.

"Just lie here, my dear," Dorothy said. "Rest here all day if you like." She brought Dot baskets of bread and ordered plates of eggs. She pressed cold washcloths to Dot's forehead and spent hours raking her fingers through her hair. Sometimes, she just lounged next to Dot, spooning her and saying, "Oh, you don't know how *good* it feels to be able to take care of you."

"I just wish I didn't get hungover every time we go out," Dot croaked.

"Don't worry," Dorothy said hastily. "Besides, I get to take care of you. This is a treat. Thomas was taken from me when I was so young."

Thomas again. Dot had so many questions, but she still thought it too indelicate to ask.

Dot's boyfriend didn't go out with them after that first night. He kept using the excuse of exams, and then lab work, and then a Phish concert he really wanted to see. "Why do I get the idea you don't *want* to come with me to see Phillis?" she finally said, aggravated. They were in the dining hall; they called Dorothy Phillis whenever they were in public. Dot wasn't taking any chances; her mother might have sent spies.

He shrugged, trudging with his tray to the next food station. Dot followed him to the salad bar, the cereal bar, and then the fro-yo machine. Finally, he sighed heavily. "I wanted to be the one who took you home that night you fainted at the club. I wanted to take care of you, but she insisted. She was a bully about it, in fact."

"Well, she's my aunt," Dot said. What a silly thing to argue about. "She's family."

"Yeah, but do you really even *know* her?"

Dot watched him. He was making a big deal of shoving a Styrofoam cup under the yogurt dispenser. "I thought you loved her."

"She's fascinating in theory. But in person she also seemed so . . ." He glanced at her, then moved to the hot food line.

She chased after him. "So *what?*"

"Forget it."

She watched as the cafeteria worker slopped mashed potatoes onto his tray. Her boyfriend went to sit down. He was eating mashed potatoes and fro-yo for dinner. He had no bearing on reality. "Are you really afraid of a fifty-year-old woman?" Dot laughed.

He looked up at her, mid-bite. "Just be careful, okay?"

Be careful. That one amused Dot for days. Be careful of *what*?

ELIZA

I OPEN MY EYES and sit up on the pavement, the sun baking my skin. "Eliza?" says a voice.

I blink hard. The sun burns a harsh circle onto my retinas. A shadow appears over me, and I smell overpowering deodorant. "You Eliza? You call me?"

The man has on aviator sunglasses, a creased, pin-striped shirt, and jeans that pull tightly across the waist. Behind him, a white Honda Pilot chugs. I look around and see the familiar buildings of the Westwood Center—the Whole Foods in particular—and it all comes back. But besides the two of us, the alley is empty. When I wince, pain explodes across my face. I touch it carefully, expecting blood, but all I feel is tenderness.

"I *said*, you Eliza?" The man gestures to his car. "You call Uber?"

"Y-yes," I manage to say, pushing up to sit. I look around one more time. No one seems to be lurking about. But there *was* someone.

"I've been waiting," the man says, annoyed. "I've probably called you six times. I was about to leave."

I stumble to my feet and stare down at myself. All of my clothes are still on. My bag is on the ground. I grab it and rifle through it. My wallet is there. So is my phone. I touch the circle at the bottom and look at the time. Only a few minutes have passed since I looked at it last.

"Someone else was just here," I tell the man. "Did you see?"

He's already walking to the Pilot. "I wasn't back here until two seconds ago. You want the ride or not?" He gives me a glare. "But you can't pass out again. And no puking."

I flinch. "I'm not drunk."

"Uh-huh." He adds something else under his breath.

I don't know what to do, and my pounding head isn't making it any easier to decide. If I leave, then I'm leaving the scene of the crime. I need to call the police now, while whoever did this is still in the area. Only, if nothing was taken, was there really a crime? All of a sudden, the details feel jumbled. The sun is too hot against the crown of my head.

There's a *whoop*, and I look up. A police car is pulling into the alleyway. Still on my ass, I watch as an officer leans out the driver's side. "We just got a call that someone fainted back here."

I whip around to the Uber driver. "Did you call the police?"

The Uber driver holds up his hands. "No way, man. I just got here."

The cop stares at us. His partner in the passenger seat peers over his Ray-Bans, then says to me, "Everything okay, miss?"

My throat feels as though it's coated with corroded metal. "Someone accosted me back here. I think a crime has been committed."

Driver Cop's gaze swings to the Uber driver. The Uber driver steps away, hands shielding his chest. "I just got here, man. You can check my GPS. I saw nothing."

"It wasn't him," I say, feeling pretty confident about that. "It was someone else." But something doesn't make sense. I assess the alley one more time. If I was alone when Uber guy found me, and if Uber guy didn't call the police saying I fainted, then who the hell did?

Driver looks at his partner. Ray-Bans gives a nod. They get out of the car simultaneously, the act beautifully choreographed. Their shoes make crisp sounds as they cross the asphalt to me.

"Uh, excuse me?" the Uber driver says. "Can I go now?"

"Not yet," the cop says. "We may need you to make a statement."

The Uber driver says something in Spanish under his breath. The cop who was driving squats down and places his hands on his knees. His uniform is a crisp black. There's a shiny badge on his front pocket that says O'Hara. The name is too lilting, too poetic to belong to a police officer.

"What's your name?" he asks me.

"Eliza."

"What happened?" Ray-Bans points to my face. I touch it experimentally and wince; I can feel a bruise.

"I fell," I say. "Someone startled me. I spun around, but I couldn't see who it was, and then I felt very woozy." After this all comes out of my mouth, I realize how flimsy it sounds. You can't arrest someone just because they come up to you and touch you on the shoulder.

"Did the person say anything to you?" O'Hara asks.

"No. I don't think so. But at the end, after I fell, the person said, *What the hell? Get up! Please!*"

"Please." O'Hara looks amused. He glances at his partner. "Polite."

I try to stand, but my footing feels wobbly, uncertain. I grab on to O'Hara's shoulder for balance, my mouth nearly kissing his cheek. O'Hara reaches out to steady me, and once I'm upright, I notice that his eyebrows have hitched up. His partner glances at him, a small sliver of a look. His mouth curls into a smirk.

"You all right there?" O'Hara towers over me, at least six-two.

"I don't know," I insist. "I might have a head injury. I feel . . .

dizzy." I look at them expectantly. Neither makes a motion to write this down. There are no efforts to call an ambulance.

"Well." O'Hara clears his throat. "I think what you need, Eliza, is some coffee."

"It's possible you might have misinterpreted whoever you saw in the alleyway," his partner, whose name tag reads *Larkin*, adds. "Maybe they were just trying to help. Maybe they were worried about you."

My cheeks burn. *I'm not drunk*, I will silently. *I might have a brain tumor. It's not my fault.* But then I remember the mead I'd drunk before leaving Steadman's. How many shots had I taken—two? Three? More than that? What was *in* mead, anyway? Was that why I was so fearless when intercepting Leonidas's phone?

"We can give you a ride home," O'Hara says, kindly. "Or to the hospital, if you want to get checked out."

"No hospitals," I say.

"Uh, can I *go*?" Uber Driver says again.

"Yeah, go ahead." Larkin waves him away.

I'm out of options. I trudge to the cruiser and slump into the back. It smells like old leather. There's some sort of paper bracelet in the footwell with the logo from a seedy strip joint. Larkin shuts the door behind me. I slump down as far as I can go in the seat. If my mother saw me now, she'd probably forcibly send me to the Oaks. I'd have no say in the matter.

I swipe to unlock my phone, then press the photos button, eager to look at the pictures I'd taken of Leonidas's call screens. One of the numbers on the list is needling at my memory—I know it, I just don't know why I know it. But when I access my gallery, the images are gone. I swipe and swipe, but they aren't there anymore.

"Uh?" I eke out, jutting my chin toward the silent figures in the front seat. O'Hara raises his eyes to me in the rearview. *There* was *a crime*, I want to say. *Something was taken from me. When I was passed out, someone went on my phone and erased photos.*

I try to compose my words, but even before saying them, I know how they will sound. I will then have to explain sneaking into Leonidas's dad's office, which seems like too much of an effort and probably not something I should be talking about. This is my punishment, I suppose, for snooping.

It just doesn't seem like this punishment fits the crime.

From The Dots

I n mid-April, Dorothy surprised Dot by taking her to a resort. It was in the middle of the desert and Dorothy loved it because she could hear coyotes howling all night.

She got a suite for them to share. It had a large balcony that overlooked the warren-like courtyard of grassy nooks, flowering planters, and sleek wooden benches. A woman sunned herself on a towel in the nude.

Dorothy turned to Dot, grinning. "There's a marvelous story about a murder at this hotel. Celebrities used to come here in the sixties, especially those who slept their way to the top. This one girl, she must have been mixed in with the wrong crowd, because someone killed her in that courtyard. Hit her over the head. And the next day, when the staff found her, they identified her as a different starlet—a more famous one. They planned this elaborate funeral for her. Friends and family from out of state came in droves. The FBI was doing a full-scale investigation. But then the starlet emerged, alive and well. Turns out, being dead for three days did wonders for her career. She made quite a few movies after that! Married a good friend of Sinatra's!"

"But what about the real murdered girl?" Dot gasped.

Dorothy shrugged. "Oh, I have no idea what happened to her. She probably got in over her head with some goons, and that's why they killed her."

"They never figured out who did it?"

"No, I don't believe so. This other girl wasn't much of a priority."

"Did the star who lived pay some sort of homage to her?" Dot asked. "I mean, it was because of this poor dead girl that her career took off, right? I hope she was grateful."

A thoughtful look crossed Dorothy's features, and then she looked at Dot squarely. "You know what would be interesting? If the famous starlet was actually the one in trouble with the goons in Palm Springs, but she sent this other gal in her place to bear their wrath. She got out of a jam *and* a career boost, lucky thing."

"Huh?"

"Oh, don't listen to me." She playfully slapped Dot's arm. "I'm just making up a plot."

When they went to the bar, Dorothy wore her sunglasses and scarf. "Why don't you want anyone to notice you?" Dot asked as her aunt checked herself out in the mirror.

Dorothy's mouth made a straight line. "I just don't want to answer questions."

"Questions about what?"

"I wear many hats, Dot. I have my hands in many pies."

Someone started playing a piano, an old-timey twenties tune with lots of trills and flourishes.

"Why does my mother hate you?" Dot blurted.

Dorothy grew still. "Is that what she said? That she hates me?"

Dot didn't answer.

Dorothy's head drooped. She made a clucking sound with her tongue. "We used to be good friends, marvelous friends, especially growing up. I mean, we didn't *see* each other much, but there was still a bond, you know? I was always the pretty one, but I was unlucky in love. Your mother's husband, your father? He was a peach. A good man. Took care of her and you. He lived in Los Angeles, which is why you all moved there. I moved to follow you. I bet you didn't know that."

Dot shook her head. She did not.

"But your mother is . . . Well, you know her. She didn't give your father what he needed. I was over a lot—I could tell what was happening to their marriage. I saw him looking at me, too. I tried to ignore it, but I had needs, too. I'd just gotten divorced. I'd just lost Thomas. I was single and rich and miserable. I only kissed him once, but your mother caught us. She banished me from then on. Said I was no longer her sister."

"You kissed my father?"

"No, darling, he kissed *me*. But he wasn't a bad man. Please don't think that. It just . . . happened. Sometimes things do. But anyway, your mother read it how she wanted to read it. I was the instigator, she thought. We didn't speak for a time. I think she understood what I meant to you and what you meant to me. She also knew how I could help out, financially. So she agreed that you and I could still visit. But she made it clear she wasn't happy with me.

"I did everything in my power to win your mother back. After your father passed away, your mother found out he had bad debts and no life insurance policy. She really did work like a dog to keep you two afloat. I *said* I'd help out, but she wouldn't accept my money." Dorothy paused to sip. "Your mother is very proud."

Dot widened her eyes. So Dorothy *had* offered to help out. She curled her fist under the table.

"From then, things started to fall apart between us again," Dorothy explained. "She enjoyed working, and she made excuses to work, but I think she sensed it wasn't right. The guilt weighed on her. She took it out on me. She was jealous of our relationship. Yours and mine. I could do for you what she couldn't."

"Did she send you away?" Dot cried.

Dorothy stared at the table. Slowly, she licked her lips. "I don't want to drive a wedge between you, dear," she said softly.

Dot snorted. The wedge was already there. "Mom says you're unwell."

A muscle in Dorothy's cheek twitched. She took Dot's hands and looked at her hard. Her eyes were so clear and violet. "What do *you* think? Do you think I'm unwell?"

"No," Dot answered. But then she thought of what her boyfriend had said. That Dorothy was a bully. *How much do you know about her?* Why was he so mistrusting?

A group of boys about Dot's age passed through the bar just then. Dot watched them carefully—they were bearded, dirty, their jeans cut skinny, their shoes carefully weathered. They were probably coming from the three-day concert that was taking place the next town over. It was the kind of concert where you camped out and took a lot of drugs; Dot and Marlon had thought about going but then had decided not to because neither of them had anything appropriate to wear.

The boys slunk up to guests in the bar and whispered in their ears. They were targeting other young people, it seemed, and each person they asked frowned, digested their question, then shook their heads. Finally, the boys made their way to Dot, but when they noticed that Dorothy was older, they started to move on.

"Wait!" Dorothy cried. The boys turned. "You guys either have something or are looking for something. Which is it?"

Dot nudged her. "What are you doing?"

Dorothy's gaze was still on the group. "I'm not a cop, fellas. I'm honestly curious."

The boys shifted their weight, stuck their hands in their pockets. They all exchanged a glance, then shrugged. "We have a bunch of flakka," the shortest and dirtiest one, his dreadlocks literally caked with mud, said. "We're looking for takers."

"What's flakka?"

"Not for you," the tallest one said quickly.

"How do you know?" Dorothy asked. Dot stared at her in horror.

The boy in the middle, who was the most normal looking, his brown hair only a little shaggy and his face clean-shaven, shrugged. "It's kinda like ecstasy, and it's kinda like a roofie, except not as dangerous." His friends nudged him and gave him sharp looks. "What?" he murmured to them. "She *asked*."

"It's not like she knows what a roofie is, dude," Dirty Dreadlocks spat.

Dorothy scoffed. "I know what a roofie is, boys. And sure. We'll take some."

"No we won't!" Dot cried.

Dorothy was already getting out some cash. Dot looked around frantically, paranoid someone in the bar was going to be wise to their drug deal. The police would come, Dorothy would go to jail, and Dot would somehow be implicated, and then *her mother would find out.*

It was over quickly, though, the exchange fluid and discreet. The boys slunk away. The biggest one's dreadlocks bounced cheerfully. They all had slow, dumb laughs; Dot wondered if they were already high.

She turned to Dorothy. "What are you trying to prove?"

"Nothing," Dorothy said haughtily. "Oh, well, maybe a little. I was teaching them not to be so ageist. Sometimes women in their early fifties like to party, too."

Dot stared at the pocket where Dorothy had slipped the pills. "It's not like you're going to *take* those, are you?"

"I don't know. Maybe." She drained the last of her stinger. "Don't worry, dear, it'll be someday when you're not around. A random afternoon when I'm feeling lonely."

"Then I'll have to stick by you every day," Dot said. "Make sure you don't ever take it. It might kill you."

Dorothy's face brightened. "Darling. That would be absolutely lovely if you stuck by my side every single day."

Back at home, Dot told Marlon the story. She told it in a joking way—*my crazy aunt! Isn't she a card?* She told him after they'd had sex, when he was in a good mood. But Marlon paled.

"Shit," he said in a far-off voice. "I'd never even *thought* of that."

"What?" Dot asked, sitting up. "What are you talking about?"

"Roofies. Maybe she's drugging you."

Dot barked out an angry laugh. "I can't believe you'd say such a thing!"

"I keep working it out in my head, Dot. That night when we went out with her? You really *hadn't* had much. There had to be something else in the mix. Something that made you pass out like that."

"My aunt loves me!" Dot cried. "She wouldn't roofie me! Take it back!"

He threw up his hands. "I didn't want to tell you this, but I looked up some facts about that Otufu story. Where your aunt visited is fairly stable. There are no warlords."

"So what? She got her story mixed up."

"Or maybe she was making *all* of it up. I talked to my grandparents, too. They said she was a real nut. Used to walk around the Magnolia grounds naked. Don't ever swim in her bungalow's pool. She used to have orgies in there." He made a face.

Dot got up from the bed and pulled on her sweatshirt. "You were asking around about her? What gives you the right?"

"I was just asking some questions. I want to protect you."

Dot glared at him. "Even if all of this is true, does that make her a bad person? A person who'd *roofie* someone?"

"I don't know. Maybe?"

"I can't believe you're saying this." She stepped into her underwear and jeans, grabbed her backpack, and headed toward the door. "Call me when you grow up."

"Come on. Don't be like that. Don't kill the messenger."

Dot stared into the grungy dorm hallway. "I think we should break up."

"Dot! I love you. I'm not saying this to hurt you."

Dot shut her eyes. She knew he did. But why couldn't he love Dorothy? Why was he trying to undermine her?

"Please don't go out with her anymore," Marlon said. "Just for a little while. Just until we can figure out what's true and what's not."

Dot stared at the door that led to the hall. There was a thin beam of fluorescent light poking through the peephole. "I can't do that."

Behind her, he sighed. His hands moved away from her; she could feel his heat recede. She flung open the door and ran, a ball lodged in her throat. She ran down the hall and entered the little nook that held the dorm's vending machines, wedged herself between the Pepsi machine and the ice maker, and rested her head between her knees for a long, long time.

ELIZA

MONDAY MORNING, I start awake, disoriented. *Where am I?* A hazy scene around me: green-and-white-striped curtains, a luxurious California King bed. But then the furniture turns to mist. I open my eyes, and I am in my canopy bed in my bedroom. Where else would I be?

Someone pounds at the door. Judging by the lack of noises to right the situation, I am guessing Kiki and Steadman aren't home. I sit up slowly, a sticky, rotting taste in my mouth. There is one message on my phone from Laura: *Uh, I got this weird voice mail from this woman who said she's your mother? She wants us not to publish your book?* Nothing from my mother, though—I don't know why I'm even checking. Nothing from Bill, apologizing for her. Nothing from Lance the forensic psychologist. Nothing from Richie the bartender.

More pounds. I glance in the mirror at myself and try to tamp down my wild, witchlike hair. Mascara is caked around my eyes, and I must have reapplied lipstick in between drinks number seven and eight, because it makes a wobbly circle around my general mouth region, hitting a good bit of my teeth, too. The knot on my head where I fell on Friday has morphed over the weekend from a garish blackish-purple to an even uglier greenish-yellow. It still hurts when I touch it.

I dart into the bathroom and scrub my face raw. With the makeup gone, my eyes are tiny, my lips puffy, my cheeks the color of raw cauliflower. I smooth my hair down my forehead and arrange it so it's kind of covering up the bruise. I down twenty varieties of vitamins in hopes that their wonder-powers will counteract all the alcohol. Then I take a deep breath and listen, hoping the knocking has ceased. If anything, whoever it is has begun to pound harder.

What if it's Leonidas down there? What if he knows I'm alone and has come to hurt me for looking through his phone?

I part the curtain at the top of the stairs and peer out the window. The Batmobile is in the driveway. I'm so astonished that I laugh. I would have thought that after Friday Desmond would want to be rid of me.

I hurry down the stairs and open the door. I find him in a dis-armingly normal black T-shirt, old black jeans, and lace-up boots that are suede and pointed and perhaps like something a minstrel might wear. He cocks his head at me. "Were you slumbering?"

"No, but I was sleeping," I mutter. "I tossed and turned all night."

"Up solving your mystery? You should have called me."

I cross my arms over my chest. "I thought you were out of the detective game."

"Oh, now, I never said I was out for good."

I remember my hope that he was coming to spin me around to kiss me. I think I'd dreamed about it last night; I have vague flashes of his pointy little face above mine, that thick, glossy hair brushing against my cheek, those little hands deft.

I place my hands in my pockets, and the shock of hair covering my bruise falls out of position and reveals the greenish skin. Desmond notices it and gasps. "What happened?"

"Just a fall."

"Onto what, someone's fist?"

He reaches out to touch the gash, but I squirm to the left. Begrudgingly, I tell him about what happened in the alleyway on Friday and that the picture I'd taken was now missing. He looks aghast. "I should have stayed with you! Made sure you got safely into the Uber!"

"Nothing *happened* to me, exactly," I say. "Except that I had a panic attack and lost consciousness. And then the police came, and they drove me home." You know. Totally normal day.

"How intriguing that the assailant deleted the file," Desmond muses. "It has to be someone who *knows* something, right? Someone who doesn't want you to figure out who Leonidas was speaking with."

I nod—this is what I've deduced, too.

Desmond places his hands on his hips. "You know, you can subpoena phone records. We should explain this to the police."

I make a face. "On what grounds? It's not like I have much proof besides eavesdropping on Leonidas's conversation."

"Hmm." Desmond looks chagrined. "We should try and *get* proof."

I nod, though I have no idea how we could do this. "I'm pretty sure a number I know was on that call list. I've tried all weekend to remember, but I can't." I sigh. "Even better, I wish I could just remember who I was talking to that night in Palm Springs. And maybe even who pushed me into the pool."

Desmond paces the room, then suddenly snaps his fingers. "I have an idea."

I suck in my stomach. There's something propositional about his voice. "What?"

"I've been reading up on how to unlock memories. Sometimes, the key is to go back to the scene of where you lost them. They can return just by smelling the same smells or hearing the same sounds. We should go back to the Tranquility."

"What, *today*?"

"I have the day off." His gaze goes to my bruise again. "Unless you're feeling too infirm."

I run my tongue over my teeth, and all at once they feel smooth and clean. It's not like I have anything else to do today besides panic. The Tranquility looms in my mind like a book I don't want to open because I'm not sure I want to know how it ends, but maybe Desmond is right. Maybe everything will slot into place if we go.

"Okay," I say. At the very least, it would be an opportunity to retrieve my car from the resort's garage. I'd thought my family was going to chariot it back for me, but as far as I know, it's still there.

Once again in the Batmobile, Desmond plays a favorite song from a CD compilation in his disc player: something heavy with mandolins. I play one next: Sleater-Kinney. I watch his expression, suddenly curious about what he thinks. "Interesting," he says, and finds another song on his CD. A lute, some mewling. I keep my expression neutral, but I notice him watching me in the same way I was watching him. I burst out laughing.

NPR, sports radio, Spanish for a few minutes, even though neither of us really knows the language. We follow an old VW Beetle, a pink stretch limo with *Happy Chicks* painted on the side, a bright blue bus of old people. Desmond waves to the old people, and many of them wave back. Toward the back of the bus, a younger, shadowed face appears, and I flinch. I'm looking at an image of myself.

"Are you all right?" Desmond asks, because I must have made some sort of noise.

The bus lags a little behind us. The angle of the sunlight changes, and the face in the window is gone. There is sweat spilling down my neck into my underwear. I chew viciously on a fingernail. "I just thought I saw something. *Someone.*"

"Who?"

I press my hand hard against my knee. *Me,* I want to say, but I know that's impossible. Out loud: "I don't know. But it was someone who looked like they knew me, maybe."

By the time we pull up to the Tranquility's sweeping front drive, I am feeling sweaty and starving and maybe like this isn't a very good idea. I still don't really *know* Desmond. Who's to say *he* isn't dangerous? Should I have alerted Bill and my mother? They'd seemed so offended that I'd disappeared to Palm Springs the last time without telling them.

We stop the car, and a valet immediately appears to relieve us.

"Good afternoon," Desmond says dramatically, using a fake, Dracula accent. He tosses the valet his keys, and I notice he has a wimpy throw. I bet he was picked last for teams in junior high gym.

"Sweet ride," the valet says, handing us a ticket. "You two staying with us?"

Desmond glances at me with one eyebrow raised. "Shall we? Perhaps a suite *par deux?*"

My smile wobbles, but I'm still feeling so out of it, so I snap, "Of course not. And I think your French is wrong."

He walks inside, and I reluctantly follow. Desmond tries to take my arm and I let him for a few seconds before dropping it. Halfway across the floor, the smell of tequila wafts into my nose, and I swoon. All at once, pieces of memories that I don't know what to do with rush my brain. I see myself, younger, sitting on a barstool, laughing at someone. Me and a person, lounging on a couch together. Leonidas?

Desmond touches my arm. "Is it happening?" he asks, excitedly. "Are you remembering?"

"I don't know," I murmur, taking a deep breath to try to steady my legs.

We walk past an indoor desert garden of waterfalls, cacti, and terra-cotta sculptures. The atrium is fragrant with floral succulents. A potpourri of people in southwestern garb probably purchased in the gift shop lounge on big chairs in front of a floor-to-ceiling window that overlooks a desert vista.

"This is truly an oasis," Desmond says, tenting his fingers. "I used to come here as a child with my father. It's why I bring my team down here—I always feel so centered in this place. You, too?"

I blink hard, the memories swirling around my head suddenly gone. "Maybe."

"Did you come here as a child as well?"

"I . . . *think* so."

"You *think*?"

It feels like something I was sure of only days ago, maybe even minutes ago—how I know of this place, my history within it, and why I'd chosen to come here on the day of my almost-drowning. It's not like it's a Ritz-Carlton. It's not like it's featured regularly in *Travel + Leisure*. It's one of those places you have to know about to find. We must have come here when I was younger: my mom, Gabby, Bill, and me. I distinctly remember hiking up that trail out back, yelling my name between the two canyons to hear the echo. It's just that what happened in between is missing.

But this isn't what I need to focus on right now. I need to think about my most recent visit. If I can just retrace my steps, I can remember who hurt me. I picture myself in the lobby. Walking over to the front desk to check in. I recall the smooth key card in my hand. I remember a woman in a crisp white shirt sliding my American Express card back across the counter with a tight smile. I remember taking a mint from a dish and popping it into my mouth. "Would you like to book any spa services, miss?" the woman had asked me, but I'd shaken my head. No massages for me. No facials or manicures. So what had I come here to do?

Drink. And drink heavily. But why? *Was* it because I knew, subconsciously, the tumor was back? I wish it were that simple. Could something have set me off, then? What had happened that day before I went? I try to think. I probably woke up like I always did and choked down vitamins and a smoothie. I'd probably talked to Kiki. I had received the boxes containing copies of my book that day. Could that be something?

"Come on," I say, tugging Desmond's arm. "Let's go to the bar I was at before the pool."

We look at a map on the wall; the Shipstead is through a hallway, past a couple of gift shops and the spa, down an elevator, and past the fanciest restaurant. Outside, the pool beckons, the cheerful orange cabana cloths flapping in the light wind. A few people are lying on the chaises, reading books. The blue water glistens. I'm surprised it's open, actually. It sounds ridiculous, but I was hoping they would have closed it off after I'd been fished out. A man glides in the water with a baby buoyed by a large round float. The baby's smile is all gums. She splashes her father giddily. Neither of them have any idea I'd been lying at the bottom nine days ago.

I wonder what the father would do if I told him.

It's 3 p.m., a dead time, especially on a Monday, and the Shipstead's bartender, who's wearing a sailor suit, grimaces as he wipes the counter by the bottles. The wallpaper features diagrams of how to tie different sailing knots. The room smells like Old Spice.

Desmond surveys the room, then looks at me. "Do you remember where you were sitting?"

I pick a stool at the bar, though I have absolutely no recollection. The bartender places coasters imprinted with jaunty navy-blue anchors in front of us, and asks if we'd like a menu. Desmond asks what sort of absinthe they've got. The bartender names a brand, to which Desmond makes a face.

"*Amateurs*," he whispers, but he orders it anyway.

I consider ordering nothing—I already feel naturally tipsy—but then I blurt out, "A stinger." It feels like the right answer. I'd had one that night.

The bartender nods. When he reaches for the martini glass, he has to stand on his tiptoes. A heady scent of deodorant wafts from his underarms.

"You aren't Richie, by any chance, are you?" I call to him.

He turns around and blinks at me. "No. Sam."

"Is Richie . . . here?"

"Nope." He adds various liquids to a stainless shaker. "Not today."

At least Richie actually *exists*. "Do you know when he's around next?"

The bartender frowns. He's handsome, but he's short, and the bell-bottomed one-piece just makes him look even smaller, almost like a child. He has tattoos of numbers in a random pattern on every finger. A phone number? Birth and death dates? "Are you a friend of his?"

"No, I was at this bar two Saturdays ago, and Richie was my bartender. I'm trying to figure out who I was sitting next to," I say in the most pleasant, sane voice I can muster. "I spoke to the person for a while that night, but I didn't catch her name. I was hoping Richie could help me."

There's half a smile on the bartender's face. As he sets down our drinks, he looks sympathetic. "That's happened to me a few times, too. I hit it off with someone, it seems like something, and he leaves before I get his phone number. You could place an ad on Craigslist, you know. *Missed Connections*. Ever read those? *Cashier at the 76 on Main Street, I'm the tall thin guy who comes in in the mornings for hot chocolate and Red Bull. You waved at me, maybe you'll see this.* You could do something like that."

My mouth, I'm sure, is hanging open. "Oh, I'm not trying to get a *date* out of this."

The bartender blinks at me. "Oh," he says, woodenly. He abruptly walks away to serve an older couple who has just come in.

Desmond pours the green liquid over his absinthe. "I used to post on *Missed Connections*. I never got a response. I don't know *anyone* who ever got a response. Kind of makes you wonder why it still exists."

I point at him playfully. "I thought social media made you sad."

"Snapchat makes me sad. Selfies make me sad. Thinking that a text message serves as a love letter makes me sad. Posting on *Missed Connections*, that was poetry."

"You're so weird." I down my cocktail and gag. The stinger tastes bitter, unlike things I usually drink, but the flavor doesn't conjure any new memories. Desmond drinks slowly, tapping his toe at the smooth, sax-heavy jazz number on the stereo. The old couple sips wine and talks quietly. The bartender ignores us, making a big deal out of cleaning the barware. In the distance, a maid feverishly vacuums the rug, her head bopping to music over her headphones.

"So tell me how you think it transpired," Desmond says in a low voice. "You came into this bar. Is that right?"

I look around. "I think so. And I spoke to someone. I'm sure of it. Someone who said *you've got to get ahold of yourself.*" I squeeze my eyes shut tightly. "If only I knew *who.*"

"Do you think it's someone you knew?"

"I feel like it, yes. But I was also surprised to see the person here. It felt very . . . unexpected."

"So maybe it was Leonidas. I mean, if you'd already broken up, you wouldn't expect to see him, right?"

"Yeah, I guess."

"Let's assume it *is* him. He sits next to you at the bar. You have a conversation. He says *you've got to get ahold of yourself.* Does that seem right?"

"It could be . . ."

"And then what? What do you think you talked about?"

"I don't know."

"Your breakup? Maybe you were really upset? Maybe that's why he said you had to get a grip?"

"Maybe . . ."

"But what got you out to the pool?" Desmond muses. "Leonidas must have said something to get you to head out there. You needed some air? Or maybe he wanted to be . . . intimate?"

He gets a goofy look on his face when he says it, and I blush. "I doubt it. I was feeling afraid, not sexy."

"Okay. So maybe Leonidas says something that frightens you. Like he's going to hurt you. You run out to the pool. You have a bigger argument, maybe about your breakup. He pushes you in." He smiles triumphantly.

"Maybe," I say, emptily.

"Maybe not?"

I swivel and look at the pool out the window. Now, a couple of kids are splashing each other in the shallow end. A woman in a black bikini dips in her long legs near the diving board. "I feel like the person who pushed me was a woman."

"Oh." Desmond frowns, studies his cocktail napkin, which is an illustration of various knots, like the wallpaper.

"But maybe my memory is wrong. I mean, Leonidas knows me. He was talking about me on the phone. It fits."

"Or maybe it doesn't," Desmond says. "I mean, I met him, Eliza. He seemed . . . Well, he seemed like a big dumb dog, no offense. So maybe it *was* someone else."

Deep down, I agree with him. It would be easy if Leonidas was the answer, but it doesn't feel right.

We don't say anything for a while. Someone is using a leaf blower outside. To blow what, I wonder. We're in the desert.

"Did you ever hear the story about the starlet who was murdered here in the sixties?" I ask Desmond, to break the silence. He shakes his head, so I explain about the mix-up. When I'm done, Desmond looks chagrined. "Poor Diana Dane," he cries.

"What are you talking about? She's the one that lived. It's Gigi Reese you're supposed to pity. Someone killed her, and they didn't even care who. Her mystery was never solved."

"I know, that's sad, too, but it's an expected sort of sad. But imagine what Diana Dane had to deal with. All those articles talking about her death. Do you think all of them were nice? Maybe someone snuck something disparaging in there, since she wouldn't be around to defend herself."

"I'm pretty sure they all sung her praises."

"Oh." Desmond blots his face with a napkin. "Still, the idea of someone mistaking someone else for you is spooky. I wonder if she had any moments of thinking, *Hey, if everyone thinks I'm dead, perhaps I am!* Public opinion can sway all sorts of truths."

"You're missing the point of my story."

"Or maybe she thought, *Hey, this gives me an out. I can leave Hollywood. Start another life. Go on a crime spree—no one will catch me because they all think I'm dead.*"

"But she loved Hollywood. She didn't go on a crime spree."

Desmond sips his drink. "Huh. There's so much more possibility to her story if she decided to run with the whole dead thing."

I squeeze my eyes shut, feeling more and more annoyed. "The point is that poor, dead Gigi Reese went unnoticed. The point is that some people are remembered only because they resemble someone else."

"If I had a double, I might go on a crime spree," Desmond says dreamily.

"No you wouldn't."

"Okay, I probably wouldn't. But I'd do something unexpected. For me, I mean."

I try to imagine what would be out of character for Desmond. Joining a fantasy football league, maybe. Adopting a child. I wonder about the anti-Eliza. I would take up residence at an ashram. I would breathe deeply and worry little.

Another stinger arrives even though I haven't signaled for it. I suck it down, wincing once again at the flavor. Who on earth would drink a cocktail with crème de menthe? The opening bars of a song peal through the room, and my head shoots up. "Low Rider." It's the same song I heard when I was here. I go very still, concentrating on each note, trying to picture the last time I'd heard the song. I might have been sitting on this very stool, looking out at this same view. And when I turned my head—

Fear ripples through me. I see a shadow. I shoot to my feet. "What?" Desmond says, sliding off his stool, too.

"Someone wants to hurt me."

Desmond's eyes widen. "Who?"

But I don't know. I have only been given this thought and only this thought exactly. And yet the fear is liquefied, coursing through my veins. Something in this bar frightened me that night. I'd hurtled off the stool just like I have today, and I looked for the first exit I could find. And that's what I do now, too. Except my body is pointed in the other direction today, so the exit I lunge for is the one into the hallway back to the hotel. I stagger there, arms outstretched like a zombie, the Muzak piping through the speakers abnormally loud.

"Eliza!" Desmond cries, stumbling behind me. "What are you—"

I hear the bartender protest something about being paid for the drinks, but I don't turn, and Desmond doesn't, either. All I know is that I have to get off this floor. *Away.* Whatever I feared a week ago is still here, now. I punch the elevator button, and, mercifully, the doors open immediately. I get in and press the button for the lobby. Desmond leaps inside as the doors are closing.

"What's going on?" he asks me, panting. "Eliza, what's happening? Tell me what you're thinking? Who are you afraid of? What did you see?"

My brain twists and bucks. I am scrambling for more, and I'm not getting any answers. I press my thumbs to my eye sockets until I see stars. When I peek at Desmond again, there is a nervous, uncertain look on his face.

"Someone you've met before?" he tries. "Who does this person look like?"

Like me, I want to say, but I don't know where this has come from. *I* certainly didn't come up with it. But then I remember that face on the bus. That face in the window at my mother's house. My face, my face, my face. Why do I keep seeing myself? I look at Desmond blankly, lost. My jaw feels unhinged from my skull.

The elevator dings. The door slides open on the lobby level. I shrink back at the throng of people waiting to get in, but Desmond leads me by the hand and sits me down on a leather chair near a large saguaro cactus that is somehow growing indoors.

"Eliza," he says, his voice cracking. "You're burning up."

"I'm okay." Sweat prickles down my spine.

"No, you're not. Talk to me, please. Who did you see? Why did you run away?"

"I don't *know*." And then, suddenly, the shakes come on. My whole body rolls with them; they travel all the way down to my fingertips, sharp little zingers. I chatter my teeth. I feel my eyeballs curl inward. I'm seizing, I can feel it. I shut my eyes and feel my head hit the leather ottoman. I can hear Desmond shouting above me, but I can't do anything to get to him or talk to him. *Just don't call other people over,* I wish I could tell him. *Just let me ride this out.* Something tells me I've had a seizure in public before. Something tells me I got too much attention for it.

And then, suddenly, it's over. My eyes focus again. Sound rushes back, and I have the use of my voice. I sit up, noting that I've left a pool of sweat from my hair on the ottoman. When I look at Desmond, though, he is staring at me in horror. Several other people stand over me, including a few men in hotel garb. "Is she okay?" one of them is saying. Beyond them, a few guests crane their necks. I hear the words *Ambulance,* and *Fainted,* and *Drunk.*

Someone clears his throat behind us. It's the bartender from the Shipstead; he's brought the bill. Desmond stands, leads him a few steps away to take care of the transaction. I sit on the ottoman, staring at the cross-hatchings in my palm, feeling cold, slimy embarrassment.

Desmond says nothing as he sits back down. "Sorry about that," I mutter, finally, because I feel like I must say something.

He pauses before speaking. "I want to call an ambulance."

I feel a bolt of shock. "Are you kidding?"

"Maybe you need a professional. Someone who can help you."

I curl my hands into fists. "I can't believe you."

"Eliza. You were *terrified*. You need to unlock what was scaring you."

"So you want to commit me? Just like everyone else?"

He looks horrified. "Of course not! I just want to know what's wrong!"

But maybe that's not what he means. It could be just a tactic to soften me up. I turn my back. "You don't know me at all, Desmond. So don't pretend that you do."

He scuttles around to face me again. "I didn't mean for you to think—"

"You know how I mentioned a brain tumor?" I interrupt. "Well, I think it's still hanging around. Messing with my head. Causing me to say things and remember things I have no control of. Causing my body to move in strange ways. It's not some psycho tic, okay? I'm not crazy."

His mouth drops open. "Oh, Eliza. Oh dear. I'm sorry."

"Yeah, well, sorry doesn't really cut it. Not now." This is unfair— I'm saying all this because I'm embarrassed and vulnerable. But I need him to leave me alone. Pretend it never happened. Coming here was a terrible idea.

"What can I do?" he pleads. "How can I help? Maybe you *do* need an ambulance, then."

"I can handle it." I cross my arms over my chest, feeling a wall come up around me. He tries to get me to look at him, but I don't.

"I'm smitten by you, Eliza," Desmond says. "You're like the Lady of the Lake. I don't understand a lot about you, but I'd spend the rest of my life figuring you out. I want to help you however I can, including figuring out what scared you so much. I want to *save* you."

"I don't need saving."

"Of course you don't. You're strong. You're impenetrable. But you want to know who hurt you, don't you? I think your brain and body just gave you a huge clue. Like I said, I've been reading up on memory, and I think just being here is working."

I glare at him. "How do I know *you* didn't hurt me, Desmond?"

He draws back. The color drains from his face. "W-what?"

"You just *happen* to be walking by and fish me out of the pool on the night of a storm? You just *happen* to have seen someone running away? You could be saying that to take the heat off yourself."

His hands are at his mouth. "Why would I do such a thing?"

"Because you're strange. Maybe I was bitchy to you in the bar. Maybe I made fun of you when we were younger and I don't remember you. You were absolutely the kind of person I would have made fun of."

Desmond shakes his head, his eyes unblinking. "You have to believe me. I didn't push you. I would never."

I pointedly turn away. I really don't think Desmond pushed me. It's probably good I threw it out there, but I know it isn't true. I just wanted to hurt him. It's too hard for me to have someone care this much. I have a coiled-up feeling that things with Desmond will end badly, disappointingly, devastatingly, and maybe it's just better to push him away before he pushes me. Maybe I've been in this situation before. With Leonidas, perhaps. But more likely with my mother.

Desmond's shoulders heave, and then he stands. "Let's have dinner and forget all about this."

"No way," I say stiffly. "I'm getting my car out of the garage, and I'm leaving."

"Don't be crazy! You just had an episode! You're in no state to drive!"

"I'll be fine."

"Absolutely not. I'll drive you."

Desmond reaches out and grabs my arm, but I wheel around and give him the most searing glare I can muster. "I said *no*."

I march across the lobby. I feel tipsy from the stinger, and not in a good way. Memories and feelings are bumping into one another in my head. Me pushing Desmond away, me feeling afraid, that seizure—a half-formed picture is taking shape in my mind, except it's still under a drop cloth. I wonder if I'll *ever* get to see what it is.

In the driveway, the same valets wait at their post. The one who took Desmond's car notices me and snaps to his feet. "Need the Batmobile, miss?" Then he chuckles. "Man, I've always wanted to say that."

I shake my head angrily. I'm even furious at Desmond's car. "No, thanks. And for the record? It's basically a glorified Buick."

"Did you have a nice stay at the Tranquility?" he asks, not missing a beat.

I consider this question. Across the drive, people are going on a hike in the blazing sun. Cacti jut out on the plateau. They look picturesque and innocuous from two hundred yards away, not like they really are: spiny, unyielding, mostly dead.

"Not really," I grumble over my shoulder, halfway to the parking garage. I'm not sure I've ever had fun at this place. Not once in my life.

From The Dots

The next Wednesday, Dot walked slowly to the Vons parking lot, not able to get any of the things Marlon had said out of her head.

How could he think Dorothy would roofie Dot? Didn't he remember all she'd told him about Dorothy's constant presence in the hospital when she was a little girl? She'd been the only one in Dot's family to come. She cared about Dot so, so much. But Dot also knew Marlon wouldn't lie to her, even if he was jealous about her and Dorothy's relationship. He wasn't Dot's mother. He loved her, honestly and truly, and only wanted the best for her.

Worrying about it kept her awake all night. She felt like she had to choose between them.

Dorothy was waiting in the car as usual, and she greeted Dot with an enthusiastic wave. "Ready for dinner, my dear?"

Dot tried to smile, but her mouth muscles wouldn't work, and she saw herself making a freakish face in the rearview mirror. The whole drive, she couldn't think of a thing to say, so she fiddled with the radio for noise. She settled on a sports announcer just because he was yelling the loudest. *Roofies.* It throbbed in her mind like an infection. Why would Dorothy have done such a thing? Why had Marlon even put that thought into her mind? Only, she'd read a little about the drug and how it made you feel. The symptoms were certainly familiar. Would the drug still be in her body? Should she get tested for it?

"What's with you today?" her aunt asked, poking her arm. "You're so quiet."

"I'm just thinking about school," Dot said. "We have finals soon."

"But aren't you an English major? What on earth could be difficult about finals?"

At M&F, the waiter had their favorite table all made up and ready. But when it came time to order drinks, Dot said she wanted water. Dorothy's head turned sharply. "No cocktail?"

"I'm not in the mood."

Dorothy scoffed. "When did you become so unfun?"

A glass of sparkling water appeared for Dot. She took a sip and swished the bubbles in her mouth as if to wash it clean. Across the table, Dorothy drank from her wineglass and gave her a cool stare. She asked Dot about the books she was reading, and Dot gave one-word answers. She tried to make up stories about the other patrons at the restaurant, but Dot didn't twist around to see who she was talking about.

She was reminded, suddenly, of seeing Dr. Koder in the wheelchair the first time they'd come here. After she'd gone home, she'd looked Dr. Koder up and learned that not long after Dot left her care, the doctor had been in a tragic fall down the stairwell of the swanky apartment building where she lived. She'd broken her neck. This was on a Facebook page set up by her husband, a man named Evan Koder—not on any sort of news site. One person commented that Dr. Koder should press charges, insinuating that the fall wasn't an accident . . . but no one followed up on that line of thinking. Dot couldn't find any evidence of a lawsuit.

"Did you do something to Doctor Koder?" she blurted.

Dorothy's head whipped up. "Who?"

"You know who. She's in a wheelchair because of a fall down the stairs. I know you were upset at how she treated us. It happened right after we left."

Dorothy's mouth hung open. It was a few moments before she could speak. "How dare you accuse me of such a thing."

"I just . . ." Dot felt tears come to her eyes. This was so much harder than she'd imagined. "The timing matches up. Her accident was on July 11. I'd just gone into the new hospital, but I still wasn't doing well. I could understand if you were upset . . ."

"July 11." Dorothy narrowed her eyes, thinking. "I know where I was that day. July 11 was my husband Milton's birthday, and I treat myself to a spa day every year in his memory." Milton was the film producer who'd passed away. "I went to The Hyacinth on Beverly Boulevard for the works. After that, I came to the hospital . . . to visit you."

"Oh," Dot said. "I'm sorry."

Dorothy crossed her arms over her chest. Her chin wobbled. "You know, I'm going to pretend you never said any of that. I'm just going to pretend this didn't happen."

"I'm sorry," Dot whispered again, feeling like a child. "I shouldn't have doubted you."

Dorothy pressed her lips together, as though to keep from crying. "You know, your dark moods remind me of the ones Thomas used to have."

Dot sucked in a breath. "Really?"

"Indeed. My, he would work himself into a lather. I felt like he was doing it on purpose." She folded her hands at her plate. "I was all he had in the world, though. Meaning I was the only person he had to push away. I tried to take it as a compliment, of course, but it hurt. I did so much for him. I was the only one who listened."

Dot marveled at how thinly veiled her aunt's words were. But maybe Dorothy had a point. Dorothy was the only person in her life, really.

Both of them reached for the last pretzel stick in the basket at the same time. Normally, faced with such a situation, Dot would withdraw her hand and let her aunt take the last piece of bread, but that day, she grabbed the stick and shoved it in her mouth.

Food arrived, big steaming plates of steak. "Ah," Dorothy said cheerfully, cutting into hers. She eyed Dot several times. Then she reached for her napkin, knocking her fork to the floor. "Can you get that, dear?" she asked. "My back isn't what it used to be."

Dot leaned down, but because it was on Dorothy's side, she had to actually kneel on the carpet and lunge to get the utensil. When she returned to the table, Dorothy was sitting heavily back into her seat as if she'd just been standing. Perhaps she'd just signaled the waiter, because he glided over quickly, and she handed him the fallen fork.

"So," she said, folding her arms and looking at Dot with an easy smile. "Now, tell me what's bothering you, dear."

Dot smeared ketchup around her plate. "Nothing."

"Is it your boyfriend?"

She shook her head miserably.

"Your mother?" Dot made a noncommittal noise. "You can tell me, darling. You can tell me anything."

Dot squeezed her eyes shut, startled at the tears that suddenly formed there. She wished that were true.

"Did I ever tell you about the lover I had in Italy who was part of the Sicilian mob? His name was Federico." Dorothy swooned. "My God, what a man."

"If he really exists," Dot muttered, unable to stop herself.

Dorothy frowned. "Pardon?"

Dot stared at her shiny utensils. "Nothing."

Dorothy set down her wineglass. "Do my stories bore you?"

Dot swallowed hard.

"Am I just some windbag?"

Dot touched the tines of the fork, wobbled the spoon.

"Because I *thought* I was important to you. You're awfully important to me. I thought you'd want to hear this stuff. But if you don't, we can end this evening right now."

Dot hated Marlon, suddenly. He'd shoved a spike between her and Dorothy. Who cared if she twisted some details of her time overseas? Who cared if she told a pack of lies? It didn't mean she was evil. It didn't mean she was hurting anyone. She gave so much love; she was the most selfless person Dot had ever met. Marlon was being narrow-minded, perhaps as ageist as those grungy kids in the bar.

"I came back just for you," her aunt said. "But if it's not worth it for you, I had a good thing going in Italy. I can go right back."

Dot's throat was suddenly dry, and she reached for her glass and took a drink. "Please don't."

Dorothy nodded slowly. "Okay, then. Good." She pointed to her water glass. "Drink. You sound hoarse."

After that, the lights brightened, and Dot felt herself unknot. Dorothy told stories, some of her best ever, and Dot began to laugh. Her limbs turned loose, and she enjoyed the dinner. Until the nausea hit her. One minute she was at the table, then in a blink she was on the bathroom floor, half in a stall, half by the sink. "Oh, dear," Dorothy said above her. Dot lay in the back of her aunt's car. Dorothy's voice floated from the driver's seat. The lights of St. Mother Maria's receded in the distance. "Just tell me if I'm driving too fast," her aunt said.

Next thing she knew, it was morning again, and she was waking up in the Magnolia. Panic clutched Dot's chest. This didn't make sense. Here was the same headache. Here was the same nonplussing blankness.

"Just rest," Dorothy was telling her, the old refrain.

Dot bolted up. "But I only had water last night. Nothing else."

"It must have been food poisoning. Or maybe you've got the flu. I wouldn't be surprised, living in that dirty dormitory."

Dot didn't feel like she had the flu. She felt hungover. She was about to say this, but then there was a knock at the door. "I bet that's our room service!" Dorothy trilled, the ends of her poppy-printed silk kimono trailing behind her. "You'll feel better once you've had some eggs."

She whipped the door open and made a strange choking sound. Dot sat up fast, head throbbing, and watched as her aunt tried to push the door shut again. Whoever stood on the other side out-muscled her, and the door flew open, banging hard against the stopper on the wall.

Dot's mother was backlit against the bright California sunshine. When she stood on tiptoes and saw Dot, her expression darkened and twisted.

"I am going to kill you," she whispered, and headed straight for Dot in the bed.

ELIZA

THE DRIVE HOME is a repeat of my flight from the Palm Springs hospital except I'm in better clothes and in my messy Toyota RAV4 instead of Bill's Porsche. I can still smell Desmond's body spray on me as though we've rolled together wildly, our skin touching in all kinds of places. I peel off one of his long, silky black hairs from my pants and whip it out the open window.

After a while, the scenery along I-10 becomes familiar. To avoid post-work traffic, I get off the freeway and turn onto a busy thoroughfare in Alhambra, passing by derelict strip malls and little shacks that sell porn on VHS. After a while, the neighborhood improves, and a hospital looms ahead. I see a familiar sight and lose my breath. Stunned, I cut across four lanes of traffic into a driveway. A neon sign looms above me.

M&F Chop House.

I park in a space, suddenly shaking. The steak house rises above me, brick and stucco and concrete and *real.* My vision starts to swirl. When I turn clockwise, there's St. Mother Maria's Hospital across the street. I must have seen this out the window or in an ad and used it for the book. It looks just as I described it in *The Dots.*

I push the door open and look around cautiously, as if I'm expecting sirens to go off at my presence. A chunky man with red blotches on his cheeks smiles at me vacantly, then ushers me through the dining room. "This table all right?" he asks. It's in the middle of the space. A menu sits jauntily next to an unlit candle and a small potted succulent.

I nod and collapse into the chair. It seems like a normal steak house: wood-paneled bar, framed photographs of old newspaper articles, brass plaques bearing regulars' names on the walls. The only problem is that I know every inch of the room astonishingly well. The place even *smells* like how I imagined it in *The Dots*: meaty, saucy, like red wine and money and sex. Perhaps because all steak houses are alike?

Sizzling plates swirl by. A baseball player cracks a hit on television, and the yuppie twenty-something bankers with their whiskeys cheer. I wrack my memory: perhaps I was here with Leonidas? Perhaps with Bill and my mother? And I must have driven out this way while researching the book. How else would I know there was a hospital named St. Mother Maria's across the street? How would I know how many floors it had, or that there was a big parking structure right next to it that was taller than the hospital itself? This isn't a neighborhood one takes pictures of or sees on the news. This isn't a neighborhood featured in movies, iconic and quintessential. It's a nothing sort of neighborhood, and yet I seem to know it by heart.

My phone buzzes, and I look down. It's Desmond. *I'm so sorry. I just wanted to make sure you're okay.*

And then another text: *I would never, ever harm you. Please understand that. You are the light of my LIFE.*

And then another: *If you don't want me to contact you again, just say the word. But I shall mourn you until the end of my days.*

Get over yourself, I finally respond. Then I turn my phone off. It's probably cruel, and maybe I should forgive him, but it's just too comforting to convert my shame into punishing wrath.

As I look around more, I'm surprised to see an unoccupied booth way in the back almost hidden from view. Something about it seems untended, maybe even condemned. I crane my neck. Could there be a secret door back there, too? I feel so loopy. How is it that this place is so *vivid*? How do I know all its nooks and crannies? Maybe I'm a better writer than I think. If my mother came in here, if she saw how well I'd captured this, maybe *then* she'd be impressed. Instead of saying, *This is what you wrote?* Instead of saying, *Other people read it?* Instead of saying, *Do something, Bill.*

Instead of saying, *Get up. Please.*

The last thought knocks over a set of dominoes. A latch gives way, opening a door. *Get up. Get up.* It's a pealing bell in my brain. Concentric rings rippling in a pond. A voice telling me to *count backward from ten.* Maybe it's the overwhelming smell of bloody meat, maybe it's my aching, throbbing head, maybe it's the eerie, dizzy awareness of fiction clashing with reality, but all at once I am standing on the pavement outside Leonidas's father's doctor's office again, and I am smiling about Desmond, and then I am on the pavement, and for a split second before I fainted I looked up and saw what I needed to see. The image has only slid into place now. *Get up. Please.*

A face stands over me. The eyes are wide with confusion. The mouth is twitchy and concerned. A hand leans down to check my pulse, and then there's a sigh of relief. The face moves away, and two hands rifle for my phone, and then tap the screen. A backing away, and then the person runs off, legs moving awkwardly. It's the run of a non-athlete. The run of a middle-aged woman.

My mother.

From The Dots

"Darling!" Dorothy said, hurrying after Dot's mother as she crossed the carpet into the hotel suite. "What a wonderful surprise!"

Dot's mother dodged Dorothy's open arms and instead grabbed Dot, who was now on her knees, by the wrist. "Get up. Now."

"Would you like some coffee?" Dorothy said, hurrying behind her. "And room service is coming soon. The eggs Benedict is divine."

Dot's mother gawked at Dorothy. "Don't say another word." She slung an arm around Dot's shoulders. "I'm calling the police."

"Darling, there's no need to—"

"Mom, what are you doing?" Dot shrieked.

"I'm calling them," Dot's mother insisted. "I should have called them years ago."

Then she pulled Dot out of the bungalow. The sun was bright in Dot's eyes, intensifying her headache. She twisted around, expecting Dorothy to be chasing after them, but her aunt stood, wilted, in the doorway. It looked like she might cry.

Dot tried to wriggle from her mom's grasp. "What is *wrong* with you? Why did you just do that?"

But her mother was stronger than Dot anticipated, and she wouldn't let go of her wrist. With her other hand, she was talking to someone on the phone. "Yes, I'd like to report that I know the whereabouts of a felon," she said briskly. "The Magnolia Hotel in Beverly Hills. Her name is Dorothy Banks."

"What the hell are you *doing*?" Dot said. "A *felon*? Have you gone insane?"

Her mother hung up and stared at Dot. She looked angry, shocked, and something else, too. Maybe haunted. Maybe sad. "I can't believe you. I can't believe you would see her, go *out* with her, without telling me."

"Why would I tell *you*? You hate her. Obviously."

"Don't you think there's a good *reason* for that?" Her mother pulled her across the parking lot and unlocked the SUV.

Dot sniffed. "Yeah, because you're jealous." And yet there wasn't as much bite in her defense as there might have been even a few days prior. Her head felt swollen. The dread lay, gelatinous, in her stomach. She wanted to love Dorothy, and she wanted to trust her, but there was that disconcerting scene back there in the hotel. She shouldn't be sick today.

Dot's mother opened the car door for Dot and indicated for her to get inside. Once Dot did, she quickly shut the door and hurried around to her side.

"I wanted to see her, and she wanted to see me," Dot growled when her mother got into the driver's seat. "I've missed her. She was gone for twelve years. You can't keep us from each other."

"*Watch* me."

"I'm an adult. I can do whatever I want." Realizing she could just leave, Dot reached for the passenger handle. But her mother caught her arm and pulled it away. She started the engine and backed out of the spot so quickly she almost slammed into the car parked in the space behind them. Dot yelped in surprise. Her mother white-knuckled the wheel and eased gently on the gas.

"How many times have you seen her?" she demanded.

Dot didn't answer.

"How long has this been going on? Months? *Years?*"

"Just a few months," Dot mumbled into her chest. "February, I think. Right around Valentine's Day."

Her mother jerkily maneuvered the car through the parking lot. "And what do you do? Where does she take you?"

"Just to dinner." Dot glowered at her nails, then started picking at one until it started to bleed. The blood looked satisfying running down her hand. "Just to this steak house. It's not like we're doing anything *wrong*. Why would you say she's a felon? You're delusional. What do you think she did, rob a bank?"

Her mother pressed her lips tightly together. "You know who *told* me about this situation? Your boyfriend. He says most Wednesday evenings he can't find you, and Thursdays you're not in your dorm room in the morning. You don't go to class. He says you've been acting strangely, and that you're not finishing your assignments anymore. He told me what you've been up to. That you've been seeing her. That you've been drinking. You're not *supposed* to drink, Dot. Especially not with her."

Dot hated Marlon. How could he have betrayed her to her *mother*, of all people? She tossed her hair as best she could, despite her throbbing head. "She's my family. And she took care of me, in case you don't remember."

Her mother let out an ugly laugh. "You really think that's what she was doing? Taking *care* of you? You really don't know?"

"Know what?"

Her mother looked astonished. "Dot, she's trying to *kill* you."

Dot stared at her incredulously, but then something on the road distracted her. "Look!" she cried, pointing. Her mother had veered into the other lane, and a truck was heading right for them. The driver laid on his horn. Mother and daughter screamed, but Dot's mother managed to steer out of his way just in time.

"Pull over!" Dot screamed, and surprisingly, her mother did.

They both breathed heavily, listening to the idling engine. Cars swept past them. Across the street, outside a 7-Eleven, a couple ran toward each other and embraced.

"I want out," Dot said, grappling at the door handle.

Her mother hit the lock button. "Don't go. Please. You don't understand how sick she is."

"She's not *sick*." Dot really didn't want it to be true. "You're just jealous of her. You've always been. That's why you sent her away from the hospital. You made her *leave*."

"Dot, she was trying to *poison* you!"

Dot gawked at her mother. "W-what?"

Her mother pushed her hair out of her face. Her features had elongated into worried ovals. There were frown lines deeply etched into her forehead. "She was poisoning you in the hospital. She gave you strychnine in small doses. It's a pesticide. It made your seizures come on, which made the doctors flock around you, and which put her at the center of a situation. She has a psychological illness. It's called Munchausen Syndrome by Proxy. Do you know what that is?"

Dot shook her head. It had gotten so hot and steamy in this car all of a sudden, like they were in the middle of a rain forest.

"It's when a caregiver either makes up or brings on symptoms in a child because they want attention. Well, and also because they get joy out of deceiving others who seem more powerful than they are, like nurses and doctors. But because they appear so caring, and because they can be so manipulative with the hospital staff and the child, sometimes people don't catch on for a long, long time." She touched Dot's arm. "It's *child abuse*. The doctors figured it out; that's why they sequestered you to the ICU. You got better there because she wasn't able to get in and put anything in your IV. We had to file a restraining order for her. There was going to be a big investigation—she was going to jail. That's why she left town."

Dot felt vomit rise in her throat. "No. She didn't do any of that. Where's the proof?"

"Your blood tested positive for strychnine poisoning. I have the paperwork, if you want to see it. Once the doctors suspected, they banished you to the ICU. There was a warrant out for Dorothy's arrest."

"She didn't poison me. It had to be one of the nurses."

"It wasn't."

"But she took care of me. She loves me."

"No, she didn't. She did the opposite. She tricked you. She tricked all of us." Her mother's voice shook.

Dot couldn't listen to this anymore. Groaning, she shifted back onto her seat, undid the lock button, and pulled at the door handle.

"No!" her mother cried, reaching for her once more. But instead of grabbing her shoulder, she grabbed the ends of Dot's hair. Dot moved one way, her mother pulled the other, and there was a horrible ripping sound. White pain shot through Dot's skull, straight to her eyeballs. She screamed out and clutched her head.

When she looked over, her mother was trembling. A few strands of hair were in her hands. "I'm sorry," her mother whispered. "Oh my God, Dot, I didn't mean to do that."

Dot said nothing, just whimpered and cradled her scalp.

"Let's just go home, okay? I'll take you home. We'll have dinner and talk it through."

"I want to go to the dorm."

"I would never hurt you, you know that!"

"*I want to go back to the dorm.*"

Dot cried silently the whole way. Her mother probably thought she was angry, and she was, of course, but the tears were from loss, too. A story like that couldn't be unremembered.

ELIZA

I AM QUAKING by the time I reach my parents' curb. My heart galumphs, and I tumble out of the front seat and onto the sloped front lawn. The sky is a disarming shade of purple. Behind me, kids who have just climbed to the Hollywood sign are traipsing back to their cars. Their giggles sound like breaking glass.

At the door now, once again, I smell the cloying scent of orange perfume. I roll back my shoulders, readying myself. I consider ringing the doorbell, but instead I try the knob. It twists easily, and then it whips open without me moving a muscle. I jump. Gabby blinks at me from inside, letting out an *oof*.

"O-oh," I blurt. "What are you doing here?"

Gabby's mouth twitches into a smile. She's in a black pantsuit and is carrying a red purse shaped like an anvil. "I came home early. I was just about to come get you, in fact."

"Why?"

"Your follow-up appointment, remember? Didn't I call you? I thought I was grabbing you at your house, but this is better. We'll get there much faster."

I narrow my eyes. "What follow-up appointment?"

"For the pool thing. Remember I said I'd take you?"

"Is it for an MRI?"

"I don't . . ." She rummages in her bag and pulls out a reminder card. "No, it's with someone named Doctor Sweitzer."

"Who's that?"

"Uh, a psychiatrist." She says *psychiatrist* quickly, like I'll gloss over it, and smiles hopefully.

I back away from the door. "I don't need a shrink."

Then Gabby notices my bruised face. "What happened?"

"Someone came up behind me and scared me. And I fell."

"*What?*"

I reach for the door to shut it. "It's why I need to talk to Mom right now, actually."

"But Eliza, the appointment."

"*I'm not going!*"

Gabby's hands curl against her chest. The crystals on the chandelier above the dining room table tinkle together. I didn't mean to yell that loudly.

"Look, I need to stay here." I temper my tone. "I need to talk to Mom. It's really important. I'm not leaving until I do."

"She's not here."

I shrug and plop down on the slipper chair near the door. "Then I'll wait."

Gabby checks her watch, then shuts the front door and walks closer to me. "What do you need to talk to her about?"

She looks so dowdy in her baggy suit. People without style have always fascinated me. Is it that they don't care? Does she think she actually looks good? I made so much fun of her as a teenager, but Gabby was begging for it. She wore Mary Janes with socks well into middle school, for God's sake. And could she not have gotten cuter glasses? Now, of course, I regret it. If I had been nicer to Gabby, perhaps she'd be a sympathetic ear now.

"I think Mom knows something she's not telling me," I explain.

Gabby just stares at me for several ticks of the clock. "Knows . . . what?"

"I saw her in this alley behind a parking lot a few days ago, sort of near her work. I think she was following me. I had a panic attack and passed out, and by the time I woke up, she was gone." I run my tongue over my teeth. "She deleted something off my phone, then left. Though I think she called the police to let them know I was back there. Nice of her, huh?"

Gabby looks astonished. "Are you *sure* it was Mom?"

I think of the fuzzy image of her face that had returned to me at the steak house. "Pretty sure."

"What did she find on your phone?"

"Something . . . important. And the only way she'd even know I found the important thing was if she was following me. Something really weird is going on, Gabby." I cut my gaze over to her. "Do *you* know what it is?"

"I don't have a clue." Gabby clears her throat. "Look, you're going to hate me for saying this, but you sort of sound like how you sounded when you had the tumor. Always worried that someone was following you. That sort of thing."

"I know this sounds the same, but it's not. I have proof this time."

"What kind of proof?"

"I *remember Mom there*," I urge emphatically. "And I need to know why." My mind has been racing ever since I made the connection. Why would my mother delete the list of numbers on Leonidas's call screen? Is her number one of them? Is *that* the number I vaguely remember? It's possible. I would have recognized our home phone number—it's been the same since I was a kid—but I don't have my mom's cell memorized.

So was my mother talking to Leonidas that day outside the Cat Show? Was she sharing some sort of worry about Palm Springs and was he talking her down? But *why*? Because she's guilty of something, obviously—it's the only thing that makes sense.

I look at Gabby. "I think she knows who pushed me into the pool in Palm Springs. In fact, I'm sort of scared *she* pushed me into the pool in Palm Springs."

Gabby smiles nervously. "Okay. That's . . . interesting. But just— go with me here. Is it possible you're blaming Mom because she's the one who's the most worried about you?"

I burst out laughing. "Mom hasn't even *called* me since Palm Springs. The only time she's spoken to me is to tell me that my book is crap. I wouldn't call that worried."

"She wants you to go back to the hospital. She's desperate for you to get better, and—"

"Gabby, instead of waiting for me to regain consciousness," I interrupt, "she *ran off*. She tampered with my phone then left me in an alley! When the cops came, they thought I was nuts!"

"—but an unhealthy part of your brain is trying to fight against that," Gabby bulldozes over my words. "You're not seeing things rationally. I mean, okay, even if Mom did run from you in a parking lot, clearly she knew you were okay, and you said yourself she called the cops just in case. Maybe she had a good reason to leave."

My mouth drops open. "What could that possibly be?"

"Maybe she . . ." Gabby shuts her mouth tightly and looks away.

I feel a shiver down my spine. "Maybe she *what*?"

"I don't know. Maybe she was late for something."

I can tell this isn't what Gabby was going to originally say, and I snort. Gabby walks across the room and looks out the window, her face hidden from view. "Eliza, I know she's not all warm and fuzzy. Your illness has been hard on her. Some people rise to those occasions. Others . . . it tears them apart. They can't handle it. It kills them, and they just crumble. She sees you acting strangely again, and it's killing her."

"Are you trying to get me to feel bad for her?"

"No. It's just that . . . I don't think you see it from her perspective. None of us can wrap our minds around what you were going through when you were sick. Yeah, she should have been there for you a little more, but she *does* care. I woke up many times in the night to find her crying in the bathroom. Or just down in the kitchen, sitting at the table, hands cupped around an empty coffee mug, just staring."

I make a *tsk* sound. "She always acted like she'd had enough of me."

"She's one of those people who doesn't know how to deal with tragedy. So she gets angry and distant. It isn't the right response, but it's just how she is."

"It doesn't change that she's hiding something. I'm still going to sit here until she's back."

Gabby looks at her watch again. "I hate to break it to you, but I don't think she's going to be home for a while. She and dad have some sort of dinner thing tonight. You'll be waiting a long time." She stands. "So how about that appointment?"

"No appointment," I say. "I'm not changing my mind."

And then we stare at each other for a while.

"Okay," Gabby relents. "We don't have to go to the appointment. But let's get out of the house. To get an early dinner, maybe. And then, afterward, I'll bring you back here, and we'll see if Mom is home then. Okay?"

I roll my jaw. It feels less satisfying, but I feel like if I say no, she'll try to force me down the appointment road again. And to be honest, maybe I haven't thought this through. I'm not sure if I'm ready for a confrontation with my mother. I *want* to ask her all sorts of questions, but she'll never admit what she's up to. She'll twist it, somehow, and turn it into *my* problem, *my* illness—this is all a figment of my messed-up head. What I need is to prove it another way. I'm just not sure what that way is yet.

"Fine," I say. "But you drive both of us. I'll leave my car here." That will force Gabby to bring me back, and maybe by then my mother will be home.

Her car, a beige PT Cruiser, is parked in the driveway. The inside of it smells like a vanilla candle. The seats have recently been vacuumed, and the footwells are clear of the wrappers and napkins and books and other bullshit that plague mine. I kick open the glove box when I climb into the passenger seat; her owner's manual is neatly stowed away. A plastic Baggie labeled *registration and insurance* holds those two documents. I bet she's the type who regularly gets her tires rotated.

I settle in the passenger seat, and Gabby swings next to me. There's a flash in the rearview mirror. A person is standing on the road, hands on hips, dark hair floating around her face. I turn around and viciously study the street behind us, but the road is empty. Sweat prickles on my body. It's that face again. *My* face.

"What?" Gabby asks, staring at me.

I look again, and of course the face is gone. "Nothing," I say, trying not to sound breathless. "I just thought . . . Nothing."

We start down the hill. I'm looking for a way into a conversation with Gabby, but I can't think of the right starting note. She sits very straight when she drives, like there's a book balanced on her head. Every few seconds, her phone buzzes with a text—I can see the bubbles appearing on her screen, then disappearing. Something else dings, too, something in her purse. "Do you need to get those?" I ask.

"It's fine. I don't like to text and drive."

When we turn on Sunset, I sit up straighter. "Are we going to the Chateau?"

"The what?"

We whip past the Chateau Marmont without turning in. Undaunted, I point to Toi. "That place makes good Thai cocktails," I sing out. "*Virgin* cocktails, I mean."

She continues past it, too. At the end of Sunset, she pulls into the valet lane and gets out, hefting her purse on her shoulder. I get out, too, my gaze on the below-the-knees hem of her skirt. Here on Sunset, she looks even more matronly. A tattooed man wearing short shorts and no shirt ambles up the street, yelling at someone on his cell phone. A convertible full of leering Asian guys cruises by, thumping rap music booming from their speakers. Across the street, a bunch of girls are wearing dresses that barely cover their crotches. Gabby's hair boings childishly.

Gabby saunters past a bunch of rock clubs and boutique hotels and five-star restaurants and walks into a place called, at first glance, *Gravel,* though actually it says *Crave. Eat, heal, love,* reads a large slogan over the window, and there's a picture of an enormous, fruit-filled smoothie. It's probably made out of pineapple, but the color reminds me of pus.

Inside, tranquil music is playing, and people are sitting quietly at tables. The only jarring sound is a blender, juicing. A hostess, pin-thin with ripped Pilates arms, glides over to an empty table and hands us menus printed on paper so thin I'm afraid just handling it will make it disappear. "This place is . . . nice," I mumble.

"I come here for dinner sometimes," Gabby says. "With friends from work."

Everything on the menu has quinoa in it, and there's not a single cocktail, not that Gabby would allow me to get one anyway. I put the menu down and look around. There is a man in the corner who's got on the full Buddhist garb. He's sitting with the most beautiful woman I've ever seen, blonde and tan, totally flawless skin. I prefer bars with hard-looking women, jowly, fast-talking actors, chain-smoking rock-and-rollers. I suppose this is where everyone comes if they want to remain preserved.

Gabby's phone pings again, and I chuckle. "They keep you on your toes at work, huh?"

She checks it and places it facedown on the table again. "I suppose."

"So how do you know so much about people's reactions to children with illness, anyway?"

Gabby gives me a strange look. "What you said about Mom," I remind her. "It was very . . . insightful."

She fiddles with her chopsticks. "My boss's son has leukemia. I'm sort of . . . dating him. My boss, I mean. Dave. Not Linus, his boy."

"That's great, Gabby. For how long?"

"Six months, two weeks, and five days."

"What's his son's prognosis?"

"Fifty-fifty. Dave's a mess about it. I'm not sure we should be together right now. His whole focus is on his son, which it should be. But I guess he needs something else. A . . . distraction."

"Something that makes him happy."

Gabby primly sips her water. "Maybe that's why Mom was so into kite-surfing when you were sick. She needed an escape, too."

Yes, but what a magical, picturesque escape, flying over the ocean on a kite. Is it terrible of me to wish she'd chosen a hobby that was a little gloomier? "I guess I wanted you to suffer as much as I was," I say.

"No. But people show suffering in different ways. And in your case and your mom's case, maybe you didn't see the extent of it, but I'm also not sure you're being fair to her."

I sniff. "And why would you say that?"

"Because . . ." Gabby looks away sharply. Red splotches appear on her cheeks. "Well, you don't remember how it was."

I sit back. "What do you mean?"

Her mouth grows very small, a perfect little button. I've seen the look on her before, when we were teenagers and she once blurted out the word *fuck* at the dinner table—something so old-hat for me, but a word I didn't even know she *knew*. "Let's just leave it at that, okay?"

Fury flares inside me. "No. I'm not leaving it at that. What do you mean? People are hiding things from me. Big things. I want to know what's really going on."

When Gabby looks up again, her expression is strangely sad. "Oh, *Eliza*." But before she can say anything else, her phone rings. She looks down at it, lowers her shoulders, and shuts her eyes. "I need to get this. Stay here."

She hurries off, snaking around the tables and pushing through the front door. She stands in front of the restaurant, near a bike rack, head bent a little, her lips moving fast.

I rake my hands through my hair. What are people keeping from me? What is it I'm not remembering? Is Gabby trying to tell me my hospital stay wasn't as I pictured? What was there to picture, though? And my mother really *wasn't* there. In fact, she texted me a picture of her on a kite board, floating above the Pacific, as though I should be proud of her, and forgiving.

Something pings in her bag, the same thing that's been pinging along with her texts. I ignore it at first, perusing the menu, flipping and flipping and still finding nothing I can imagine eating. There's a second ping, and then a third. Something is lighting up inside her bag. I shift my chair over and peek inside.

It's an iPad. I don't even need to take it out to see that the texts from her phone have also shown up on the screen. *Doing okay?*

It must be Dave, the boyfriend. I want to write to him to say he should make sure to sit with his son at the hospital, even through stupid moments, even when he's sleeping, because he really needs someone there. *From one sick patient to another.* And, oh yeah. Don't lie to him. Don't cover shit up. It's not very much fun.

There's another ping. When I look down, there's something in this text that I didn't notice on the first one. A name is attached. For a moment, my brain doesn't make sense of it, and I assume that it's only what I *want* to see, simply because I've been too much in my own world lately, too engulfed in my own problems. So I look again. And one more time, because it's not a name you see very fucking often.

Leonidas.

I read the second text. *The cops haven't called you, have they?* My heart goes still.

Outside, Gabby is still talking on the phone. She probably hasn't checked the texts that have come in yet, but I'm guessing they show up on this device and her phone simultaneously. Her back is to me, so I slide the iPad from her bag. I stare at Leonidas's name in the bubble. And then something else flashes to me, hot and flinty in my mind. That's why one of the numbers on the screen shot I'd gotten of Leo's call screen seemed familiar. It was Gabby's. He'd been talking to Gabby . . . about *me*.

I try to remember what I'd overheard Leo saying at the Cat Show. *I mean, why would they ask you? And you don't need to bring up Eliza or Palm Springs.*

Another text pings in. Leonidas again. *If they do, remember what we talked about,* it reads. *Just stay the course.*

I grip the iPad tightly, wishing I could type something but knowing that as soon as I swipe the screen a password request will come up and those texts will disappear. I stare at the words, willing for more to come up. Anything to explain this.

A shadow falls over me, and I jump. Gabby has her phone in one hand, the texts clear on that screen, too. She stares at her open bag and my fingers wrapped around her iPad. When I meet her gaze, her expression is eerily calm—not caught, not frantic, not bumbling, not scrambling. It is as though she was expecting this might happen, and as though she formed a plan in case it did.

"Gabby," I whisper. She grabs the tablet from me, whirls around, and runs.

■ ■ ■

"Gabby," I call out, bursting onto the street. "Gabby, wait!"

Gabby is scrambling in her suit and heels, her purse bouncing against her back. She banks around a corner, sweeping right past her parked car.

"Gabby," I cry, chasing after her up the long street. She keeps running. "Gabby!" I scream. "Stop! I need to talk to you!"

"Just go, Eliza," she calls over her shoulder. "Please."

"I'm not leaving. Not until you tell me what the fuck is going on."

She has run into an alleyway, and there's no way out. She halts and spins around, shielding her hands against her chest. She looks frightened of me. Which is ridiculous, because it should be the opposite. Right now I have no idea who I should be afraid of. Maybe everyone.

"Tell me why Leonidas is texting you about the police," I demand.

"It's all a misunderstanding."

"Bullshit."

"Just let it go!"

"I'm not letting it go! You *know* something. Just like Mom knows something. How do you even know Leonidas?"

"We've been friends for a while. Out of worry for you."

"Why is everyone so *worried*?" This last word explodes off my tongue, salty, fizzling.

Gabby's bottom lip twitches. She is digging her thumbnail deeply into her palm.

"Why are you and Leonidas talking about Palm Springs?" I press. "Why is he talking about the police? What are you guys trying to cover up?"

Gabby juts her chin toward the sky. "Eliza, this isn't some kind of conspiracy!"

"Really? You could've fooled me!" The blinking neon lights on the hotel across the street are only enhancing my dizziness. I turn away from them. "I know you have answers, so you'd better start talking. What are you keeping from me? Tell me what you know!"

I'm inches from her face now, my breath mingling with hers. Gabby tucks her chin into her chest. Her shoulders heave up and down. "Eliza," she squeaks out. "Trying to figure out this pool thing, you're just harming yourself. It's making you so paranoid. So *troubled,* like before. We're not trying to hurt you. We're not the bad guys here. You're sick. Whatever was happening to you before your brain incident is happening again."

There's part of me that wants to buy into what she's saying—after all, I think it might be true, too. But I keep seeing those texts on the iPad screen. *No.* This *isn't* just my brain. Not all of it. "I'm not just randomly falling into pools. And I heard Leonidas saying something sketchy on the phone the other day, and I *remember* Mom in that parking lot. I know you know something, maybe everything. You can be arrested for withholding evidence," I warn her. "You know that, right? If you know something, you have to tell me. I can go to the police."

Her eyes are shut. "Don't go to the *police.*"

"Because that would get you in trouble, right?"

"Just let it go!" Her hands flail in front of her face.

"I *can't!*" I scream.

I back away from her, my whole body heaving. I don't realize I'm crying until the tears hit my mouth. We both stand there for a few beats, hardened in our shells. After several ragged breaths, Gabby looks at me again. Her eyes are dark and wet. "It was me, Eliza. I did it."

My hands fall to my sides. A garbage truck passes by, and I concentrate on that for a moment, staring at the red plastic string of a trash bag that got caught outside the hopper. I try to imagine what could be in that trash bag. Porn magazines? Yogurt containers? Body parts?

When I turn back to Gabby, her head is dipped so low I can see her straight, neat part. "*What* did you do?" I whisper.

"I was at a conference at the Tranquility the same day as you. I-it was a weird coincidence to see you there. You were in the bar, and you were acting so strangely. Like you were going to have another seizure. I tried to calm you down, but you got violent with me. I realized you were really, *really* drunk. So I walked you outside to get some air. But you kept freaking out. You were just so drunk, and you were acting so ridiculous, and I was afraid you'd say . . ." She takes a big breath. "I wanted to sober you up. I wanted you to just . . . rest. So I pushed you in the pool. It was a knee-jerk reaction." Gabby peeks at me. "I'm *sorry*. I am so, so sorry."

"I was talking to you at the bar?" I try out, digging around in my brain. I wish I could remember this. I wish I could remember *her*.

"Yes. That's right." Her syllables come out choppily, like she's pulling them, taffy-like, from her throat. "But then I walked you outside. I just didn't want you making a spectacle of yourself. I was trying to do you a favor, but I realize now that it was a terrible decision."

"What was I freaking out about?"

"I don't really know. I couldn't understand you."

"So you pushed me into a pool just because I was drunk and being ridiculous? When you knew I couldn't swim?"

"I know. It's awful. I wasn't thinking." She covers her face with her hands.

"Is it because of what happened when we were young?"

Her head shoots up. ". . . *What?*"

"How I . . . wasn't nice. The vodka thing. And when I put you in the closet. And the time you needed stitches and never told on me."

Gabby places a hand to her mouth. "Oh God, Eliza. *No.*"

I choose to believe her, because she looks honestly confused. "Okay, but why push me into the *pool*? Jesus, Gabby, if you wanted to sober me up, you could have shoved me down an elevator bank or thrown me in a fire. At least people wouldn't have immediately assumed I did it to myself."

"I wasn't trying to *frame* you. It just . . . happened. You were standing by the pool, practically ready to dive in yourself, so . . ."

"And then you just left?" I'm still so stunned. I really, really didn't think Gabby was capable of this sort of thing.

Her eyes dart back and forth. "I was about to dive in after you, but then I heard someone coming. So I took off." She tilts her head up to the pinkish sky. "I shouldn't have. I was freaked about it the whole night. I was ready to say something the next morning at the hospital because I thought they'd have the whole thing on camera and figure it out anyway. But then I found out that the—"

"—security cameras were out because of the storm," I finish for her.

Gabby nods. "Right. Still, I should have said something. I know how it looked. Only, by then you were saying someone was trying to kill you, and *that's* not what I was trying to do, and then that guy who works with the police came, which *never* happened before because it always was so clearly a suicide attempt, and then . . ." She puffs her eyes and blows out a breath. "I'm awful. I know. I let everyone believe you were trying to kill yourself, and you weren't."

"Uh, I *know* I wasn't." I say this wearily, though, not triumphantly. I wish I were feeling something grandiose right now—I've solved it!—but I just feel numb. This doesn't solve everything, after all. It doesn't solve the piece about me being completely and totally healed. It doesn't make up for the memories I've forgotten. "So Mom knows about this, too, I guess? This is why she tracked me down in that alley and deleted those pictures off my phone?"

She nods sheepishly. "We were on alert after you mentioned Leonidas last week—he knows about what happened in Palm Springs, too. It was me he was talking to on the phone that day you overheard him. But we didn't think you were going to actually *confront* him. But then Leonidas called Mom to say something strange happened at his office—some guy tripped and made a big scene, and when Leonidas came back to his desk, his phone had been moved. Something felt off, he said. He had a weird feeling you'd just been there."

I grit my teeth. I knew Desmond shouldn't have been so histrionic. And had I really been that obvious?

"So Mom walked over from her office to see if you were in the area . . . and you were. She found you in the alley. She didn't intend to *scare* you, Eliza. She just wanted to talk to you."

"But instead she deleted a screen shot of his phone with your number on it. She was trying to protect your needs over my sanity." I sniff. "She always did favor you over me."

"Don't be silly." Gabby looks embarrassed. "We were worried that you finding out I was involved might make you even more paranoid. But you have to understand—I was trying to help you that night in Palm Springs. You might not have tried to kill yourself, but you were still out of control that night. Self-destructive. You're supposed to be taking care of yourself. You *do* need the help Mom keeps recommending."

"You know, for someone you were afraid was paranoid, this definitely *isn't* the way to help them—by making them feel even *more* paranoid."

"I know." Gabby's head hangs low. "I realize that now."

"And you didn't five minutes ago? When you were telling me how sick I was? When you were saying I sound just like I did before the tumor?" I put my hands on my hips. "It's not fair."

"I know," Gabby says, kicking at a pebble. "I'm sorry."

Someone has inscribed his or her name into the sidewalk; it looks like either *Anna* or *Anne*. Anger broils in my stomach, and at the same time, my heart is broken. I picture all of them sitting in the hospital waiting room in Palm Springs before I woke up, concocting this plan. *Okay, so we'll just say that she did it to herself. Even though she didn't, it's clear she's still messed up, and it's best just to send her off again. Right? Yes, right. Okay, break.*

On one hand, I feel oddly comforted by the fact that I have a family who cares enough to concoct complicated scenarios to help me. On the other, it's hurtful that they thought I was so gullible that I'd just buy into the idea that I was crazy without asking questions. They don't know me at all. They don't *understand* me at all.

Gabby is quietly crying. I cross my arms over my chest, trying not to care. "I love you, Eliza," she says. "I truly think of you as a sister. I've always cared about you, even when you've been a difficult person to care about. But I get it if you hate me. And if this happened to me, if I fell into a pool and woke up and had people telling me I'd done it on purpose, I'd be clamoring for answers, too. Mom and Dad are going to be furious I came clean with you, but I'm glad I did. Now maybe you can drop it. Now maybe you can just live your life. Be happy."

"Be happy," I spit out. "*Poof.* Just like that."

"It's all any of us want for you. Just to live your life. To not be scared. To not be . . . sick." She steps a little closer to me. I can smell something coming off her pores, soap and sweat. "Are you going to tell the police? They've asked me a few questions. They know I was there. I haven't told them what really happened, though. I guess that's in your hands now."

I think of all those calls to the tip line. All those unanswered messages. All the hours I've spent obsessing over this. All this time, Gabby was lying to me. It makes my head pound.

But I also think of the MRI that's scheduled. I can buy that I was drinking at the Tranquility because there was something wrong again in my head. I can also buy that the paranoid feelings rushed back, too—symptoms of the tumor. Maybe I fell into a death spiral of self-loathing. Maybe I began to think someone was after me. I consider my bike ride in Santa Monica again. That day, I'd been overcome with the certainty that someone was pursing me on a bike, and I'd become so afraid, I'd hurtled into the ocean. I remember standing on the pool's edge at the Tranquility gripped with the same sort of fear.

It's not improbable to believe my family's been right all along. Maybe it *is* happening again. And maybe, in a backward way, Gabby pushing me into the water is her way of calling it to my attention— and my family's attention—so that I can get the help I need.

I clear my throat. Part of me wants to say that yes, I'm going to tell the cops. I've been manipulated, after all. Lied to. But part of me just feels tired. I do want it to be over. I'm sick of being angry and paranoid. "No," I say. "It's fine."

Her face opens like a flower. "Really?"

She throws her arms around me and hugs tight. We stand there for a while, in the middle of Sunset, rocking back and forth. "I'm sorry," Gabby keeps saying. "I just want you to be better." I think she means to say *happy* but is too distraught to realize her mistake.

We break apart. Gabby insists on driving me back to the house, but all at once there's somewhere I want to go, and I don't want to waste the time stuck in traffic just to get my car. I can pick it up to-morrow. I've done all right without it for this long, after all.

I feel scooped-out and ravaged, betrayed and shocked, but also calmer than I've felt in weeks. Gabby is right. Maybe I do need to find happiness, or at least something to distract me from the pain, just like how her boss is dating her so he doesn't have to think about his sick child every moment of the day. I suppose that's all anyone can do, though it's not something I'd indulged in. Instead, I've been crouching and shrieking and panicking at every turn, my whole life one big anxiety attack. Maybe that's no way to live.

After I get inside an Uber, I give the Westwood address of the apartment building I've looked up online several times since Des-mond told it to me. When I get there and peer into the lighted win-dows, I spy Desmond pacing back and forth in the front window, talking to someone out of view. It's like in the movies. When I ring the buzzer on the street, I see him stop through the glass and peek out the curtain. His expression is startled for a moment when he sees me, and then he mouths something into the phone and dis-appears from view. And then there he is, in the lobby, flinging the front door open, his smile surprised and pleased. And I fall into his arms, deciding that my happiness, my real life, hopefully full of love and joy and truth, starts right now.

ELIZA

DESMOND LIKES EGGOS for breakfast. Blueberry, specifically, with Mrs. Butterworth's syrup, and when he handles the bottle he speaks to Mrs. Butterworth with deference and is very careful not to touch her plastic breasts. He sleeps in his socks, and if even a day goes by without shaving he has dark stubble that makes a sandpaper sound when you rub it with your palm. I got him to shave off the Guy Fawkes facial hair, and already he looks much better. His lips are full and sensuous—I have no idea why he was hiding them. I catch him glancing at himself in the mirror, though, rubbing his smooth upper lip and chin in lament, but I choose to ignore it. I'm working on him getting a haircut next, but when I delicately mentioned that he could use a trim he looked horrified and backed away from me, pulling his hair into a hat, as though he thought I might set it on fire then and there.

He sleeps in a bedroom full of light in a big, well-made bed with a tufted headboard. I am told it's his parents' bedroom; they're both ambassadors and rarely here. The apartment has a lot of leather chairs and fiddly French cabinets, courtesy of his parents, but some of the design elements are of his choosing. Like the bowls of potpourri on the high shelf. When I'm alone in the room with it, I take the strange dried fruit pieces out of the bowls one by one, trying to crush them between my fingers, but they won't yield.

There is a jar of Sea Breeze on the vanity. His shower curtain has tiny printed sailboats, which were so incongruous to his being they made me laugh. "Oh, my brother, Stefan, hung that," he says. I meet Stefan, his brother the dabbler, a portly guy with kinky hair to his waist and huge nostrils. He looks nothing like Desmond, though apparently they are biologically related. Stefan wears stained T-shirts and wrinkled khakis and carries around a jug full of whole milk that he slowly drains through the course of a day.

In the little hallway just outside the kitchen is a cabinet full of Desmond's authentic absinthe collection and a bunch of vintage absinthe spoons. He keeps the cabinet locked because, he says, one time Stefan got in there and drank a whole bottle and almost died.

"You don't cross wormwood," he says spookily. "It has a majestic power over all of us."

His windows look out onto a courtyard with a Roman fountain filled with pennies and dimes. He has an owl sculpture made out of tin on his mantel; if it were to fall, its beak would impale a toe. Over the couch is an afghan his aunt knitted for his parents when they got married. He tells me these things on days two and three, as we drink coffee, as we rub each other's feet, as we kiss and kiss and kiss, his mouth so big and different, his movements surprisingly sure, his body engulfing mine in bed, despite its smallness everywhere else.

He admits he writes poetry. I tell him about Kiki's awful sonnets. Together, we look through his high school yearbook—he looked like Guy Fawkes even then and was even skinnier.

We cook dinners together, weird gourmet things that involve cheesecloth and double boiling and cauldrons—one of the nice things about living in an apartment actually owned by fifty-year-olds is that they have nice cookware. On day two of our courtship,

Desmond builds a special shelf for my vitamins, and I move them in. We read from a book of epigraphs from fifteenth-century tombstones. We put on Halloween masks (a gorilla and a pug, from Stefan's closet) and sit on the balcony, waiting for people to notice us. The masks smell organic, like skin and dairy. The smell of sour milk leaks out of Stefan's pores.

Desmond shows me a layout for the next Comic-Con and explains the new exhibits and the big draws; I pretend to be interested, but mostly I'm just disappointed nothing like *The Addams Family* will be there. I talk to him about my time in the hospital. Desmond listens. And he adores. I wake up some mornings and he's just staring at me, starry-eyed. He stands close to me in the elevator. He sneaks his hand up my skirt whenever people's backs are turned and sometimes even when they're not. When we go out to dinner, I feel his fingers tickling my thigh, and I jokingly swat him away. I find his woolly eyebrows strangely sensuous to lick. He buys me an *Addams Family* cartoon book from the 1940s, and together we look through it, marveling over the artwork.

On our second Saturday together, I'm sitting on the couch, looking at my cell phone, daring myself to open a review of *The Dots*. More people have read the galleys, and the opinions were starting to trickle in.

"They're good," Posey told me. "You really should read one." But I'm not sure I'm brave enough yet.

Desmond is in the shower, preparing for work, and while I'm staring at my phone, wondering if I can do it, Stefan lumbers into the living room with his JanSport backpack and his jug of milk. I have been told that this week he is working as a production assistant on a cable-channel zombie show, though other weeks he works in lighting or sound or even at the commissary, making tacos. Stefan doesn't limit himself to Hollywood stuff, either, Desmond explained. Last year, he took a job as a trumpet player on a cruise ship and was gone for six months. Before that, he aided a veterinarian who specialized in giant, exotic, illegal Hollywood pets, like white Bengal tigers. Some big-time director had a rhinoceros in his backyard, and Stefan helped it give birth.

Stefan plops down on the couch opposite me and pushes his dirty water–colored hair behind his ear. "You're nice," he says, looking at me carefully.

I give him a guarded half smile and glance toward the shower door, hoping Desmond finishes up soon. "Thanks."

"No, I'm serious. My brother's a fucking freak. We all know it. He knows it. But you're nice. You seem to get him. You're way nicer than Paul."

Paul. I know that name; after a moment I remember why. "Paul, the guy from work?" *The guy who was there when I drowned.*

"Paul's a girl. It's short for Paula." Stefan peers into his backpack, gives me a mysterious look, rearranges something in there, then zips it up. "They had a thing for a while. Des took it hard when it ended. He seems better now." Then he stands and shoulders the backpack. His feet are dinosaur-heavy as he plods toward the door, and before he steps into the hall, he jabs his finger toward my forehead. "So don't wound him, okay? I'll have to hurt you."

The door closes, and I stare at the God's-eye someone has hung on the knob. I feel slimy and sour, like Stefan has coated milk on my face. Is it because Paul, my co-rescuer, is a girl—and Desmond's ex? Hadn't Desmond deliberately hinted that Paul was a guy, though? Does he still see Paul? Do they work together? I curse Desmond for not having a cell phone. It's so hard to spy on him.

I stop myself mid-thought. I'm being dramatic. Creating problems where there aren't any. So what if Desmond lied about Paul? He didn't want me to assume he was attached. And Stefan was giving me a compliment, as backhanded as it was: I have cured Desmond of his misery. I understand Desmond, and that's something to be celebrated.

Of course, worrying like this doesn't mean I *love* Desmond. Not yet. But maybe I will, eventually. We're on our way to becoming two peas in a pod. We are on our way to finishing each other's sentences.

Now where have I heard that before?

■ ■ ■

It's MRI day, finally. I feel like I've been waiting for years. I need someone to accompany me in case I have a bad reaction from the injectable dye, but I can't imagine asking anyone in my family. I don't want to give them the satisfaction of admitting I, too, believe I'm sick again. I'm not sure they even know that I know the truth about the pool; I doubt Gabby had the balls to tell them. Really, I *should* call my mother and tell her what I know and that I'm never speaking to her again—for a lot of reasons. But maybe it's not worth it. She'll just say they lied for my own good. And she'll have an explanation for the incident in the parking lot, too—she'll say she was trying to protect me. She'll say whatever bullshit she needs to.

I want to bring Desmond to the appointment, but it's crunch time at the convention and he can't take the time off. So I ask Kiki. I have to tell her everything, all the truths I've kept hidden, and I expect her to panic, but instead, she receives it with calm. "It fills in some holes," she tells me. "Now I understand why you're you. Now I understand why you don't remember going to yoga."

"I *didn't* go to yoga that time," I argue with her, but then stop myself. Maybe I *did* go to yoga. Maybe it didn't matter that I didn't remember.

We meet at my house before the appointment. The inside seems unfamiliar when I walk in, and then I realize why: it's clean. There isn't any dust on the Theremin. The baseboards don't have a layer of grime. The place no longer smells like a dying horse.

Kiki's in the kitchen drinking a glass of lemonade. She's in the same rainbow skirt she wore when we met at the writing group, and her hair is tied back with a yellow ribbon. She looks scrubbed, young.

"I had three Elsa parties yesterday," she then grumbles, sinking into a seat at the table. "It's been a nightmare." Then she peers at me. "It's lonely without you in the house!"

"I didn't mean to stay away this long," I tell her. I would like to offer for Desmond to stay here, but the idea of him having a run-in with Steadman nauseates me. It's bad enough I've had to cross paths with him four times at the curiosities shop. Kiki doesn't ask why we haven't come to the house, either. She probably knows.

"So what's Desmond like?" Kiki leans forward, fluttering her lashes. "He's so handsome."

My mouth drops open. "You *think*?"

"Of course. Don't you? He's so . . . swashbuckling. Definitely a step up from Leonidas."

"Leonidas wasn't that bad," I mumble, not that I really know. Thinking about him still freaks me out—I don't like that there are so many blank spaces in my memory about him, but I've decided to think it's a minor blip, a boyfriend obliterated by lack of brain function. I have to believe Leonidas is a good person, a person who worries about me, just like Gabby. I hate, though, that he was in on the who-pushed-Eliza ruse. I still get the crawling feeling that they're all snickering behind my back, or else covertly filling out the forms to send me to the Oaks.

"But Desmond is . . ." I search for adjectives for Kiki, and all at once there are too few and too many. ". . . lovely." I tell her about his role at the convention and his place in Westwood. I describe the dates we've been on, real dates where he shows up with flowers and holds the door for me. I thought I wouldn't be into that sort of thing, but it's quite charming. "He even bought me a gift," I say. "A nineteenth-century baby carriage and two of the scariest kewpie dolls you've ever seen."

Kiki grins. "Classic!" Then she leans closer. "That said, you need to hold on to him. You need to be careful."

I frown. "How so?"

She fiddles with her straw. "Don't go out as much."

"What are you talking about?"

She studies me carefully. "Steadman saw you at this club he likes. Kosmos, I think? You were talking to some guy."

I give her a crooked, incredulous smile. "That's impossible."

"That's what I said, but he was sure it was you. Just watch it, okay? He said Kosmos has this website where they take pictures of the crowd. Don't get snapped in one. I'd hate for Desmond to find out."

"Kiki. There's nothing *to* find out. I haven't been to any of those places."

Kiki looks at me carefully. I can tell what she's thinking. *How do you really know, Eliza, if you can't remember everything else?* But I have a witness. Desmond can vouch for where I've been every night, because every night I've been with him. Except for the few nights when he's had a conference emergency, but even then I'd hung back at the apartment and watched TV. A doorman could corroborate my whereabouts. Or Stefan. Right?

At the imaging center, an assistant smiles at me and hands me a form to fill out. I list that a year ago, I'd been at UCLA for surgery. I list my doctor, Dr. Forney, and his address and phone. Kiki checks her phone while we wait; after its battery dies, we pass the time by watching Rachael Ray force her guest, some actress I've never heard of, make duck ragout with her. There's a lot of fake laughter that makes me feel jittery.

They call my name, and I walk through the door and into a long hall. In a small room, I change into a gown and lie down on the table. They start the IV of dye, which warms my body slightly but otherwise feels like nothing. After a few minutes, I'm led into another room where they slide me into the long, dark, metal tube, the walls closing around me. I wince at the ear-splitting sounds of machinery and play Beethoven's Ninth loudly in my head. The lyrics and melody of a 311 song I may have listened to with Leonidas come back to me in a rush, and I let the whole thing play out, realizing I know every word. I feel an itch coming on, and I'm about to scratch it, when I hear a voice: *Don't scratch. They'll be mad at you. They'll sequester you to the ICU for this.*

My eyes open wide inside the tube. The clicking sounds of the MRI machinery rush back, loud and urgent, as though I've woken from a dream. The ICU. But *I* was never there. Dot was, as a child. So why was the memory so vivid? Why did I suddenly and distinctly remember the pull in my chest as a nurse pushed my wheelchair down the hall? Where was I going? Is it just a dream? I follow the memory to its end. I remember glancing at my face in a mirror as we passed. There's a child staring back. Eight, nine years old—a knockoff Wednesday Addams—but it's my eyes, my face. Only, there's no way. I wasn't in a wheelchair at nine.

Was I?

Count backward from ten . . .

The banging sound stops, and the silence is earsplitting. Slowly, the tube moves, ejecting me. I blink in the beady overhead lights. The nurse smiles above me. "We're all done. You do okay in there?"

"Yes," I think I say. I feel my arms, my legs, and my stomach to make sure they're still intact. I want my body to feel different, smaller, lighter, more slippery. Like that of an arachnid that's just fumbled out of its egg, blind and ignorant to the world into which it's just been thrown. But it's just the same old me.

■ ■ ■

It's Sunday. I am lying on Desmond's bed, my ear against his stomach. It is dusk; lavender light has cloaked the room. I can hear the gurgle of his digestive juices. I can also hear him turning the pages. I'm letting him read *The Dots*. It's time. The book comes out in two days.

He is focusing so intently on the page it's as if he is turning each of the words upside down and shaking them for change. I want to get up and go somewhere else—it is torture, lying here, *watching* him read, trying to gauge what he's thinking—and yet I cannot move. I can't go into another room and pretend to occupy my thoughts. I want to know immediately, the very moment he finishes.

Finally, he marks a page, closes the book with a slap, and looks at me. "Well."

"Well?" I practically shriek. "That's all you can say? *Well?*"

"Well." He runs his hand over his hair. "It's . . . exigent. Like a pandemic."

"Is that bad?"

He gathers me in his arms. "Of *course* not. That's good. I'm not quite at the end," he adds. "But I feel like it's going to be tragic."

I nod. He is right.

"But in an apropos way. Shakespearean, yes?"

"Don't compare me to Shakespeare." I let out a sigh. "So why does my mother hate it? Did I make the mother too unyielding? Too much of a bitch?"

"It's definitely raw, but she's not that bad. I mean, she's sort of absent, she's sort of angry, but she clearly cares."

"So why did my mother get so offended?"

"I guess it hit too close to home for her." He scratches his chin. "Roxanne's going to ask you that, you know. How your family is taking it, if you have any regrets."

I nod. *Dr. Roxanne* is in two days, and I'm no less anxious about it. I'm afraid she's going to ask cutting questions. Or I'm afraid she's going to say, to her live audience, that she didn't like the book. I'm afraid of explaining why I wrote it. It's a stupid concept, surely—a girl with a brain tumor who has a crazy aunt. The only reason it's getting buzz is because I made a fool of myself by being pushed into a pool.

Desmond seems to sense my panic and clutches my hands. "You don't have to go on the show, you know. Seriously. I'll still think you're the most amazing vixen ever, even if you don't. Don't let the people you work with push you around. Do this on your own terms."

"Posey would kill me. Laura already said that if I did, she'd probably never sign me for another book."

"But I thought you didn't want to write another book."

"I probably don't, but I at least want the opportunity."

Later that night, I wake up alone in a puddle of pillow-drool. I sit up and squint at the digital numbers on the clock: 10:30. There are soft murmurs in the hall, Desmond and Stefan. They're whispering conspiratorially, maybe about something interesting. I slide off the bed and tiptoe to the door, half because I have to pee, half because I'm curious.

"I don't think that's a good idea," Desmond is saying. He sounds upset.

"Why not?" Stefan's voice. "What do you even know about her? All those . . ." He speaks even quieter, and I can't hear.

"But it's a big deal," Desmond says. "Isn't there something else?"

His voice trails off. Stefan responds, but the air-conditioning comes on then, rattling loudly. I press my ear to the door, but the voices have been drowned out. I think of Stefan leering over me the other day. *My brother's a fucking freak. We all know it. He knows it.* And the lie he told me about Paula. Or was it just an omission?

The door shoots open, throwing me backward. I scuttle to the bed, pretending I wasn't listening, but Desmond has come in too quickly and I probably have a guilty look on my face. "Oh," he says, stopping short. "You're . . . up."

"Yep. Just now!" I hate the chirpiness in my voice.

Desmond walks slowly to the bedside table and turns on a lamp. His expression is guarded and suspicious. My gut burns with acid.

"What were you talking about out there?" I blurt out. "Was it about me?"

Desmond's face tightens. He gets a look of annoyance I've never seen before. "What makes you think that?"

"I . . ." My hand rushes to my chest. "What were you talking about, then?"

"It doesn't matter." He opens a drawer.

"Why can't you tell me?"

He turns. His eyebrows knit together. "Are we really having this discussion, Eliza?"

"I just . . ."

"It was boring work stuff. Stefan is helping with some of the convention details." He pulls out the blue silk pajamas he loves to wear and begins to pull them on. Halfway through the process, his shirt off, his hairless nipples winking at me, his eyes meet mine. "You aren't *that* kind of girl, are you? The kind who's suspicious about even her boyfriend? I like that you question things, but you don't need to question *me*. You strike me as way more highly evolved than that."

I know I should smile back, too, but I can't make my lips do it. I feel wrapped very tight in invisible bandages. The shaking has extended to my arms and stomach. *Come on,* I tell myself. *Snap out of it. Stop this right now. You have nothing to worry about.*

I swallow down the paranoia. "Of course I'm highly evolved. I'm Darwin's dream."

Desmond seems to visibly relax. "That you are." He leans down, and his hair tickles my cheeks. "That you are."

ELIZA

IT'S TWO DAYS later. Book release day. *Dr. Roxanne* time.

I'm at my house. Desmond is on his way here to meet me, and we're going to go together to *Dr. Roxanne* in a limo the studio is sending. I'm trying to figure out the answers to the questions the studio has sent. *What inspires you? Does any of* The Dots *stem from your real life? What's your writing process?* I am trying to decide whether I outlined this book or went with the flow instead of freakishly writing it in one vomitus go, start to finish, with barely any shifting of scenes. I am trying to come up with a creation myth on how this story came about, but really, it just poured out of me, maybe always there.

But amid all this, something is bothering me. There's a detail that just doesn't make sense. I can't believe that Gabby was at the bar at the Tranquility. Or, rather, she might have come in at the end, and she might have pushed me into the pool, but I spoke to someone else at the bar, too. It was that someone else who riled me into hysterics.

I can feel it. I *know* it.

I hate that my brain is fighting against what Gabby told me. I hate that reality has begun to shift again, like sand. I want to think that my tumor, surely there, is playing tricks on me, fucking with my happiness, but I know that isn't true. There was someone else at that bar. More happened at the Shipstead than Gabby's saying. Whatever happened before, whoever I was talking to before Gabby came in, *that's* why I was so panicked when she found me.

And that's who I need to be afraid of.

After all, who filmed that video of me in my hospital room? I'd asked Gabby, and she swore up and down it wasn't her—she'd gone back to the hotel for the night, and my parents could corroborate the alibi. And who do I keep seeing lurking about? And who sent my novel to my parents? A different person might have let this go. You could say I chase strife and welcome complication. And yet, after I dial Gabby for the seemingly zillionth time and yet again get her voice mail—so she's avoiding me? She knows that I know there's more to the story?—I find myself dialing the Shipstead bar again and asking for the elusive Richie.

It's the Aussie who answers, and I swear when he hears my voice he starts to snicker. I hang up and toss my phone to the mattress. But then I grab it again and type in the website for the Tranquility resort—if Aussie is lying about Richie being there, then maybe I can file a complaint. A picture of a stucco archway surrounded by succulent desert flowers serves as the resort's homepage. I consider the navigation options, settling on "amenities." A list of the bars within the resort pops up along with pictures of each. I click on the Shipstead and narrow my eyes at the familiar swaths of polished wood and the rigging ropes. No list of bartenders, though. Not even a name of a manager to whom I can grouse.

Still, I can just ask for a manager of the hotel and go from there, right? I click on a link marked *Management*, and pictures pop up. When I notice the face in the upper right-hand corner, my gaze brushes over him fast, the way it does when I see him in real life. But then I blink and look again. I'm confused. This guy belongs *here,* in Burbank. Not grinning in a suit next to a bunch of old guys in a photo titled *From Our Family to Yours.*

It's Andrew. Dirty, Random-Sex Andrew from the whorehouse bar down the street.

I click on the photo to make it larger, gawking at his oily grin. How has Andrew snuck into a photo of the resort's founding family? Is this some kind of joke?

There is no caption on the picture, but I notice a link titled *Legacy.* I am led to a page about how the Tranquility resort was built by the Cousins-Glouster family of hoteliers and how it's the Cousins-Glouster family's pride and responsibility to keep their resorts intimate, luxurious, and exclusive. There is a roster of Cousins-Glousters who keep the resorts afloat: *George Cousins, second generation,* balding and paunchy and pink-faced. *Marvin Cousins-Glouster, second generation,* taller and handsome, with an overbite. More old men, an incredibly old man, and then *Andrew Cousins-Glouster, third generation,* with that lascivious prep-school smile and that scar cutting across his eyebrow that I have focused on quite a few times while having a post-coital cigarette.

I gawk for a few still moments. *Andrew?* As in the guy who always buys the cheapest whiskey the bar sells? As in the doofus who wants to be part of a TV writing staff? An heir to a hotel fortune? A cog in a *From Our Family to Yours?* How did I not know about his connection to the Tranquility? *Did* I know?

The front door creaks open, scaring me. I run to the landing, almost expecting it to be Andrew, somehow instantly knowing what I've figured out. But it's Desmond, fresh from work, carrying clothes he's going to change into in a garment bag.

"Hello, mistress," he trills, dropping a kiss on my forehead. "I'm going to take a quick shower and then we'll go, yes? Are you excited?"

"Uh, sure." I take too long to answer.

Desmond frowns and steps back. "What's the matter?"

Don't tell him, a voice in my head begs. I chew on the side of my hand and make a distracted *mm.*

He starts to massage my shoulder. "If you're nervous about the show, don't be. You're going to be great."

I dig my nails into my leg. I just can't hold it in. "Say you just found out someone you know has insider knowledge on the Tranquility. Maybe access to security cameras. And say this person is more than likely down the street at the wine bar that used to be a brothel right now. Would you maybe call that person, or pop in quickly, and ask some questions?"

Desmond sinks onto the couch. "Why does it matter?"

"But it would prove unequivocally what happened."

"But didn't Gabby tell you what happened?"

"Maybe not everything. Maybe there's more. I think Gabby only came at the end. She might be lying about what else I saw . . . or she might not know. If I had a video feed, something, I would know for sure what all went on."

Desmond looks shaken. "But didn't that guy you were talking to from the police say the cameras had been out during that time because of a storm?"

"So we ask a bartender. Just something to prove I spoke to Gabby and only Gabby."

"But why does it *matter*? Gabby's the one who pushed you in the pool, right?"

"Yes, but I want the whole truth. I want to make sure . . ." I'm not sure *what* I want to make sure of. I've lost so many memories; it's puzzling why I'm so driven to get this particular one back. Or is it?

"Eliza." Desmond's eyebrows knit together. "You know I totally support you on unlocking your memories. But maybe today isn't the right time. Your mind should be clear. You should be thinking about being on TV. It's going to be live, after all. You have to be at your best."

"I know, but it's not like this would take very long, and . . ."

"Don't," he advises. "This seems like sabotage. It's like you're setting yourself up for failure. Besides, isn't the limo picking us up soon?"

"Yeah, but I just thought . . ." I trail off and sigh.

"Drop it. At least for today. If it's still bothering you tomorrow, we can ask this guy. But for today, just focus on being on the show. Focus on everyone loving your book. Focus on being amazing, because you *are* amazing."

I lay my head on the couch pillow. Desmond is right, of course. Why can't I just be happy? Why can't I just accept what I've been told? Why am I so dreadfully mistrustful?

"I'm going to take a shower," Desmond says again. "I'll be out in a second, okay?"

He goes upstairs, and soon I hear the water start to run. Desmond hums a minstrel song he has on auto-repeat in his car. I lay on my back for a moment, trying to relax, but it feels like there are pins driving into my skin.

I rise, walk to the second floor, and look out the window. From up here, I have a perfect view of the bar down the street. There are a few cars in the parking lot. One of them might be Andrew's. But even if he's there, there's no guarantee he knows the information I need. And just going there, just risking seeing him, opens a can of worms I'd rather keep closed. I know what Andrew's terms will be for giving me the information. I don't want to have to be faced with that decision.

Then again, I don't want to spend the rest of my life wondering.

My phone pings with a new email. I glance at it, eager for distraction. It's from the Imaging Center. *Your MRI results are in.* I frown. It's a whole day early. And what, the place is so cheap they don't have someone call you and personally tell you you're dying?

I peer down the hallway, knowing I should wait until Desmond is out of the shower, but there's no way I can keep the email closed for another second. I select it, then open the attached PDF. At the top, it says my name. In the radiologist's notes, most of it is medical mumbo-jumbo, but I know which line to look for: the radiologist's impressions at the bottom. I blink several times, unsure of what I'm looking at. *No abnormalities.*

It can't be possible.

I check my watch—half-past four, meaning the office is probably still open. I dial the number, and a nurse answers. "This is Eliza Fontaine, and I just got some results that I think have been switched with someone else's," I say in a rush.

The nurse asks me to spell my name slowly and give my date of birth. I hear keyboard tapping. After she asks me to respell my name and go through about fifteen different security indicators to prove that I am, indeed, Eliza Fontaine, she says, "Ah, yes. An MRI. We sent the results today. What did your PDF say?"

"Negative. Normal."

"Well, it *is* negative. The radiologist signed off on it—I see it right here. So there you go."

"But that's not possible."

She laughs incredulously. "I'm sorry?"

"The tumor I had a year ago isn't gone. I can tell. I'm having symptoms. I can practically feel it inside me. I really think my scan got confused with someone else's."

"I don't think so . . ."

"Look, can I just speak to a doctor?"

"Hold on," the nurse says, a slight groan in her voice. She clicks off. Muzak lilts into my ear. I rub my fingertips against my silken pillow. Desmond is still humming in the shower. I feel a pang in my head and touch a spot between my eyes. I want it to be the tumor, I realize. I want it to still be lurking in there, messing things up.

"Miss Fontaine?" A man's voice. "This is Doctor Geist, the radiologist on staff. How can I help you?"

I go through my spiel, explaining my tumor and surgery. I try not to sound hysterical—or like I completely mistrust doctors. After

I'm done, there's a silent gap. "Where did you say you had surgery earlier this year, Miss Fontaine?"

"I wrote it down on my forms. UCLA."

"With which surgeon?"

"Doctor Forney. He's on staff there."

"No, he's a neurologist. I mean your neurosurgeon. Who operated on you?"

"I don't . . ." I'd been so out of it. A guy with glasses, maybe? "Isn't it in a chart?"

"That's the thing. We tried to get your chart from UCLA so we could compare your new scan to an old scan. But you *have* no chart with UCLA."

"*What?*"

"You have no recent records at UCLA. Certainly nothing about brain surgery."

My legs go numb. As do my cheeks. I feel dizzy, too, so I slide off my bed to the ground until my butt touches the carpet. "What about the neurologist I just mentioned? Doctor Forney?"

"He says he's never heard of you."

I press my hand into the carpet fibers. Hadn't I spoken to Dr. Forney before? Wasn't that who discharged me from the hospital? "But I was at UCLA. I *remember*."

"We checked the system, Miss Fontaine. We have access to UCLA's records, and they do a good job with patient data. There's no record of you there."

I pinch the skin on the top of my hand hard, hoping this will steady my memory and bring back the right details. But I can't locate anything. All I remember is the day I left the hospital. My mind was clear. I sat up, swung my legs over the bed, got dressed, and went back to my parents' house.

My parents. They must know, then. They were in the room when I was discharged. They paid all my bills. They can straighten this out. Or *can* they? If they were lying to me about Gabby and the pool, then what *else* are they lying about? After all, why didn't they insist on my getting an MRI when I was in the hospital in Palm Springs? *Because they knew nothing would show up,* a voice in my head tells me. *Because they knew the doctors would say I'd never had surgery in the first place.*

I can't believe I didn't think this through sooner. But maybe I didn't want to. Maybe a deep part inside me urged me to just look the other way.

I shudder with fear. A second fear nestles into me, too, iron-cold and blade-sharp: it was comforting when I thought the errant wiring in my head was what led to my skewed decisions and the memory loss and the recent delusions. So where does this leave me *now*?

Dr. Geist advises me to check my insurance company—perhaps I was at another hospital and have the names confused. But somehow, I know that isn't the case. I hang up and look at the blank screen, then dial my mother's number. She doesn't answer. Heart in my throat, I try Bill, Gabby. Nothing. It's like they know I'm looking for them. It's like they realize I've found out.

But *what* did I find out?

I walk into the hallway and listen to Desmond in the shower. I want to tell him the news, but I'm afraid of what he'll think. Bizarrely, a clear scan is terrible. Because what was that recent freak-out at the Tranquility about, then? The one where I ran from the bar, from Desmond, and started trembling in the lobby? If my messed-up brain wasn't synthesizing the fear, then what the fuck was making me afraid?

I try my family again, blam, blam, blam, all in a row, but still they don't pick up. I need answers, though. I need the answer to *something*. I walk to the window again and stare at the bar down the block. All the same cars are still there. The neon Budweiser bottle blinks in the window.

It's not a good idea. I stare down Olive, then at the Batman symbol superimposed over the WB water tower. It's really, *really* not a good idea. I squeeze my eyes shut once more, begging the memory out of me. *Any* memory. But nothing comes. There's only darkness, a blank hospital, a drunken day, "Low Rider," and a few useless words.

From The Dots

On a Monday morning, Dot was getting ready to go to class. Her head hurt, but not because she'd drunk with Dorothy last night. She hadn't seen her aunt in a few weeks, actually—not since what her mother told her. Instead, the night before, she'd nursed a bottle of Stoli Vanil in her dorm room, draining almost the whole thing by herself. She knew this was self-destructive behavior, but she was hoping, praying, that drowning her system with that much alcohol would change what was real. What she *feared* might be real. And also, she just liked the escape.

Marlon eyed her soberly from the chair in her dorm room. A lot had happened in the past month. At first, things had been chilly between them. Dot didn't confront him about how he'd betrayed her confidence; instead, she conveyed her fury by giving him one-word responses, or by taking the last chocolate-chip cookie in the dining hall (the only real edible thing there), or by denying him blowjobs. He kept trying to bring it up—"I'm sorry," and "What happened?" and "I just love you so much. I was just so worried"—but Dot would always change the subject, loudly solving the puzzle on

Wheel of Fortune, or yelling out a quote about Hinduism from their World Cultures textbook.

But then she looked up Dorothy's past. Before, when Dorothy was missing, Dot had always concentrated on looking into what she was up to in the present—she'd always taken Dorothy's stories about her history at face value. She went to the largest branch of the public library, a place she hadn't been to in years. There, after hours of searching, she found a photo of Dorothy in a *Life* magazine article about a place called Bridgewater Hospital.

The article was dated January 14, 1979. It featured a photo of Dorothy—and it was *definitely* her, with her porcelain skin and almost identical haircut and that saucy little upturned mouth— sitting in a faded gray gown in what looked to be a music room. The picture was blurry, and she wasn't looking at the camera—it didn't even seem like she knew the camera was there. According to the article, Bridgewater was a psychiatric hospital in Menlo Park, California. Some say it was the inspiration for *One Flew Over the Cuckoo's Nest.* The article was about the deinstitutionalization of mental hospitals to community mental health services, though Bridgewater, at that time, was still very much an isolated institution whose staff used manipulative and coercive methods. Most of the patients in the hospital had severe mental incapacities and were considered dangerous and unsuitable in other hospital environments.

So there was that.

Dot kept searching. Wading through the records for the county of Los Angeles, she found a protection order filed with the court against one Dorothy Banks. Protected in that order was her niece, Dot, and, surprisingly, Dot's mother. Dot sifted through documents to see if the order had ever been lifted or revoked or whatever you'd call it in legal-ese, but she found no record.

Dot felt furious. She didn't want her mother to be right about any of this. She also felt devastated. If her mother *was* right, then who was she to her aunt? A pawn? Did Dorothy ever love her?

Did Dorothy love anything? Or perhaps this was all some sort of complicated ruse. What if it was her mother who was pulling the strings here? Perhaps creating a story of Munchausen Syndrome by Proxy, and convincing the nurses of it, too, and getting Dorothy sent away, and drafting that restraining order out of spite? But there was the record of the strychnine. Could her mother have drugged Dot *herself*, and then pinned it on her sister?

What was the truth? Who could she trust?

She didn't know what to do. She found herself spinning into violent rages over so very little—a guy who cut her off on the freeway, a snappish sales clerk, how the Q button on her keyboard kept sticking. She threw books. She didn't like this new version of herself. Finally, two nights ago, she told Marlon everything she'd found, including her mother's accusations. How they matched up, dreadfully, with her experience in the hospital when she was young. In her dreadful research, she'd found out that in California, she was still well within her statute of limitations of bringing what her aunt had done to her to trial. Or her *mother* bringing it to trial, if it came to that.

And maybe it would come to that. Her mother had called the police, after all. Had they gone to the Magnolia? Was Dorothy in jail? Dot kept scouring the news, but she found nothing. Wouldn't a Munchausen story be interesting to the local public? A glamorous ex-socialite behind bars for torturing her niece? Finally, she called the Magnolia Hotel and asked if Dorothy Banks was still staying there. "No, she checked out several weeks ago," a concierge said. But was that true, or was the Magnolia protecting her?

That morning, as she was nursing her hangover, a hangover that felt authentic and nothing like the obliterating fog that hung over her on the mornings she woke up in Dorothy's suite, a knock sounded at her dorm room door. Her boyfriend looked up but didn't stand. Dot walked calmly to the foyer, but a few feet away, she froze. Dorothy was on the other side. Dot just knew.

She turned back to her boyfriend, her eyes wide. Her heart was thumping in her throat. He cocked his head. And then: "Dot?" Her voice. "Darling, can you let me in?"

Her boyfriend paled and half stood. Dot licked her lips and motioned for him to remain still.

The pounding began. "I know you're in there. I saw you through the window."

Dot met her boyfriend's horrified gaze across the room.

"I miss you, darling," came Dorothy's voice. "What's going on between your mother and me is our business—she shouldn't be putting you in the middle of it. I just want to see you for a moment. I have something for you."

Dot was biting down so hard on her knuckles—she knew there would be teeth marks in her skin. Finally, she walked to the door and opened it a crack. Dorothy stood on the other side. Her face was drawn, and her hair was shot with gray. There were bags under her eyes and wrinkles corrugating her forehead and around her mouth. She smelled sour and unwashed. A mink stole hung limply on her shoulders. It was as though she hadn't slept or eaten or done her makeup since the last time Dot had seen her. Dot wondered, suddenly, if she had fled from the Magnolia—from the police. Maybe she'd been living in her car. It was probably a risk for her to be here.

Relief flooded Dorothy's face when Dot opened the door, and she threw her arms around Dot's neck. "Oh, darling," she breathed. "I missed you so much."

Dot let her arms hang at her sides. Her heart was pounding very hard. "Um, I have class soon."

"I understand. But here." Dorothy rooted around in her tote and handed Dot something wrapped in red paper. Dot went to tuck it away, but Dorothy bobbed her head, indicating she open it now. Slowly, Dot pulled the paper off. Inside was a dusty copy of *The Bell Jar* by Sylvia Plath.

"It's a first edition, first printing," Dorothy explained. "A collector's item."

Dot raised the book to her nose. It smelled like mustiness and paper, an old bookstore. She'd read *The Bell Jar* already. The choice felt oddly significant, eerily canny, like Dorothy knew what Dot had found out about her.

"Have dinner with me," Dorothy whispered, clutching Dot's hand. Her fingers felt cold and bony. "Tonight. Please, darling. At our place. Please, and I'll explain what's going on. I'll tell you why your mother is doing this. I need you to hear my side."

"Aren't you worried about the police?"

"Oh, honey, there's no concern about the police. Your mother . . . that was just to scare you. And me. Please. You won't be doing anything wrong. Please meet me. It's very important."

Dot could feel her boyfriend shift his weight in the chair. A flare of pain pinged in her head, then fizzled out. "Okay," she whispered. "I'll see you there."

She shut the door and turned back to her boyfriend, her knees shaking. Her boyfriend gawked at her. "What the hell is wrong with you? We should call the cops right now!"

"No, I have an idea. A way to prove if it's actually happening. And if it's true, then we can go to the police."

She told him the idea. He pressed his hands over his eyes and shook his head. "No, Dot. No. You can't do that." He went through all the reasons why. Dot nodded. Maybe he was right. It probably was dangerous, even illegal. What they should do is wait until Dorothy came to them again at the dorm. Then they would call 911. Dot's boyfriend said he would stay with her every night to protect her. He would make sure she was never alone here.

Dot's boyfriend's watch went off. It was time for him to go to class; her too. "You promise you won't see her later?" he begged her as they parted at the quad.

"I promise," Dot answered.

His expression was guarded, haggard, and sad. He pressed her little hands between his big ones just as Dorothy had done. "All right. If you need anything, call me. I'll keep my phone on. I'll check it every ten minutes."

"Okay."

"And I'll see you in eight hours, right?"

She nodded. "I'll be here."

But eight hours was a long time. Dot tried to wait it out, she really did. Seven hours in, she changed her mind and left campus. If she didn't go, if she didn't try her plan, she would always wonder.

She needed to know the truth.

ELIZA

I PUSH THE DOOR open to the bar. Andrew is on his regular stool, thank God. He jack-in-the-boxes up as he sees me. His eyes gleam hungrily, traveling up my legs, around my waist. My heart hammers in my chest, and though this goes against every instinct I have, I slither toward him and smile.

"I have a proposition for you," I say, sliding into the stool next to him.

"Don't you always," he answers with a smarmy smile.

I tell him I know who he is. I explain what happened to me, what I want. Andrew seems surprised. "*You're* the girl who fell in the pool?" he says. "My dad said you were pretty fucked up."

I choose to ignore this. "I'm looking to talk to the bartender who was at the Shipstead that night. It's important. I want to know who I was talking to at the bar."

Andrew stares at the popcorn machine in the corner. He sits back on the stool and takes a long sip of his drink. The Rolling Stones rock through us, the bass jacked so high my teeth ache. He drums on the side of his leg, then taps the air as though he's hitting an imaginary high-hat. He looks at me for approval, and I obligatorily laugh. I hate that I have to laugh. I hate that I need him, and I hate that I have stooped to asking this of him.

Finally, after letting me twist in the wind long enough, he says, "I can probably get that sort of information. If you're willing to . . ." He juts his chin toward the bathroom.

"Make the call first," I demand. "*Then* we'll discuss."

Andrew leans back a little, suddenly wary. But I don't care if he's afraid of me. Maybe it's a good thing.

Sighing, Andrew pulls a cell phone out of his pocket and dials a number. "Chris?" he says after a pause. "Hey! Andy." (*Andy*? I'm struck, too, by how *smooth* his voice sounds. Assured and assertive.) "Yeah, man. I'm good. Listen, can you give me the Shipstead schedule for . . ." He looks at me. "Four weeks ago?"

I nod.

"Four. Well, four and a few days. It was on a Saturday. Shipstead. Yep—I'm looking to see who was on Saturday night."

"It was Richie," I say out loud. I knew *that*.

Andrew pauses, listening. He hangs up and looks at me. "Richie. Look at you."

"Yes, but I want to *talk* to him."

Andrew groans, but he dials another number. I listen to him talking to someone else this time and explaining who he's trying to reach. After a minute, Andrew asks me my phone number, the first time he ever has. He repeats it into his phone, then hangs up. "Richie will call you in an hour."

"An *hour*?"

"That's the best I can do. His boss tried to reach him, but he didn't pick up. But he's working tonight, so he'll be at the bar in an hour. Then he'll call you."

"Can I at least get Richie's number in case he *forgets* to call me?"

Andrew's smile is the same smarmy one I saw on the Tranquility website. "Sorry. I didn't happen to get it."

"Can you call back?"

"Liza, he *said* he'd call. Don't be such a freak."

Then he reaches for my waist, wanting what I've offered in exchange. I recoil, curling my fingers into a fist.

"No fucking way."

I slide off the stool fast. I hope it's the last time I ever see Andrew. The bar is more crowded than when I came in; people stare at the baseball game on TV. Brian the bartender hands out shots; his gaze meets mine as I snake toward the door. He yells my name, saying something I can't make out.

"What?" I ask, inching closer to him.

"Someone's here for you," he says, jutting a finger toward the front.

My head swivels to the window. The Batmobile is outside. My heart jumps into my throat. Then I see Desmond sitting at a bistro table next to the Lotto machine. I stop and try to think of something to say, but my mind has gone terrifyingly blank.

"Hi" is all I can muster.

"Eliza." He laces his fingers together. "I thought you weren't going to chase this today."

I run my hands over my hair. "I know. I'm sorry. I just knew I could check quickly, so . . ." I shrug. Offer an apologetic smile. Out of the corner of my eye, I can see Brian the bartender glowering at me, probably ready to call me a cunt under his breath.

"Well, did you find anything out?" Desmond asks.

"Nope. So let's get out of here, okay? You were right. I should be thinking about the show. And the limo's going to show up soon."

Desmond frowns at someone behind me. When I turn, Andrew is there. He's not standing particularly close, but his skin smells like my perfume. There's also a huge hickey on his neck—not from me, but it could *look* like it was from me, it's so red and fresh.

I notice Desmond's gaze on the hickey, too. My cheeks blaze. *Go away,* I will Andrew silently. Instead, he leans even closer, cupping his hands to my ear so I can hear him over the noise. "Found this on the floor, Liza."

He presses something into my palm. I open it up and stare. It's a gold earring. I touch my ears. One earring hangs jauntily, but the other earlobe is bare. To my horror, Andrew touches my cheek and adds, "Richie will call you in an hour."

And then he disappears into the crowd. Nauseated, trembling, I turn back to Desmond. I try and smile innocently, but all at once I can tell what Desmond's worked out. His face has gone pale. He blinks his eyes rapidly. He hops off the stool and backs away from me, all the way out the door to the Batmobile at the curb.

"Desmond." I follow him and touch his sleeve. He wrenches it away. "What's wrong?"

"What's *wrong*?" Desmond spits, his gaze momentarily meeting mine. His eyes are black. I've never seen them so narrowed. Shaking his head, he walks to the opened driver's side, falls into the seat, and pulls the door down. I try the passenger side, but he's locked it.

"Desmond!" I cry, pulling at the handle. "Come on! Open up! It's not what it looks like."

Desmond stares at me through the glass. I press my hand to the window. The glass is so cold, like it's been sitting in a refrigerator. Which doesn't make sense, given the late-day heat. I can think about only this, because everything else is too difficult and too terrible to ponder.

Desmond starts the engine. Then he rolls down the window. "Desmond," I say desperately, feeling a whoosh of air-conditioning sweep my cheeks. "Desmond, *please*. I'm sorry. There's something wrong with me. Something huge. My MRI scans were negative. I might not have even *been* in the hospital. So I need to talk to you. We need to figure this out. You said you'd help me, remember?"

A few beats go by. Desmond's eyes are still so dark. Finally, he ducks his head. "No, Eliza. I can't help you. From now on, you're on your own."

From The Dots

M&F had had a staff change in the few weeks Dot had stayed away. The baby-faced bartender was gone, and a pudgy, surly Scot had taken his place. There was a thin, dark-haired guy in charge of the waitstaff, and a waitress took orders. She wore a men's white shirt, same as the boys, with long pants and wingtips. When she gave a special to the table next to Dot and Dorothy, she spoke in a deep, masculine voice. Dot focused on the waitress as a way to dispel her nervousness. She pictured the waitress changing into a dress later, slipping out of those clunky shoes, and going somewhere with her boyfriend or girlfriend. Living an easy, uncomplicated life.

Bernie was still there, though, and he swept over to their table first thing and made a huge deal out of how his two favorite ladies were back.

"Drinks on me," he said lavishly. He didn't seem skittish in the least about Dorothy being there. Dot looked around; there were no cops barricading the door.

"I'll have whatever she's having," Dot called out, faking joy.

Dorothy raised a surprised eyebrow. "Two stingers, then, please."

As Bernie mixed the drinks, Dot tightened and untightened her calf muscles, desperate for release. Dorothy seemed nervous, too, unfolding her napkin and then folding it up again, rooting around in her purse, twisting her earring on her lobe.

"I'm glad you came, darling," she said. "After that last incident— well, I wasn't so sure. I don't know what your mother's told you, but it's all lies."

Dot shrugged. "She's just worried about me."

Dorothy pressed her fingers to her temples. "She never understood me. Never at all." She glanced at Dot, her face pained. "Lucky for me, though, there was Thomas." She stares morosely at the jungle-animal mural behind us. "He was an angel. He had the sweetest disposition when he wanted to. And boy did he love his mama." She lowered her head. "The day he died, something inside me died, too."

Every cell in Dot's body went very still. "And was that why you had to go to Bridgewater Hospital?"

The skin around Dorothy's mouth slackened. "Pardon?"

"I saw a picture of you there. A *Life* article."

Bernie set down the drinks and then backed away. Dorothy stared into her cocktail glass, then picked off the mint garnish and dropped it to her napkin. "So you've done some digging, I see. A regular investigative journalist."

"I looked you up because I was afraid there was something I didn't know."

"And you found it." Dorothy dabbed at her mouth. "Yes. I went there after Thomas passed. I needed some . . . time. To think. To get away from my life."

Dot nodded. Okay. Maybe that wasn't so bad. It was the best possible reason to have gone to a place like that. A good answer, an understandable answer.

"Losing a child is the worst tragedy one can experience. And then consider how he died—well. I just felt so . . . *empty*. So alone.

I suppose I should have explained to your mother, though, because since then, she's worried there's something *wrong* with me." Dorothy met Dot's gaze, and Dot must have been unconsciously nodding, because she added, "It's not true, though. There's no more wrong with me than there is with anyone else in this world." She laced her hands together. "God, how I've wished to tell you for so long. But I was afraid you'd be afraid of me. I was afraid you'd judge me without asking questions, just like your mother did." She raised her glass in a toast. "Anyway. To being strong enough to tell my wonderful niece the truth."

"To being strong," Dot answered, touching her glass to her aunt's. She tried her hardest to take a hearty sip of the minty-smelling liquid, but Dot had always thought stingers tasted like the gum one chewed to cover up the bite of bile.

"Your mother is prejudiced about my time at Bridgewater," Dorothy went on. "And then, when I left you, she thought it was just a further example of something wrong with me. She said to me, *You're breaking her heart if you leave.* And then, a few years later, *If you come back, you'll just confuse her. You're a bad influence.*"

"Wait," Dot interrupted. "You spoke to her while you were away?"

Dorothy blinked. "Just to see how you were doing. To make sure you were doing okay. She owed me that."

"And you didn't want to talk to *me*?"

Dorothy set her drink back down and placed her hands flat on the table. Her rings glittered. "Darling, your mother wouldn't let me."

"Why not?"

"Because . . . well, it's complicated."

Dot jiggled her legs under the table. *Restraining order, restraining over.* The document was real, all right. But were the reasons it was drafted real? How could she even *think* such horrible things? Dot's throat caught as she swallowed.

When Dot looked back up, her aunt's smile was composed and endearing. "You look so overwrought. You might want to go to the bathroom and freshen up."

"I'm fine," Dot insisted. She wasn't sure her legs would hold her if she stood.

"Take my word for it," Dorothy said firmly. "You need a little break. Go compose yourself, and then come back and let's have a nice dinner, like we always do."

Like we always do. Dot opened and closed her fist. Maybe this was an opening. An opportunity—for both of them. She shut her eyes, knowing what sort of courage she needed to summon. It was now or never. Slowly, surreptitiously, she lined up her cocktail glass so that it was even with the M initial on the M&F dinner plate. Then she stood, trying not to give anything away in her expression. Her heart was pounding so hard.

"Okay, I'll be back," she said, gathering strength.

The bathroom was a long hallway of black-and-white tile and old-fashioned bronze sinks. Dot grabbed a mint from a bowl on the counter and banged into a stall, slumping on the seat, sucking on the mint until it became a flat, sharp disc. She thought about Dorothy out there, alone with both of their drinks. What was she doing? Nothing . . . or something? In a twisted way, did Dot *want* her to be doing something? After all, a normal aunt wouldn't suit Dot any more than a plain cotton T-shirt from the Gap. Was she fulfilling her own fantasy? But that was silly, too—she was fulfilling no fantasy, because Dorothy wasn't going to follow through with it. She loved Dot. They were soul mates.

A stall door banged, a toilet flushed, and then Dot's mind tipped again. Thomas fluttered into her thoughts. *Yes, it was after Thomas died,* Dorothy had just said about the Bridgewater Hospital. *I just felt so empty. So alone.*

But did Thomas *have* to die?

All of a sudden, Dot pictured the little boy from the photo she'd seen playing baseball with his friends, pretending to make a toy airplane fly by hurling it across the lawn. Then she remembered what Dorothy had said once about how she was sure there was something wrong with Thomas's brain, but the doctors wouldn't listen. She pictured him in a hospital bed, slowly wasting away, slowly growing more and more bipolar. "Doctors are all morons," Dorothy always said. "Morons and crooks. I *knew* he was going to do something like take his own life if we didn't get answers. And then, look—he did."

She almost choked on the mint in her mouth. The similarities were so clear. Dot couldn't believe she'd never seen it before. All this time, she'd felt sorry for Dorothy for having lost Thomas. Maybe it was Thomas she should have felt sorry for instead.

She rolled back her shoulders and emerged from the stall reenergized. Her pupils were very small in the bathroom mirror. Her chest heaved up and down. She used her shoulder to shove the door open and walked into the back hallway. It was empty, but all of a sudden, she thought she heard the tiniest wisp of a breath behind a defunct phone booth. She stood on her tiptoes. The shadows were opaque. Nothing moved.

"Hello?" she called out.

The only sound was the low hum of voices in the dining room. The hair stood on the back of Dot's neck, but she couldn't make out anyone hiding in the depths of the hall. Swallowing hard, she whirled back around toward her table.

Dorothy had her hands folded in her lap, but even from far away, Dot could tell her glass was no longer lined up with the M on the plate. A voice inside her head begged that it could be nothing—maybe Bernie had moved it. But she was starting to ignore that voice more and more.

"Well, you look much better," Dorothy purred as Dot sat. "I always say taking just a moment to freshen up in the restroom does wonders."

Dot nodded and eyed her drink. It didn't look tampered with as far as she could tell, but what was she expecting? Metamucil-like granules floating on top? A color change?

"I ordered for you," Dorothy breezed on. "The burger, mushrooms, no bacon. Medium-rare. Is that okay? Did you want a salad? I got you fries."

"No, fries sound great. Hey, doesn't that guy look exactly like Salman Rushdie?"

Dorothy frowned, then followed her gaze toward the bar. Dot knew she only had seconds before her aunt's attention returned to her. Luckily, they both had drunk about the same amounts of their stingers—unless Dorothy had ordered another. A few quick movements and it was over.

"That looks nothing like him at all," Dorothy said, turning back to their table. "And believe me, I know." She cupped her hands around her drink, seeming none the wiser. Dot almost felt bad for her. She'd just pulled the oldest and possibly stupidest trick in the book on her aunt, and she'd fallen for it.

"You *do* know," Dot said, leaning forward on her elbows salaciously. "Didn't you say you used to party with him?"

Dorothy's eyes twinkled. "Darling, do I have a story for *you*."

Dot sat back to listen. All she had to do now was wait. And try not to inwardly combust.

ELIZA

I CHASE DESMOND'S car for a block, yelling his name. He drives right past my house, but he doesn't stop, making a right at the dead end and looping around the other street in the neighborhood. I can hear the Batmobile's engine growling, but houses block my view. I slap my arms to my sides, baking on the lonely sidewalk. My face blazes with anger for Andrew's petty little stunt. I trusted him— and for what? I haven't yet gotten the information. There probably *is* no information. I was probably blathering on at the Shipstead to myself. Except it's not a tumor that made that mischief—it was just *me.*

An engine hums behind me, and I turn. A limo is waiting at my curb. The driver leans out the window. "Eliza Fontaine?"

"Y-yes."

"I'm Sal. From *Dr. Roxanne.* I've been calling."

I look at my phone, and yes, there are four missed calls from a 310 area code I don't recognize. I can feel sweat running down my back. There's no way I can do *Dr. Roxanne.* I have to cancel. I consult my phone, readying myself to call Laura, who will be furious, and Posey, who will probably start crying or go into spontaneous

257

early labor as a result of her distress. Only, almost comically, my phone is at 1 percent battery life. As I'm looking at it, the thing shuts down.

The car's engine purrs. Sports radio plays softly out of the speakers. "First time on the show?" Sal asks. When I don't answer: "First time on *any* show?"

I make a small squeak of confirmation.

"It'll be all right. Believe me, I've picked up tons of nervous guests in my day. Way more nervous than you—and they do great."

I take the bait and look up. "Anyone I'd know?"

He smiles mysteriously. "I've been sworn to secrecy. Now, you ready to get inside?"

He gets out, opens the back door, and gestures me in. I peer at the interior. Leather-on-leather. An open bottle of Perrier rests in the center caddy. There's a bunch of trashy magazines in the seat pocket.

I do as I'm told and sit stiffly. I don't bother to buckle my seat belt. Maybe we'll get in a crash. Maybe I'll perish. Though unbidden, the incident at the bar with Andrew runs in my head on a continuous loop. I open my palm and realize that the earring Andrew gave back to me is still there; I've been clutching it so hard it's made an impression in my skin. Shakily, I thread it through the hole in my ear. My throat starts to close, and I shut my eyes, wondering where Desmond has gone. If he's ever going to speak to me again. Why I'm always such an asshole. Why I couldn't have just let it go for one day.

"So, you an actress?"

I meet Sal's gaze in the rearview mirror. "An author."

"Yeah? What sort of book? Self-help?"

God, I don't want to talk right now, but his grandfatherly voice gets to me. "Fiction, actually."

"No way! I've always thought I have a book in me. What's it about?"

I poke a finger through a hole in my jeans. Hopefully they'll have clothes for me to change into at the show. *The show.* My chest clenches again. Why am I going through with this?

"Love," I manage to answer. "And having to rewrite your entire past."

"Hey, now I know that firsthand," he says as he merges onto Route 5. "My first wife? Cheating on me through our entire marriage. With—get this—my freaking *brother.*" He chuckles. "All this time I think she's crazy for me. And I think when she says she's got a headache and doesn't want to have sex, she's really got a headache. Now I gotta believe there was no headache. She was just sore from banging Nico. Excuse my language."

I shut my eyes, which the driver interprets as a quick attempt for a nap, for which I'm grateful. When we stop, I look around. *Dr. Roxanne,* I was told, is shot on the CBS lot, but we're in a completely different part of town. Sal puts on his blinker and turns up a long, pretty driveway. *The Magnolia Hotel,* reads an old-fashioned sign that's nestled between a jungle of blindingly green palms.

The hair on the back of my neck rises. "What are we doing *here*?"

"She's shooting on location this week. You ever been to this place? Pretty swanky." He glances at me in the rearview. "Honey, you need some water? You're looking kinda piqued again."

"I'm fine," I think I say, though I can't be sure, because everything has gone muzzy. It's the tumor, I desperately want to think, except I can't think that anymore because it isn't true. Yet this place is awakening parts of me I didn't know were there. I have no knowledge of ever being at the Magnolia Hotel in my life, but somehow I know that the road will bend at the top and two valets will leap out from behind an invisible post—and they do. I also know that when I step out of the car it will smell like orange blossoms—and it does. I know that the valet who greets me—bulbous nose; bristly, wheat-colored hair; trim in his uniform—will have a deep, cranky voice with a slight accent from somewhere in the middle of the country. And look. There he is.

I know this because I wrote him. I wrote about this whole place. But it isn't supposed to be *real.*

"Eliza? Eliza Fontaine?"

My head swims as it turns. A PA in a *Dr. Roxanne* ball cap rushes up. "Thank God you're here. Let's get you to hair and makeup."

The nameless grunt grabs my arm and guides me to a trailer on the other side of the parking lot. In the distance, I can see the tree line that leads to the bungalows. In the late-day heat, the buildings shimmer and dance. I continue to smell that orange-blossom scent even though I don't see a single blossom anywhere. Unconnected brain pathways bang together like the metal balls in a Newton's cradle. I swear I've never been here, but I've *been here.* I looked at plenty of photos of this place online for research for *The Dots*, but once again, my descriptions were so accurate. It's like my fiction made this place real.

In the trailer, everyone talks to me at once. The makeup lady, a small, spidery woman with sad eyes, sits me down and starts caressing me with a powder puff. "Water?" asks a PA wearing heavy perfume. Another PA takes my phone from me and plugs it into a charger. A young, pretty blonde with a headset and a clipboard sidles up next, pumping my hand forcefully.

"Roz Lowry," she says. "It's awesome to meet you. Your agent reached out—I'm so happy we were able to make this work."

"Uh-huh." I try not to sound suicidal. My hand is slick with the lotion from her palms.

"Pretty cool that we're doing this here, huh?" She sweeps an arm out the trailer's tiny window, gesturing to the monstrous hotel structure behind us. It is the color of raw chicken. It is an association I've made before.

Amanda, the makeup artist, has me tilt my head back so she can apply false eyelashes. "So you're going on first," Roz says somewhere above me. "Taylor Swift is on after you, so Roxanne might ask you if you're a Taylor fan, which I hope you reply yes. Then she's going to ask you some pretty standard stuff about yourself. How old you are, where you went to school, that sort of thing. And why you wanted to write the book. You know, the questions we sent ahead of time. Try not to get too complicated with your answers—it's a live taping, so we won't be able to do retakes."

"Uh-huh," I murmur, feeling feathery makeup brushes swipe across my eyelids.

"I just finished your book today, by the way," Roz says. "*Amazing*. And really heartbreaking." She offers a gleam of perfect white teeth.

When my phone, sitting on a counter being charged, bleats, I jolt up. I see another number that I don't recognize, except this one is from Palm Springs. A sharp, hot feeling darts through my chest. I glance at the makeup artist. "Uh, can I take this?"

"Sure thing, honey." She lets me slip out of the chair. "Just make it quick, okay? We're on in about ten."

I walk outside the trailer and start across the parking lot before I pick up. "This Eliza Fontaine?" It's a guy's voice.

"Y-yes . . ."

"This is Darrell from the Tranquility resort. Andrew Cousins-Glouster called us—said you're looking for a security image?"

"That's right." I stare down at my shadow. It slants crookedly across the lawn. I look like I've been dismembered. "At the Shipstead bar." I give him the date I'm looking for.

"Well, unfortunately, I don't have security footage from that night—our cameras were out. But I have Richie on the line from the Shipstead with me, and I think he can shed some light on what you need. Richie?"

"Hey," Richie says, reluctantly, his voice gravelly and cautious.

"Hi." I can feel sudden sweat on my lower back.

"So yeah, Andrew described you, and I remember you. I mean,

sure I do, because of the pool, you know? You were drinking sting-ers, which we rarely make." *Stingers!* "And so was the lady sitting next to you."

"The blonde?" I ask incredulously. There was no way Gabby was drinking stingers. There was no way Gabby was drinking *anything*. My heart rockets. I can almost taste the stinger in my mouth. I can hear, once again, "Low Rider."

"Nah, you met with a blonde, but she came in later. This lady had dark hair, like you."

My mouth opens. "Are you *sure*?" I don't remember that at all.

"Your name's Eliza, right? I made a joke that she looked like your twin. It was like a second Eliza sat down. I called you two the Elizas. Then the black-haired lady looked at you and said something that must have really pissed you off. You looked livid."

"*Please. Stop staring*," I whisper.

"And then she left. And then your friend with the curly hair ar-rived." There's a pause, and a cough. "So, yeah, that's what I've got."

"Thank you, Rich," Darrell breaks in. I'd forgotten he'd been lis-tening. "Miss Fontaine, does this help? I want to make sure you have what you need. Any friend of Andrew's is a friend of ours."

I whisper something that might be a yes or might be a no, and the call ends. I let my phone slide from my fingers; it clatters to the grass. A dark-haired woman. Another me. I'm less shocked than I should be, and that's what frightens me the most.

I root around in my memory, and a few lights come on. I can sense someone sliding into the seat next to me. I'd smelled her drink first, then gazed at the brownish liquid in the triangular glass. I turned and looked, and she was sitting there, next to me, so poised and composed. I'd sucked in a breath.

It was me. Me exactly. My same face. My same body. My same smile. "I've been looking for you," she said. And then: "Please. Stop staring."

My heart isn't pounding anymore. I'm not even sure that it's beating. I've stopped next to a parked Range Rover. When I glance at my face in the window, I see *her*. Her eyes. Her mouth. Her cheekbones. Her skin, even her expression. I whip around, swallowing a scream, and then her name. Except it's my name. And she isn't behind me. She isn't anywhere.

But she was. At that bar. I just don't know who she is.

From The Dots

Dot tried to pay attention as her aunt told her about her partying days with famous writers in New York, but it wasn't easy. Dorothy kept sipping at that stinger, more and more of it disappearing down her throat. Nothing seemed to be happening. So that was a good thing. A very good thing.

But then, at one point, Dorothy leaned on her elbow and gave Dot a soapy smile. "I'm so happy you came out tonight, dear. Have I told you how much I missed you?"

And then Dot saw it. A slump of her aunt's head, her chin slipping off her palm. "Oops," Dorothy said, giggling. Dot took stock of the way her own body felt—she'd drunk half her stinger, but she was still lucid. Her hands weren't shaking. Her vision wasn't doubled.

Her heart cracked inside her chest. So there it was.

Like an old roof that could no longer withstand hurricane-force winds, Dorothy suddenly lost her composure. Her cheeks went from pale to flushed in seconds. Her eyes began to water. Her movements became florid and haphazard. When she smiled, she couldn't quite control her lips. Dorothy stared at her palms as if she'd never seen them before.

Dot glanced around the restaurant, terrified that someone was on to what had happened, but all of the businessmen and doctors and first dates were caught up in their own worlds. She was grateful for Dorothy's paranoid need for concealment. But Dot's expression must have given something away, because when she looked across the table, Dorothy was staring at her in sober understanding.

"What did you do?" her aunt growled.

Dot licked her lips. The stinger had formed a thick coating at the back of her throat.

Dorothy stared at the drink in front of her. It was possible she saw two drinks instead of one, or maybe the drinks were spinning. Then she looked at Dot again. "What. Did. You. Do?"

"What did *you* do?" Dot asked quietly. "That drink was meant for me, not you."

Dorothy's eyes widened. "How *dare* you do this to me?"

"How dare you do it to *me*?"

"Did you know I have cancer?" Dorothy exploded. "Ovarian. I was going to tell you tonight. And now you've done it. You've probably ruined my chances of surviving." She jumped up from the table For a moment, she just stood there, peering around the restaurant, her eyes narrowed on a back hallway that led to the kitchen. Then, clutching her chest, she took off for the back door, the one they always came through.

Dot leapt up, too. She had no idea whether to believe the cancer story or not. But before she followed her aunt, she glanced at the remainder of Dorothy's drink. She plucked it from the table, carried it to the bathroom, and poured the rest of it down the sink. She could feel the bathroom attendant's eyes on her, but she didn't look over. She didn't look at anyone.

Then she went outside.

Dorothy was half in the shadows in the alleyway behind the restaurant, bent over at the waist and making retching noises. She wiped her eyes, stood, and glared at Dot. "What do *you* want?"

"Do you need me to get you a doctor? Do you need your stomach pumped? Before we call the police, that is. Because I *am* going to call the police."

Dorothy blotted her mouth with her sleeve. Her nostrils flared. "You win. You win, Dot."

"It isn't about winning."

"This wasn't what you think. I was trying to help you."

"*How?*"

Dorothy stuck her nose in the air. "Your drink wasn't going to kill you—it was just going to knock you out long enough that I could get you out of this town without you protesting. I was going to get you a doctor. You were going to be fine."

"You expect me to believe that?"

"You should."

"And where were we going to go?"

"Bolivia."

Dot scoffed. "Why *there?*"

"Have you ever been? I spent some time there a few years ago. It's so beautiful. And private."

"I thought you were in Africa."

Dorothy's eyes were glassy. "We were going to have a wonderful life."

"Why do you think I would want to have a wonderful life with you after what you've done?" The alley led to a busy avenue. Cars rushed past, their headlights bright, but she and Dorothy were in a pool of shadows. Dot doubted that a single driver saw them. "And who's to say you wouldn't keep doing this to me? Keep drugging me. Keep poisoning me. All to keep me in your *control.*"

Dorothy looked disappointed. "I'm sorry you see it that way, dear."

"How *else* can I see it? You slap me so that I'll cry and then you can hug me. You poison me so I can get sick and you can take care of me. It's . . . it's *insane.*"

"Clearly you've been listening to your mother. This is exactly the kind of thing she would say. I nursed you back to health, dear. It's not my fault you can't hold your liquor."

"So why not take me to a fucking *hospital?* Why hide me in your room and bring in creepy Doctor Singh whenever I need an IV?"

"Doctor Singh is an old friend, and—"

"Stop talking!" Dot roared. "Just stop, okay? I know what's going on. I've tried to put this puzzle together a million different ways, hoping that *this* isn't the answer, but it's what I keep coming up with every time." She felt tears come to her eyes. "How long have you been hurting me? Did you come back just to hurt me some more? Did you hurt Thomas, too? Did you give him something to make him crazy? Were you the one who shot him?"

Dorothy stepped away from her, her footsteps clumsy and heavy. She had a pinched, cruel smile. "So many questions."

Dot's blood turned cold. Just like that, she knew she was right. "How could you shoot your own child?"

Dorothy rolled her eyes, then turned on her heel and ran across the alley. Her fur trailed behind her like a tail.

"Hey!" Dot cried, running after her.

Dorothy crossed the avenue. On the other side was a little bridge that overlooked the busy freeway below. Under the streetlight, her skin looked gray, and there was a sheen of sweat on her forehead. Dot had never seen her aunt sweat before. Dorothy was also clutching her throat as though she was choking. Her eyes were bulging out, too. Dot was pretty sure she was doing it for show. *She'd* never felt that way all the times she'd been drugged.

"You were going to kill me, too?" Dot cried. "You gave me something to bring on those seizures. Something to make my condition worse. Something that would get you on the cover of *Los Angeles* as the saint who saved her niece's life."

"I can't believe you'd say such a thing," Dorothy sputtered. Her vocal cords sounded pinched. "I would never do that. If it looked like that, it was set up that way."

"By whom?"

"The doctors. Those nurses. And your mother. Oh God, most definitely your mother. They all had it in for me. They had it in for me from the beginning."

"No, they *didn't*."

Dorothy staggered to the overpass barrier. She curled her fingers over the ledge, peering into the traffic. "They hated me. All of them hated me. Wouldn't let me in. *No one* would let me in. But I had one over on them. They were all so stupid." Saliva spewed from her mouth. Her head lolled on her neck. Maybe this was the real, true Dorothy, Dot thought with a pang. Maybe the woman she'd seen and known had been an elaborate act. A look-alike.

"It's why we've had to be incognito," Dot persisted. "You're not supposed to be here. You're not supposed to be out with me. You could get arrested."

"Yes, because of your moth-*er*." Dorothy rolled her eyes. "Have I told you that she was a pill even as a child?" She broke off and clutched her throat, making a gagging sound. Her mouth opened wide. Dot watched as she tried to draw in a breath. The color began to drain from her face. Dot wasn't sure how Dorothy could fake *that*.

"Dorothy?" Dot asked tentatively, taking a small step toward her. Now her aunt was gasping. Her eyes rolled back toward her skull. She staggered backward toward the overpass railing. Her legs started to crumple as though her bones had been removed. She grappled for her throat. She was just supposed to pass out, Dot thought. Like Dot always did. This poison wasn't supposed to make her lose function. It wasn't supposed to kill her.

Dorothy slumped against the guardrail and gagged. This time, bile came up—Dot could smell it. Her aunt spit a long string of stomach juices and saliva all the way down to the moving traffic. Horrible sounds emerged from her lips. She burped raucously, then gagged again, then threw up some more. Even in the dim light, Dot was pretty sure it was blood.

"Dorothy," Dot whispered, trying to pull her up by her waist. Her aunt wouldn't budge. Out of options, Dot reached into her pocket and found her phone to call 911. She didn't look forward to the aftermath of this—her mother finding out again, the doctors testing Dorothy's blood, a police investigation, a finger pointed at Dot, and then, of course, Dorothy herself going to jail. Maybe *both* of them going to jail. But she couldn't let her aunt *die* out here.

Her fingers trembled as she pressed the buttons on her phone's screen. Light illuminated against her face, and she pressed the 9. Then, the overhead light burned out. Dot looked up, staring at the streetlight, willing it to flicker back on.

"Dorothy?" she called nervously. She could barely see a few feet in front of her. She heard footsteps, someone breathing.

A hand shot forward and grabbed her wrist, knocking Dot's phone away. Dot felt her hipbone smash against the guardrail. She could smell her aunt's perfume and bile breath, so close. With surprising strength, Dorothy pushed Dot against the metal barrier and held her there.

"If I'm dying, then you are, too," Dorothy growled. It didn't even sound like her voice, and it barely looked like her face. Someone else had taken over her body. Someone possessed.

Dot felt her hips tip over the edge of the guardrail. Her head twisted, and she stared woozily at the traffic below. The cars swept by so obliviously. If they happened to look up, all they'd see was blackness.

Conjuring strength, she pushed hard against her aunt. Dorothy staggered backward with a grunt. Dot managed to tilt herself upright before Dorothy came raging back for her. She slid off the guardrail and ducked to the side, avoiding Dorothy's charging form. What made her grab her aunt's thin, shapely calves, she wasn't sure. What made her hoist those calves up, tipping the top half of her aunt's body at the guardrail, she couldn't say. She didn't intend to tilt her aunt so forcefully, and when she let go, she had no idea

Dorothy was angled so far over the guardrail that most of her body dangled over the edge. As soon as her fingers freed themselves from those ankles, though, Dorothy's whole body slipped away effortlessly. Dot whirled around and gasped, instantly understanding what she'd done. She lunged for her aunt's tumbling feet, but it was too late. Her fingers grappled darkness and air.

Dot peered over the guardrail and screamed. It was so dark, and there was no sound of her aunt's fall, but maybe that's because the highway was too far down for her to hear. The cars kept rushing, their headlights betraying nothing. But Dorothy was definitely down there. Soon enough, someone was going to hit her. And soon enough, they would be looking upward, trying to figure out what had happened.

She turned and ran.

ELIZA

OH GOD, THERE it is, there it is: I'm dizzy, my vision is cloudy, I'm wavering in my seat at that bar, but I can make out a body sliding into the stool next to mine. I smell the bergamot oranges and the sickening creamy mintiness of the stinger. Everything inside me goes still, and when I look over, there she is. Me, and not me.

It can't be possible. It *can't*. It was part of a dream. The worst part is I don't even know who I'm afraid of. Myself? A clone of myself? An evil twin?

Stop staring, she said. I knew the voice. *I need to talk to you. I need you to listen.*

"Miss Fontaine?"

Roz is touching my arm. I realize I am standing in the parking lot with my phone in my hand. She looks at me cautiously, her clipboard under her arm. "We need to get you back in hair and makeup." Her mouth makes an O when she peers into my face. "Are you okay?"

I am desperate to muster a smile, but it's probably more of a snaggle-toothed cringe.

Roz pats my shoulder. "Hey, it's going to be great. Just relax. If it's any consolation, Katie's out there right now getting the audience drunk. They're going to think everything you say to Roxanne is positively scintillating."

She extends her arm and leads me back to the trailer. My stomach heaves, and for a moment my vision tilts, but I manage to remain upright. Somehow I get up the stairs. The makeup artist says nothing about my greasy face. She hums as she puts on my lipstick. "Now go like this," she says, popping her lips together. I pop, too. I'm amazed I can pop.

"Roxanne's about to go on for her introductions," Roz says. "You're first, Eliza. Get ready!"

I'm a zombie as she walks me down the trailer steps and across the lawn. When we get to a blue curtain, she tells me to stop. "Wait here, and she'll call your name, and then you'll walk through there." Roz parts the curtain just slightly to reveal a makeshift set inside a gazebo festooned with flowers. Six cameras are trained on Roxanne, who has ash-blonde hair cut to her chin and wears a white doctor's coat. I wish, suddenly, she was a *real* doctor, and that I could be lying on a bed, hospitalized.

I wipe my sweaty palms on my pants. A sound tech rushes over and rechecks the microphone he's threaded up my blouse and into my ear. But when I turn my head just so, I see *her.*

It's just a flash of light and skin. A wink from a full-length mirror a few feet away from the curtain. When I look closer, I see my face staring back. Only, the me in the mirror flashes an eerie smile I don't think I know how to make. I yelp and turn around so quickly that the cord of the microphone goes taut in the sound tech's fingers. The microphone clip leaps off my blouse.

"Oops," the sound tech murmurs. "Can you stay still for me, honey?"

I stare into the mirror again. The reflection is gone. I glance at Roz, who's looking at me questioningly. "Are guests allowed backstage?"

"Nope, they're all in the bleachers. And you got off easy—it's a small group compared to when we shoot on our normal set." She studies me, then tucks in her chin and speaks into her microphone. "Amanda, can you get out here? Eliza needs a touch-up."

"Already?" I can hear the makeup artist complain through the headset. Yes, Amanda. Already.

I study the mirror again. Still nothing. But it doesn't matter. I saw it. I know she's here. Now that I believe in her, I suddenly believe in everything—all those shadows I wrote off as nothing, all those feelings I was being watched, all those eerie, uncanny prickles on the back of my neck. The mysterious video on my phone in the hospital room. The reason I felt so afraid when I ran toward the pool at the Tranquility; the reason I fled from the bar at the Tranquility when I was with Desmond. It's *her.* This strange second Eliza is everywhere, as magical and omnipotent as Santa Claus.

Someone on the other side of the curtain calls for quiet. There's saxophone music and applause, and the host begins to talk. Roz hears something through her headset and scuttles away a few paces. I look around freely. There are more cabanas behind us, chaises and thick palms. She's crouching somewhere. I can feel her readying a laugh. I want to comb through the plants until I find her.

"Eliza." Roz is back by my side, poking my arm. "*Go.*"

The host must have called my name, because the audience is clapping. I am pushed through the curtain. The cameras swivel over and record me as I stand, transfixed. I try to smile, but my fear has taken control of the muscles of my face. Past the cameras, I see an audience sitting in grandstand-style seats. One figure stands out from the others. My heart jumps all the way up to my brain.

I point at her. *"You!"*

The me in the audience touches her breast. Her lips part. Shapes rearrange, and it's a middle-aged woman, well-dressed, with red lipstick and a big handbag on her lap. The kaleidoscope turns again. Now it's all Elizas in the audience. A hundred clones of me, out for blood. I blink. It's back to bleachers of strangers.

I wheel around to Roxanne. "Help me," I whisper, not loud enough for the microphone to pick up.

"Eliza?" Roxanne beckons from the couch. "Come over here, darling, and let's talk about this amazing new book of yours!"

I see an excited expression on her face, but I don't know how to respond to it. I can feel the sweat running down my forehead. "I know you're here," I say, loudly. "I know what you're doing."

"Pardon?" Roxanne asks.

My gaze sweeps the set again. Cameras. Tech people. Audience. Blue Los Angeles sky. "Just come out. Show me who you are."

"Eliza!" Roz hisses from the wings. "*What the hell?*"

Roxanne, still standing, smiles at the audience. "Uh, I believe we're having some technical difficulties, so this might be a good time to break for commercial."

"*No!*" a voice hisses from stage right. "*Keep going! This is great!*"

Roxanne presses her lips together. Behind her, I see a glint of light followed by a flash of dark. It's the other me. I lunge for it. The audience screams. Roxanne steps away from my outstretched arms, stumbling in her high heels, but I barely notice her. I reach the chairs and shove them aside, their legs making angry scrapes against the concrete. I peer behind the *Dr. Roxanne* banner; there's a small, landscaped Eden full of flowering plants. A rippling pond burbles happily. I *know* this pond, I realize. I sat here, one morning, wickedly hungover, and pitched pennies into its lowest tier.

No, you didn't, a voice inside me shouts. *Dot did. Not you.*

But I did. I *did.*

I fumble out from behind the curtain and face the audience. "Where are you? Come out so I can talk to you!" I can hear my ragged breathing. I can sense the expression on my face. And yet I can't stop myself. I can't stop any of this.

"We're going to commercial," Roxanne decides, walking straight for the camera.

There's that loud *buzz*; the director reluctantly yells cut. The audience's murmurs grow louder. Everyone is staring at me. Roxanne scuttles off the set. Roz hurries over to me. "Eliza," she whispers. She doesn't sound angry anymore. More like shaken and frightened. "I think it would be best if you came backstage with me, okay?"

"No." I say it so forcefully spit flies out of my mouth, landing on her cheek.

"You're clearly having some sort of . . . *moment*. It's upsetting our guests."

"I'm being hunted. It's not going to stop until I'm dead."

Roz notices my microphone and pulls it off my shirt. "If you just come backstage, if you have some water—we'll get this sorted out."

"Don't you understand?" I scream. "I'm in danger! *I'm. In. Danger!*"

A gasp from the onlookers. "Stop!" someone else screams, and I feel hands pulling me backward. "Eliza, *stop!*"

I stare down at myself. Somehow, I've grabbed Roz's shirt, and I'm shaking her. "I'm sorry," I start to say, but Roz has already turned backstage.

I turn around to assess whoever has pulled me backward. A tall, hefty security guard with a shaved head takes my arm. "Time to go, miss."

I stare at his dark, fleshy fingers around my biceps. "W-where are you taking me?"

"Off the property. If you go quietly, no one will press charges."

I dig in my heels. "Don't leave me out there alone. She'll find me."

His expression hardens. "You've created enough of a disturbance. Let's go."

"Please!" I beg. I can feel the tears running down my cheeks. "Please, I'm scared!"

We push through the cut in the curtains. The whole production team is standing there: Amanda the makeup lady; Cathy, who blow-dried my hair; about fifty PAs. They are staring, slack-jawed. I sense the Eliza vibration again, and the world starts to wobble. Nerves snap at the surface of my skin. I can feel my legs crumpling, and suddenly I'm on the ground. I can't move. At least if I stay here, I'm around people, and she won't get me.

"Miss Fontaine." The guard yanks at my arm. "Get up."

"I can't," I whisper. "Don't make me. Don't leave me alone."

"*Get up.*"

"I've got her."

It's a new voice, one I know. Bill stands above me. I peer at him, fearful, paranoid—why is *he* here? I wonder, suddenly, if *he's* also in on the plot—maybe they all are. Maybe they all know who this woman is who's lurking around, ready to hurt me. Maybe they're all best friends.

I scuttle away from him. "Leave me alone!"

But Bill is quicker, and he scoops me up under my arms. I kick my legs, trying to get free. "Eliza. Honey. Stop, okay? Please stop. It's me. I'm not going to hurt you."

"How do I know that? How do I know *anything*?"

"I knew this was going to be too much for you. Your mother and I both said. We're going to get you help, okay? You're going to be fine."

He drags me past the craft services table, where about twenty more people who work on the show stare at us in astonishment. "But she's *here*," I say. "I know it. And she's going to follow me out here. She's going to follow *us*."

"Just . . . come on. Let's not talk about this here."

Still holding me, Bill drags me away from the set and down a leafy path. The sun bores down on my head. In the distance, I can hear the audience applauding. It's strange to think that *Dr. Roxanne* has gone on as though nothing is amiss. Meanwhile, my life is crumbling before my eyes.

Bill takes me through a pool gate and sits me down on a lounge chair. The pool area is empty. Every table offers a neat stack of towels. A hot tub burbles to the left. It's tranquil, but the desolation unnerves me. As soon as I sit down, I start to tremble from head to toe. "Why are you here?" I ask Bill. "What are you doing?"

Bill sits next to me. "I was afraid something like this might happen. Gabby told us what she told you about the pool. We had a feeling you might start putting the pieces together."

"What pieces? What are you talking about?"

"How about you start by telling me who you're afraid of? And maybe I can explain."

There's a lump in my throat. So he *does* know who she is? Part of me wants to bolt, but his voice is so trusting and gentle. I want to believe he won't hurt me. "This . . . woman. She looks just like me. I've seen her everywhere. I think she wants to hurt me. For *real,* Bill. Not like the other times. At least I don't think so." I peek at him. "You know who she is, don't you? And you're not telling me. *No one* is telling me. Am I right?"

Bill's hands loosen from my legs. A look I can't decipher at first floods his face. Regret, maybe. Devastation. He takes a long breath. "You're right. I do know her. I believe you're talking about your aunt. But . . . she's dead."

I recoil. "What aunt?"

"Your mother's sister. Her name was Eleanor. Eleanor Reitman. You two look exactly the same."

I jolt away from him. "What are you talking about?"

"It's natural you're terrified of her. She's been trying to kill you for years—in the hospital, when you were young, and then after. But she's dead, Eliza. She really is. She was hit by a car when you pushed her over that overpass."

I rear back. "No. *No.* That was Dot and Dorothy. From my book. That was *in my book.*"

"Eliza. Calm down, okay? Calm down. She *is* Dorothy. And you are Dot. You're the *exact same*, just with different names. You disassociated. You created Dot and your book as a way of dealing with what happened to you. Don't you understand? This is why we were so upset about your book when we finally read it. This is why we didn't want you to publish it. This is why your mother unsuccessfully tackled you in that alleyway. She was hoping . . . well, I guess she hoped you would come with her willingly. And that she could convince you, somehow, to call your editor yourself and pull the book. We hadn't really planned it all out. We just knew we had to do *something*."

I feel like my whole body is tumbling down a deep, deep well, its sides slick and full of spiders, its bottom miles away. "None of this is possible. I can't have forgotten a whole fucking *aunt*."

"But you did. It's *understandable,* Eliza. Explainable. Horrible things happened a year and a half ago. Horrible things we should have stopped, had we known. All we could do was try to cover it up after the fact and protect you from further damage—hide what you did from the police, try to find you treatment. We all understood why you did it, honey—we knew what she was doing to you unfortunately when it was too late. So we sought out a doctor to remove those memories. He had this method that he used on PTSD patients, a mix of drugs and a whole lot of psychotherapy—it was *supposed* to work. What it did instead was shove the memories into a bottom drawer. They were always there, though. And the *emotion* was always there, the fear. It broke through in your book. And now it's breaking through for real in other ways, too."

There's suddenly a tinny taste in my mouth. "*What* happened a year and a half ago?"

"Everything in your book. Aunt Eleanor hurting you in the hospital. Aunt Eleanor coming back to town. That dinner out. Her . . . death."

I stare at him. "Are you suggesting what I wrote is true?"

He looks pained. "Yes."

"Even the part where Dot . . . where I . . . ?" I can't even say it out loud.

Bill's hands grip mine hard. "It's why you kept diving into those pools. You felt guilty. Responsible. And unsettled—there was no body for the service. You kept thinking she was still alive, and that terrified you. So like I said, we got you help. You couldn't go on like that. We had to do something."

I widen my eyes. More pieces snap together. "I didn't have a brain tumor, did I? That's why there's no record of me at UCLA. I checked, you know. I made a fool out of myself, claiming I was sick when I wasn't. I even got an MRI because I thought the tumor came back!"

He licks his lip. "You had a mass as a child, but it was benign, and everything was removed. But not last year. That's just what we told you. It was a more rational story. And no, you weren't at UCLA. You were somewhere else."

I'm horrified. "Doing that *other* thing? That PTSD bullshit?"

He looks wrecked. "It's very cutting-edge. Scientists have targeted genes that make proteins that either enhance memory or interfere with it. There's a new drug that acts on those genes, turns them off so certain memories are suppressed. You talked to a therapist a lot, too. He had you do hypnosis a lot, and for a while, you seemed cured. You forgot . . . and that seemed like the best thing for you. We thought we were protecting you. From the police—and from yourself."

Bile rises in my throat. "I wouldn't agree to that. It sounds like bullshit."

"Well, we forced you to. We got a court document and everything, but you probably don't remember. And . . . well, it was bullshit, kind of, because instead of you forgetting, you created Dot." He presses his hands to his eyes. "We thought the process had worked. You seemed so well. So happy. And we thought that when you were writing a novel, it was about something else. We should have asked to see it far sooner than we did. We shouldn't have believed you when you said it wasn't going to be published for a long time. We just didn't want to push—we were afraid you were fragile. So we let it go. But we're afraid people will read it and realize that it's true. We don't want anything to happen to you, Eliza. You shouldn't be punished for what you did."

"I *didn't* do it," I insist. "I mean, Dorothy—*Eleanor*—isn't even dead! She was with me at the Shipstead at the Tranquility the night Gabby pushed me into the pool. A bartender saw her! And she's here, now. I've seen her everywhere." Something else strikes me. "For all I know, she's impersonating me, all over town. People have seen me out and about—at yoga studios, at the shop I work at, at clubs—but I distinctly remember *not* being in those places. It's like she's trying to take over my life!" Just saying it chills me. Could it be true?

Bill shakes his head. "Eleanor is dead. I promise you."

I look at him through tears. "How can you be so sure?"

"Because the police told us so. It was her ID. But she was taken away. I guess she didn't want any of us to see her. But it was *her*, Eliza. I promise you."

I blink hard, trying to let this sink in. It just doesn't seem possible. "And you're sure *I* did it?" He nods sadly. "*How* are you sure?"

"Because you kept saying so. You said it over and over. You were like Lady Macbeth. Possessed."

I shut my eyes. All of a sudden, an image swims against my closed eyelids. I see two women standing near a highway overpass. One of them is an older, pretty woman wrapped in a fur. Her shoulders are hunched, and her mouth is open in a scream. Behind her is the guardrail; to the left glows the sign for St. Mother Maria's. Orbs of neon headlights gleam below.

Then I look at the person next to her. She's yelling, too. And though I can't see what she's wearing—something in the foreground cuts out the lower half of her, only showing her face—she looks awfully familiar. She is standing in the same way I pictured Dot in those final moments. It's possible she's *thinking* what Dot was thinking in those final moments.

I look at Bill in horror. "It wasn't me. *It wasn't me.*" But even as the words spill from my mouth, I'm not sure I believe them anymore. Because it *was* me. It couldn't be anyone else.

This seems to unlock a door, because memories smash through a wall. The feeling is almost palpable; I want to cover my head to protect myself from the deluge. All Dot's memories can't be mine. They *can't.*

But then I try it out. Eleanor Reitman. My aunt. And there it comes, spilling over the dam. Little me, prancing through a beautiful room at the Magnolia Hotel, trying on gowns in Eleanor Reitman's closet.

Little me, playing Oscar Night, coming out in a gown way too long for me, answering Eleanor's questions about who I was wearing ("Wednesday Addams Couture," I always said) and what my beauty tips were ("No sleep, lots of cookies").

Little me, playing Funeral, lying in that silk coffin, the two of us giggling, my arms reaching out for my mother to come play, too. Sometimes she'd join in, but others she'd rush off, late for work.

Little me in the hospital, miserable, terrified. Aunt Eleanor bursting through in that silk wrap dress, carrying that Chanel bag, making everything perfect.

Stella the look-alike taking my blood pressure. *Los Angeles* magazine. The ICU. Me hearing my doctor's voice yelling at someone outside the hall. Eleanor's frostiness. Her paranoia. *Don't tell them anything.* I hear her voice through the phone.

Bill and Gabby coming to the door of our house, me pouring that glass of vodka, Gabby looking on with wide, spooked eyes. *Maybe you shouldn't be doing that,* she'd said—but not because it was taboo. Because I'd been *sick.* Because she felt sorry for what I'd been through. They'd told her everything—including the part about Eleanor. That's why Gabby took the blame. That's also why Gabby didn't want to rehash it, days ago.

Memories come back of my mother changing on me, growing silent, angry. Telling me Eleanor was in France, then taking it back.

And then I see myself meeting Eleanor in the parking lot near school. My ass in that booth at M&F, taking that sip of champagne. Leonidas—*there* he is!—and I going out with Eleanor to that club. My mother hunting me down the morning I awoke woozy and sick in Eleanor's suite. Telling me the truth. Me not believing it. Doubt creeping in. Leonidas making me promise not to see her that last night. But I went anyway.

I can hear myself screaming, but I can't stop. I cover my ears to block out the sound, but it just echoes inside my head. I can feel my knees buckling again, and from the end of a long, long tunnel I have the vague sense that Bill is trying to lift me to stand. My legs are limp and boneless. I can't move.

The memories bulldoze on, crashing, crashing. Details I'd packed into the novel: Aunt Eleanor handing keys over to my mother so she could take possession of her chopped-up, meringue-like house in the Hollywood Hills.

"It's the least I can do, Francesca," she said. "At least accept *this*." And my mother looked so angry, so doomed, but we'd moved in, hadn't we?

Waking up in Eleanor's bed at the Magnolia and seeing her slow-dancing with Dr. Singh in the front room. And afterward, after she was dead, Leonidas looming over me at that pizza parlor, which I'd stumbled to, fled to a back hallway, and stayed there. I remember smelling Eleanor's bile on my hands and nearly puking. Leonidas was furious at me because I'd gone against his wishes, but he said that at least we could go to the police now.

"No, we can't," I said. "She's dead! She's dead!"

"*Quiet!*" he hissed, glancing in horror over his shoulder. We were only steps away from the pizza ovens, but the music was cranked so loud, it didn't seem like the guys working behind the counter heard us. Still, Leonidas dead-lifted me and dragged me out an emergency exit at the back. "You can't go around saying that," he moaned. "Eliza, we have to get you *out* of here."

But instead of going back to the dorms, I found myself at my parents' front door. My mother opened it and went pale. Bill pushed through and grabbed me by the arms before I fainted.

"What did you do?" he whispered. "Eliza, what did you *do*?"

I blurted it all out. Everything, in lurid detail, starting with Eleanor showing up at my dorm that morning. Then I got to my revelation about what she'd done to Thomas, and then how Dorothy—Eleanor—had confirmed it. My mother went white.

"No," she said. "Thomas shot himself. With that gun."

"You really believe that?" My laugh was cruel. "Eleanor did something to him to poison his mind—and then took him to doctor after doctor, trying to get pity, trying to get attention, exactly in the way someone with Munchausen Syndrome by Proxy works. *You're* the one who schooled me on this disease—you should have made the connection. Maybe he pulled the trigger of that gun, we'll never know—but *she* was the one who basically put it in his hands." I shake my head. "How can you not see? How can you look at my situation and not understand what she did to him?"

My mother pressed her hand to her mouth, but there was a light in her eyes. All sorts of emotions crossed her face. Horror. Guilt, maybe. Regret.

And then she shot into action.

"Get inside," she told me, pressing her hands on my shoulders. "You're not talking to anyone else about this. *No one.* We'll do the talking for you. What you did, you did out of self-defense, but it's better if people don't even know about it. Okay, Eliza? Okay?"

Then the memories come to a screeching halt. My brain goes still and silent. I open my eyes and look around. Bill has sat me down on a chaise inside the pool area. The water is flat, untouched glass. I can hear a Taylor Swift song lilting from the *Dr. Roxanne* set.

I have to stand. I have to move. I jiggle my legs and arms wildly, hoping to shake the memories free. I need to get rid of this brain, rid of myself. That I have forgotten something so huge, so devastating, seems like a crime in itself. I rise and stagger away from Bill, half-blind.

"Eliza?" I hear Bill calling out. "Eliza, what are you—"

And then I see it: a rippling, blue, welcome respite. I tumble toward it, arms wheeling around, and then I leap. The space between ground and water is lovely. I wish I could open my arms and fly.

As soon as I hit the water, the pain inside me begins to dull. The voices stop, the memories subside. I open my eyes and enjoy the blue bubbles. I give in to sinking. My lungs start to give out, but something inside me tells me that I just need to wait. It will feel bad, but then it will get better.

And then the pain will be gone.

From The Dots

That same evening, Dot felt drunk as soon as she opened her eyes. The room wobbled vertiginously, and her stomach burned with acid. She was in her old bedroom at her parents' house. She couldn't quite remember how she'd gotten here.

Something was happening outside the house. She pushed back the curtain on her window. A police car rolled into the driveway.

She cracked open the bedroom door and listened as an officer stepped into the foyer and talked to her mother. The cop said Dorothy's name. Dot's throat tightened, everything she'd done tumbling back to her. This was it. She had to confess.

She opened the door wider and readied herself, but then her stepfather appeared from out of nowhere and clapped his hand over her mouth. "*Shhh*," he whispered, widening his eyes in warning. Dot stared at him, puzzled. He pushed her back into her room.

Downstairs, soft murmuring: "Can you describe your relationship with your sister?"

Dot's mother answered, but Dot couldn't make out what she said. The conversation lasted another minute or so, and then the door shut.

Her mother appeared up the stairs, her head bowed. Dot's step-father moved aside to let her into Dot's room. Dot scrambled back to her bed, afraid of what was to come. But Dot's mother's face was kind when she entered the room. She walked up to Dot and took her hands.

"That was the police," she said evenly. "About Dorothy. They have her body at the morgue."

Dot breathed in. She searched her mother's face, but her mother wouldn't meet her gaze. "Oh," was all she could think to say.

"The police wanted to talk to you, but I said you hadn't seen her in ten years." She finally looked up at Dot. "Do you understand?"

Dot licked her lips. "But that's not true."

"Yes it is."

"But I—"

"No buts," her mother said steadily. "We talked about this."

Dot swallowed. She watched as her mother and her stepfather exchanged a glance over her head.

"But people saw us," she said softly. "People at the restaurant. That steak house."

"I don't think that will be a problem."

Again, Dot tried to catch her mother's gaze, but she wouldn't look in her direction.

"Can I see her body?" she asked. She needed to prove to herself it had really happened, that Dorothy was really gone. It was still unthinkable that any of it had happened. The poisoning, the manipulation—to *her*, Dorothy's alleged favorite. How could she have done such a thing? How could Dot have let it go on for so long? Would a smarter girl have caught on sooner?

Her parents exchanged a shocked glance. "Absolutely not," her mother said.

And then her parents stood up and left the room. *Stay here*, they told her. *Don't you dare leave.*

To Dot's horror, there was a memorial held for Dorothy, and

Dot's family insisted she go. Not going would arouse suspicion. *Just act normal*, they told her. *Don't talk to anyone*.

It was held at M&F Chop House. There were steaks for all, and unlimited drinks. The mood was buoyant and Hollyweird. Bartenders in white jackets and turbans mixed martinis. Someone circulated with a platter full of Cuban cigars. There was a woman walking around with a monkey on her shoulder; both were wearing tiaras. A couple of Vegas showgirls performed, and then a burlesque dancer, and then a Frank Sinatra impersonator. The place was crawling with writers, but some of them Dot had been sure were already dead—James Joyce with his little glasses, Oscar Wilde in a topcoat, a ghostly Virginia Woolf. There were people there who looked as though they might be dressed up for Halloween: a leathery-skinned man in a cowboy hat and with a handlebar mustache, a large-eyed woman in a peacock-colored caftan with a crystal ball under her arm, a huge black man with a tattoo on his face and a bone through his nose.

Dot wandered through the crowds of revelers double-fisting drinks. Just being confined between these walls made her skin crawl with guilt. The only respite was that Bernie the bartender and all the other normal staff members were nowhere to be seen. Oddly, when she dared to ask the bartender on duty where Bernie was that day, he looked at her blankly as if he'd never heard of him.

Eerily, there was no body in a casket. Dot asked and asked, and finally her mother admitted that Dorothy's will stated that a friend pick up her body from the morgue and dispose of it as she wished, and apparently those instructions didn't include putting her body in a casket for a funeral. Dot wondered if Dr. Singh was the one who'd retrieved Dorothy from the morgue. She peered through the crowd for him, hoping to get some answers. But he hadn't come.

At one point, a woman in a fortune-teller's turban holding a half-drunk martini teetered toward Dot.

"Oh, Dorothy, this is so *like* you to stage a funeral when you're not actually dead."

Dot had stared at her, sickened. "I'm *not* Dorothy."

The woman blinked woozily. "Oh," she said. "Of course not. You're a few years too young. Still, what a wonderful party trick!"

Dot felt so disgusted. She broke away from her and ran, finding herself opening double doors into another dining area. Though the whole restaurant had been rented out for the funeral, this room was empty. The tables were set neatly with linens and napkins, but no one sat at them. Her footsteps echoed noisily as she crossed the wood floor to the bar.

She peered into the antique mirror behind the bottles. She had never looked more like her aunt in her life, maybe because she was guilty of something now, too. What would it be like if she went back to the memorial and pretended to *be* her, for real? How many people would buy it? She wondered what she might do in Dorothy's name. Hideous things she'd never dared, or nice, sweet things to make up for her aunt's transgressions?

Staring at herself, something new pressed down on Dot, a bone-shaking frisson she couldn't help but peek at sideways. Even if Dorothy deserved it, someone was going to figure out what she'd done. If not the police, then Dorothy's ghost.

In the mirror, as if in answer, a shadow shifted behind a curtain across the room. Dot whirled around, heart in her throat. "Dorothy?" she called out.

Shifting, shuffling. Dot crouched down, eye-level with clean glassware. "Dorothy?" she cried again, her teeth chattering. It had to be her over there. She was still alive. Maybe her body had never been in the morgue. Maybe her parents were lying. Maybe the police were confused. Maybe that was why Dr. Singh wasn't here, either—he was keeping a secret. This was all a ruse.

The curtain shifted and fluttered. Dot pressed her hands over her eyes, knowing Dorothy was going to fling it wide and come for her. She bolted out from behind the bar, down the back hallway, and into the alley. But the scene was too familiar and haunting—this was where they'd had their fight. A few doors down was the pizza parlor, where Marlon had found her. Her gaze swung to the hotel on the next block. Out front, surrounded by a little gate, was a swimming pool for guests. At present, it was empty, the pool lights making the water glow a brassy gold.

Footsteps rang out behind her. Goose bumps rose on Dot's arms. She could think of nothing but the pool and its welcoming water. She hurried toward it. The fence was high, but she was able to climb it without much problem. When she turned, a figure in silhouette rushed over the fence, too. She let out a yelp and stretched her arms out, falling headfirst into the pool. She sank so fast that her head hit the bottom.

She shut her eyes at first, but then rolled over and opened them. Someone stood above her on the pool deck. To her horror, the figure jumped in. Dot fought to swim away, but she was running out of oxygen. She felt her body being dragged to the surface. Her lungs gasped for air, and she gagged once she was on the concrete. Her hair made a wet fan around her face.

As soon as she saw her mother, she started to cry. "She's coming for me. She's coming."

Her mother pressed a towel against Dot's chest. "No one's coming for you. I promise."

"That's not true. She's not going to rest until I make this right."

Her mother's face broke. "You haven't done anything wrong. Sit up. Look for yourself. No one is here. She's gone, Dot. She's really gone."

Weak as she was, Dot did what she was told. The pool area was empty. The street was empty. She touched her face and wet hair. Her legs were so cold they were starting to shiver. She looked at her mother, something breaking inside her. "I can't keep this to myself," she blurted. "It isn't right."

Her mother's eyebrows knit together. "You have to."

"No. I *can't*."

"Dot. You *have* to." Her hands clutched Dot's forearms. "Promise me. Please. I can't lose you."

It was the kindest thing Dot's mother had ever said to her, and through her sinking quicksand of panic, Dot felt a small flare of recognition of that. But it passed quickly through her, hardly making an impression. "I can't go on," she said again. "I can't be haunted."

"Then we'll find a way for it to un-haunt you."

"How?"

"I don't know. But we'll figure it out. Together."

Dot stared. She'd fallen prey to comforting words before. But she found herself leaning against her mother's chest anyway, cradled, comforted, feeling, at least briefly, that she was safe.

ELIZA

MY CHEEK HITS the leather seat of Bill's car. My wet hair snakes around me, soaking my neck; droplets plop onto my palm. Bill, wet too, tries to put the seat belt around my waist, but it's awkward with the way I'm lying, so he gives up and leaves me unbuckled. I shut my eyes, awash in misery. I don't want to be breathing. I don't want to be alive. I wish Bill would have left me in that pool.

Sometime later, I see a slice of blue sky out the window, half of a tree. I hear Bill speaking to someone on the phone, but I can't tell what he's saying. I must doze off again, because the next thing I know I am slumped over in a wheelchair, and Bill is speaking to a triage nurse: "Do you think she's suicidal?" And then, Bill: "Yes. She jumped into a pool, and she can't swim." "Let's get her back there, get her checked out." A hand on my arm. "Honey?" Hot breath, the smell of latex gloves. Hair tickles my earlobe. I try to look toward the sound of the voice, but my eyes won't cooperate.

"She's not moving," comes the woman's voice.

I am lifted under my arms and hefted onto a mattress; I roll to my side and curl in a ball. Around me: Beeps. Dings. Footsteps. Sighs.

"Hello?" I call, much later, raising my head. It is dark, and I am alone. I am seven years old again. I am wearing a charm bracelet of skeletons. I've just knocked over a plate full of chicken and carrots. I'm seeing double of everything. "Is anyone here?"

"I'm here." A squeak of the chair. My gaze focuses, and it's my mother standing above me. A blanket is pressed over my body. Her touch is warm on my forehead.

"Where am I?" I ask, my mouth cottony and my words slow. "Is my tumor back?"

She breathes out a small puff of air. "Oh, Eliza. It hasn't been back for years."

■ ■ ■

In some ways, the Oaks Wellness Center is worse than I imagined. The rooms are too cold and there are too few blankets—maybe the staff thinks the patients are going to knot them together and climb out the window, I'm not sure. For the first week, when I lie on my bed, curled up and feral, resistant to talk or medication or sleep or food, not a single staff member is nurturing.

"Up, you have to shower," the nurses say gruffly. Or: "On the toilet, now. There you go." Or: "If you don't eat something, honey, we're going to have to give you a feeding tube. Your choice."

I try to argue with them that I just want to die, but apparently dying isn't an option here. They have rough hands and slam the doors and speak loudly when I want quiet, and on day eight, when I start making tiny requests—for a drink, for a walk down the hall, to talk to someone—they sometimes forget what I've asked for. Desperate for water, I try my door to find it locked. I spend hours shut in my room, rocking on my coccyx bone, until finally a nurse sweeps in and rolls her eyes. "Get *up*."

Or maybe my mind is playing tricks on me, because when the fog starts to clear, the staff members are all quite pleasant.

The third week in, I start to mingle with other patients. If I want to be out and about, there is no way to avoid them: we eat meals together, watch TV together, and I'm even forced to go with some of them to Group. Some of them descend on me, leechlike, chattering about their stories, who they are, what landed them here. It surprises me how many people talk unapologetically. Peter says almost proudly that this is his third visit to the Oaks. Angela shows me self-inflicted burns up and down her arms. A girl younger than me whose name I can't remember boasts that during her last breakdown, she smeared herself in shit. On the other hand, some of the patients seem completely normal, just sort of worn-out: like Jim and Pablo, who play chess in the corner. Like Felicity, who wears the silk bathrobe—she'd be so pretty with makeup on, and she's always talking about her kids. Like Caroline, who knits and smiles at everyone and says that in a previous life she was really talented at baking cakes.

In some ways, though, the Oaks exceeds my expectations. I have my own room with no roommates—a terror at first, when I needed distraction from my screaming mind, but now it's an incredible gift to escape from the others. There are a lot of channels on television and decent books on the shelves in the common rooms. The staff lets you spend a lot of time outside, tilting your head into the dry desert sun, thinking about nothing.

My therapist is a thickly muscled, goateed, African American man named Albert. He looks like he could asphyxiate anyone who came close by just sitting on their chest, which I appreciate. I need a big, strong man around me. I still can't get Aunt Eleanor's cackle next to me on that barstool—or that flash of her face in that mirror on *Dr. Roxanne*—out of my mind.

Albert is slowly unwinding my memories, explaining that I distanced myself from them as a form of self-protection—and because I was manipulated to forget. He shows me a picture of the man who tried to literally excise Eleanor from my existence, and it's Herman Lavinsky, flasher guy from the café with Posey. The Freak Show who wrote the pamphlet-book at my parents' house. What the pamphlet didn't mention was that aside from being a faith healer or some shit like that, Herman is also a neuroscientist, and he developed a few experimental psychopharmaceuticals he was trying out on people. He and his team of people hypnotized me—*count backward from ten*—put me into an MRI machine, asked me to spew forth my memories of killing Aunt Eleanor, and then carefully targeted this chemical he developed to turn off the memory gene. And then, *poof!* Memories gone.

I would have been better off with a trephine.

Of course, those weren't the only things Herman tried. Along with whatever chemical he stabbed into my brain, he also used antiquated drugs like ether on me, and some weird Native American herbs. My central nervous system was put on ice. I had electrodes stuck to my head. Not that I remember this—Albert just reads it back from various papers and articles written about his process. Herman spent hours in my room every day—a room that wasn't in UCLA at all but in a hospital all the way in the Mojave, where I guess they allowed him to do this nonsense, unexamined—cataloging all of my memories with Aunt Eleanor in them and rewriting them, one by one, so that Eleanor was no longer there. In the case of me having a brain tumor as a child, apparently that was too tainted with Eleanor to salvage, so it was wiped away completely. Why would someone want to remember a childhood brain tumor, anyway?

The problem, of course, is that my memories were too strong for Herman's method, and they were screaming to get out—hence *The Dots*, and hence various pieces clawing through at inopportune moments, though I'd tricked myself into thinking I'd had the brain tumor I thought was present last year but that had only existed when I was a little girl. Albert hasn't yet read my book, so I have to try and explain my story to him all by myself. Much of it is still foggy to me; I can't figure out where Dot ends and I begin. Part of me still denies any of it happened to me. Another part thinks some of it happened, but in a very different way.

"Really, your family shouldn't have tried to hypnotize your memories out of you," Albert says. "It doesn't exactly work that way. It's much better to work *through* your memories. Try and make sense of them. Try to see their significance, and try to decide what you believe. This business of erasing them? Well, it leads to a lot of messiness later on."

Messy as in losing one's mind on *Dr. Roxanne.* But I don't comment—I don't want any insight on *that,* either.

So we work through my memories, all shitty seven zillion of them, reversing Herman's freakish effects. And I see Aunt Eleanor, brighter and stronger, with every moment that comes back. Love of my life, Aunt Eleanor. Lovely little addiction I clung to again and again. I know I should be furious at her, and I definitely *am*. But on some early mornings, I have dreams of our old conversations, the back-and-forth banter from when I was a child—her telling stories, me telling a joke, her telling me I was the smartest girl alive. She hugs me and says, "All of it, darling, is a lie. I love you, I love you, I love you."

But I always wake up, and I always tell Albert about it, and he always tells me that I did feel love for her, and that's okay, and maybe I always will, but I also have to recognize that she is the bad person, and it was all her fault, not mine.

"You were talking about Eleanor when I found you in the bar," Gabby says on a day when she and Leonidas visit. Well, when I finally *let* them visit. "God, you were so freaked out. *She just left,* you said. *Jesus, Gabby, she's still alive, how is that possible?* I was heartbroken. You were supposed to forget her, but it was like you remembered everything, and it was killing you. So I had to stop you. I had to try to . . . set you right, I guess. I said you couldn't talk about her anymore. And you said, *but I* have *talked about her. She's in my book.* It's why I made Mom and Dad get your book. I was in a panic."

"And then what? After you found me in the bar at the Tranquility?"

"You got up and just ran out of there. I didn't know where you were going. You stopped at the pool, but you were still raving, and it seemed like you . . . *saw* someone. You were so scared. You said Eleanor wasn't going to stop until you made it right. You said this was why you'd come to the Tranquility—something had led you here. It was so you could remember, and so she could find you. You remembered everything in that instant. It was like everything we worked so hard to suppress broke through."

"Though I guess I forgot it all when I woke up the next day," I grumbled. "I bet that made you happy, huh?"

"Oh, Eliza," Gabby says, lowering her eyes.

But I feel so bitter, tricked, betrayed, duped, obfuscated. Complex lies upon lies have been spun, all by people I'm supposed to love. I'm not sure if I can ever really trust them again.

"Look, I made a promise not to ever mention Eleanor, and I took that promise seriously," Gabby admits. "Remembering her would be a huge trigger for you. It was why we erased so much of your life that would remind you of her, too. We went through your room and removed all your mementos. And later, we even took down your Facebook page—there were a few spots where you made a reference to the book Eleanor was writing. We didn't want to leave anything to chance."

"Hmmph," I grumble, though at least this explains what cuckoo Eliza Facebook page Kiki was talking about looking at when she first met me.

"And anyway." She smiles wryly. "Anyway, it's not like you *really* saw Eleanor at the bar. It's impossible."

I tap my teeth together. Was it? Then I look at Leonidas, who, so far, has stood there numbly, like a post. He's no longer a stranger, all the feelings I had for him rushing back like a beloved book I've just reread, but I'm angry with him, too.

"So why were *you* involved in keeping all this a secret?" I snap, feeling embarrassed to be talking to him with my stringy hair and unwashed armpits.

He shrugs. "Because I knew everything. You told me you were going to kill her before you did, and then I was the one who rescued you the night it happened."

"And were you at Palm Springs, too?"

"No. Gabby just called me to talk about it later. She was frantic."

I stare at the ceiling and let out a breath. "How did you find me that night it all went down, anyway?"

"You were gone when I got to the dorm. So I drove to M&F—I had a horrible feeling. I saw you running into the pizza place, and then you just blurted it all out."

"And then you yelled at me for not doing what I was told and dumped me at my parents', is that it?"

Leonidas looks tormented. "I should have stayed by you that day. I worried all through class—I *knew* you were going to go to dinner with her. But maybe if I'd stayed, you wouldn't have seen her."

"Or it might not have mattered. She was out to get me. It would have happened another day. The story would have ended in the same way." Well, in *sort of* the same way. Except that maybe I would have heard a *thump* when Eleanor hit the concrete on the highway. And a horn honk. A *crunch* and *pop* as a car hit her.

Instead, I'd heard nothing. The only evidence I had she was gone was the cops showing up at my parents' later that night, saying they had her body at the morgue.

"And as for breaking up with you." Leonidas clears his throat. "I was told by the doctors your parents hired that I had to. They said that ties to the past, especially to *her*"—he makes a face, so I'm assuming he's talking about Eleanor—"would be detrimental. Your doctor wanted your mom to cut ties with you, even, but she said absolutely not." He walks to the window. "I hated dropping you like that, though. Not that you care, but I went through a lot of pain. I missed you terribly."

Someday, perhaps, I will care about Leonidas's feelings in all this.

But now, front and center, is the *How Eliza Was Duped* show. Everything else is on another network, one I'm not watching.

But then, after they leave, I am given another memory, one that hasn't come back yet. A few days after the singular evening we went out with Eleanor together, Leonidas and I were on a drive somewhere. I still felt like shit—whatever Eliza gave me created a hangover that went on for days. I waited for Leonidas to tell me *I told you that you shouldn't have drank*—I would have, had the roles been reversed. But instead, he drove silently until we reached Santa Monica. He parked near the amusement park and unlocked the doors.

"What are we doing?" I asked.

"We're having fun," he answered.

He bought us tickets for the rides, and we went on all of them, which sounds dreadful with a hangover, but somehow, combined with soda fountain Coke and two huge, steaming-hot pretzels, made the headache and nausea evaporate. We held hands on the Ferris wheel, screamed on the roller coaster, threw darts at balloons and won a giant Scooby-Doo. By the end of the day, we were tired, we were laughing, we were talking about normal stuff. It was his way to cover up a night he feared had been laced with duplicity. It was his way of saying, *Whatever that shit was, it was adult and weird and I'm not ready for it. I still want to be a kid.*

I want to be a kid, too, even now. With my childhood tumor memories returned to me, I feel like I never got to be a kid, not even for a day.

■ ■ ■

After Albert and I straighten out reality, we straighten out the truth, especially the unraveling of what was tumorous inside of me and what was brought on by Eleanor's wild, sick head. I'd had a tumor, yes, when I was young, but it had been benign. My mother was busy with work, even more stressed now because there were hospital bills to pay. Eleanor volunteered to hang out with me while I recovered, and my mother begrudgingly said yes—she didn't have money for a nanny, and Eleanor *seemed* okay. Well, sort of okay. "I mean, yes, she'd had a son who killed himself, and she'd had mental issues years ago, but she seemed recovered," my mother admits one day, when she and I are in a joint session with Albert. "And she was always lying to you about who she was when she was young, but I didn't see it as dangerous, really. Just sort of . . . childish."

I demand to know what she means. Apparently, Eleanor's fabulous New York youth, how she worked at a circus, how she was a spy in DC—they were just tales. "All her life, your aunt *wanted* to be fabulous, but she was mostly on the fringes of things," my mother says. "She might have been acquainted with some interesting characters in New York, for example—our mother certainly was, and Eleanor *idolized* her. But she was always too needy, too desperate. That was a turnoff to most people. Even I saw it, as a younger sister. She required too much. She needed so much hand-holding and attention. She was never let into the group. Some people rejected her very viciously—it was almost bullying. But she continued to try. She was so desperate to be loved."

There hadn't been a Contact Lens Baron or a DC spy. Eleanor had moved to California with us once my mother married my father. She met her husband out there, but he'd been a construction worker, not something more fabulous. Shortly after she had Thomas, her husband died in a freak accident on the job site—an I-beam disengaged from a crane and fell from a great height, crushing him. With the insurance settlement money, Eleanor bought the beautiful house in Hollywood—the house I *grew up* in, though it had been excised from my mind that the house had once been hers. But of course it had been hers! Who else would have written those crazy death facts on my closet wall?

"She tried to ingratiate herself with the neighbors when she lived there, but it was clear she wasn't one of them," my mother continues. "So she sold the place to us for a steal and moved to the suite in the

Magnolia because she was sick of feeling like a social pariah. At a hotel, she could pay people to make her feel like the star."

I'm stunned. "Why didn't you tell me any of this? Why didn't you correct me when I went on about how great she was?"

"Because you loved her," my mother answers simply. "And when your child loves something like that, you don't want to be the one to burst the bubble. I thought you'd blame me. Besides, you two had so much in common. She delighted in you, and you delighted in her. I didn't want to be the one to end that."

I feel sad about this new version of Eleanor. The truth doesn't come as so much of a surprise, but I hate that everything I'd adored about her was fiction. When Eleanor couldn't impress her peers, she turned to an impressionable child. I suppose I should find it flattering that I was her audience, but I see it all as a big, complicated sleight of hand.

But there was more to this, a complicated question of identity. So much of my personality was based on Eleanor. Playing Funeral in her suite stoked my love of death. Playing Oscar Night in her gowns convinced me that only melodramatic people were interesting. Would I have attempted to write a novel if she hadn't paved the way first with *The Riders of Carrowae*? It wasn't that I regretted who I turned into, but I couldn't help but get trapped in a solipsistic quandary about the way fate slides and shifts. If I'd known the *real* Eleanor, who would I have developed into as a teenager and adult? A different person? I might have ended up like Gabby, working in an office, grabbing smoothies after work, driving a PT Cruiser. It's not likely, but maybe. Maybe any of us could be anybody. Maybe it just depends on who we surround ourselves with.

I wonder if Eleanor thought about it this way, too. I might have been a nine-year-old, but I was a nine-year-old she could unquestionably shape. How powerful that must have felt! How deity-like! I saw her as an icon. Which was better than being a mother, because I didn't notice her flaws. Until it was too late.

Of course, if that's the way Eleanor saw it—if that's what she understood she was doing—then why the fuck would she poison me?

"After you recovered, I assumed you knew more than you let on," my mother says in another session. "I figured you knew that you were poisoned, and you were furious at me for letting Eleanor handle your care for so long. I thought you'd decided that I'd let it happen. Which was untrue, of course, but I didn't know how to explain to you that I had no idea without getting into what she actually did."

"Uh, *no*." I look at her like she's crazy. "I had no idea she poisoned me. Do you think I would have seen her when she came back if I knew? Do you think I would have asked you all those questions about where she was if I knew?"

"Yes, I realize that now." Her mouth puckers. She stares out the window. "I wish I'd made the connection about Thomas. His situation was so different, and he *was* a strange boy. I wish there was something I could have done to help him. I feel like I let it happen— *all* of this happen." She bites down hard on her fist.

"I wish you would have told me the truth about her," I say quietly, plunged once again into a particular brand of despair I've felt so many times since coming to the hospital. Betrayal and anger, sadness and disappointment all rolled into a sour, heavy feeling that stalls the rest of my thoughts. "*Everything* about her."

My mother smiled sadly. "You would have never believed me."

I pause a moment, thinking this over. "I guess you're right. I wouldn't have."

ELIZA

A FIGURE LOOMS in my doorway a few days later. It's a woman with a beehive hairdo and slapped-on makeup and hips that could birth several babies at once. I like high heels, but I could never walk in the shoes she's got on, and by her unsteady gait, she can't really, either. Her bag is a waxy Chanel knockoff with two huge interlocking Cs across the front. I blink at her blearily. I wonder, with a start, if she's my new roommate.

"Eliza, yoo-hoo," she says. "It's me. Laura."

I cock my head.

"Your *agent*?"

I stare at her as I might an artifact in a museum, astonished that such a creature could exist. Here I had been expecting a polished, fingernail-thin suggestion of a woman, all flash and fragrance and white teeth. Laura has a million bobby pins in her hair, and most of them jut haphazardly. When she sits down across from me, I see she's wearing nylons with a run on the left calf. Her eyes have the cross-hatchings of a woman in her forties, and there's a plain gold wedding band on her chubby finger.

"I suppose this is *one* way to get me out to LA," Laura grumbles, plopping her monster of a purse in her lap. "But oh well. I could use some sun right now. As for *you*. How're you doing, kiddo? Hanging in there?"

I stare down at myself. At least my hospital gown isn't gaping open, but I'm sure my hair is slicked with grease. I haven't shaved my legs in a week. My breath probably stinks from the weird drugs they've got me on. None of that has me that embarrassed, though. Laura knows what happened to me at *Dr. Roxanne*. Everyone does. It's a morsel of gossip that's been kept from me since I've been here, but I'm cognizant enough to recall the harsh, mortifying details. The cameras had been rolling, and I'd been standing there on that stage, losing my shit.

"Don't be embarrassed," Laura says, perhaps sensing my feelings. "All the good authors go bananas here and there. You're just keeping with your milieu."

"I'm not an author anymore," I say quickly.

Laura gives me a circumspect look, then reaches into the bowels of her purse and pulls out a huge container of Tic Tacs. "You allowed to have one of these?" she asks. I nod, and she shakes one into my palm. "Of course you're still an author," she says as she pops a few in her mouth. She bites into them like candy. "Your book's out, darling. And it's doing great."

I sit up. "It's *out*? You let them publish it? My parents *let* you publish it?"

Laura chuckles. "I have to say, your mother called quite a few times saying we should pull the plug. But I told her it was too late. And anyway, I don't know what they're so worried about. Posey's thrilled. The critics are thrilled. Everyone has enjoyed it thoroughly."

My head starts to feel like it's been plunged under six feet of water. "It can't be out there. My mother was right. It says too much. People are going to assume . . ."

Laura cuts me off with a wave of her hand and gives me a hard look. "It's fiction."

"But it's *not*." Clearly Laura understands this. Clearly she gets that it's the reason I'm stuck in here, ironing out the differences between reality and imagination. "Most of it isn't. I didn't understand that before, but now I do." I stare into my lap. "I'm sorry. I gave you the novel under false pretenses. It's *not* a novel at all."

Laura shrugs. "So what if it's kind of real? Most novels have some truth to them. But this is the big secret: nothing is one hundred percent *real*. This is just your version. It's real to you, but you're also—pardon me for saying this—delusional."

"Thanks a lot," I grumble.

"It's a good thing!" Laura cries. "Think of how Eleanor would have written this book had it been from her perspective. Completely differently, right? Think of how your mother would have written it, or a nurse at the hospital. Or even that guy who always shepherded you into the steak house—what was his name?"

"Bernie."

"Right. Him. They'd all have their own versions. This is your version. It's not like you've written a biography where people are going to dispute the facts. And to be honest? This book has helped Eleanor Reitman's sales, too."

"What do you mean, *sales*?"

She reaches into her bag, this time pulling out a wad of papers. The first one she hands me has a bunch of numbers running across the top. "She self-published that novel you write about her working on a few months before she died. *The Riders of Carrowae*. See those numbers?" Laura points. "It earned a little money last week. If she were alive, she'd get a royalty check in a few months, though I guess it'll go to whoever handles her estate. That you? Your mom?"

"I don't know." I keep staring at the book's title on the page. I'll be damned. She actually wrote it. That exact name had poked through the scrim of my memory and made it into the book unscathed. Funny what I'd remembered verbatim: Eleanor's book, Thomas's name, Dr. Singh. Part of me is dying to read Eleanor's book. The other part needs to stay far away.

"So all's well that ends well!" Laura crows. "Really, I'm just in here to see when you're getting out. Your publisher really wants to talk to you about doing another book. And Roxanne wants you back."

"After that train wreck?" I sputter, turning my head at the memory.

"Not a train wreck." Laura points at me. "Your appearance got them the highest ratings they've had in years. People DVR'd the shit out of it! It's gone viral on YouTube! Every morning show has featured it! They've even done segments on artists and mental illness! You're part of a national conversation!"

"Oh my God," I groan into my hands.

"Oh, please. Don't worry about it, Eliza. You're famous! You're eccentric! You'll come out of this and everyone's going to be like, *There's that crazy-interesting writer who lost her marbles on* Dr. Roxanne! *Wonder what she's going to do next?*"

But I don't want to be the crazy-interesting writer. Eleanor Reitman was that person. It seems like the worst thing to aspire to.

"Oh, before I forget." She rustles in her bag and lobs me more papers. "I don't know if you actually *know* this clown, but someone's done a tell-all about you. It actually came out the same time as when your *Dr. Roxanne* appearance aired—I think he was trying to scoop them. It got lost in the shuffle after your breakdown onstage, so we only dug it up now."

I turn the paper over. *My love affair with Eliza Fontaine,* reads the headline. And then: *Dating an artist can be strange, interesting, and sometimes even exciting. And with Eliza, you really had no idea what was around the corner—but all of it was incredible.*

Leonidas, is my first thought—but I hadn't been an artist with him, had I? And besides, he knew how Eleanor died—he had a lot to lose by exposing himself. Then my gaze lands on the picture at the bottom of the page. It's Desmond's quirky smile. I'm standing next to him, my cheek smashed into his shoulder. It's a selfie of us that he'd taken with his phone the second day we'd spent together.

I let the paper drop to the bed with a yelp. But then I immediately scoop it up and read everything. Desmond wrote about fishing me out of the pool (*she emerged from the abyss like a mermaid, moonlight on her lashes*), how I have a merry-go-round in my backyard (*she was whimsical, original, and artful*), how I'd come on to him at my house (*good Lord in heaven, how I longed for her, but I was so afraid!*), and Steadman's junk shop (*a woman who can be around petrified cat penises all day is a woman after my own heart*). Stalking Leonidas's dad's office was, apparently, the sexiest date he'd ever been on. Even my seizure at the Tranquility was transcendent. Caesar himself would have chucked aside Cleopatra for a chance with me.

Desmond concludes the article saying that we'd parted ways, not dropping the Andrew bomb at all. It's as though he forgot it. And then he signs it, *Love you always.* By the end, my face is wet. I feel foolish to be crying, and yet I can't stop.

"Don't feel too bad," Laura says. "It's flattering, really. And I doubt anyone's going to read it." She plucks the article from my hands and tosses it into a rolling Dumpster of trash that happens to be passing by my room. But after she leaves, I chase that Dumpster down, hurl myself into the can, and dig the article out, picking off a banana peel and dirty Kleenex and empty pill wrappers until it is flat and clean and mine and mine alone.

■ ■ ■

And then I can smell Desmond before I see him: mothballs, capicola ham, the carpeted interior of the Batmobile. He peers in tentatively, and because I'm turned away from the door, he darts backward. Then I roll over and sit up. "Oh."

"Okay if I come in?" His voice cracks. "You're not sleeping?"

I don't say anything, but he takes that as an invitation and sits on the green plastic chair farthest away from my bed. A bouquet of roses wrapped in crinkly cellophane twists in his hands.

"Those are hideous," I say dourly.

"I know," he says in a small voice. "I wanted black tulips, but to be completely truthful, I came here on a whim. I didn't even tell work, and it's *two days* before the conference. This is all that was available in the gift shop."

I sniff indignantly and face the wall. I suppose I'm supposed to feel like he's made some sort of sacrifice by missing his precious pre-conference prep?

"You know, I forgive you," he says. "For that . . . fellow. In the bar. I understand why you had to do that."

I'm glad he can't see my red cheeks.

"I understand why you had to know. I like your determination. I always have."

"I suppose that's why you wrote that article, then?"

There's a pause. "I had to," he says. "Stefan was going to write something awful."

I turn to him. "Your brother?"

He has bent a few of the rose stems because he's holding them so tightly. "It's another thing he dabbles in. Gossip pieces. He chases minor celebrities for the tiniest speck of dirt. When he found out I'd met you, he started grilling me about what you were like. I told him I didn't want to be part of some sort of tell-all. Then I found out he was working on a story anyway. It was all based on things he'd overheard us rehashing or things he found on the Internet. So I had to write something first, something about all of those things, so that when he wrote his own piece it sounded . . . lame. *As told to the roommate brother* sort of bullshit. And because I'd written something so positive, no one would want what he had."

I cross my arms tightly over my chest. "So you didn't actually *mean* that stuff you wrote, then."

"Of course I did!" Desmond moves to my bed and sits down. I shift away from him, but not before our calves touch. A shimmer goes up my back. "I meant every word."

Outside my room, the girl who so proudly talked about shitting herself shuffles by, doing an arm-flap dance that sometimes overtakes her. Crystal. Her name suddenly pops into my head. Desmond watches, too, and then turns back to me, offering a real smile this time instead of something posed and uncomfortable. "Is that what most people here are like?" he asks, gesturing to the hall.

"Pretty much."

"I bet you walk around with your hair in your face, scowling at everyone."

I snicker. "Yeah, well."

"I bet you're like, *If you dare talk to me, I'll bury your cat alive.*"

I glare at him, about to say, *As if you know me?* But then I realize. He does. Kind of better than anyone. I can tell, for instance, that he understands the truth of who I am. That he knows my book is true. That he's put the pieces together. I will ask him, tomorrow, when he comes back, and we will talk through it all, and I will tell him everything, but it will be surprising how much he has already guessed.

All of a sudden, as if he understands what I'm thinking, he stands and presses his hand to my shoulder. I feel that taut string between us, still there. I squirm away and say, with vitriol, "Watch out. I might just be dangerous."

"Well, if you are," he says, spinning me around so that I am facing him. He catches my wrist and holds it tight, entwining his fingers in mine. "I would love to be one of your victims."

■ ■ ■

"My family thinks I've done something," I tell Albert in a session a week later.

"Something good? Something bad?"

"Something bad. Something you've probably heard. The only problem is that I'm not sure it actually happened."

Albert pauses to sip his tea. The whole room smells like Earl Grey. "Do you want to talk about it?"

I'm surprised I've brought it up. So far, I've stayed away from this topic, primarily because I don't know what I think about it, exactly, and I don't want to talk about a potential crime I might have committed. I have to believe that my fate played out like Dot's: I freaked out at the funeral, I started jumping into pools, I begged to confess, and my parents told me not to, and when I refused, they found a method that would erase what I'd done. It shocks me, now that my memories have returned, how much I'd wanted to kill Eleanor. How *rid* of her I needed to be. Ignoring her would have never been enough.

And yet.

"I have such a blurry memory of that night," I answer. "I mean, I have what I wrote, and I think that's the truth, but why didn't I hear Eleanor fall onto the highway? And when I look back on that memory, Eleanor's face is a caricature—there's something so *odd* about her."

Albert cuts me off. "What do you mean?"

"I don't know, really. It's just like she transformed into a demon in those last moments. Into someone I didn't know at all."

Albert spins in his chair. "Maybe you don't *want* to recognize her in your memories. Maybe if you can shape-shift her into something else, you'll feel less guilty."

I stare at my lap. "You're probably right."

"The mind is very mysterious."

I pull a pillow close to my chest. It's embroidered with a large question mark; Albert told me a patient cross-stitched it for him. The mind is mysterious, and don't I know it. There are some days when I wake up and have this overwhelming feeling that *none* of this happened to me. The memories that have come back are simply the ones in the book replacing dull, drab scenes of me stuck in a hospital somewhere, perhaps. I mean, hell, for all I know, I could have been sick for *years,* right? In a hospital with brain issues for years, and only recently let out, and to supplant years of monotony, I made up this fantastical story.

It's possible, isn't it?

But mostly, I choose to buy into the memories, though sometimes I think my interpretation of them is incorrect. There are times when I wonder if Eleanor was the victim. I've read my book again; I see how Dot desperately wants to think her mother's the one in control. What if *that* is the truth? Could my mother have fabricated Eleanor's Munchausen-by-Proxy behavior? Could she have fed the nurses lies to get Eleanor evicted? It wasn't as if there was documented proof that Eleanor had, beyond a doubt, been in possession of strychnine and figured out a way to get it into my body, causing the seizures—the police would have only started an investigation when the claim was filed, and by then, Eleanor had taken off. Yes, there *were* my seizures, and my blood tests were positive for strychnine poisoning. I don't want to presume my mother was in charge of fabricating the tests, too—or, more horrifyingly, giving me the strychnine herself—but I'll never really know. What if she did it for my own good? But would she go to such great lengths?

This still doesn't explain Eleanor's return, either, or my strange wake-ups at her suite, and the powder she'd put in my drink the last night I ever saw her. But some days, those scenes feel embellished, too. Had there even been a drink switch? Maybe I just invented that scenario after the fact to justify what I'd done next. *She was going to poison me, so I killed her.*

Maybe I am a terrible, terrible person.

"So why did that bartender say another Eliza had been sitting next to me at the bar?" I ask Albert, once I gather my thoughts. "Who was he talking about?"

"That I don't know. And maybe you'll never know, either."

"But I *want* to know. Clearly the bartender saw someone. What if she *is* still alive?"

He clicks his pen on and off. "I think it's highly unlikely. There was a report about her death."

The report was given to me a few days into the hospital stay, when I still refused to believe anything I didn't remember was real. *Eleanor Reitman*, it read, *aged 52, dies from tragic fall in Alhambra*. There wasn't much more to it than that. A lot of the story was about how traffic was tied up for a good portion of the night. The writer touched very briefly on the fact that Aunt Eleanor was a resident of the Magnolia Hotel and that the staff adored her, and that her memorial wishes state that a remembrance ceremony would be held at M&F Chop House. There was no talk of foul play. There was no talk of the legacy she left. No family was mentioned. It wasn't a police report, either. There was no talk of a body being found. For all I know, my parents fed the writer every detail. And they could have said anything.

"But say you really did see her at the bar," Albert goes on, "and say you've seen her lurking around, as you've said. What do you think she wants after all this time?"

I can't believe Albert would ask such a silly question. "I guess to kill me."

He stares into the middle distance. "Are you *sure*?"

I run my tongue over my teeth. I felt so sure of this at the hotel, during *Dr. Roxanne*. And I'm pretty sure I felt certain at the Tranquility when I saw her. But now that I have the whole story, it feels jumbled. "In my book, she said that if she was going down, I was going, too."

"Right. So okay, she could be after you. But maybe there's another emotion at play here. Maybe you keep seeing her because you secretly miss her."

I stare at him.

"Come on. You admit that you still love her. And face it: for a long time, you didn't *know* she was hurting you. You loved your time together. You modeled yourself after her. And then, suddenly, this whole alternative truth about her, this *hideous* truth, is revealed to you, unequivocally. And then she's gone. Shortly after she left, it's erased from your memory, so you don't even have time to properly grieve and work through your feelings. There's just this . . . *hole* inside of you. You never got to say goodbye. You barely got to voice your fury. You never got to hear her side of things, not really." He sniffs. "I mean, come on. You want to, don't you? Even if it's manipulative bullshit. Even if it's the craziest thing you've ever heard. There's no shame in wanting to know her thoughts. And there's no shame in missing her, either."

I get a pang. It's true. I do miss her. "But isn't that a self-destructive feeling? If she did poison me, I should hate her. Not miss her. Not love her." I take a breath. "And *why* did she poison me? How could she have done such a thing?"

"Control. She worried about you leaving her. It was a way of getting attention. And a way of keeping you close."

"But I *would* have remained close to her. She was my favorite person in the world."

Albert reaches for his teacup again. "Well, she was sick. I can't explain Munchausen by Proxy. I don't know what drives people to do it. What drives child molesters? What drives people who abuse their spouses? It's a terrible thing. But you have to accept that that's who she was, too."

"I'm not sure I *can* accept that," I say quietly.

"Well, then you've got to let her go."

My heart squeezes tightly. Letting go doesn't mean loving or hating, it means feeling nothing. How could I possibly get there? And more than that: there is a film reel inside me still running, unfinished. I could be fooling myself, but I can still sense Eleanor's pulse. I can still hear her thrumming energy if I put my ear to the ground.

"She's still out there," I repeat to him. "She's still looking for me. She still wants to settle the score. I can feel it."

"Eliza, she's not. It's a symptom of your ripped-out memories. It's your mind playing tricks on you. You're seeing a ghost you've created. If you want to be a functional person in the world again, if you want to go on with your life and be happy, then you need to try and exorcise her. Exorcise this *feeling* that she's after you because you've done something so terribly wrong."

"So how do I do that?"

He taps his chin. "Maybe you should do what Dot does in the book."

Albert eyes the copy on his shelf. It is definitely new as of today; I would have noticed it before. Several copies of *The Dots* have been circulating around the hospital; I've caught nurses, administrators, doctors, and patients reading it. I guess I shouldn't be surprised Albert has a copy, but it's still discomfiting to imagine him reading it.

I consider what he said. The ending of *The Dots* is the only thing that hadn't happened to me. "I'm not doing *that*."

"But maybe you want to. Maybe it's why you wrote it. It might give you closure. You'd be free. Just like Dot is. You could admit what Eleanor did to you and why you had to take action." Here he pauses, and I realize for sure, just like I realized with Desmond, that he understands my book is an autobiography. "You could let someone decide your punishment."

". . . And go to jail. I can't take that chance."

The chair creaks as he sits back. "And yet you let Dot take that chance."

"She's a fictional character."

"She is?"

I let out a snort, stand, and start toward the door. Albert glances at the clock—we have ten minutes left, but he doesn't move to reel me back in when I walk out. "I understand your reaction, Eliza," he calls out. "But maybe, with reflection, you'll see I'm not so crazy for suggesting it."

"I'm sick of reflection," I grumble over my shoulder. "All I've *done* is reflect." I bump into the coffee table in the waiting room and knock off a stack of *Yoga Journals*.

I walk down the cold hall with the ugly lighting, past Jim and Pablo playing chess again. Maybe they're more fucked-up than I think—they're at that chessboard day and night, starting a new game the moment they've finished the first. I never see them in Group or at meals. What a stroke of fate that they'd found each other here. Maybe it's not like that for them, and there's probably no romance to their kinship, but it's comforting to think so. And suddenly, I feel a longing for Eleanor again. Kinship is what I thought I'd had with her. Understanding. Connection. Could I get that with someone else? Desmond, maybe? Or was what she and I had unique? Or was it all bullshit, because it had been built on lies?

Desmond knows no lies, though. But maybe that isn't such a good thing, either. He might love me unconditionally, but I'll always be this person to him—not the girl in the facility, after a time, but the girl who got away with something. How will that affect our relationship going forward? Every time he holds back, every time he steps away from me as though flinching, every time I think he's walking on eggshells, I'll be afraid that he's seeing the murderer in me. What if he resents me for walking free? What if he thinks I should pay for what I did? Because I *did* do it. Whether Eleanor died, whether she's still out there, I'm almost positive I used my hands to push.

And then it hits me. It's not just Desmond who knows that I did it. It's *everyone.* Yes, wink wink, the novel is fiction. But I've peeked at some of the reviews. People are pointing at the factual similarities between Dot and myself and Dorothy and Aunt Eleanor. They are taking pictures of the M&F Chop House and posting them on Amazon as an additional picture for the book. Bernie, the waiter, has been interviewed, saying that yes, there's a back entrance to the restaurant for high-profile clients, and he remembers Eleanor and me there, though he had *absolutely no idea* she was in trouble with the law. That *Los Angeles* cover has been dug up and posted. If the meat of the book is the truth, why then would the ending be a lie? I'd made Dorothy die exactly the same way. I didn't change a fucking *thing*—because I hadn't realized, at the time, that it had happened. Had I known, I would have altered some details. I would have had her fall into a canyon, or into an alligator's mouth at the zoo.

Had I known, I wouldn't have written the book at all.

The police haven't come storming the hospital, an investigation hasn't been started, no one has come out and *said* what I've done, but they've got to be thinking it. It's only natural. So can I go on living my life after committing such a crime? Dorothy did, after harming Dot. Eleanor did, after harming me. But I don't want to be like either of them. On the other hand, can I bite the bullet and come clean? What was the right thing to do?

I open the door to my little room and let myself in. Books are piled on my nightstand. I've ripped off the blinds, so light streams onto the floor. The staff finally let me have more blankets, and my mother brought an afghan from home. I pick it up and press it to my nose, smelling bergamot oranges. A pang so overwhelming rises in me, and I think of Eleanor yet again. I think of her splashing perfume on her pulse points. I think of her spritzing an atomizer toward me and saying, "Now, walk into the spray. There you go. Now you'll smell delicious."

Sighing, I reach toward the books on the nightstand and pull mine from the bottom of the stack. The binding cracks as I open it for the first time . . . I flip all the way to the last chapter, and I read.

Afterward, I sit very still until the light from the window wanes and turns gray. I ignore the knocks on my door for dinner, I ignore the soft footsteps that pass down the hall. I ignore the lights flicking off, another nurse popping in with a plastic cup of meds. She knows I'll take them, so she leaves it on the bedside table without a word. I sit still until the room is filled with inky blackness. I turn the words I'd written over and over in my head. I am giving myself a great power, choosing to heed my author self's instructions or take another path. Whichever I choose, it is all my decision, though. I'm the one in control now. I'm the one forging the path that will become the truth.

From The Dots

wo weeks after her aunt passed away, Dot went to
the airport and did that thing she assumed people
only did in movies: picked an international flight off the Depar-
tures board, slapped down her Amex at the ticket counter, and got
a seat. She wasn't sure why she chose Dublin except for the fact
that people spoke English there and she had no Irish ancestors.
She didn't want to go to a place where anyone looked like her.

Rain pissed on the plane's windows when they landed. A stew-
ardess came through one last time practically giving away duty-
free cigarettes and booze. Dot contemplated a bottle of Baileys Irish
Cream, but didn't buy it. The idea of alcohol sickened her now. She
hadn't had a drop since her aunt's funeral.

Off the plane, the airport was small, humble: an airport that
might be seen in a fairy tale or a children's book. Its shops sold
questionable sandwiches wrapped in wax paper and the smallest
bottles of Coke Dot had ever seen. She waited for a bus that was
an hour and a half late. When it finally came, Dot and the other
tourists—Italians, some Scandinavian varietals, a plump couple
from Texas—lumbered aboard. The radio loudly played a pop song

she'd never heard of. The rain dripped steadily, and though she was safely inside a vehicle, she still felt damp.

At the hotel, the concierge slipped her a list of things to do and tour, but Dot didn't feel like actually seeing the city—she just wanted to be away and alone. She lay in bed and watched TV, much of it American reality shows and Australian soaps. On CNN, there was a report of another school shooting. Out the window: buses, more rain, men with identical pasty, doughy faces quickly hurrying down the sidewalks. In the afternoon, after a snooze, she took a walk around Temple Bar. She stamped through puddles on Grafton Street and listened to a busker playing Beatles songs on a piccolo. Then, in a used bookstore window, she saw a copy of *The Bell Jar*. It had the same cover as the book Dorothy had given her the day she died.

Well, it seemed Dot couldn't get away from Dorothy, after all.

She sank down onto a bench, the water on the seat soaking through her jeans. What had happened blazed inside her, and her perspective on the crime flip-flopped a few times a minute. Had it been an accident, or had she meant to do it? Was she a liar, or was she a fool? Was her aunt poisoning her, or had it been a colossal mistake? Were her boyfriend and mother demonizing an outlier because they felt threatened and jealous of her, or did they have true cause for concern? Was Dot going to heaven for what she'd done, or was she going to hell? On second thought, Dot didn't believe in heaven. Hell, though, was another story. Hell wasn't a myth. Hell was inevitable.

Was Dorothy in hell now? Dot had to think she was.

Two days later, she took a flight to London and stayed at a hotel in Pimlico. But on a newsstand: an article about Dorothy's death (*Troubled Recluse Dead on Highway*). The *Los Angeles* cover was unearthed. A woman next to Dot at the newsstand was reading the same article, and Dot, afraid of being spotted, pulled her hood over her head and darted away.

Another picture of Dorothy at a rest stop in Brussels. A news spot on television in Amsterdam. Dot made a bunker for herself in a hash bar, eating spiked brownies and smoking spliffs until she couldn't stand. The door swept open, and a black-haired figure stepped in: *Dorothy?* A short woman with protruding teeth took a seat on a high stool and perused the menu. Dot's eyes dropped closed. Wherever she went, there was Dorothy.

Staggering home that night, she noticed an Amsterdam police officer on horseback giving her a strange look. She shot up straight, suddenly sober. Could he know? Was she an international criminal? He gave her a nod, asked her something in Dutch. Dot shook her head and moved on, but once she got back to her room, she curled into a ball and felt her heartbeat thudding against her knees. The police had never asked her questions about Dorothy's death, but maybe they should. Maybe her family protecting her wasn't fair. Maybe her promise to her mother to keep quiet wasn't right. A life had still been taken, after all, and Dot had important information to put the pieces together. Even if she had done it in self-defense, Dorothy's death wasn't a suicide. But it wasn't as if turning herself in would preserve her aunt's reputation. Turning herself in would *destroy* it. All those people who were pitying Dorothy now for falling into traffic would understand what a monster she was.

The spooky gleam from the red lights in the prostitute's windows across the street continued to burn. The women behind the glass pivoted and posed all night, it seemed, disappearing only to take a client. Dot rolled over on the stiff mattress. Maybe the world needed to know what a monster Dorothy was.

But she knew what telling might mean. She steeled herself for this decision, wondering if she could handle it. She'd already endured so much. And yet, just imagining getting the secret off her chest gave her a surprising sense of relief. People would know everything, bad and good, about Dorothy and about her. There would be no secrets anymore. No questions. If Dot had to suffer a little while—or maybe a long while—because of it, maybe that would be okay.

She packed up her suitcase, leaving behind a few knickknacks she'd picked up during the trip. The bag bumped against her shin as she walked into the slick, wet night.

Over a canal bridge, and then another. A late trolley wobbled down the tracks. Drunk kids hooted, coming home from a bar. The police officer on horseback was in the same spot Dot had left him. When she touched his calf, he flinched—he'd been looking the other way. He looked down, and his face blossomed with recognition when he saw her. "*Benyeh oak?*" he said in Dutch. At least that's what it sounded like.

"English?" Dot asked.

"Yes, okay," the cop said, and Dot felt relieved. "Is there a problem?"

Dot breathed in. It was the last breath she would take, she realized, as a free person, as a person with secrets. But maybe that was okay. Maybe this was growth. "There is a problem," she said. "I hope you can help."

EPILOGUE

Three Years Later

I'VE NEVER BEEN to the Hotel Vetiver before now, and for that I am grateful. When I came here a few months ago to scout a location for this party, I'd walked through the dining rooms and ballrooms as a stranger—there were no associations, no tickles of memories. The hotel is so brand-new it still smells like Home Depot. All the staff is so young they were probably still in high school three years ago when I was cycling through my troubles, and all of the guests are so old and moneyed that they probably have no time or interest in the *Dr. Roxanne* show or contemporary fiction. I hate that three years have passed and I'm still on the lookout for people I might know or who knew me—past ghosts, past oglers. I've run into a few women who'd been at that *Dr. Roxanne* taping; a couple of them came up to me right away, recognizing me, gushing about how good I look, how healthy, and that they loved the book. Others back away quickly, their mouths puckered in a half laugh. I only know they were in the audience because I hear the whispers. If you were at that show, you won't forget it anytime soon. Probably the only person who doesn't have a crystal-clear memory of that day is me.

Desmond and I walk into the ballroom together hand in hand. Posey, rail-thin, her three babies long since evicted, greets us as promised in the lobby.

"There are a lot of people here already. We'll do dinner first, and then the silent auction, and then you'll say a few words. Read from your new novel if you like. Everyone is dying to hear what it's about."

I feel that same jump of nerves I always get before getting up in front of a crowd. It hasn't gotten much easier for me, but at least now I can actually *do* it.

Posey's neck turns sharply toward her phone, which is ringing. "Gotta take this." She scampers away.

Desmond touches my arm. "You'll be fine," he says into my ear. He smells like sandalwood; his hair has been cut to show off his angular face and his blazing blue eyes. I've only seen him in a suit a few times, but he looks deliciously handsome. When he came out of the bathroom with it on, I'd jumped on him and tore it off, so beguiled by his tall, thin body in all that black wool.

"And if you're not fine, if you need to get the hell out of here, I scoped out all the exits," Desmond continues. "There's one only about fifteen steps away to your left. And there's another to your back that will lead you through a really long hallway and out into this Dumpster area—that one might be best. No one will be gawking at you out by the trash cans."

I grin at him, then kiss his cheek. "Thank you."

There are about twenty round tables that seat ten people each. Desmond seems to know the way, guiding me to a front table marked with the number 1. My mother and Bill are already sitting. Gabby's with Dave, her old boss and now fiancé. His son, Linus, a boy as pale and fragile as I had been at his age, sits next to them. Kiki has brought the new occupant of my bedroom in Burbank, someone named Theo I'm not sure if I like yet. Even my old friend from high school, Matilda, has come out, dressed in the same black spidery gown I used to borrow from her. I don't dress in so much black anymore, though. My hair has a few highlights in it, even. It's just something I'm trying. A new version of myself.

Everyone smiles when they see me, each of them expressing varying levels of enthusiasm—Bill braying and opening his arms for a hug, Gabby clutching Desmond's and my hands, my mother coolly nodding though at least looking half-decent in makeup and a dress, Kiki cheering and sharing news of Steadman, whose store burned down last year in a blaze of animal hair and bone and who moved to Tunisia. It was my mother's idea to have the release party for my new book, *Pawns*. Personally, I would have preferred something a little less stuffy—this has the feel of a fund-raiser or a reception for a wedding where the bride and groom aren't 100 percent sure about getting hitched—but as my mother was the one who planned it all, I can't help but feel flattered.

Waiters deliver endive salads and bottles of wine. In the center of the table is the cover of *Pawns:* stark white, with two black chess pieces side by side, a pen-and-ink of an institutional building in the background. I started work on the book about a year after *The Dots* came out. Not because it took me that long to come up with the idea—the idea came, actually, at the Oaks, as the story is about two men in a mental hospital who bond over their love of chess and their messed-up heads and lives. Jim and Pablo, the original chess players, were invited to this, too, invitations sent to the Oaks, where they're both still living, but they declined to come. I don't think they ever leave that place. It took me so long to start the new novel because I had to completely recover, and once I did, I had other things to do first. I ended up doing exactly what Dot did in the novel— exactly what Albert suggested. I turned myself in.

The Dots ends before we find out what happens to Dot—is she extradited to the States? Does she go to a Dutch prison? I wish I'd written a scene—at least it would have given me a template for what I was about to do. As it happened, I had to go in blind.

I was still a patient at the Oaks when I spoke to a detective at the station. They had to scramble around to find someone to take my call—Eleanor Reitman's death didn't have a file, as it was considered a suicide. Finally, when Detective Carson answered, he sounded dubious, and when I told him he had to visit me at the Oaks all the way in Palm Springs, he almost hung up on me.

But he came anyway. Detective Carson met me outside, on a bench. He had graying hair and a jowly but friendly face. His bright eyes were so light blue they were almost translucent. He was the kind of man I could see roughhousing with grandchildren; he probably had a trampoline in his backyard. We sat on the lawn; he took out a pad and pencil and asked me to explain my story. I was soothed by the old-school way of documentation, his scratchy pencil marking up the page. And so I told him. I told him what Eleanor had done to me when I was a child in the hospital, how she'd been banned from the nurses, how none of it had been communicated with me, how she'd returned and started drugging me in other ways. I explained our last dinner, how I'd switched the drinks—I didn't realize what she'd put in my cocktail would be so dangerous. I just wanted to see if she'd planned to do it to me. I told him the story exactly as I'd written it in the book. I'd decided to buy into that version of the truth, mostly because I didn't have a clear sense the truth could be anything else.

Detective Carson was not familiar with *The Dots*. He had to read passages from my book as a form of evidence; I waited for him to finish the passage where Dorothy catapults into traffic. "So she charged for you?" he asked, then slapped the book shut. "At that guardrail? And you pushed her over?"

I shrugged. "I guess so. I mean, I don't remember any of this very clearly, though my therapist says that I'm *choosing* not to remember it. I remember *wanting* to push her, that's for sure."

"So you're admitting to her murder, then?"

I took a deep breath. "I'm admitting to . . . *something*."

"But you don't remember."

"No, but I don't see how it couldn't have happened."

The detective pulled his bottom lip into his mouth. "I just don't understand why someone would write a confession in a novel. Even someone who was mentally compromised, as you were. It seems to go against every instinct we have as humans."

"I confessed because I thought it was fiction. I went through treatment, and the memories were taken out of me."

"Yes." He frowned. "Your family was in charge of that, right?"

"They were, but . . ." I stared at my trembling fingers. Maybe I hadn't thought all this through. I didn't want my family getting in trouble. "They were worried about me. They've been worried for a long time. But it's not their fault. It's mine."

It was difficult to say all that. It wasn't like I *wanted* to go to prison, but I'd resigned myself to it. I couldn't walk around with a murder on my conscience. I couldn't have people thinking I'd killed and gotten away with it. Like Dot, I needed to own up to it. It probably sounded naïve—prison was going to be awful, I knew—but I really felt like that was how the story should end.

Detective Carson stood and brushed a few pods that had fallen from the trees off his pants. "The thing is, Miss Fontaine, the way you describe the incident in your novel doesn't sound like murder. It sounds like self-defense. If I were your lawyer, that's how I'd frame it."

"Huh?" I snatched my book and leafed through the pages to the end.

"Eleanor came at you first. She *poisoned* you. There might not be empirical proof that she was the one who did it, but when she left, you got better. *She's* the one who should have been in jail—for child abuse. And even that night—all you did was switch the drinks. You didn't know for sure that she'd put anything in yours. And at the guardrail, you wrote that she charged at you and tried to push you over. There's no picture showing otherwise. I have a report of the accident here, which describes that we identified Ms. Reitman's body by her driver's license. It details the state of her body while the department still had access to it in the morgue. There are no signs she was choked or hit or bludgeoned or struck in any sort of way by you. We don't even know if she was poisoned by that drink you gave her—we weren't able to do a drug screen on her. It could have all been an act.

"It doesn't add up to much," he said. "I mean, sure, you can claim you did it, I can send you to prison, but do you really want that?" He touched my shoulder gently. "You seem like a nice girl who just had some shitty luck. I'd go live your life. Stop feeling guilty. It's not your fault. None of it is."

"But—but—" I stammered nonsensical vowels and consonants. "My therapist told me to confess to you. He said this was the right thing to do."

The detective had a hint of a smile. "Maybe he told you to do that because he knew I'd say what I'm saying. Maybe he hoped you'd listen to me. It's not your fault, Eliza. None of this is. You're the victim, okay? And that's hard, too. Because now you have to heal."

He extended his hand, and I realized after a moment he wanted me to take it. Once I did, he squeezed hard. I felt like he was *my* grandfather, comforting me after a bad dream. "Now, I read that this place serves really decent coffee," he said. "Mind if I stop in and get a cup?"

I'd walked him into the Barn, which was what we patients called the main facility building where all of the therapies took place and the meals were served. I felt like I was slogging through mud. I'd been so ready to accept the blame. I had visions of being handcuffed and riding away in his car. I almost felt cheated of that moment.

I got the detective coffee. He stopped and spoke to one of the nurses, coincidentally an old neighbor from where he grew up. As he was about to leave, something struck me, and I ran after him. "Why weren't you able to do a drug screen on Eleanor?"

He reached for the keys in his pocket and a silver gum wrapper fell out. As he stooped to pick up the litter, he said, "She had strict orders in her living will not to perform an autopsy, no matter her cause of death. We're used to that around LA—a lot of celebrities have unusual death directives. But we couldn't keep her body for very long, either—the living will also stated that we had to call a man immediately, and he would dispose of it as she wished. The report says her man showed up the next morning, and that was that."

"Doctor Singh."

He squinted at the report. "Yes. A Doctor Vishal Singh signed for her body. Pretty standard procedure. Like I said, we thought it was a suicide, anyway—and honestly, it *was* a suicide. She *wanted* to die. You have to believe that. She was on the run. She was going to be arrested. So we didn't look into it. Doctor Singh showed up, took the body, and that was that." He shrugged. "I appreciate your honesty and candidness, but really, this conversation doesn't need to go any further. You can let it go."

But I couldn't let it go. I wanted the answer. I wanted to find Dr. Singh and figure out where he'd taken her body. I wanted to know why she hadn't wanted an autopsy. What was she hiding?

The problem, however, was the Oaks had very limited Internet privileges, and they wouldn't give me a special pass to do the research. So I asked my mother to look into it. She called every Dr. Vishal Singh in Los Angeles County. There were quite a few of them. None of them claimed to know a woman named Eleanor Reitman. None of them had claimed her body.

My mother also unearthed several boxes of things Eleanor had left behind from the Magnolia that she'd been keeping in an upstairs room, hidden from me. She brought the boxes to the hospital so I could look through them, too. Peeling off the tape, a sharp scent of bergamot oranges filled the room. I almost fainted. It was like letting a genie out of a bottle. I could see her before me, hale and hearty, wearing a fur, drinking a stinger. I could hear her croaky voice. I could feel her laugh.

We poked through the boxes. There were negligees, bathing suits, a lot of elaborate hats, a box of expensive perfume with a name I didn't recognize. Several mystery paperbacks, a DVD of *The Third Man*. At the bottom, costume jewelry, a fringed flapper dress, a bunch of *Vogue* magazines, and a tiny knitted baby shoe. I held it up, my eyes wide. "Was this mine?"

My mother squinted. "Maybe?"

A card for the concierge at the Magnolia. A card for a literary agent in San Francisco. No writings, no paperwork, certainly no will. Not even a bill for her cell phone or her health insurance, if she even *had* health insurance. But no card for Dr. Vishal Singh. No indication they'd been friends. It was like he didn't exist.

"Just let it go, Eliza," my mother advised me. "What's done is done."

I tried to. It wasn't worth looking into, I told myself. I'd done my part, too—I'd confessed, I'd gotten it off my chest, and now at least I could tell this story as part of my interviews, as I'd had to do a few after I was released from the Oaks. Yep, I might have pushed her, I said, but the cops know and they don't think I'm guilty. It legitimized me, sort of. I still walked around worrying I'd done something horrible, but at least I wasn't repressing it anymore. At least I remembered most of everything. And for those things I didn't remember, those ephemeral, wobbly moments at the guardrail . . . well, maybe that was okay that I never got those gory details back. They wouldn't do me any good.

Except I still felt unsettled from time to time. There were still a few loose ends, a few things I can't make sense of. Who was it people kept seeing around town? Who filmed me in the hospital? Why, leading up to my psychotic break, did I feel followed? Maybe *I* was the one around town, after all—maybe my personality had split. And maybe my paranoia was because my guilt was poking through, beginning to show itself. These are the logical answers. And yet . . .

We work our way through the meal, though I'm too nervous to eat much. Posey steps to the podium and breathes a few times into the microphone, getting everyone's attention. "Thank you all for coming," she says. "It's my great pleasure to be here at this launch party, celebrating a new novel by a young talent. As many of you know, Eliza Fontaine achieved notoriety with her last book, *The Dots,* and it has sold almost a million copies worldwide."

Everyone applauds. I duck my head, still astonished at the number. I don't look at Amazon ranks. I don't read reviews. The only thing I read is mail fans send to me. Rarely are those letters critical. And usually, those people actually *read* my book, as opposed to the multitudes who bought it only because I'd made a name for myself for falling in the pool and acting like a maniac on *Dr. Roxanne.* I hate that that's how I achieved the sales I did. I hate that people think I'd done those things on purpose because people need a gimmick, these days, to sell books. I hate that it's kind of true that you need a gimmick to sell books.

"Now, Eliza is here to read from her new book, *Pawns,* which comes out next week. Once dessert is served, we'll have her up here for an excerpt and for a signing. So until then, enjoy, drink, be merry, and please buy a copy of Eliza's book in advance if you want it signed. Thank you."

There's a smattering of applause, and the music comes back on. My mother smiles at me from across the table, but I'm too jittery to smile back. Downing the rest of my water, I drop my napkin on my chair and head to the bathroom. I need cold water on my face and pulse points. The last thing I want is to faint up there on the stage. I pass a table covered with copies of *Pawns* and about twenty Sharpies in varying colors and styles. My stomach tumbles. This time, I have to actually promote a book, go on tour, give interviews. But I can do it, I think. I can tell the truth. Mostly because I know what the truth is.

The bathroom is filled with women, and I head for a stall, nervously smiling at one of my mother's friends who looks like she wants to corner me and tell me that *she's* got a good story for my next book, if I'm interested. Toilets flush around me, and I just sit for a moment, relishing the privacy. One by one, the sink taps turn off. All the feet vanish from the counter. I step out of the stall. A figure shifts to my left, and when I notice her, my heart freezes solid. It's her. Dressed in a bathroom attendant's uniform, slimmer, with shorter hair, but *her.*

I scream and back away. Part of me has been ready for this meeting. Part of me has never let go of the idea that Eleanor is out there, lying in wait. Well. Here she is.

The woman looks back at me and tentatively smiles. "Hello."

I have backed up the whole way to the paper towel holder on the other side of the room. The voice coming out of Aunt Eleanor's mouth is higher, more singsong. It breaks through a blanket-thick layer inside me, conjuring up my hospital bed, the scratchy sound of the blood pressure cuff's Velcro as it was ripped from my arm, and the smell of antiseptic. I am so relieved I want to laugh.

"Are you . . . Stella?" I say slowly.

She nods gravely, seeming unsurprised that I know. "Yes, I am."

And I see her, suddenly, so clearly: sitting on my bed at St. Mother Maria's, watching the gauge, acting flighty when my aunt came in and demanded to know who was prettier. It was so long ago. So blurry. I'd never thought she was actually real.

"I was in St. Mother Maria's Hospital," I tell her. "A long time ago. You were a nurse's aide."

Do you get ovarian cysts from time to time? Is your eyesight just a touch myopic?

The voice is so clear in my mind. And then, when Stella left, *You'd think she would have enjoyed that. Not everyone has a doppelganger.*

It's Eleanor's voice. Not Dorothy's. A real voice, a situation I witnessed. And in this moment, it is as though the two strings of my consciousness, real and fiction, thread and lock together, becoming one for good. Other people had bled over from my real life to the fictitious one I created, but Stella had actually been *in the hospital with me*—far more than my mother was. She probably saw things. And for some reason, looking at her now, I believe undeniably that everything people said happened to me really happened. I had a benign tumor when I was young. I was poisoned. I was abused. I was lied to. And then I killed.

It all happened just like that.

For so long, even in the past three years, I have *wondered*. Nothing I have found has satisfied me completely in believing that what I wrote and what I remember and what I've been told match up. I have, from time to time, still questioned my mother's intentions, cooking up ideas of conspiracy. When I get a twinge of a headache, sometimes I think, *Ah, it's the tumor.* When I pass UCLA, I still believe I was in there for surgery. It has been difficult for me to shed the memories of Eleanor, but it's also been difficult for me to shed the memories that replaced her, too. At best, they exist in tandem with one another, fighting for prominence.

Until now. Now, I just know.

I step toward Stella, discomfited by the coincidence. What is she doing here, of all places? My mother would have never allowed this—she would have never unleashed an Eleanor look-alike on any of us. It has to be some weird kink in the universe.

I swallow hard. "You look so much like my aunt. She passed away, but maybe you remember her. She stayed with me in the hospital. She asked which of you was prettier."

She gives a slight, brief nod—still unfazed. "And I saw you, not that long ago. At the Terranea Resort. You were cleaning the rooms. I thought you were my aunt again. I could have *sworn* it—you were wearing the leopard scarf she loved." These are details from *The Dots,* but they are details from my life, too. I close my eyes, and there they are, vivid and sharp.

A muscle in Stella's cheek twitches. "Ah. Yes. That scarf."

Her tongue darts out of her mouth to lick her lips. She looks nervous, suddenly. When she meets my gaze again, my skin prickles. All at once, I feel like I'm on the precipice of something huge. I don't know what it is, but my gut is clenched, and my intuition screams that I cannot leave, not yet. There is something more here.

I grab her hand. "Come with me."

She follows willingly, more or less. We pass a few women on their way into the bathroom, there for my reading. I duck my head, and they don't notice it's me.

Instead of turning toward the ballroom and my podium, I lead Stella in the opposite direction, to an empty back hallway that butts up to the swimming pool and the gym. The air smells faintly of chlorine, and I can hear an exercise machine whirring on the other side of a wall.

I sink down onto a small leather couch and pull her down, too. My heart is pounding. She looks conflicted, but not confused. It's like she knows what I'm going to ask.

"My aunt gave you that scarf, didn't she?" I ask quietly.

Stella's throat bobs. She tucks a piece of hair behind her ears. "Well . . ."

"Please tell me the truth. Tell me *why*."

The wind presses against the big windows only a few feet away from us. I picture Posey pacing, wondering where I am.

Stella lowers her head. "I've been trying to tell you. I've showed up where I thought you'd be—I needed this off my chest. It was hard to find you. But then when I did, I chickened out."

"What were you trying to tell me?"

She doesn't seem to hear this question—her eyes are glazed, and she's staring at the floor. "I tried to film a video of myself on your phone, thinking you'll have it as a confession—but I *still* couldn't do it! I was worried you'd wake up and see me and panic. I worried you'd take all of it the wrong way."

I open my mouth, then close it again. *My phone. The hospital.* Had *she* made that video? She'd been in my room, handling my phone?

I don't have time to process this because Stella straightens up and looks at me head-on. "Your aunt made me an offer. I was to spend a whole day at the spa under her name, and she'd give me an Hermès scarf and one thousand dollars in return. It was too good to be true. Of course I told her I'd do it. But then I found out what happened." She pauses, her face crumpling. "That poor doctor did nothing to deserve it. I know why your aunt pushed her. There was talk in the hospital of what was going on. The doctor suspected, too."

It takes a few seconds for me to process. In real life, Dr. Koder's name is Dr. Richards—but I checked, and just like Dr. Koder, she suffered a paralyzing fall down a flight of stairs shortly after I left her care. If a doctor suspected Eleanor of poisoning me, of course Eleanor had to get rid of her. I'd wondered about this accident, wondered if Eleanor had had something to do with it, but I'd had no way to prove it until now.

"Eleanor made you go to the spa in her place so she could hurt the doctor," I say slowly, putting the pieces together. "She used you to establish her alibi. Because you look like her. It was foolproof."

Stella nods. "I only realized that afterward. I shouldn't have been so stupid. I *knew* your aunt was bad news. And then the doctor didn't remember what happened. She thought the fall was an accident. I threatened your aunt that I was going to tell on her, and guess what she said? *I was at the spa all day, wasn't I? My name is in the appointment book. People saw a woman who looked like me. But what about you?* I was the one who didn't have an alibi that day—I'd even taken the day off work to go to the spa. I worried I was the one who'd get in trouble—the doctor might remember a face, *my* face, because we looked so similar. Your aunt told me that I should quit my job at the hospital to be safe."

"Oh my God," I whisper. "So you've been following me, trying to tell me this?" All at once, it makes sense: with a quick glance, people could mistake this woman for me. We are the same build. Stella has more lines around her eyes, but they're not very obvious. She takes care of her skin, her hair. It was Stella at the yoga studio, at Steadman's store, maybe even lurking at my parents' house. And then it hits me, like a thin, strong beam of light: "You were the person I spoke to at the bar in Palm Springs!"

Stella nods vehemently. "Yes. I needed to tell you. I followed you to the resort, thinking we could talk there. But at the bar, the moment you saw me, you panicked. You thought I was her—and that I was going to hurt you. So I ran, but it gave me even more of a reason to get through to you. You needed to know the truth."

I narrow my eyes. "The truth about what? That my aunt pushed my doctor? That she was crazy?"

"No . . ." Stella stares down at her hands. She studies them as if trying to memorize every tendon, every wrinkle. I have no idea how much time passes. Two minutes? Ten?

"She called me again, years later," she finally says. "Said she had something else she needed me to do. I told her no way—but she threatened me. Said she'd send the doctor an anonymous letter accusing me of attacking her on the stairs. Said she had *pictures* from a surveillance camera—she bribed some guy in management to get them. This was probably a lie, but who knows?

"I felt trapped, so I said yes. She said she wanted me to hide at a restaurant where she was having dinner, and when she got up to leave, I had to slip into her place, order one more drink, and sign the check." Stella's chest heaves in and out. "I had no choice. So I went. But then I saw that she was having dinner with a young girl. *You*. I became afraid that she was going to do something awful to you. You're so *young*."

My throat catches. Is she talking about that last dinner? I close my eyes and put myself in Dot's place, remembering that small flicker of movement she'd sensed in the hallway just before going back to the table to switch the drinks. Had that been Stella? Had she been hiding, waiting?

"You saw us," I said, trembling. "You saw what happened."

Stella's gaze is off to the left, on a generic print of a beach scene. "Yes. I didn't take her place at the table, like she wanted me to. When you two left, I followed. And I listened. That woman was a monster. She deserved to die." She whips around and looks at me head-on, her green eyes wide and unblinking. "And she *did* die, Eliza. She did. She's gone. I saw her fall."

The words sink into me, fizzling like acid. "You saw me push her," I eke out.

Her expression tells me all I need to know. "I'll never tell on you. That's not why I'm here. I'm here because you need to know she's *gone*. I wanted to get to you much sooner, right after it happened—but your family took you away. As time passed, I couldn't bring myself to say what I knew." Stella gives me a hard look. "But here I am."

I sit back, resting my hands on my thighs. "Wow. *Wow*."

Stella's smile is crooked and small. "Yes. Wow. And I'm so very sorry."

I have so many more questions for her. So many more tiny things and big things to ask. But just as I'm gathering them up in my mind, my phone rings. It's Posey. I wince.

"I'll be there in a sec," I say as I answer. "Two minutes."

I hang up and give Stella an apologetic look. "I don't want to stop talking."

"No, go," she says, waving her hand. "I shouldn't have taken up this much of your time."

"Are you kidding?" I cry. I linger on her for a moment. I want to hug her, sort of, but instead I just touch her hand and mouth *Thank you*, and then hurry back to the ballroom.

Waiters are placing plates of crème brûlée on the table. Posey gives me a worried look when I approach the stage, but I shrug her off. She returns to the microphone and introduces me, and I try to pull it together as I take my place at the podium. My purse carries a marked-up copy of my book. But as I open it to the right page, I hear voices in my head.

It was like I was in the presence of a paranormal event! It's Eleanor. Dorothy. *I'd split in two! She should play a look-alike of me at parties.*

Or you could play a look-alike of her, I answered.

Then the story of Gigi Reece and Diana Dane pops into my mind. *There's a marvelous story about a murder at this hotel,* Dorothy had said. Eleanor said it, too. And they both said, later, in the same dreamy, faraway voice, *You know what would be interesting? If the famous starlet was actually the one in trouble with the goons in Palm Springs, but she sent this other gal in her place to bear their wrath.*

Had Eleanor been trying to tell me the whole time? Of course she used Stella to her advantage. She was her look-alike. She was a get-out-of-jail-free card.

But what if she took it even further? If my aunt used Stella as a convenient stand-in for an alibi, and if my aunt had Stella at her disposal the night she planned to kill me, what if she also used Stella in those last moments? Yes, Stella had told me, moments ago, that she'd only been there to slip into Eleanor's seat at the table, and that she'd watched me push Eleanor over the guardrail. I could believe that at face value—but should I? After all, in my murky recollection of what happened, Eleanor had looked so *different* in those last moments before she fell. Like herself . . . but also *not* like herself.

Was it possible that, amid our scuffle, Eleanor had wrested Stella from the shadows and forced her to take her place?

I can't exactly wrap my head around how Eleanor could have convinced someone to do this, or why Stella wouldn't have immediately revealed to me who she really was. I also don't know how Eleanor could have recovered from the poison, because of all the memories that are blurry, those images of Eleanor vomiting bile moments before her fall are still crisp and vivid in my mind. And yet . . .

What if the woman I'd just spoken to wasn't Stella at all?

I start to shake. *Stop it. It was Stella. Let it go.*

Detective Carson told me the police had identified Eleanor Reitman by her driver's license. For the crazy scheme I have just cooked up to have happened, my aunt would have had to slip the ID into Stella's pocket before she fell into traffic—or else Stella had had it on her person all along. But it *could* have happened, right? No blood had been taken to prove it was Eleanor. No autopsy had been performed. Dr. Singh, who I'd never been able to find, came to the morgue, took her away, and disappeared, too.

I look up. My audience is staring at me expectantly, waiting for me to start.

"I'll be right back," I say.

There are murmurs as I step off the stage. Posey grabs my arm. "What's going on *now*?"

I smile bravely. "Just . . . the bathroom again."

I jog away. I have to pass my family; Desmond is looking at me in alarm. He knows me best—he probably can sense the panic on my face. I only pray he doesn't come after me, though when I peek over my shoulder, he isn't.

I want to run, but I don't want to draw attention to myself. The distance to the ladies' room seems farther than the first time I walked here. I fling open the bathroom door, heart thumping. I'm prepared for anything from an uncomfortable confrontation to a gun being shoved in my face. All I know is that I need to talk to Stella— or whoever she is. I just need to make sure.

When all I see is an elderly woman staggering out of a stall, struggling to pull up her panty hose, I'm struck dumb. "Oh!" the woman says when she looks up. "Goodness, I'm sorry." She yanks down her skirt so that her underwear isn't showing. "These damn nylons. They're all twisted."

I stare at the corner where Stella had been. Even her toiletries are gone. "Did you see someone here?" I ask breathlessly. "A bathroom attendant?"

The lady smiles. "Now wouldn't *that* be nice? Maybe she could get me a new pair of panty hose. Now I've got a run."

"So you didn't see where she went?"

The woman just smiles at me daftly. I scurry over to the spot where Stella was standing. It's wiped clean. Was she ever even here?

Whirling around, I head back into the hall, desperate to see Stella's—or Aunt Eleanor's—bobbing black head. I press my hand to the wall to steady myself.

"Eliza?" Posey has appeared at my side. "What's going on? Are you all right?"

"I just needed the bathroom," I say shakily. "I'm fine."

And I try to be fine. I stand at the microphone again. I apologize for my little break. I try to make a joke about it—a little too much water at dinner! A nervous bladder! I thank everyone for coming, open the book to the page I've marked, and start to read. I know the pages so well, I don't have to concentrate very carefully to get through the reading, so my mind is left to race.

I get to the end of the passage, indicating I'm finished by closing the book shut and giving a nod. The group applauds. I smile. Posey reappears and announces that signing will begin and everyone should form a line. I step off the stage. I'm furious at myself. Furious I'd rushed back into the ballroom so quickly. And where could Stella have gone? What does this all mean?

I take one more look into the crowd, wondering, for a brief spell, if she's maybe just *out* there, watching benignly, no longer interested in doing harm. It could be the old Aunt Eleanor of my mind, the one who enjoyed me so much, the one who only wanted to love me unconditionally. I know this isn't feasible. That's not who Eleanor is. But still, when I see a black head close to the door, my heart lifts, and part of me wants to leap from the table and run to her, arms outstretched, and tell her how sorry I am, and how all I want is for things to go back to the way they used to be, the way I used to believe them to be.

Her eyes meet mine. Her head arches up then, revealing thick cords in her neck. She gives me a thin, mysterious smile that could be interpreted as conspiratorial . . . or mischievous.

My throat is dry and raw. I look to my mother, but she isn't studying the crowd—she's looking at me with alarm. There must be something telling in my expression, something that gives away that the ghost has wormed her way back into me, that I'm possessed again, that I've *seen her.* Her face pales perhaps to the shade of mine. She widens her eyes in disappointment and heartbreak, because it's so clear what I think I know, and it's even more abundantly clear that I'm still not to be believed.

"No, you don't understand," I start. "It's . . ." But then I trail off.

Drop it, a voice in my head tells me. Finally I have real answers, and here I go turning them on their heads. A woman notable only because she looked like someone else has just unburdened herself to me—that's all this is. I've hunted down the truth because it has haunted me and because I have something of a disease, but I've also romanticized the truth, too. Romanticized *Eleanor.* How could I not?

I think of all the stories she told me about her life, stories I desperately wanted to be real. All her adventures. All her dalliances. She might have been mad and damaged and eccentric and psychotic, but she had a magical imagination, and I suppose that's something I should treasure. Only someone like Eleanor could make me believe in the impossible. Only someone like Eleanor could shape-shift, cajole, wrangle, manipulate, poison, and come back from the dead.

But Stella had said it best—she hadn't. That was just the myth she wanted me to believe, not what was real.

I stand on my tiptoes, meeting Stella's gaze again. She gives me another short nod as if to say, *Yes. Good choice.* And then, turning on her heel as elegantly as Eleanor used to, she heads for the doorway and disappears.

I let her go, knowing I'll probably never see her again. From now on, she'll only be marvelous, effervescent fiction.

ACKNOWLEDGMENTS

Many, many thanks to many, many people for their help with this book. First and foremost, huge thanks to my editor, Johanna Castillo, who took a chance on this manuscript and steered it in the right direction with intuition and wisdom. To Andy McNicol, who championed the idea early on and probably read at least twenty-three versions of the novel. To my early readers: Lauren Acampora and Cari Luna—it's very nerve-wracking to place a half-formed novel into the hands of such smart people, but your comments and suggestions were invaluable. To Michael Gremba, my husband, who stayed with me in the neighborhood in Burbank that served as the inspiration for Eliza's neighborhood in the novel, and to Ali Shepard, my sister, with whom I took my one and only trip to Palm Springs. To my parents, Shep and Mindy, whose old-Hollywood influence (and absinthe drinking) gave this book its vibe. Also to Kristian and Henry—not because you really helped me write this book, but the more books I write, the more toys I can buy you.

Also, this book is dedicated to my late grandfather, Charles Vent, who I still think of all the time. I think he would have gotten a kick out of this book when he wasn't busy making dogs smoke cigarettes, narrowly escaping the police, or stealing things off people's front lawns.

ABOUT THE AUTHOR

Sara Shepard is the #1 *New York Times* bestselling author of the series Pretty Little Liars, which was developed by ABC Family (now Freeform) into a television series of the same name. She is also the author of the adult novels *The Visibles* and *The Heiresses* and lives in Pittsburgh, PA, with her family.